THE ENDING SERIES

LINDSEY POGUE   LINDSEY FAIRLEIGH

Into the Fire
By Lindsey Fairleigh and Lindsey Pogue

Editing by Sarah Kolb-Williams
www.kolbwilliams.com

Cover Design
Deranged Doctor Designs

L2 Books
101 W American Canyon Rd. Ste. 508 – 262
American Canyon, CA 94503

978-1949485028

For our first fans—you're the reason we write.

Maps

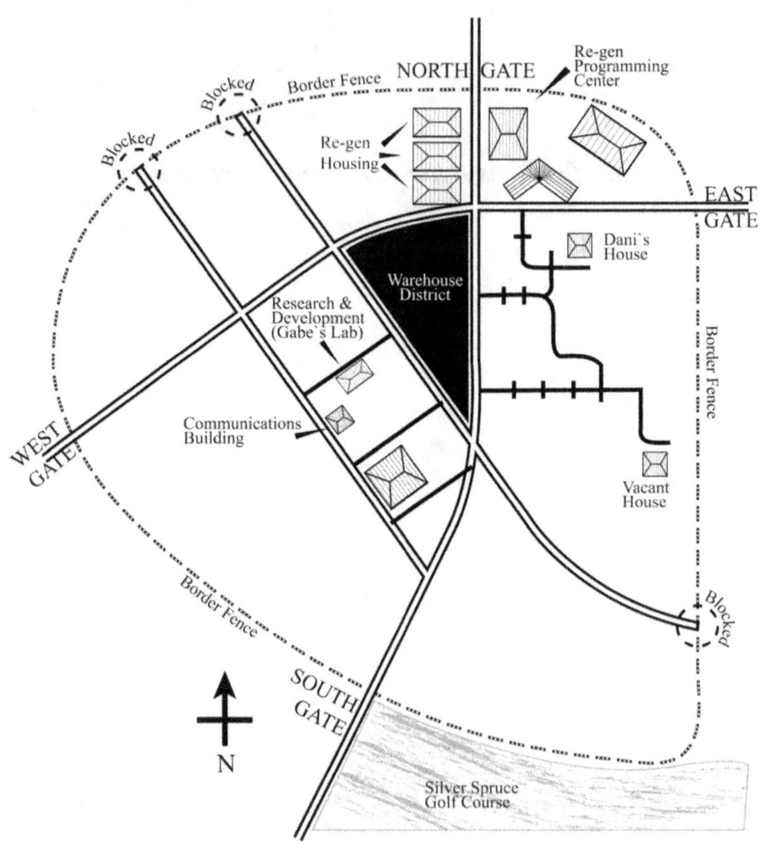

MAP OF THE COLONY

MAP OF COLORADO

PROLOGUE

MASE

JANUARY 5, 1AE

"I'm just sayin' the General freaks me the fuck out, Mase, and…" Carter stopped talking—for once—as he shifted the beam of his flashlight to shine down the next aisle. "D'you hear that?"

Carter could be dense, but if he thought he heard something, there was something to be heard. Thanks to the Virus, the guy had the ears of a dog.

Mase lifted his left arm and made a fist, and the other two members of his fireteam froze behind him. Ahead, Carter stood, head cocked to the side. As one, they listened. Mase barely caught it—whimpering. After giving Carter a curt nod, he signaled for all three men to follow him, raised his M4, and crept closer to the noise.

Patrolling the supply warehouses had been their duty for over a month, ever since the Virus had wiped out almost everyone, and they'd yet to find an intruder. General Herodson's standing order was that only select personnel could enter the warehouses to guard, inspect, and distribute food and other supplies. Unless Mase was grossly mistaken, they were the only patrol on duty at Warehouse F until the shift change at midnight, which was still hours away.

It looked like they'd found their first intruder.

As they crept down the aisle between two towering metal shelving units stuffed with pallets of shrink-wrapped supplies—paper towels, toilet paper, plastic cups—they swept each side with the lights attached to their rifles. Halfway down the aisle, huddled on the cold cement floor, was the intruder. The girl was hugging her knees and hiding her face like she was trying to disappear. Mase scowled.

Slowly, the girl raised her head, and when Mase saw her dirt-smudged face, his breath hitched. It couldn't be *her*...not in the Colony. Her long, dark hair was ratted and clumped, tear tracks trailed down her cheeks, and confusion filled her eyes. Mase knew they were hazel from memory, even if he couldn't see their color in the darkness.

"Stand down," Mase said to the other soldiers before turning his attention to the young woman. "Camille? What are you doing here? Are you hurt?" His voice was always deep, gravelly, but concern or maybe fear made it even harsher. Hesitantly, he took a step closer to her.

Camille flinched, becoming an even tighter ball of folded limbs and tangled hair on the dirty cement floor.

For the first time in his two years as a Ranger, Mase regretted spending so much time lifting weights. She was afraid of him. But he *knew* her. He had to help her.

Clearing his throat, he put on what he hoped was a comforting smile and took another step closer.

"We won't hurt you," he told the teenage girl as he knelt down in front of her. "I promise." When he touched Camille's arm, she flinched again. "I promise we won't hurt you," he repeated. Intruders were to be taken straight to headquarters—to General Herodson—but he couldn't do that. They tended to disappear after that. Of course, if the bastard found out Mase had disobeyed his orders, Mase would disappear himself . . . but it was Camille.

When she finally peered up at him, Mase did his best to look less intimidating by hunching his shoulders, hanging his head, not scowling. She watched him carefully, blank curiosity filling her face.

"What are you doing here, Camille?"

She opened her mouth to speak, but no sound came out. She tried again. "Who—who is Camille?"

Surprised, Mase sat back on his heels and studied her. *It* is *her, isn't it?* She was older—more a woman than a child, unlike the last time he'd seen her. Camille was a few years younger than him, so now she had to be at least seventeen. She still looked like a perfect little doll, though. There was no question in Mase's mind that he was staring at the young woman he'd lived next door to nearly his entire life.

"You," he said. "You're Camille. And I'm Mase." He remembered the day her parents brought her home from the hospital…the afternoon she fell off her bike and chipped her tooth on the sidewalk…the Valentine's Day she gave him a card made out of pink and purple construction paper…the day he taught her how to coast on his skateboard without falling…the night she ran away crying after meeting one of his girlfriends. But if Camille could remember any of that, she was hiding it well. She just stared, not responding, and began to shiver.

Mase heard his men whispering and shuffling around behind him. He ignored them. "It's okay, Camille," he said, doing his best to soften his voice. "We're friends. We were neighbors, remember? Back in Minneapolis? I used to look after you when your parents—"

The other men chuckled, Carter bursting into open laughter. Mase flipped them the bird over his shoulder. They only laughed harder.

"You…" Carter couldn't stop laughing. "You…you used to *babysit*?"

Rising, Mase spun and pointed threateningly at Carter. "Shut the fuck up." He glared at each of the men, warning clear in his eyes, until they quieted. "Nobody touches her. Nobody says a fucking word about this. Forget you ever saw her."

Their amusement vanished, and they stared back at him with identical expressions—fear mixed with pity and regret. They knew what had to be done.

"Mase," the nearest said. "We have to turn her in. The General's standing orders are to—"

"I know the orders," Mase snapped. "Fuck them. She's not going anywhere near Herodson. Forget. You. Ever. Saw. Her."

After a brief hesitation, all three men nodded.

Letting out a relieved breath, Mase turned back to Camille. She was watching him with eyes widened in interest, not fear. He knelt in front of her and explained, "It's not safe for you here. You're going to have to hide until I can get you registered as a Colonist."

Surprising him, Camille reached out and touched the side of his face with her fingertips, frowning when he flinched. "Where am I?" she whispered.

Mase glanced back at his men, silently warning them to keep their mouths shut. If Camille didn't have any memory of the Virus—of nearly everyone dying—he didn't want to be the one to tell her. At least not yet. "You're in the Colony. It used to be a military base. You'll be safe here as soon as I get you registered." He hesitated for a moment. "You have no idea how you got here?"

Quietly, Camille said, "No. I have no idea." She studied him with eerily calm eyes.

A metallic bang stole Mase's attention, and then the overhead lights flared to life. Someone else was in the warehouse. While the others stood nearby, rifles raised, Mase helped Camille hide between two pallets of paper towels. She was barely out of sight when the newcomers rounded the far end of the aisle. Mase's stomach dropped when he saw *him*.

"Atwell! How is your patrol going this evening?" asked the man leading a dozen soldiers. Dressed in his usual officer finery, General Herodson strolled down the aisle toward Mase…toward Camille.

"Nothing unusual, Sir," Mase reported, stepping away from Camille's hiding place before the General was close enough to see her in the shadows.

General Herodson inspected Mase and his fireteam closely. "So it seems," he said, giving Mase an instant feeling of *holy-fucking-shit*. Casually, the General glanced around, his gaze lingering near Camille's hiding spot.

"How are the Ability transfers going?" Mase asked, hoping to distract him.

The General looked at him with cold, gray eyes.

Mase returned the man's stare, refusing to look away. "Have there been any new developments? I know some of the men would like to get outfitted with regeneration or telekinesis."

General Herodson bared his teeth in a smile. "Not yet, no. However, we *have* had an interesting breakthrough on another project. We're calling them 'Re-gens'—they're reanimated corpses, more or less. They even retain their Abilities, though they're altered somewhat from what they were during their first lives." He paused, glancing up at the lights thoughtfully. "But the process wipes their minds completely clean, making them *very* easy to influence." He rubbed his hands together briskly. "No need to deal with pesky memories or morals."

Reanimated corpses. It took effort for Mase to keep his expression blank.

Abruptly, General Herodson said, "As you were," and turned to leave.

Mase watched him walk away, reluctant to move. Why had the

General told him about the Re-gens? Why had he come into the warehouse in the first place? Something wasn't right.

As they neared the end of the aisle, General Herodson and his guards halted. "CL-one," the General called out as he turned to face Mase again. "Come here, CL-one."

Shocking the shit out of Mase, Camille wriggled out from her hiding spot and hurried to General Herodson's side.

Mase clenched his jaw, realizing he'd just signed his own death warrant.

"CL-one is a particularly amazing Re-gen, don't you agree, Atwell? We just finished her the other day." General Herodson watched Mase like he was gauging every minute change in his expression. Mase kept his face hard and cold, like the General's. "Take their weapons, my dear," Herodson said to Camille.

Even at a distance, Mase could see the confusion on Camille's face. "Why, Father?" she asked softly.

The General stiffened. "Because I told you to, *my dear*," he said with strained affection. "These men must be arrested and put on trial. They broke the law. *My* law."

"Oh," Camille said, sounding sad, or maybe confused. "What will happen to them after the trial?"

It seemed to take a conscious effort for General Herodson to suppress his simmering anger. The man hated being questioned. "The other three will be banished from the Colony," he said through gritted teeth. "Atwell will be executed and turned into a Re-gen."

"Okay," she said, smiling contentedly. She took a deep breath, then shut her eyes. Her mouth thinned to a flat line.

As Mase looked from her to General Herodson, hatred flooded his veins, quickly followed by adrenaline. His muscles vibrated with the unnatural strength that had increased steadily over the past two years. He was the strongest, fastest person he'd ever heard of —not that it would help him now. The General knew about his Ability. Mase figured that was probably the only reason he wanted to bring him back as a Re-gen: to be used…owned. Mase ground his teeth together and tried to think of a way out of this clusterfuck.

Suddenly, his M4 tugged out of his hands and floated upward. He tried to yank it back down, but it continued to float higher. Moving quickly, he untangled his arm from the rifle's strap before it forced him up onto his toes. From the sounds of his men cursing behind him, he knew they were being remotely disarmed as well. Mase watched as their weapons glided into the hands of the General's guards. His attention was drawn to Camille, who was still concentrating. *She* was doing it.

She opened her eyes and left the General's side, a coy smile curving her mouth. Mase watched her approach him, frozen in remorse at what he'd caused. His men wouldn't be "tossed out of the Colony"—they would be executed, regardless of what the General had claimed.

It felt like minutes, but finally Camille reached Mase. She caught his gaze, a spark of sharp intelligence lighting eyes that had once been hazel but were now gray. Almost inaudibly, she whispered, "Do not be afraid, Mase. I will take care of you, just like you used to take care of me. And with my friends, we will take care of Father."

Mase barely registered her robotic intonation. He couldn't believe what was about to happen. Soon, he would die, only to be brought back as something else. As some*one* else.

The reanimated young woman stood on tiptoes and lightly touched her lips to Mase's cheek. "My friends *really* do not like Father."

March - 1 AE

I

ZOE

MARCH 14, 1AE

N*o! No! This can't be happening!*

"Dani!" My voice carried throughout the eerily quiet field as I sprinted along the pasture fence, away from the barn and toward Dani's bone-chilling scream. Jake was right behind me, the light from his flashlight dancing around my bare feet. Each breath was so loud, so raspy, it was like I could hear nothing else.

My mind started to feel odd, momentarily distracting me as I ran, but I ignored the feeling along with the frigid air biting at my skin and the jagged rocks poking the bottoms of my feet. My eyes blurred with unshed tears, and I stumbled over something, barely catching myself before colliding with the unyielding ground. I shook my head, trying to dispel the disorienting fog that was steadily creeping into my mind.

In the darkness a few yards ahead, I could see Jason's shadowy form. His flashlight and gun were pointed in front of him as he swept into the forest with Jack, Dani's German shepherd, leading the way.

I slowed, hesitating at the edge of the forest. Seeing Jason's pistol raised scared the shit out of me. *Did he find something? Who's in there?* What's *in there?*

"D!" I cried out.

In an instant, a strong hand wrapped around my arm. I whipped my head around to face Jake. "What—"

"We *have* to be quiet, Zoe." His voice was low and severe. He pointed into the woods, and I realized all I could hear was the sound of flapping wings and a hoot from an owl off in the distance. Jason wasn't calling out for Dani; there were no voices.

I nodded, feeling stupid, but I still wanted to call for her. I needed her to know that we were nearby…that we would find her. *Why is this happening to us? Why can't we catch a goddamn break!*

Turning back to the woods, I concentrated on controlling my breath and regaining some clarity. *Why can't I focus?* Sanchez, Harper, Chris, and Carlos passed me, bouncing flashlight beams lighting their way into the dense forest. I vaguely noticed Biggs, Ben, and Ky following them, Biggs muttering curses under his breath. My head started to throb under the massive influx of foreign emotions. I shuttered myself against the onslaught and rushed into the woods, hardly feeling the scraggly branches poking and scratching me.

"What was she even doing out here?" I rasped. I stopped inside the tree line, wishing I had been levelheaded enough to grab a flashlight and a pair of boots like everyone else.

Jake stopped beside me, but Cooper trotted passed us, his nose skimming the ground for a scent. He locked on to a trail and began to follow it. I heard a barrage of whispers around me before everyone broke off into groups, but I focused on the dogs; they were following two different scent trails.

After what felt like an hour of following, searching, and waiting for Jack or Cooper to find some sign of Dani, both dogs' trails converged at a narrow, jagged tree stump. Jack whined, and

Cooper sniffed the pine needles around the base of the stump. The dogs had found something. Instinctively, my gut balled into a knot.

Ben, who was helping to keep his brother upright, began to say something. "I think—"

"Here," Harper said, aiming his flashlight at the exposed roots of the stump. Crouching, he shifted a fist-sized stone and picked something up.

Chris stepped up behind him and peered over his shoulder. "Jason," she said ominously, glancing at my brother.

He moved to her side, and hesitantly, I followed. I stopped almost instantly. Jason's dread washed over me, a wave of nausea making my insides lurch, and I had to close my mouth and hold my breath to avoid vomiting. Every hair on my body stood on end at the thought of what they'd found. "What is it?" I croaked. *Please don't say a body part...*

Stiffly, Jason squatted beside Harper, taking whatever Harper had found from his hand. *A yellow piece of fabric?*

"It's just like the ones we saw back at Lewis-McChord," Chris said quietly. Rising from his seated position next to Jason, Jack stretched out his neck to sniff the cloth and whined.

Chris glanced around at our confused faces and explained, "It's an armband, or at least part of one. Some of the personnel were wearing these when they put our base on lock-down." She shook her head. "We stole a few; it was the only way we could get off the base. The people wearing these"—she snatched the armband out of Jason's hand and clenched it in her fist—"had something to do with the Virus."

"I've seen those before too, on people from the Colony," Jake said. He'd been trying to convince us that the supposed safe haven was dangerous since we first met up with him at Fort Knox. "It must've been them..."

An image of his sister's dark hair and violet eyes flashed through my mind. He was remembering her. He was remembering the men who'd promised to help her, the men who had frightened her enough that she'd taken her own life before *they* could.

Everyone looked at Jake, including my dangerously quiet brother. "Why would they take Dani?" Jason asked as he rose and took a menacing step toward Jake. "How would they even know we're here?"

I didn't like Jason's accusing tone, but Jake didn't seem to notice. Never taking his eyes off the yellow armband, he answered, "I don't know how they knew we were here, but if they wanted her bad enough to kidnap her…their resources are—were…" He paused. "It wouldn't have been difficult for them to take her." The images of his sister's final breath played through his head… through mine. A gut-wrenching feeling of loss took root in the pit of my stomach.

"You seem to know a lot about them," Jason probed, taking another step toward Jake. "Maybe you know more than you're letting on. Maybe you—"

"You think I'd save Zoe's life back at Fort Knox just to put her in danger again? You really are a piece of—" Jake inhaled and then emitted no further sounds, like he'd decided holding his breath for a while was the safer option. He was probably right.

He met Jason's challenging stare a moment longer before turning his angry gaze on me. "I warned you not to come here." His words stung with truth.

"Then how the fuck did they find us?" Jason's voice was damning, his glare focused solely on Jake. I didn't like it and felt a sudden desire to punch my brother in the face.

"How the hell should I know?" Jake snapped. "We've been here over a month and nothing. You get here and now they know where we are."

Jason made a noise that was part exhale, part growl. "How *exactly* do you know so much about them?"

"Because they tried to take my sister, and now she's dead," Jake replied hotly.

The two men were standing less than two feet apart, Jason's rage barely contained. He didn't lose control often, but when he did…I shuddered, recalling the worst of the fights between him and our dad. Jason cracked his knuckles, an ominous sign I was all too familiar with, and I feared my brother wouldn't be able to rein in his temper.

I stepped between them. "It's not Jake's fault, Jason, so back off!"

My brother ignored me, instead turning his aggression on Chris. "Stay the fuck out of my head," he ordered, obviously feeling her cerebral fingers trying to manipulate his mental state into something more stable.

Jake and Jason weren't the only ones on edge. Biggs was worrying about Sarah and their unborn baby, and Ky was in pain, practically folding under the weight of our collective panic. Ky's Ability to feel volatility—to sense and internalize everyone's destructive emotions—was physically debilitating him. He reached for the flask in his pocket without a second thought. Abandoning Jason, Chris ran to Ky's side.

The weight and amount of negativity Ky was picking up on frightened me; it was as if he wasn't just sensing our group, but all of the fear and hostility surrounding us. *From Cañon City? From the Colony?* Like Ky, I was pulled in all directions by the mounting unease and fear of everyone around us, as though I were being emotionally drawn and quartered. I wanted to scream.

The looming fog seemed to thicken in my brain, tangling with the barrage of emotions. *What the hell's going on?* I searched my convoluted mind for something I could grasp on to—something other than anger and fear and resentment. I'd been so fucking naïve to think everything would be okay once we found each other. *Keep it together, Zoe, Dani needs you.*

Closing my eyes, I took a deep breath, inhaling the scent of the forest—the sharp smell of pine needles, damp soil, and wood. The fog continued to spread its tendrils through my mind in a horrifyingly familiar way. I felt trapped in my own head, unable to escape the encroaching numbness. The only other time I'd felt such an overwhelming loss of mental control was when my mind had been invaded by Crazies in the hospital back at Fort Knox. *What if we're wrong? What if it isn't the Colony?*

Feeling a sudden jolt of panic, I opened my eyes. I could see the lichen coating the tree trunks in the dim moonlight, like spots on a leopard. But there were no snarls or howls or voices beyond our group. There were no fiendish sounds of Crazies cackling in the distance. There were no signs giving me cause to think anyone was there at all.

But someone *took Dani.*

A bolt of anger shot through me, jostling me from my statue-like state. I took a step toward my brother. "What the hell was she doing out here, Jason?" He'd always been big, bad, protective Jason—so why had he let Dani go outside, alone, in the middle of the night?

In the faint moonlight dappling his face, I could barely make out the hard set of his features. "Peeing," he answered lamely.

"Peeing? Alone? In the woods?" My anger flared, fury consuming my disbelief and fear. "I can't believe you, Jason! I just got her back, and now you—"

"Fuck you!" He pointed at me in warning, his eyes glinting silver in the darkness. "She was just peeing," he muttered.

"I can't believe someone was just standing here," Biggs said and began pacing. "Were they just waiting for us this whole time? Sarah…the baby…" He looked up at Sanchez abruptly. "We need to get out of here," he said evenly. "It's not safe here anymore. We've—"

"Do what you want," Jason growled. "I'm going after Dani."

"You think you can just walk into the Colony and get her? We need a plan first," Jake said, facing Chris and Sanchez. "We need—"

"Need to what? To wait for them to hurt her? To do worse?"

Jason's tone was scathing as, once again, he took a step closer to Jake.

"Calm down, Jason." I placed myself between them again. "We need to come up with a plan first. I mean, what if it's Crazies and has nothing to do with the—"

"It's *not* Crazies," Jake and Jason said at the same time. They exchanged an irritated glance.

I rolled my eyes. "If it *is* the Colony, they'll outnumber us and—"

"Then you stay here and *plan*," Jason said with a smirk. "I'll go find Dani."

"Get over yourself already!" I seethed. "You think I'm not worried about her? Like I haven't been waiting to see Dani for months? Like I haven't been worrying about her since all this bull-shit started? Like suddenly I don't care about her anymore because *you're* in the picture? She's my best friend, remember? Or did you forget that, since everything's always about you?" My voice was riddled with bitterness and jealousy, and my words were laden with twenty-six years' worth of resentment.

To my surprise, Jason remained silent.

Sanchez cleared her throat. "Look," she said deliberately. "If we want to find your friend, we need to be rational. So grow the fuck up and stop arguing, and then we can come up with a plan that *won't* get us all killed."

"We can't do much else in the dark," Harper said, his voice breaking through the tension. "The sun'll be up in an hour or so, then we can continue searching for signs of what happened."

"I'm not finished looking for her," Jason muttered and turned toward his tent.

"I wasn't implying that any of us were finished looking for her," Harper clarified, but Jason continued stalking away. The rest of us dispersed, some making their way back to camp, but Jake, Harper, and I stopped at the edge of the forest, watching…thinking.

"Look how close they were to us," I said with a shaky breath. I gauged the distance between where we stood and the barn. Although far away, I could see the dim embers of the night's fire and the outline of the hay bales and chairs surrounding it. I watched the dark figures of my companions as they moved around the camp. "We never even heard them."

Suddenly, as if my skin had become animated, creeping over my bones and muscles, I shivered. The thought of never seeing Dani alive again after everything we'd been through—journeying across the country, surviving homicide attempts and Crazies—caused a rogue tear to roll down my cheek. *Determination, Zoe,* I told myself. I hurriedly wiped the tear away.

With my brother out of earshot, I turned to Harper. I recalled the fleeting look of unease that had flashed over his dark, handsome features when Dani had arrived the day before. Whatever he'd seen was startling enough to have made his green eyes flare with apprehension.

"You had a vision earlier…yesterday, when you were hugging Dani, didn't you?" I knew I wasn't going to like his reply the moment he closed his eyes in…*regret*?

Harper didn't look at me when he spoke. "I saw her in darkness," he said quietly. "I don't know if she was sleeping or—"

"Unconscious," I finished for him, refusing to hear him utter the word "dead."

2

ZOE

MARCH 15, 1AE

I sat on one of the hay bales arranged around the campfire and brushed off the bottoms of my feet to pull on my socks. My eyes drifted to Dani's cup from the night before, sitting on the makeshift table Jake had made. It still held about an inch of white wine. Then my gaze moved to the empty liquor bottles and red plastic cups stacked on the boulder a few feet away. The sight was enough to make me sick to my stomach all over again. I couldn't believe how stupid we'd been…how careless. We weren't safe, and we never *had* been.

Cooper licked the back of my hand, and I looked down. He was watching me with downtrodden eyes, his tail moving in a half wag. "Thank you for your help, Coop," I said, rubbing his velvety ears. I hadn't seen Jack in a while, but I assumed he was still in the tent with Jason.

"What if whoever took Dani is waiting for you guys in town?" Sarah said to Biggs as he, Harper, and Sanchez noisily readied our weapons behind me. "I mean—"

"They won't be, baby," Biggs said, trying to soothe her. "They have better things to do than wait around for the likes of us." His voice was cool and easy, and I wondered if Sarah believed him. *I* wanted to believe him.

I glanced over my shoulder in time to see Biggs give Sarah a kiss on the forehead. She smiled, rubbing her bulging belly anxiously. Their unborn child had grown so much in the past month that Sarah was limited to sweatpants and loose shirts, a look that was so out of character for the former fashionista, I almost smiled.

"Are we at least moving camp?" she asked him, practically pleading. "I mean, what if they come back and take someone else?"

"Dani might come back," I interjected before Biggs could formulate an answer. I knew he wanted to leave. "Besides, they could've hurt us last night if they really wanted to. They're not interested in the rest of us." At least, I assumed they weren't.

Sarah tucked a strand of curly hair behind her ear and absent-mindedly chewed on her fingernails—a new nervous habit she'd adopted within the last couple months since learning she was pregnant. Realizing I was watching her, she focused on me and lowered her hand from her mouth. "I guess that makes sense," she said and wrapped her arms around her belly. It was like she was protecting the rapidly growing fetus from the gloomy shadow that had settled over us all.

As Sarah retreated into the barn, an image of her house in St. Louis flashed through her mind, and I knew she was missing her home. She hadn't wanted to leave, but she'd done so for Biggs… for me. A fleeting pang of guilt gave me pause, but there was little I could do. I turned back around and picked up my right boot. *Dani's out there somewhere, in the hands of…who knows. That* was my focus.

Three miles to the east, Cañon City was the closest place to search for maps, plans, and anything else that could help us come up with a way to get Dani back. Jason didn't like waiting, but most of us agreed we needed to be strategic if we were going to have any chance of rescuing her. *Assuming she's still alive.*

"I think we should assume these 'Colony' people want something specific from Danielle," Grayson said, practically reading my mind. He sat on a hay bale on the other side of the dying fire. Although his face was grim and his weathered skin seemed particularly pinched around his eyes, his presence provided a sense of comfort. I couldn't quite pinpoint why. Maybe it was because Grayson reminded me of home, of my past.

I thought of my dad and Jason, of how they used to be, but that only conjured a mess of unsettling memories. *I can't believe Dad's really gone.* Then, I remembered the box Jason had brought from Bodega Bay—our dad's box. I glanced toward Jason's tent on the edge of the woods, assuming it was in there with him.

In my peripheral vision, I spotted Grayson watching me. I looked down at my boot instead of meeting his knowing, apologetic eyes. Satisfied that the laces were tied well enough, I pulled my pant leg down and raised my other foot to tie my left boot.

"They wouldn't have gone to all this trouble," Grayson continued, "just to kill her, or—"

I swallowed another wave of nausea. Once the sun had risen, we'd searched the woods surrounding our camp for what felt like endless, heart-wrenching hours, only to be left with nothing but broken twigs indicating there'd been a struggle, the torn yellow armband, a cigarette butt, and five sets of boot prints, not including our own. We'd wasted the early hours of the morning getting nowhere. It was difficult to remain hopeful when I could feel everyone's concern and even some of their doubt.

I gathered my hair behind me and started weaving it into a French braid, wondering what was taking Jason so long to get ready.

"—saying. They knew what they were after, and they must have planned it ahead of time." Grayson leaned forward to stoke the fire with a scrap of cardboard.

"If they were after *her* specifically," Harper said, drawing my attention to him, "they must've known about her 'Ability'." He was rifling through an ammo-filled duffel bag behind me. "It's the only thing that makes sense."

"But what would they want with her Ability?" Carlos asked as he, too, joined us, donning his leather jacket. Though the sun was up, it was chilly. "A lot of you have an Ability, you know, so why take her instead of…" He shrugged.

Grayson nodded thoughtfully and scratched his brow. "True. There are other, more accessible victims they could've taken." He glanced at Sarah as she waddled out of the barn, her cheeks packed with the last mouthful of her second breakfast.

Carlos tossed a piece of straw into the fire. "And…how'd they know about *her*? How'd they know *anything* about us?"

"Well, I suppose the first thing we need to consider is who, outside of us, knows anything about the people in our group." Grayson reached behind him, pulling a couple saddlebags up into his lap, and he began packing them with water and granola bars.

Carlos crouched down near the fire, his eyes squinting from the brightness of the sun. "Hmmm…"

Sarah stopped at the edge of the campfire and tossed her paper napkin and plate into the pit. The flames grew. As I leaned in toward their heat, I scrubbed my face with my hands and took a deep breath. I watched the dancing flames until they died back down, recalling the weekend bonfires Dani and I used to have on the beach back home.

The beach... The memory of a dream flickered to life.

I was lying on an incredibly soft mattress, candles glowing all around me, illuminating the fire burning in Jake's eyes. "I'm going to do things to you, Zoe," he whispered against my cheek with delicious promise. His fingertips skimmed across my belly, lingering at the waistband of my boy shorts, and his lips were soft and moist against my neck as he kissed me. I closed my eyes in anticipation.

"I'm definitely *going to do things," he said again.*

"Yeah?" I giggled. "What sort of things?"

"I'm going to..." His warm breath caressing my skin turned into a chilly breeze, and the heat of his body against mine vanished. A bright, blinding light seared through my eyelids. Instinctively, they flew open, and I sat up. Wait…what?

I was lying on a beach—a seemingly familiar beach that Dani and I spent long summer days lounging on back home—and I was suddenly wearing a purple bikini. I closed my eyes and sighed. So much for a salacious dream tonight. *I stretched out on my towel in resignation.*

"Hi, Zoe."

I opened my eyes and sat up with a start. Dani was sitting on a green towel beside me, her legs crossed and her hand raised. She waved casually. Her hair was poofier and redder than usual, and she seemed more subdued.

"Uh...hey, D." I flashed her an awkward smile, and then realized she wasn't the only thing in my dream that seemed off. The cypress tree up on the ridge to my left was too small, and the ocean stretching out in front of me was too blue, too vibrant.

"Hey, Zoe." Dani said again, and I looked back at her. Her grin suddenly grew...too big. I frowned.

Is there a glitch in the matrix or something? *I plastered a tolerant, perhaps sad smile on my face.* It would be nice if any of this was real. *"Hey, D."*

Dani donned a pair of sunglasses that appeared out of nowhere and lay down on her towel, her strangely too-red curls fanning out behind her. As she adjusted her bikini top, I noted she was much curvier than in real life.

I started chewing on the inside of my cheek. "This dream is really creeping me out."

The breeze died down, and Dani suddenly vanished.

"That's my fault," a man's voice echoed around me. "I was

trying to recreate a scenario that would be comfortable and familiar to you."

Startled, I scanned the beach. There was no one there. "Who are you, and what the hell are you doing in my dream?" My eyes narrowed as I again scanned the endless beach, expecting to see someone walking toward me.

He chuckled. "I think you know who I am."

It was strange having a conversation with someone I didn't know...and couldn't see. "Do I?" At first I wasn't convinced, but when he chuckled again, I thought about the mystery guy from Dani's dreams. Is it possible he's real? *"MG...?"*

"According to Dani, yes, that would be me."

"And you're in my *dream because...?"*

"I'm doing a favor for our mutual friend."

Relieved, I smiled. "Really? Then she's okay?" I hadn't heard from her in weeks, not since she'd gone off on her own. "Is she still alone?"

"Yes, she's okay. She's with her friends, and she wants to know where you are. They're on their way to meet you, but it might take them a while...they're on horseback."

Ignoring a fleeting feeling of distrust, I told him where we planned to set up camp once we made it to Colorado. Dani was alive, and I knew MG was the only hope I had of finding my best friend and my brother.

"I knew I shouldn't have trusted him," I spat.

Six heads whipped in my direction.

"Trusted who, Baby Girl?" Harper asked.

"The bastard from her dreams. Mystery Guy or MG or whatever she calls him," I said. In my moment of clarity, I'd bitten the inside of my cheek too hard, and I could taste salty blood welling in the break of my skin. "I told him where Dani could find us... where we'd be." I lowered my face to my hands. "I can't believe I was so stupid! It had to be—"

"But he helped bring us together," Carlos reminded me. "Why would he do something like this?"

"He was playing us," I snapped. "He's the only one who knew we were here. And, outside of us, he's the only one who knows about Dani's Ability." I shook my head, still staring into the fire pit, which was once again a smoldering mess of embers and weak flames. "Why was he in her dreams to begin with? How did he even find her?" *Was he* hunting *her?* Herding *her to the Colony?*

"Wait." Still crouched, Harper pivoted to face me. "Didn't Dani *ask* him to find us, to find you?"

Carlos stood up defensively. "She did. And he helped her learn how to use her Ability. He's her friend."

The reminder made my skin crawl. *Was he grooming her? Molding her into a toy, something he could play with?* I groaned. Not knowing what MG wanted with Dani filled me with dread.

Understanding widened Harper's eyes. "He had to have known we'd figure it out eventually—"

"Right, and now that we know who he is…we still don't know who he *really* is," I bit out, wanting to scream. "It's fucking perfect."

"Which is why we need to leave," Biggs said forcefully. "He knows we're here, and if he's got the whole Colony to back him, we can't protect ourselves if he comes back for us."

"But he could've killed us already," Harper argued. "He could've killed us, taken Dani, and never given us a second thought. I mean, it makes sense that he's the one who took her, but the repercussions of letting us live…" He shook his head.

"We're nothing to them. There are only a dozen of us and only half are trained to fight." I counted to five and then to ten, trying to breathe away the tremors of outrage.

Jake strode over from the stable, oblivious to our collective realization. "You ready?" He dropped a pistol holster next to me on the hay bale. "This one straps to your thigh," he explained. "Chris had an extra. It'll make lugging your duffle bag around easier."

I gave him a weak, grateful smile, loving his thoughtfulness and the way his warm, brown eyes made me feel a little less pissed off. "Thanks."

Sanchez cleared her throat and we turned to her. She was focusing on the small, fold-up map in her hands. "I know the Colony is set up at Peterson, but what about this other base—"

"They were going to take Becca to Peterson," Jake said. "Dani's situation doesn't seem so different."

"What happened to her—your sister, I mean?" Carlos asked. I could feel his growing fear.

After a moment, Jake shrugged. He was as exhausted as the rest of us, and naturally, he wasn't eager to relive the moment his sister died in a bloody heap in his arms.

"We need to know everything we're up against," Grayson told him.

Jake's expression was blank, but he nodded slowly. I reached for his hand and pulled him down to sit beside me. He started by telling them that his sister was like Harper, that the Virus had changed the way her mind worked, and that she had visions of the future.

"But I didn't know it was real. I thought she was losing her mind." He paused and looked down at his hands, picking idly at the callouses that had formed on his palms. "Gabe—my best friend—was a contracted geneticist at Peterson. He swore he could help her, that he could fix her."

Jake continued, his natural reserve making it difficult to speak openly about what was easily the worst night of his life. His words faded to a steady hum in my ears as his memories of the events surrounding his sister's death played out in his head, drawing me deeper into his mind. His remorse cloaked my own emotions, and I could feel the excruciating depth of his emptiness, his crushing regret. Feeling Jake's pain helped fuel my determination to make sure Dani's fate wouldn't resemble Becca's. Unbidden tears accumulated in the corners of my eyes, and I blinked them away.

"Becca saw what the people at Peterson were going to do to her, and she chose death instead." Jake ran his fingers through his short, dark brown hair.

With the exception of a hawk screeching somewhere in the distance and the crackle of the dying fire, it was completely silent.

After a long moment, Sanchez said, "We should probably go or we'll run out of daylight before we get back."

"He's gone!" Chris called from behind me. I turned around to see her jogging back from the stable. "Jason's not in his tent and his horse is gone." She glanced out at the woods. "So is Jack."

Carlos jumped up from his seat on the other side of the fire. "He left?"

"I should've known," I muttered. "He's going to try and get Dani…on his own. He's going to get himself killed, and then Dani's going to blame herself for his death, just like she did with Cam." Terror jolted through me, and I stood and started pacing. *My brother is going to get himself killed.*

Carlos hurried over to Chris. "We have to go after him. We have to—"

"We can't go after him," she said sympathetically. "We don't know how much ground he's covered or which route he took. We have no idea where he is, and even if we do find him, he won't come back with us." She squeezed his shoulder. "Jason knows how to take care of himself. We need to stick together, and we need to focus on getting Dani back." She turned her attention to Sanchez. "I'll stay here and wait for Jason in case he returns. Get to Cañon City. Find out everything you possibly can about Peterson, and get your asses back here."

"I'll finish getting the horses ready," Carlos offered, jogging toward the stable.

As I turned to follow him, Jake's strong fingers entangled with mine, giving me a momentary wash of comfort. I peered at him, a tired but grateful smile spreading across my face, and he glanced toward Jason's tent. "He'll be back," he said, trying to reassure me.

No he won't. I knew how my brother was, but I nodded without arguing and continued on to the stable.

Wings stood out among the group of grays, chestnuts, and bays. I smiled. Of course Dani would ride the most vibrant Paint horse I'd ever seen. Wings's colors were rich and pure and bold, like her owner. Taking a slight detour, I stopped by a galvanized tub that held a few small apples and snatched one before heading over to introduce myself to my new riding companion.

"She's all ready for you," Carlos said as he double-checked the cinch around Wings's belly.

I unwound her leather reins from the metal railing. "Thanks."

Carlos gave me a quick nod and started toward the barn, toward Chris.

"You're not coming with us?"

He shook his head. "I'm gonna wait with Chris."

I shrugged and turned my attention back to Wings. Thoughtfully, I looked into her watchful, pale blue eyes. They were inquiring and cautious. "Hey, girl," I whispered. I couldn't communicate with animals like Dani, so I was left to my own devices to win her favor. I placed my palm below her velvety nose so she could smell my scent.

Wings's nostrils flared as she studied me. Slowly, she lowered her head to my palm. Her ears—one white, one coffee-brown—angled toward me, and her head bobbed a little, almost like she was nodding with approval.

"I know I'm not Dani, but I like horses, too. I'll take good care of you for her," I promised, stroking her chin and patting her thick, mostly-white neck. I held out the apple and offered it to her in my flattened palm. Eagerly, she reached for the treat with her lips, pulling it into her mouth. When it was gone, she nudged me. Wings suddenly seemed excited to have me as a riding partner, and I couldn't help but grin at my small but very important victory.

"Ready?" Jake asked, his deep voice interrupting me from my celebratory moment.

"Yeah." I smiled, stroking Wings's sleek neck once more before moving to her side and climbing up into the saddle with surprising ease—I hadn't been on a horse in years, but walking would take too long and cars weren't a viable option. Carlos had gauged the length of the stirrups perfectly. I pulled back on the reins ever so slightly, backing the mare away from the hitching post and positioning her toward the rest of the group.

"You're pretty good at that," Jake said enviously as he struggled with the reddish-brown horse he was riding…or trying to ride.

Grinning, I observed his valiant attempt at horsemanship. I was no expert, but I'd taken enough riding classes with Dani to have some know-how. "Your reins are too tight," I offered, stopping Wings beside him. "Give him some slack and he'll like you more." I lifted mine to demonstrate.

"I need to give him an apple so he'll like me more," he muttered, and my grin widened. Jake loosened the tension of the reins so the horse could move his head in stride as he walked, and then his gaze met mine, a playful glint in his eyes. A slight smile curved his lips. He opened his mouth to say something but closed it again when Harper guided his horse up beside us.

"Let's go," he said, waving for us to follow him.

Still sitting atop our mounts, we paused in the cover provided by two houses, grateful to have reached the outskirts of Cañon City. The ride had taken just under an hour, but my butt was paying the price.

"Downtown's a little ways that way," Jake said, pointing to the southeast through a ritzy suburban neighborhood that stretched out ahead. He continued to speak, but I was distracted. I couldn't tear my eyes from the serrated, snow-covered peaks of the Rocky Mountains to the north and west of us. I had been surrounded by their majesty for over a month, but the sight of them still enthralled me. Colorado was untamed and beautiful—so different from the colonial grace and sprawling greens I'd left behind in Salem.

Sighing, I threw my leg over Wings to dismount.

"What're you doing, Baby Girl?" I glanced over my shoulder to see Harper's eyebrows raised in curiosity as my boots hit the ground with a thud.

"Getting off my horse so whoever's here doesn't hear us clomping in a mile away." I walked Wings through a gate into a large, overgrown backyard. She followed me happily, eyeing the tall, untended grass. I waited for everyone else to follow suit. When I looked back at them expectantly, they dismounted from their horses—some with more ease than others—and did the same.

We secured the horses and unloaded what supplies we needed before heading toward downtown. After almost an hour of mostly silent slinking around, ducking under windowsills and crouching behind delivery trucks, we spotted the row of stone and brick buildings lining Main Street. It was easy to imagine the city in its heyday, booming with miners and cowboys in the decades after the gold rush. But now, windows were shattered, neon graffiti colored century-old brick walls, and cars were covered in dirt and grime, the only remnants of the season's final snow.

With the exception of our footsteps and hushed exchanges, Cañon City was quiet. There were no barking dogs, no Crazies mumbling incessantly, and no soldiers patrolling the streets. *This seems a little too easy.* My gaze veered up to the rows of windows on the second floor of the buildings, suddenly sinister and foreboding. *Where are all the Crazies?* That was one thing we'd come to expect.

"Something's not right," Sanchez said inside my head, and I assumed she was speaking telepathically to the others as well. Even though her Ability wasn't as strong or multifaceted as Dani's, it was still useful. *"Where are the Crazies?"* she asked, echoing my thoughts.

"There are worse things than no Crazies," I offered, not wanting to give the others too much time to consider turning back.

My companions exchanged apprehensive glances before we continued on to Main Street.

Staying true to our usual, cautious methods, Jake and I paused in an open, brick alley between two buildings, waiting for Harper and Sanchez to scout the nearby parking lots and shops. The cinderblock museum and history center, the most promising place to search for useful information about the Colony's layout, was a few blocks further down the street.

A gust of wind whooshed through the empty, stinking alleyway. The brisk air bit at my skin, and I shivered. My sweatshirt wasn't cutting it, especially since I'd stopped walking. Sunlight reflected off of a storefront window ahead, and I squinted in the glare. An antique shop was nestled between a pool hall and bridal shop.

"Ready?" Jake asked, looking back at me. He nodded across the street in the direction Harper and Sanchez had gone, but I was focused on the figures in the antique shop's display window. Sunwashed mannequins posed—one wearing a 1950s floral-print, halter sundress, the other in faded blue jeans and a vintage, olive-green bomber jacket. Its distressed leather looked worn and soft and enticingly warm. It looked so comfortable, I was practically salivating. I glanced up at the hand-painted sign: *Alice's Attic*.

"Hey," Jake nudged my shoulder with his. "What's up?"

"I'm cold," I said, glancing up and down the street. I looked over at Harper and Sanchez, who were moving toward the antique shop. "Where are we going?" I asked, happy to be moving closer to the shop that held the jacket and my potential warmth, but confused to be headed to the right, away from the museum.

"Pit stop," Jake said, pointing to the sign that hung three stores down from the antique shop. *Tommy's Gun Exchange*, read bold red and orange letters. *Perfect.*

Jake reached for my hand, entwining our fingers, and we

hurried across the street toward the others. Sanchez was already inside *Tommy's*, rifling through what remained of the store's stock, while Harper waited just outside the entrance, his sidearm drawn and aimed as he scanned up and down the street for movement.

Once we reached Harper, I pointed my thumb over my shoulder in the direction of *Alice's Attic* and said, "I'm going to grab a jacket."

Stopping a few steps inside the store, Jake glanced back at me with an agitated smirk.

Harper chortled. "Why am I not surprised."

I shrugged, equally annoyed with my inability to withstand the cold, and flashed them both an innocent smile. "Sorry," I mouthed.

"Jake," Sanchez called from the back of the store. "Bring me that bag, would ya?"

Harper looked from Jake to me. "I'll go with her." He nodded toward *Alice's*. "Come on, Baby Girl," he said with a nudge and started down the sidewalk, rifle drawn and each footstep light and calculated.

I glanced back at Jake, who nodded hesitantly. "Be quick about it."

Harper and I reached *Alice's* in less than a minute. The glass door was shattered, allowing us to slip into the shop easily.

I climbed up into the window display, unnerved by the antique mannequins, whose eyes were too wide and animated and whose mouths were too small for their heads. With a scrunched face, I unzipped the jacket, hoping the sleeves would be long enough for me. Harper helped me maneuver the plastic person's arms, jerking it toward me a few times, clearly entertained each time I recoiled. It was just…creepy.

Finally, I freed the jacket and shrugged into it. The moment I zipped it up—the bottom snug around my waist and the stand-up collar closing around my neck—I sighed. It fit perfectly. Unzipping the pockets, I stuck my hands inside and posed. "How's it look?"

Harpers eyebrows waggled in playful interest, and he flashed me a killer smile. "Not too bad," he said with a wink. "Alright, let's get this show on the road."

He was making his way for the door just as the rumble of an engine echoed down the street. We were hugging the shadows on the walls in milliseconds, my body tense and my heartbeat quickened.

"Shit," I hissed. Harper reached for my hand and pulled me closer to him.

The engine noise grew louder until a military Jeep sped past and continued through downtown.

"Damn, they're in a hurry." Harper whispered. "Let's move before—"

The sound of roaring engines grew louder, and another truck passed the antique store and stopped somewhere not too far down the street. Hearing the engines turn off and the doors creak open, I prayed the newcomers weren't planning on hanging around. We shuffled closer to the door and watched five men unload their things and settle into a store a few buildings up from us on the same side of the road. *Shit.* They had duffel bags and thermoses of what I assumed was coffee, or possibly booze, to warm their insides and help alleviate their boredom. *So…not just a quick stop then.*

With the soldiers out of sight, Harper and I hurried down the street to the gun exchange. Once inside, the four of us fell into a heated debate over whether we should stay and keep searching for helpful information or go back to camp.

"What other options do we have? We need information…*something*, otherwise this trip was pointless," I said anxiously. We'd come so far and now they were considering turning back. "There are only four of us. There's gotta be a way we can get to the museum without being seen."

Sanchez and Harper considered it for a moment, and finally

Sanchez nodded. "Fine, but we need to stay off the main road. We'll go in from the back."

"There's probably an alley," Jake said, and he found my hand and led me to the back of the gun store. He unlocked the back door and slowly opened it. Loosening his grip on my fingers, he let go and leaned out for a better look. A moment later, he closed the door. "The back alley runs along all the buildings. If they stay inside, it's doable."

Sanchez took a deep breath. "Let's get this over with," she said bitterly.

Within minutes, we were darting behind the buildings, crouching and ducking wherever we could. We were getting close. Just as Jake and I slipped behind an enormous delivery truck, a screen door flung open. It was the back door to a café—crates of coffee filters and paper cups were piled beside the dumpsters like they'd been unloaded but never delivered. Sanchez and Harper were up ahead, but Jake and I were stuck behind the truck, waiting for whoever had come out of the café to go back inside.

"I thought we were giving her a few days to get the intel," a man with a lisp said. Curious, I peeked through a slat in a stack of empty crates behind the truck just in time to see him unzipping his pants. I shrank back. The man—a soldier wearing green fatigues with a black armband wrapped around each sleeve at the biceps—had dark hair and a goatee. I could smell the tobacco smoke from his cigarette amidst the other rank smells of rotting food in the dumpsters.

"I mean, I don't get it," he said. I could tell by his muddled words that he was holding the cigarette between his lips as he used his hands to pee…at least that's what I assumed he was doing. "Just seems a little excessive, don't you think?"

"Apparently she's something special. He wants her back sooner," another man called from inside.

"She better be great in bed for all this trouble we're going to. I thought he had a thing for the doctor, but I guess he can get away with more than one piece of ass." The man cleared his throat. "Either way, I heard his newest flavor is a redhead." He groaned. "I love redheads."

A redhead...that could be Dani! So, who's the "he"? MG? The soldier's second groan made me want to walk over and kick him repeatedly in the groin, especially when the men inside the café only laughed.

"So, the raid's moved up to tomorrow night?" After goatee zipped up his pants, I heard him take a deep drag on his cigarette and cough.

"Roger that. We've got to get his toy home safe and sound, though. God, have you seen that bitch naked? I swear, I've never gotten a chub so fast."

"Hey, fuck-wad," another man called. "Are you taking a piss or a dump? If you're taking a shit at least shut the fucking door!"

Goatee laughed. "Shut up, dickhead, I'm done. Don't get your panties in a bunch."

Once the screen door slammed closed, I looked at Jake. The dread I felt was mirrored in his eyes. *A raid?* Assuming Dani was the "redhead," I couldn't help but think they were likely talking about us.

"A raid? Tomorrow?" I mouthed.

Jake shook his head, not wanting to think about an impending catastrophe while we were in the middle of another.

Carefully, we continued on toward the museum. Once we were inside, luck seemed to throw us a much-needed bone—a regular post-apocalyptic miracle. The museum contained ample information about Peterson Air Force Base.

We rummaged through the mini-exhibit and gathered a few maps of the base—they were vague and had obviously been created for tourists, but helpful nonetheless—a few history and general information books, and some black-and-white photos that had been taken on the base.

After nearly an hour, we cautiously found our way back to the horses, hoping that the café outpost was the only one we needed to worry about. It was another hour before we made it back to camp, leaving us with only a few hours before dusk.

Chris was the first person we saw as we rode up behind the barn. She'd apparently been waiting for us.

"I was starting to worry," she said, then let out a nervous laugh. "I never thought I'd be so happy to hear Sanchez's voice in my head." She surveyed our group, her eyes assessing, and I figured she was making sure we'd all made it back in one piece.

Jake's boots hit the ground with a dull thump, and he started unloading the duffel bags and backpacks of weapons, ammo, books, and maps. I dismounted and patted Wings on the neck, thanking her for being so steady and fast.

"We saw soldiers…I'm assuming from the Colony. They had trucks and were wearing armbands, but these ones were black instead of yellow." I frowned, feeling slightly ill as I recalled the perverted comments they'd been making. "We overheard them talking about a redhead…and, well, they mentioned a raid that's supposed to happen tomorrow," I told Chris while, around me, the others were unsaddling their horses. "We think the raid's gonna be here."

"Great," Chris breathed.

"Seriously. We were talking on the way back and we think we should leave. We can't take any chances. Especially with Sarah so—"

"Carlos is gone," she blurted.

I froze, my mouth gaping open. "What?"

"I'm sure he went after Jason."

"Jesus," I muttered, resting my forehead against the side of the barn.

Chris ignored my melodramatics. "So…Ky and Ben went after Carlos. Ky felt responsible, since Carlos must've ridden right past him." Her eyes drooped with exhaustion, and she shook her head. "This is such a damn mess."

I could sense there was something else she needed to tell us.

"What is it?" I groaned, straightening and dropping my hands to my sides. "What else happened?"

"A woman showed up this afternoon. She's not a Crazy, but something's not right about her. Her mind is…off, somehow. Cooper heard her walking around in the forest and…" Chris shook her head again. "Anyway, she was unarmed, confused, and seemed like she hadn't bathed or eaten anything in a while. Sarah and I got her cleaned up and fed her."

Sanchez took Wings's reins from me, and Chris matched my stride as I headed for the campfire.

"She seemed so lost and helpless," Chris added.

As we rounded the corner of the barn, I slammed into Jake's stiff, motionless body. "Jesus, Jake…" I half expected him to turn around and reach out to steady me like he'd done so many times before, but he didn't move. I righted myself and glared at him. He was completely unfazed that I'd just crashed into him. "Good thing I'm not as delicate as I used to be," I muttered tartly, but he didn't notice. Shock and horror—*his* shock and horror—trumped all preceding thought, and goose bumps prickled my arms.

I shifted my eyes in the direction of his to find the woman Chris had mentioned—our uninvited guest. The duffel bag Jake had flung over his shoulder slid to the ground with a heavy thud.

"Oh my God," I rasped, and Jake said, "Becca?"

3

DANI

MARCH 15, 1AE

FROM THE JOURNAL OF DANIELLE O'CONNOR:

Apparently I was attacked by a roving band of Crazies. That's what MG says, anyway. There was a patrol of Colony soldiers nearby, and they stopped the Crazies from doing whatever their insane little minds desired. I don't actually remember it, probably because I got knocked out and now have the mother of all headaches.

Honestly, all I remember is stepping out of the tent for a minute in the middle of the night, then waking up in a hospital with absolutely no idea of how I got there. I guess the Crazies really did a number on my head. At least the Colony patrol was around. Lucky me...

Yes, I know I should be grateful and super

happy that I didn't get maimed or killed by the Crazies, but this place is kind of weirding me out. It's not the hospital that's bothering me, exactly, but the fact that it has electricity, which I haven't seen in months. I've decided I hate florescent lights.

Mostly, I just want to get back to Zo's camp. Jason and Zo and the others are probably freaking out, and I can't even use my telepathy to let them know I'm okay. I mean, my Ability's working, but it's not strong enough to reach across the fifty or so miles separating us. FML.

Thin paper crinkled beneath me as I shifted my butt on the padded exam table. I was sitting on the edge, my legs dangling over the foot of the table. It was my first official trip out of my itty-bitty hospital room since waking this morning, and MG had escorted me down a single flight of stairs and all the way to…an even smaller room. *How lovely.*

At least I had a change of scenery. I'd exchanged a hospital bed, beeping monitors, and a cramped bathroom for an exam room containing only a padded table, a rolly stool, and a cabinet-counter-sink-desk fixture that looked to have been manufactured in the 1980s.

I sighed heavily. "I still don't really remember what happened," I told the doctor, who was standing in front of me. She leaned close as she shined a small, painfully bright penlight into my eyes. She was middle-aged, her gray-streaked, black hair was cut in a tasteful bob that reached just past her chin, and her eyes were a deep, ocean blue. They hardened at my words. *Well,* excuse *me.*

She clicked the light off, stuck it in the breast pocket of her lab coat, and shook her head, making her sleek hair sway. "You'll have to ask your Domestication Officer. I'm not up to date on your background information."

"Doctor..."—I glanced at the front of her coat, double-checking the silver name badge pinned to her lapel—"Wesley, I'm not asking for special treatment or anything. I'm just...confused." I took a deep breath, then shivered, thinking they had enough power to bump the thermostat up a few notches based on all the lights glowing throughout the building. "I mean, I was in the woods, and then I woke up in a hospital bed...I don't remember getting attacked by Crazies...I don't remember getting saved by the soldiers...I don't remember coming here...I don't remember *anything*. It's strange."

The taupe walls of the cramped exam room seemed to be closing in on me, awakening a newfound claustrophobia. All the shiny instruments and disposable utensils on the counter took on a new, menacing purpose, and I shivered again. A thin, bleach-white cotton robe was the only thing covering my peek-a-boo hospital gown. It wasn't doing much to stave off the chill.

"You remember something from before you were—" Dr. Wesley snapped her mouth shut as she stepped over to the counter a few feet away from the foot of the exam table and flipped open a folder. "Hmmm...you're not a...usually I only deal with..." She shook her head. "This is very unusual." Her intense blue eyes studied my face, and the delicate lines spider webbing across her temples and around the corners of her mouth deepened.

"Unusual" wasn't quite the word *I* would've used, but her acknowledging the oddness of my lost hours made me feel a little vindicated. "That's what I'm trying to tell you. I mean, is it normal for a concussion to lead to memory loss?" I asked the doctor. "All I remember is stepping out after...um...hanging out with my friends." Blushing, I recalled the delicious sensations I'd experienced at Jason's fingertips—and other parts—only a few minutes before getting knocked out. "I remember walking a little further into the woods, and then I woke up here. I don't think I even have a...whatever-you-called-it officer."

"Domestication Officer," Dr. Wesley said absentmindedly before shaking her head and whispering, "Gabriel. I should have known." With renewed interest, she returned to the first medical chart in the folder and scanned it from top to bottom.

Dangling over the edge of the exam table, my feet were cold despite the thick, white socks I was wearing. I rubbed them together idly and grumbled, "We never should've left Bodega Bay...should've just had 'em come to us."

As she read, the doctor transformed into a living ice sculpture, not moving, apparently not even breathing. *Did she find something alarming in my charts?*

"What is it, Dr. Wesley?" My head *was* pounding. It felt like my skull was being used as an anvil by an angry blacksmith. *Am I dying? Do I only have days to live? Only hours? This is so unfair!*

The doctor shook her head, and like she was shaking off sheets of ice with that simple gesture, the rest of her body regained movement. She set the folder on the counter. "I just thought something looked off, but I was wrong. It's nothing. Tell me what you remember from before you woke up. Maybe I can help."

I didn't bite, at least not at first. Instead, I eyed her warily, wondering what had caused her sudden change of heart; she'd been aloof and dismissive only moments before. *Maybe it has something to do with MG—Gabriel?*

I shook my head, which only seemed to enthuse the miniature blacksmith pounding away inside my skull, then squeezed my eyes shut and concentrated. *What was I thinking about? Oh yeah: what to tell the doc.* Was it entirely wise to tell her, a stranger, about my friends...about our little camp? But, if I made nice with the doctor, befriended her, maybe she really *would* help me remember what happened. For some odd reason, I felt like I could tell her, like I could *trust* her—though my processing ability *was* slightly limited at the moment.

I opened my eyes a little wider than usual and raised my eyebrows just a touch, hoping to look innocent and naïve. "We were traveling for a few months…from my hometown. We could've stayed there—probably should've—but hindsight is twenty-twenty, right?"

Dr. Wesley nodded and brought the bright, evil penlight up to my eyes again. "Follow this light, but don't move your head," she directed.

Sharp pain lanced the front of my skull as I tracked it from side to side. "Just so you know, it feels like you're sticking knitting needles into my brain through my eyeballs," I told her, gritting my teeth.

"Mmm…I'm not surprised."

Then why are you doing it? I wanted to shout.

"You have a pretty nasty concussion. You were struck here," she said as she gently brushed her fingers over a tender spot behind my left ear. Finally, she returned the torturous light to her breast pocket.

I was tempted to snag it and snap it in two.

"Tell me more about your trip," she prompted, dropping her latex gloves into the trash before opening one of the cabinet drawers. "You said you had companions who came with you from your hometown—what was it?"

I blinked. "Oh, right, Bodega Bay…yeah, that's where I'm from, sort of. But my friends, they're mostly from an Army base in Washington, that's where I was going to school…in Seattle, not the army base. Sorry, I feel like this isn't coming out well. My brain feels all mushy."

With the distinctive ripping sound of Velcro, Dr. Wesley deftly opened a blood pressure cuff and wrapped it around my upper arm. "It's fine. Tell me about them, about your friends. Maybe it'll help jog something."

"Well, they're really tough, even Mr. G, who was one of my teachers back in high school. We found him in Bodega Bay. And then there's Ky and Ben, they're brothers, and Chris. She's amazing…was an Army Ranger. We picked up Carlos from a bad group of people along the way…he's just a kid, sort of. And then there's Jason." Pausing, I pictured my handsome, brave, sometimes tender, and always lethal Jason, and the corner of my mouth turned up. "He and Ky were Green Berets…in the Army, I mean. They can be a little intense sometimes, but you probably already know all about that." After all, the Colony was a former military base.

The Colony. My barely-there smile turned into a definitely-there frown. According to Jake, the Colony was a very dangerous place. *Maybe I should take off soon.* I needed to get back to my friends as soon as possible; Jason was probably losing it. He tended to be protective, especially if—okay, *when*—I was in danger. He'd blown the brains out of the last person to threaten me. Of course, Mandy *had* been a cult leader who'd mentally and physically raped a large group of unwilling followers, including my sweet Carlos. So it's not that she hadn't deserved it, but still… brains…and skull chunks. Ew…

What does he think happened to me? Does he think I'm dead? Cringing, I realized Jason was probably blaming himself for my disappearance, especially since his temporarily over-excited nulling Ability had prevented me from sensing human minds. In reality, it had been my fault. I never should have wandered off. *I'm such an idiot.*

"Well," Dr. Wesley said, offering me a genuine smile, "those sound like pretty formidable people. They must not have been nearby when you were attacked, otherwise…"

I shook my head, gently for once. "Jason…" *…was nearby, but I guess not close enough.* "Oh God, Zo…the others. What if the Crazies went after them, too? Some of them are pretty vulnerable." *Like Sarah.* "Do you know…did the patrol notice anything? Are they okay?" I asked, imploring her with my eyes.

"You're the only one our patrol found, according to the note in your file." She glanced at the papers in the folder again, then shook her head. "Yep. Just you. There's no mention of anyone else. I'm sure they're fine. It would have been noted in your file if you'd been found near a bunch of fresh bodies."

As I looked into her deep, blue eyes, I found no hint of concern. *But what if she's wrong? She thinks their fine, but...*

Feeling anxious, afraid, and a little nauseated, I studied the white-speckled beige institutional floor tiles like they held all the answers. *Jason...Zo...Chris...everyone...what if they're all hurt... or worse?* I thought miserably.

"Lay back, please," Dr. Wesley said, placing her slim hand on my shoulder and easing me backward on the exam table. "We do general, holistic checkups on everyone who enters the Colony from the outside." Her tone was businesslike.

From the outside? I frowned.

"This includes an exam of the patient's reproductive organs," the doctor explained. "It's required, so I hope you don't mind." That shut me and my thoughts up for a good five minutes while she poked and prodded my most personal parts. When she finished and let me sit back up, she asked, "Have you been sexually active since you were infected?"

Rearranging my thin, borrowed robe to cover myself, I blushed, wondering if she'd been able to tell just by looking. *Well, this is embarrassing.* "Um...yeah."

"Have you considered procreating?"

I almost laughed, but instead emitted a part-choke, part-cough. "No."

"The human population has been drastically reduced. We've started a program here to help keep us from the risk of extinction. There are quite a few desirable men here, and you're a young, healthy woman. You might consider—"

My eyes narrowed involuntarily. "You mean, you guys started a breeding program?"

"That's not exactly—"

"Thanks, but no thanks. I'm not a broodmare. Besides, I've got my hands full with Jason. And you *really* don't want to see what he'd do to any of your 'desirable men' if they, you know, tried to 'breed' with me." And yes, I used air quotes. I suddenly wished I had my knives and my little pistol. But I'd left all my weapons in the tent with Jason. *Damn, I really* am *an idiot.*

A minuscule smile curved the doctor's lips, and she moved her head in the barest of nods. "You're lucky to have found so many people from your hometown who survived. Bodega Bay is quite small, if I'm not mistaken," she commented. She sat on her black, wheeled stool and moved my folder to her lap to make some more notes.

Is she fishing for information? It felt like she was, but I didn't really care. I was tired, concussed, and felt ill at both the possibility that my friends were hurt and the idea of being passed from man to man in an attempt to impregnate me. Finally, I answered, "Not exactly. Like I told you, pretty much everyone is from other places. There were a handful of survivors back home, but not the people who really mattered to us." *Not Grams…not Zo's dad…*

"Interesting." Dr. Wesley continued writing on one of the pieces of paper in the folder.

Is she writing down what I'm telling her? It was time for a subject change. "I, um…I'd really like to get back to my friends. Do you know when I'll be able to leave?"

"We'll want to make sure your head is healed, and it'll be at least a week before we'll be certain you're back to normal."

"And if I want to leave earlier?"

Dr. Wesley pursed her lips before responding. "You'll have to ask General Herodson about that. He makes all final decisions regarding arrivals and departures."

What is this, a freaking airport? "And when will I be able to see *him*?" I asked. From what I knew, generals were sort of high up in the don't-give-a-shit-about-nobodies-like-me hierarchy.

There was a soft knock on the door. Dr. Wesley turned her head toward it and called, “Come in.”

MG—blond, well over six feet, and easily one of the most intelligent people I’d ever met—eased the dull gray door open. He was handsome, with bold features and pale blue eyes, and his hair, reaching mid-neck when loose, was pulled back into a low, tidy ponytail. With him was another person, a slightly portly young man wearing light blue scrubs and a blank, complacent expression. MG turned to the side, letting the other man enter the room. He did so silently, stopping beside Dr. Wesley.

The doctor held out her hand in MG’s direction, her pointer finger upraised to halt his words before he had a chance to speak. She looked up at the other man. “AJ, can you please prep this for me?” she asked as she tore off a sheet from a prescription pad and handed it to him.

The young man—AJ—accepted the slip of paper. “Of course, Dr. Wesley. Would you like me to do this immediately?” His voice was monotonous, sounding almost robotic.

“Yes, thank you.”

“Very well, Dr. Wesley. I will do it right now. Is there anything else you would like me to do?”

With a small smile, the doctor shook her head. “Thank you, AJ.”

“You are welcome,” AJ said before he turned and left the room. The entire exchange was just…odd.

“Lively new assistant you’ve got there, Wes,” MG said. He flashed Dr. Wesley a breathtaking smile, earning a glare. “Sorry I didn’t explain about Dani earlier. It probably surprised you when you realized she wasn’t your normal type of patient.”

“Yes, well, a heads-up would’ve been nice, Gabriel,” the doctor replied tersely.

“C’mon, Wes, I didn’t have a chance. You’ve been busy with Re-gens and T-Rs all morning. I just wanted her to see the best, and you know brains better than anyone.”

Dr. Wesley snorted delicately and shook her head, but I could tell she was trying to hide a smile.

MG's eyes flicked to me, and I was almost certain I glimpsed worry in their pale blue depths. "So, are you done with Dani?"

"Yes, I am." Dr. Wesley reclaimed my gaze. "I believe the answer to your question of when you'll get to see General Herodson would be: right now. Gabriel will take you to him."

4

DANI

MARCH 15, 1AE

After shooting one last, thoughtful glance my way, Dr. Wesley left the sterile examination room, shutting the door with a soft click. I hopped down from the exam table and wrapped the thin robe around me more tightly. Neither the hospital gown nor the robe was very substantial, and MG was still in the room. I was feeling more than a little self-conscious.

Gone was the flirty, self-assured MG I'd befriended in dreamland months ago. As the door had shut behind Dr. Wesley, MG had transformed into a brooding, somber man I barely recognized. An ever-present crease had formed between his eyebrows, and he exuded tension. So, what had changed? *Is he unhappy to see me? Does he not want me here?* That was fine with me; I was eager to get back to my friends anyway. *But I thought* we *were friends.*

Clearing his throat, MG handed me the canvas sack he'd brought with him. When I peeked inside, all I could think was, *Hallelujah!* He'd given me clothes—glorious, much more substantial clothes. Not that my current attire really counted as "clothes," but still. Out of the bag I pulled a t-shirt, a sports bra, cotton underwear, sweatpants, and a hoodless sweatshirt—all gray—and set each item on the padded exam table. Both tops had *AIR FORCE* written across the chest in black, blocky letters. There was also a new pair of soft, white socks and some equally bland sneakers. It was like my birthday, post-apocalypse style.

"Thanks," I said, setting the empty bag on the floor. I flicked my eyes from him to the door and back. I was thankful for the clothes, but not enough to do an impromptu strip show. "Um...do you mind?"

MG cocked his head to the side, and the crease between his eyebrows deepened.

"I'd like to change...*without* an audience," I clarified.

A normal MG reaction would've included a flirty quip accompanied by a devilish smile. I received neither. Frowning, he mumbled, "Of course. Sorry," and slipped out of the room.

I locked the door and twisted the knob to double-check the lock before shrugging out of my thin robe and thinner hospital gown. The new clothes were generic, but clean, and far better than my previous attire. To finish the couch potato–chic look, I secured my wild auburn curls in a fluffy ponytail using a rubber band I found in one of the drawers below the counter.

"Ready," I almost said when I emerged from the little room into a hallway, but the word died on my lips. MG was nowhere in sight. In fact, I couldn't see anybody at all. There were only shut doors, and faint whispers. I could hear people talking softly a short ways off.

I concentrated on my Ability, planning to open myself to what Chris called "observation mode" to figure out where the whisperers were and whether or not MG was one of them, but I hit a mental wall. It was like the telepathic part of my brain was partitioned off, and I couldn't access it *at all*. It was exactly how I felt when Jason was nulling my Ability. Genius that I wasn't in my concussed state, it took me longer than necessary to realize there were three options: the strength of Jason's Ability had increased massively and he was nulling everyone within a fifty mile radius of camp, Jason was nearby, or somebody else on the base had an Ability similar to his. I was betting it was the last.

Alright, I told myself, *I'll just have to do this the old-fashioned way.* Sneaking around and eavesdropping have always been two of my strongest skills, so I started sneaking and prepared to eavesdrop.

The hallway outside the exam room was barren, extending in both directions for a noticeable distance. Moving to the left, I hugged the far wall. Ever so slowly, in absolute silence, I crept toward the voices. They were soft, muted to a whisper, and completely unintelligible and unidentifiable. I couldn't even tell if they were male or female. There was only one solution—moving closer.

I peeked around the corner. As far as I could tell, the conversing pair was in another exam room, just a few yards down the hall. The door was cracked open, muffling their words. As I listened, I became as still and silent as humanly possible.

"—you sure?" one voice whispered.

"I think so," the other responded.

A sigh was followed by the first voice saying, "Damn, Wes. I was expecting more of a fight. What made you agree so quickly?"

Wes...that's what MG called Dr. Wesley. At least I knew who I was spying on. Still, I didn't announce my presence.

"She's a perfect candidate, that's all," Dr. Wesley whispered.

A perfect candidate for what, *exactly? That breeding program?* My face scrunched in disgust.

"Besides," she continued, "I figured this was what you wanted when you sent her to me instead of the doctor she'd been assigned."

"Wow, Wes. I mean, I expected your usual, 'Caution, Gabriel, caution,' and 'Patience won't kill us, but a mistake will.' I'm pleasantly surprised," MG whispered, closely followed by a chuckle. "No need to glare."

"With you, there's always a need to glare." After a brief

moment, Dr. Wesley said, "I need some time to prepare it, to tune it to her blood. It should be ready in about twelve hours."

Tune it to my blood? Tune what *to my blood?* I wondered. *Crap! I shouldn't have told her anything about the others.* I was starting to feel a whole lot less comfortable about being in the Colony, and a whole lot more excited about meeting with that General person and bidding the unsettling place adieu. And I'd already been *very* excited about doing that. *God, Jason and Zo had better be okay...*

"That long?" MG asked.

"You forget, we haven't had a new candidate for weeks," the doctor explained. "I don't have any of the neutralizer ready. I can't just leave it around…"

Neutralizer? As I listened, I was getting more and more wigged out. I considered hightailing it out of the hospital and trying to find my own way out of the Colony without MG, Dr. Wesley, or whoever this General guy was. *Maybe nobody'll even notice me leaving?* But then I remembered what the doctor had said about the General—that he makes the final decision on all arrivals and departures. If nobody came or went without his approval, I was betting there were some pretty heavy measures preventing people from just walking out. *Nightfall.* It would be much safer to sneak out on my own after nightfall. I could wait that long.

"It's fine, Wes. I owe you," MG said softly, no longer a whisper. I'd heard his voice sound like that, kind and caring, in my dreams. I knew exactly what expression he was wearing—his forehead wrinkled, and his eyebrows drawn together. "I'll come by your office first thing in the morning to pick it up, alright?"

"Gabriel." The doctor said MG's true name like it was a warning. "Don't look at me like that."

"Like what?"

"Like you want to save me."

"Wes, I—"

"No! I don't deserve—"

"Wes," MG repeated, his tone dropping.

"Enough, Gabriel. You have things to do, as do I. I'll have it ready in the morning. Until then, I'd suggest you…"

Wanting to *not* get caught snooping, I backed away from the juncture of hallways, reopened the exam room's door, and shut it loudly. "MG?" I called, purposely looking in the opposite direction—down the hall to the right.

"Dani," he said as he rounded the expected corner. I turned to face him. "Are you ready?"

I shrugged, aiming for nonchalance, even though I felt anything but. "Sure, now's as good of a time as any. So where's this General guy? On another floor or something?"

"Uh, no. He's in another building. It's a short walk, about a half mile," MG said, stopping a few feet from me.

Hugging myself, I slouched and whined, "A half mile? But my head feels like it's going to explode."

Abruptly, Dr. Wesley came bustling around the corner. "That's what this is for," she said, holding up a syringe. "And these," she added, proffering a small, orange prescription bottle.

I took a step backward. Needles didn't bug me, but after the conversation I'd just overheard, I wasn't letting her inject me with anything. "Uh, thanks, but I'm not big on shots."

She shook her head and pressed her lips together. "It's just Toradol. You'll thank me for it. I shouldn't really be giving you this anyway, not with the concussion, but in your case, it'll do more good than harm."

For the briefest moment, I gazed at the syringe in longing. *Pain relief...* And then, I backed away another step. Any crazy drug could've been in that plastic tube. I didn't know what MG and the doctor were involved in, but it had sounded like they were planning to induct me—involuntarily. "Like I said, I'm not a fan of needles. I can live with the pain."

The doctor raised one shoulder. "Suit yourself." Handing me

the prescription bottle, she said, "Ibuprofen. You can start taking them in the morning. And, whatever you do, don't go to sleep tonight."

I groaned, already feeling like I was about to fall asleep standing up.

"I mean it," Dr. Wesley said. She gave my former dream invader a meaningful look. "Gabriel?"

MG raised his hand, boy scout–style. "I'll make sure she stays awake by any means necessary. I promise."

Again, the doctor's lips pressed together in a thin, flat line.

Wearing a wide grin, MG said, "And on that note, we'll just be on our way."

Before following him down the hallway, I spared a few seconds to study the doctor, trying to discern what her deal was. She'd gone from standoffish to helpful to considering me as a candidate for something unknown to me and wanting to attune a *neutralizer* to my *blood*. She returned my stare, her own eyes searching. *What's she looking for?*

It wasn't until I'd rounded two corners—one left, one right—that I caught up to MG and fell in step beside him. He slowed so I didn't have to jog to keep up with his much longer strides. The corridors were far more vacant than any hospital, doctor's office, or clinic I'd ever visited before the Virus, and the emptiness gave me the willies. That, and the electricity.

Evenly spaced lights shone from the ceiling with a bright, artificial glow. They hummed. It was annoying. For several months, I'd been without electricity of any kind. There had been no overhead lights in the middle of the night, no showers spraying deliciously hot water, no microwaves, and no washing machines. My people and I had reverted back to the basics and had grown accustomed to a simpler way of life. I couldn't get over how loud the electricity was; it buzzed incessantly, threatening to drive me insane.

"What? No elevator?" I asked as I stepped through a doorway

behind MG. Seconds later, the door thudded closed, leaving us alone in a gray- and white-toned stairwell.

MG chuckled. "We make an effort to conserve the energy we have."

Right, I thought, *keep telling yourself that.* To power the hospital alone, they needed a mini power plant. I frowned. *Where* are *they getting the energy?*

"It's just one flight down. The elevators use too much power to be worth it," MG explained.

"Hmmm…" I mumbled, slowly making my way down rubber-edged, cement stairs. With every step, it felt like glass shards were slicing through my tender, mushed brain. My face scrunched in an extended cringe.

MG caught my arm, stopping my descent. "I can get us a car if you don't think you can make it." Worry coated his voice, cracking through my pain and temporarily shelving my wariness.

I met his eyes—his gentle, caring eyes—and wondered if whatever he and Dr. Wesley were involved with wasn't really a bad thing…or maybe it was a *really* bad thing. The plan was to play it cool and get the General's permission to leave. The backup plan was to play it cool, then get the hell out of this place once the sun went down.

"I'm fine," I told MG. "You know, it's crazy that you could just do that…get us a car."

"I forget that things are different out there," MG said as we continued down the stairs. Even though we moved slowly, our footsteps still echoed in the stairwell above us, along with our voices.

We reached the door at the bottom landing, and I pressed my hands against the cool metal of the push bar. On the other side of the door, I found another hallway and a wall of windows—it was all that separated me from the outside world. After spending so much time outdoors over the past few months, being confined within layers and layers of walls was almost abhorrent. I couldn't escape fast enough.

Finally, I stepped out into the late winter sunshine, closed my eyes, and took a deep breath…and then I took another. The cool air tasted heavenly.

"You sure you're okay?" MG asked.

"Yeah, breath of fresh air and all that. So"—I opened my eyes and found him standing in front of me, still looking concerned—"where to, MG?"

"Gabe. My name is Gabe." He sounded tired.

"Okay…*Gabe*." The name felt wrong on my tongue; he would always be MG to me. "Where are we headed? There?" I asked, pointing to a large, boxy concrete building across the street. I knew it wasn't our destination—he'd already told me *that* was a half mile away—but I needed to get my bearings. Familiarity could breed a lot of things, including a better backup plan.

"No." MG began walking up the right side of a mostly empty two-lane road, and I followed, staying close to his side.

"What's there, then?"

"It's a storage warehouse now…before, I don't know what it was."

"Oh?" I asked. I pointed off to our right to a row of houses at the edge of what was obviously a residential area. "Do you live in that neighborhood?"

"Yeah…along with pretty much everyone else."

"Do all of the houses have power, too, or just the important buildings like the hospital?" Because that would be a lot of power, more than just a mini-power plant could provide. *Do they have enough people to man such a thing?*

"All the houses, the warehouses—everywhere has it," he explained.

Hmmm… "So where does it come from?"

Out of the corner of my eye, I could see MG shake his head.

"It's…complicated. And, honestly Dani, that's not my area of expertise."

"Well, you must know where it comes from." After a moment of thought, I added, "Wind? A dam? Solar?" Did they have some sort of nuclear power plant nearby? Had they come up with a new way to generate electricity? I watched his face as we walked, even though it made me feel dizzy.

"I hate to disappoint, but I really don't know how to explain the system. I spend most of my time in my lab, not interrogating the engineers about their power sources."

"Okay," I said with a shrug. I squinted and resumed looking ahead. There were a couple people on the other side of the street, yelling about something, and I could hear several engines rumbling in the distance. "It's effing loud here."

"Is it?" MG made a show of listening, but didn't seem impressed.

"Yep. I haven't heard a car engine in months." Suddenly, everything about the Colony felt very, *very* wrong. I stopped and grabbed his wrist, my fingers clutching at the rough sleeve of his jacket.

MG halted. When he glanced down at my hand, I released him.

"It's great that you have a place that's so"—I floundered, searching for the right word—"er, accommodating, but you have to understand what it's like out there for everyone else. It's not bad, exactly. Well, it sort of is. But this—" I waved my arms around at the buzzing power lines and parked vehicles. "It's like you're all living in a bubble. How could this possibly be sustained?"

Studying me, MG took a deep, contemplative breath. "I don't know. That's not my—"

"Area of expertise," I finished for him with an exasperated sigh. "I know."

MG frowned and continued walking. "As far as I've been told, the plan is to draw in enough survivors that we can use the infrastructure already in existence in and around Colorado Springs.

We just need enough people to make it work. It'll be a mini version of the world we knew."

I shook my head, ignoring the pain. For such an intelligent man, I didn't understand how MG could be so blind…unless he wanted to be. "And how many people would that take? A hundred thousand? Two? More? How would you feed them all? The stuff you scavenge is going to run out, and you can't grow and raise food for that many people in just the area around here. Are you going to ship it in? From where? *Everyone* is dead. Where will you get medical supplies? Hell, where will you get the basic things that people need to stay healthy? Are you going to build factories to produce toothpaste and toilet paper? What about—"

"Okay, Dani. I get it," MG said sharply. He caught my eye then quickly looked away. "I've been focused on other, more immediate things. I haven't spent much time thinking about the future."

"Sorry," I said. "I didn't mean…I know that none of this is your fault and that you don't run this place. It's just frustrating, you know, seeing all this. It feels so wrong and makes me that much more eager to get out of here."

Turning to face me, MG leaned in, his eyes fierce. "I know you want to get back to your friends, but when we get to Colony Headquarters, *please* don't behave confrontationally toward General Herodson. No matter what he says, just don't. Please, Dani."

I thought about arguing. I really, *really* wanted to argue. But he just seemed so sincere…so concerned. "Don't worry, MG." I shook my head. "I mean, Gabe. I'll be the perfect little Colonist… who just happens to want to leave."

He sighed and reached out a hand to squeeze my shoulder. "I just hope that's good enough."

We walked the rest of the way in silence, me looking around at everything, logging the layout and details of the Colony as best I could, and MG thinking. Eventually, we turned right at an intersection and approached three enormous, extremely modern buildings. Each looked imposing and completely unique, like the three structures didn't really belong together. We passed the first two, aiming for the third, the darkest.

"General Herodson is expecting her," MG told the two men posted on either side of the building's reinforced glass door. Both were dressed in green and tan fatigues with yellow armbands, and both carried assault rifles.

The man on the left nodded, and the one on the right opened the door for us.

I started to follow MG into the building, but I was halted by the guard on the left. His hand gripped my upper arm, his hold firm and unwelcome. "Why don't you come find me after your meeting with General Herodson. I'll help you *settle in*." The way he emphasized the last two words left no question as to his meaning. I was so shocked I could only gape at him.

MG clenched his jaw and stepped closer, looking like he wanted to attack my detainer.

I finally shook off my astonishment and rolled my eyes. Placing my free hand on MG's chest, I said, "Hold on, cowboy," before turning my attention to the man who was still holding my arm. I took my time looking the stranger up and down, then curled my lip. "Not interested."

Apparently it was the wrong response, because his grip tightened. *Damn.* "We'll see if you feel the same way after your meeting."

I scoffed and checked him out again, noting the name stitched onto his breast pocket. "Trust me, *Grant*. I will. And don't *ever* touch me again."

He stiffened, and a glint of challenge flashed in his eye, but he also released me. It took a conscious effort not to shake out my arm, but I refused to give him the satisfaction. *What an asshole*, I thought as MG and I continued into the building. *At least I'll be gone by morning.*

As we neared a stairwell door, MG eyed me sideways. "You've changed."

I shrugged. “Had to.”

He didn’t say anything else as we ascended two flights of stairs and emerged into another bland, beige and gray hallway. Evidently the military hadn’t been big on creative interior decorating.

MG stopped before a reinforced door. Its gold placard read, *General Herodson, President of the New United States.*

“I guess I missed the vote,” I said.

Without warning, the door opened.

“Welcome. You must be the young woman my people rescued last night,” a man said from inside the room. He hadn’t been the one to open the door—that was another camouflaged soldier reminiscent of the two guarding the entrance downstairs. No, the owner of the voice was seated behind a wide, metal desk that was equally cluttered and organized. Piles of papers, file folders, and notebooks were neatly stacked along the desk’s surface, as well as on the bookshelves and tables arranged around the periphery of the office. It was very Spartan—all function, no fluff.

The speaker tapped a few final keys on the laptop he was using, then gently shut it and handed it to the woman standing behind him, who exchanged it for a sleek tablet. She, too, was wearing camouflage fatigues. Shocking, I know.

The seated man, however, was decked out in a far more intimidating uniform. Made from a blue fabric so dark it was nearly black, his jacket was decorated with a rainbow of badges and medals over the left side of his chest, and it had garish bronze buttons. A stripe emblazoned with four gold stars and outlined in even more gold was tacked to the edge of either shoulder.

The appearance of the man himself was unremarkable, though his intense presence was undisputable. He was trim, his face narrow, and though it was etched with lines that had likely come from a life of stress and frowns, it was not unpleasant. I guessed he was in his late fifties or early sixties, though his hair showed no signs of his late-middle-aged status; it was brown and short, and only a little lighter than his neatly trimmed mustache. Overall, he was quite average. But then there were his eyes. Cold and gray, they seemed to see inside me, measure the essence of my being, and refuse to divulge their findings. Even with the smile spreading his thin lips, his stare made me want to shiver. There was no doubt in my mind that I was staring at General Herodson, supposed President of the New United States, leader of the Colony, and the one man who controlled whether I stayed or left. *Delightful.*

"Please, come in. It's Danielle, isn't it?" he asked. His voice was soft and calm in a way that made my skin crawl. MG's hushed warning to hold my temper was suddenly making a lot more sense. The General was dangerous—like swimming-in-a-shark-tank-while-bleeding dangerous.

Hesitantly, I stepped into the office, and MG followed. Or at least, he tried to follow.

"Thank you, Gabriel, but I'd like you to wait outside while I meet with the newest addition to our little settlement."

MG looked like he wanted to argue, but with great effort, he held it in.

"You may leave," the General said, and though the tone of his voice hadn't changed, irritation was evident in the tension around his eyes.

I glanced back at MG, trying to imbue my face with reassurance. Unfortunately, I was pretty sure it came across more like constipation. I was feeling neither reassured nor reassuring. When I turned back to the General, I relaxed my features; my blank face could have easily rivaled Jason's usual stony expression.

"Thank you for seeing me," I said, stepping further into the room. "I'm sure you're really busy with running this place and everything." I heard the soft click of the door shutting behind me and sat down in the empty chair in front of the desk. The General's right eye twitched minutely when I sat, making me wonder if he'd expected me to wait for his permission. *So he's a control freak.* I scoffed inwardly. *Figures.*

General Herodson rested his elbows on the desk and steepled

his fingers under his chin, unabashedly studying me. "I make it a priority to meet with every person who enters the Colony or plans to leave indefinitely."

The woman to whom he'd handed the laptop closed a file cabinet behind the General and walked around the desk to stand behind me, presumably next to the man at the door. It bothered me that the two armed soldiers were behind me—a lot—and I itched to turn and see what they were doing. With a herculean effort, I managed to restrain myself.

"So, um, thanks for rescuing me and for the medical care," I said, breaking the protracted, very uncomfortable silence. I was fairly certain my discomfort was the whole point of the silence, that and the soldiers standing behind me. *I think I'm ready to go now...*

"Of course," General Herodson said. "I like to make sure all of my Colonists are well cared for." He graced me with another of his eerie smiles. *Ugh...* instant heebie-jeebies. "Well, now that you're safely within my grasp, I'd like to offer you permanent residency here in the Colony. It's the heart—the Capital—around which the New United States will be built."

"Oh...um, thanks. But I already have somewhere I belong outside of here."

General Herodson put on a tolerant expression, his voice dripping with condescension. "Please don't make any permanent decisions until you hear everything I have to offer you."

"Listen, I really appreciate—"

"I have a house already set aside for you—it's quite comfortable, and I'm sure far better than whatever your accommodations have been over the past few months. I also have a position as a communications specialist denoted just for you. I know it would utilize your Ability perfectly."

Um, okay...how does he know about my Ability? Has MG been blabbing about me? I felt a sudden, sickening pang of betrayal in my chest.

"Also, we have the technology and personnel to help you increase the strength of your telepathy," he continued. "You're a very special woman, Danielle—your Ability is exceptional and very unique. It could greatly increase our numbers here."

That he knew so much about me, about my telepathy, was just another notch on the General's creepy belt. I felt like I'd been stalked. I made a mental note to interrogate MG about everything he'd told General Herodson.

Plastering on my friendliest smile, I said, "I really do appreciate the offer and everything the Colony has done for me so far, but I already have a place I belong. I'm happy there." It was hard to find a way to say what needed to be said without sounding like an ungrateful brat. His people *had* saved my life, after all. "So, if it's not too much trouble, I'd prefer to leave as soon as possible… or whenever's convenient." *And if you say no, I'm outta here tonight, you creepy, creepy man.*

He sighed, and his chilling, almost dead eyes latched on to mine. "I'm very sorry to hear that, Danielle. I had really hoped you would feel more at home here and that I wouldn't have to bend your mind like all the others. My most loyal are those who choose to follow me of their own accord. Oh well. You will do exactly as I say…"

As he spoke, a fog seeped into my brain, coating my senses and thoughts, dulling them… numbing them. His voice droned on, but I was having a hard time focusing on the sounds, comprehending the meanings. They jumbled together, turning into a mind-numbing hum. My vision slowly unfocused, becoming a blur of colorful, unidentifiable shapes.

Suddenly, my brain fog evaporated and the General asked, "Does that sound acceptable?"

I shook my head, trying to make sense of what had just happened. "Um…yeah," I heard myself say as my lips stretched into a grateful smile. *I'm so happy to be here.* "I think that sounds perfect."

General Herodson's answering grin was radiant, washing away a strange sense of anxiety.

"I'm very glad to hear it," he said. "Now, I'm sure you'd like to see your new home and settle in."

I nodded. *My new home.* "Yes, that would be great. But I don't know where it is."

"Not to worry." He stood and rounded the desk, then reached for my hand, pulled me up from the chair, and draped his arm over my shoulders. Compared to me, he was tall, though he was probably still a little under six feet. "I'm sure Gabriel will help get you settled. I'll be sure he knows to introduce you to the other communications specialists as soon as you've recovered."

"Okay," I said, feeling absolutely content with my new situation. I'd felt so lost and alone for so long, it was nice to finally belong somewhere…to be around other people.

When the female guard opened the door, Gabe came into view. He'd been leaning his back against the opposite hallway wall, but he straightened as soon as he saw me. His handsome face lost all expression, going completely and utterly blank. "Are you finished, Sir? Can I take her back to the hospital?"

"Actually, Danielle has decided to stay. I believe you know the house we prepared for her. Please take her there and help her settle in." General Herodson removed his arm from my shoulders and nudged me through the doorway. "And make sure she wears these at all times," he said, handing Gabe a pair of yellow armbands that matched those I'd seen on pretty much everyone.

Gabe's expression remained blank as I neared him, which irritated me. Shouldn't he have been happy that I was staying in the Colony, that he'd get to spend more time with me? I was certainly looking forward to getting to know *him* better…a lot better. But his eyes held a hint of something resembling unhappiness. *He doesn't want me to stay?*

"Yes, of course, Sir." Gabe accepted the yellow fabric, then reached out and placed his arm around my shoulders much like

General Herodson had done. Except Gabe's embrace felt different—more protective, possessive, even. I figured it was just because he was noticeably taller and stronger than the older man.

As Gabe started to guide me down the hallway, I looked back at the General and smiled. "Thanks again," I told him.

5

ZOE

MARCH 15, 1AE

Walking closer to the fire pit, I could distinctly hear the shock in Jake's voice as he confronted our mysterious visitor, his sister.

"I—I thought you…" He stared into Becca's eyes. I could feel the concern and guilt washing over him in waves, and I hesitated, not wanting to intrude. "You were dead." He reached for her, but she raised a hand to block him. He froze, clearly distraught. "Where the hell've you been?"

And just as Jake's mind fled to memories of the past, Becca's did as well, sweeping me along with it.

"We found the telepath," a slender, stern-looking man said as he rose from behind his large metal desk. His voice held a tinge of victory, although his eyes remained empty. He was a middle-aged military officer with brown hair and a slightly darker, cropped mustache. His navy blue, medal-adorned uniform looked pretentious. I noticed a raving gleam in his eyes as he glided over to Becca, who was standing in front of his desk wearing pastel green scrubs.

"The one you've been searching for," Becca said, only a hint of

emotion in her raspy voice. Her dark hair was twisted into a tight, fist-sized bun atop her head, and her eyes were a dull mixture of blue and gray...not the violet I recalled from Jake's memories.

"Yes, the very one." The officer nodded and walked the few feet between the edge of his desk and Becca's position in front of it. His lips curved into a knowing smile as he placed both hands on her shoulders. "Everything is turning out exactly *like I wanted...we just need to wait a little longer," he added. "So prepare yourself for a special task." He leaned in closer to her.*

She raised her chin a notch, honored that he'd chosen her *to help him. "Of course, Father. Anything you wish of me, I will do."*

He gave her shoulders a slight squeeze. "Yes, I know," he said. He straightened and strode to a large window, his hands clasped behind his back. "Sometime soon, you will be going to their camp to find out everything you can about them. We need to know how dangerous they are, and how useful they may be. We need to know if they're special—like you, my dear." He flashed her a false smile over his shoulder. "And we need to know what their plans are. Will you do that for me, RV-one, and do it well *this time?"*

Taken aback by his tone, she nodded and smiled. "Of course, Father," she repeated.

"Leave me now." He shooed her away without even a glance back up at her. "Don't let me down again, RV-one." There was an edge to his voice, a warning. "You will regret it."

The telepath. "Dani," I whispered. *What are they going to do to her?*

"I said, 'where the hell've you been,' Becca?" Jake's hands clasped her shoulders.

Becca straightened, looking startled. "I am not Becca." Her raspy voice sounded official. "I do not know you," she said slowly and stepped away from him. "And please do not touch me."

Jake frowned. "Don't touch you?" Although he dropped his

hands to his sides, he didn't step away. "Jesus Christ, Becca…are you alright? What happened to you? I thought you were dead."

She held his gaze for a moment longer before turning her attention to the fire.

After a few breaths of silence, Jake took an uncertain step closer. His eyes were wide, and his lips were parted like he was struggling to find the right words. "You had no pulse…you were bleeding all over the place…" His words were quiet and unsure, like he was questioning his own memories. "You *were* dead," he said under his breath.

Becca's eyebrows rose infinitesimally, but I couldn't feel her emotions clearly enough to interpret them. "I do not know what you are talking about," she said stiffly. Her strange speech pattern was jarring. "And my name is *not* Becca; my name is R—Rachel." Idly, she rubbed the skin beneath the cuff of her sweatshirt, and I could just make out some black marks on her wrist. *A tattoo? Like Dani's?*

Jake hesitated before he spoke. "Your name *is* Becca. It's Rebecca Marie Vaughn," he said, and though she recoiled at his intensity, he continued, "You're twenty-four. You like to swim, but you love snowboarding. You were born in Durango, but when Mom died we went to live with Gabe and Lizzy in Colorado Springs. Your birthday is September twenty-fifth, and your favorite color is red. You said you had fun at your prom because you knew that's what I wanted to hear, but secretly you hated it." He shook his head. "I *do* know you. I've known you your whole goddamn life. You're my little sister," he stated, his words pained, almost pleading.

Becca watched him for a moment, her eyes narrowed in question.

"You were dead, Becca," Jake said, still unable to grasp the reality of her being there and standing in front of him.

She shrank away. "Please stop calling me that. I have already told you, I am *not* your sister. I do not know what happened to her, but I assure you, I am not her." Her voice was slightly harder than before. "Please stop calling me Becca." Her steady tone was breaking, and I wondered which emotion might surface first. *Confusion? Anger?* She turned back to the fire. "Call me Rachel." There was a hint of sadness in her voice as she made the request.

I backtracked slowly and leaned against the barn. I wanted to stay, to help Jake in some way, but I didn't know how. I glanced back and forth between them, watching Jake's expression change from disbelief to sadness and then to confusion. I could feel his apprehension warring with the overwhelming need to pull his sister into his arms, to assure himself she was really there. I wished I could take away the pain and regret that filled his heart, but I couldn't. All I could do was feel it with him.

After a second's pause, Jake took a much-needed step back, turned, and strode past me and into the barn. Cooper, who'd been sitting quietly by the fire, rose and trotted after him. When Jake finally reappeared, stalking toward Becca with a small square of paper held between his fingers, my heart seized. *Oh, shit.* Assuming it was a photo of the two of them, I held my breath, waiting to see how their interaction would play out.

Jake stopped beside Becca. "Look at it," he said evenly, holding the picture out to her. When she made no move to accept it, he sighed. "Just look at it."

Becca pried her eyes from the flames and slowly reached for the photo. I could feel her mounting curiosity. She studied the image for a moment, her expression giving nothing away.

Unexpectedly, her head snapped up, her eyes locking on to Jake's, and she thrust the picture at him. "Take it back," she said brusquely. Her display of frustration was the first sign of any intense emotion she'd shown since she'd arrived. "I am not *her*." She tugged anxiously at the hem of her tattered black sweatshirt.

Jake's mind was a cesspool of draining emotions—his anger and confusion twisting with concern and despondency. He shook his head and walked away, defeated.

His words, or the pain behind them, must have affected Becca, because she watched him fixedly as he took one slow, brooding step after another into the barn. He passed me again without a glance in my direction, and I wondered if he even realized I was there.

Unbidden, another of Becca's memories surfaced.

"Where was she, RV-one?" Father asked, eerily calm. He clasped his hands behind his back and turned away from her, heading toward his cluttered desk. "She was in your charge. I gave you specific orders."

Becca's eyes closed in shame. "Yes, Father. I know I have let you down."

"Yes, you have."

Her face was expressionless, but when her eyes flew open, they were filled with a sickening regret. "She was in the cafeteria," she offered. "CL-one is new. She did not understand why she must wait. I was only in the restroom a few minutes. I do not know why she left."

"Interesting." He sat down in his leather desk chair, calm and collected.

"I will speak with her, Father," she said with only a tinge of panic lacing her words. "I will determine the right course of action—"

"No, you won't." Father picked up a pen lying beside a stack of files and began writing something, seeming completely unaffected by her heightened sense of fear.

"Father?"

"Your carelessness is unacceptable," he said distractedly. "Grant," he called.

I could practically taste Becca's terror as the name rolled off his tongue.

The door opened and a guard stepped inside. "Sir?"

"Take RV-one to the interrogation room." He absently gestured

to Becca with the top his pen, his focus intent on the file in front of him. "Make sure she realizes how important my orders are and what happens when they're not obeyed."

Becca stepped forward. "Father, I will—"

"No," he said, finally looking up at her. "And never let this happen again. I won't be as kind next time." He glanced at the guard. "If she struggles, do it again."

After the guard nodded and pulled Becca's hands behind her back, the memory changed.

Becca was lying on a slanted board, her feet restrained above her and her arms tied at her sides. Muted rays of light shone through the fibers of the rag draped over her head. Her eyes were blurred from the remnants of water that still seeped through the wet cloth onto her face and trickled down her throat. Every attempted inhale was like breathing in scorching fire. Tears of pain mixed with the water as it streamed across her temples.

When Becca heard the sloshing of water and realized her momentary respite was over, she tried to scream, to beg for the guard to stop. But it was no use.

Again, water seeped through the rag, running into her nostrils.

Again, her mouth involuntarily opened and she attempted to breathe. Water gurgled down her throat, making her lungs seize, her chest heave, and her throat burn as she choked, almost suffocating completely.

Again, the primal instinct to breathe forced her body to thrash against the board. She couldn't help but struggle between bursts of panic.

Again, she was choking on water as she all but drowned. Terror completely consumed her.

My mind stirred defensively, shutting out the suffocating feeling that had begun to consume me.

Becca was standing alone by the fire. She inched closer to the flames and tentatively raised her hands to their warmth. It was like she'd never seen fire before.

What else did they do to her? I drew an unsteady breath. *Oh my God...what are they going to do to Dani?* I continued searching through Becca's mind for a memory that might help us figure out what "Father" wanted with my best friend.

A cafeteria flashed in my mind, and I saw Becca sitting among a sea of others dressed in scrubs like her, but in different colors, each with two letters and two numbers tattooed on their wrists. They all seemed socially stunted, innocent, and overtly unanimated —like Becca.

She was in a classroom—in a speech class of some sort—and she was learning how to pronounce vowel sounds. She was wearing white scrubs, just like the rest of the people sitting at the desks that filled the room. Colorful posters covered the walls, like those you'd find in a foreign language classroom, except everything was in English. A middle-aged woman with black armbands was weaving among the desks, praising and correcting her pupils as needed.

A few more of her memories flashed in my mind's eye before I blinked myself free of them. My Ability had been strengthening over the past month, allowing me to see more of people's memories and feel more of their emotions than I necessarily wanted to. Unfortunately, my control hadn't been increasing at the same rate.

I'd felt and seen enough from Becca to know her mind had clearly been tampered with. As far as I could tell, her memories only spanned back a few months. She'd been rehabilitated, trained in basic self-defense, and taught to speak and how to act within a matter of weeks.

I studied her face from a distance. It was just as I remembered it from Jake's memories—only her eyes duller and lifeless—and I painstakingly waited to glimpse an irrefutable memory of Jake to force her to admit, even to herself, that she *was* who she denied to be.

But her mind was an impenetrable vault of things forgotten, possibly gone forever. There was nothing in her mind connecting the two of them; it didn't make sense.

In the distance, gravel crunched under horse hooves, followed by a whinny and the sound of clanking metal bridles.

Jason? I straightened and started walking toward the noise, an unexpected string tugging at my heart. But the rider wasn't my brother.

Carlos and his horse, Arrow, clomped through the line of trees edging the northeast side of camp, their outline barely visible in the dying afternoon light. Ky and Ben followed directly behind them. Not surprisingly, Ky brought his flask to his mouth as he swayed atop his horse. He tipped his head all the way back to savor every remaining drop.

Chris ran out from the barn, and I caught sight of the scathing look she shot Carlos. As he dismounted, his eyes met hers, and I felt her relief before her expression softened. Jack barked and trotted toward us with his tongue hanging from the side of his mouth. Jason, sitting atop his nameless horse, brought up the rear. *Thank God.*

My brother eyed me for a moment, his gaze lingering before shifting to Chris. She was fretting over Carlos, her hands hovering around his body as she inspected him for injuries. Wiping a smudge of dirt from his cheek, she scolded, "I had no idea how to find you. You're lucky—"

"It's my fault," Jason said evenly. "Blame me."

Chris glared at him. "Oh, I do." Pulling away from Carlos, she rounded on Jason. "Get your head out of your ass. What were you thinking?" She snorted, her arms flailing as her anger flared to rage. "Oh, that's right, you were thinking about *yourself.* It's not like no one cares what happens to you, but you just go off, oblivious to the repercussions of your stupid actions." She peered up into the sky, her claw-like fingers balling into fists. "I can't even look at you right now." She reached for Carlos's arm and led him into the barn.

Even though Jason was nulling me, I could see the defeat in his eyes as Chris and Carlos disappeared inside. I didn't know why my brother had come back, but I was grateful that he had.

"What'd we miss?" Ky asked, climbing clumsily from his saddle. "You all look like you've seen a ghost." Then he flashed a crooked, drunken smile. "Or is it just that you all missed me terribly?"

I couldn't help but laugh. "We have a visitor," I said quietly, and nodded toward the campfire and Becca.

Jason handed his reins to Ben, who led the horses to the stable, and then my brother turned his attention to the stranger by the fire. "So who is she?"

"Jake's sister," I said.

"He has two?"

I shook my head.

Jason eyed Becca. "I thought he said she was dead."

"She was."

"Come inside," Chris called from the barn. "I'll fill you in."

"I thought you couldn't stand looking at me," Jason said.

She barked a laugh. "I don't have to look at you to talk to you."

I followed Jason into the barn, wondering what plan the others had come up with in the hour since we'd returned from Cañon City. Grayson, Carlos, and Sarah passed us on their way out as we stepped inside, leaving Chris, Harper, Biggs, and Sanchez huddled around a workbench. Jake wasn't there. *How's he doing?* A horrifying thought crossed my mind. *Is Father toying with us? With Jake? Does he* know *who Becca is to him?* Based on her memories, it didn't seem likely.

"Toy." It suddenly made sense. I took a few hurried steps closer to the workbench. "H," I said, reaching for Harper's arm.

He turned to me. "What's up, Baby Girl?"

"Becca—she's his 'toy.' The men in Cañon City said they had to 'get his *toy* home safe and sound.' It's gotta be her. I've seen the man I think they're referring to in her memories." I quickly filled them in on the disturbing scenes I'd gleaned from her mind. "They're sending a retrieval team for her tomorrow, and they're going to raid us. *For sure*." I glanced at Biggs and then out at the fire, where Sarah was chatting with Becca. I didn't miss the way Becca's eyes narrowed and lingered on Sarah's round belly. "Whatever happens, we've gotta get Sarah outta here."

"Who the hell *is* this broad?" Biggs asked. His easygoing attitude had been completely dormant since we'd first heard Dani's scream.

"It *is* Becca," I told them a little defensively. "She just doesn't have any memories past a few months ago. It's like they've been wiped away—or she has amnesia, maybe?"

"Then how do you know it's really her?" Sanchez asked, clearly unconvinced.

"I've seen her in Jake's memories. She looks exactly the same."

"Well, clearly she didn't die then," Sanchez mumbled and then swore under her breath. "This is unbelievable."

"Where's Jake?" Harper asked, placing his hand on my shoulder.

I shrugged just as Ky and Ben walked into the barn. Ky was a little wobbly and steadied himself on a central support post.

"Take it easy, Ky," Ben told his brother, his Japanese accent faint.

"Should he…sit down, maybe?" Sanchez asked, smirking.

"I'm fine," Ky said hoarsely.

"You're not fine," Chris said as she turned to walk back outside. "I'll get you some water." The edge in her voice worried me. With Jason and Carlos back, I figured she'd feel less anxious, but Ky's frame of mind was deteriorating; I could feel it, and I knew Chris could too. She was doing all she could to keep the surrounding negativity at bay, but the Colony was too close and too strong to ward them completely away from Ky's absorbent mind.

"Actually, I feel pretty good right now." Ky smiled to himself and closed his eyes as he leaned against the post.

"Sit down before you fall on your ass," Jason said, sounding exhausted, and he pointed to a hay bale near the entrance.

Ky saluted Jason playfully and did as he was told, wavering the entire way.

When I turned my attention back to Harper and Biggs, they were in heated discussion. I didn't like the ominous look on Harper's face.

I took a steadying breath before I asked, "What is it, H?"

He swallowed. "We need to trade—" he started to say before Sanchez held up her hand to stop him.

She strode to the entryway, confirming no one else was in earshot. "We only have one option," she said, returning to the workbench. "There's really only one way to get your fr—"

"Trade?" Jason asked, interest clearly piqued.

Harper stared at him for a moment, then nodded. "We trade Dani for Becca, or Rachel…or…anyway, the Colony's coming for her, we already know that. They're risking lives to extract her." Harper looked back at me. "You've seen how important she is to them, and you overheard their conversation today. They want her back. We can use that to our advantage."

Waves of dread rolled through me.

"It's a good plan," Jason said, looking around, measuring our resolve. "What are we waiting for?" He turned toward the barn doorway.

"Jason, wait!" I clutched on to his arm before he could walk away. "It's Jake's sister, we can't just…" *…hand her over.*

But it could bring Dani back. "We need to think about this more," I said. "I mean, don't we?"

He turned on his heel. "What the fuck, Zoe. You—"

Chris reentered the barn, murmuring something under her breath as she set a cup of water next to Ky's unconscious form.

"Just give him some time. He'll be fine," Jason told her.

"No, he won't," she said. "Not if we don't get him out of here."

Hearing Sarah's laughter, I glanced outside to see Becca and Grayson smiling with the mother-to-be about something. "We can't do this to Jake, you guys. That's his sister sitting out there."

"What other choice do we have, Baby Girl?"

As if on cue, Jake strode out of the stall we'd been using as our room and down the corridor, running his hands over his head fervently. "No," he said, his voice as cold as ice.

"Jake," I breathed, and when our eyes met, his darkened.

"No."

Sanchez took a step toward him. "They'll be here within the next twenty-four hours. We need to get some of these people out of here—Sarah, Grayson—and we need to move camp."

"Fine, but you're not using Becca."

"She's important to them," Harper said, trying to get Jake to understand. "If we use her to—"

Jason opened his mouth, but before he could say anything, Jake rounded on him. "Would you do that to Zoe?"

"It's not the same. For all we know, that woman isn't even your sister."

When Jake's eyes met mine, they were pleading with me to understand or to back him up, but I was starting to second-guess my initial certainty. *Do we just* want *it to be her? Is it just a coincidence? Is it just a resemblance?* "Jake, I—"

He shook his head and strode out of the barn, leaving the rest of us staring after him in momentary silence.

"What do we do?" I whispered. I trained my eyes on the doorway, wishing Jake would come back, that we could figure this out together.

"We vote," Sanchez said. "It's all we *can* do." I turned to face her as she continued, "We already know what Jake's vote is." Her eyes swept around the group, giving us a moment to think. "Who thinks we should use the woman as a bargaining chip to get Dani back?"

Biggs raised his hand, then Jason and Chris. Sanchez's eyes rested on me, waiting. My mouth was suddenly dry and my heart racing.

"Uh, guys…" Harper pointed toward the doorway.

We all looked over to see Becca standing there. *How much did she overhear?* With her arms crossed over her chest and her eyes fixed on us thoughtfully, I could tell she'd heard enough.

"What does it mean, 'bargaining chip'? Who is Dani?" Becca's tone was flat, like she was trying to act offended, but I could feel a genuine curiosity stir inside her.

"She's my best friend, and your 'Father' has her," I spat, my concern for her melting away a little, but only for an instant. Her eyes widened with surprise, and her curiosity was replaced with something that felt almost like concern. "She's the telepath he was looking for…the one you were so excited that he'd found."

Becca stood there quietly, her cobwebbed mind coming to life.

I could hear someone moving around behind me, but my eyes were glued to hers. "What's he going to do to her, Rachel?" Her false name felt strange on my tongue, but I didn't want to argue with her.

Becca took a few steps inside, the conversation she'd had with "Father" about the telepath replaying in her mind.

"You know what he's capable of," I said, my voice breaking a little. "What—"

Simultaneously, Jason sidled up to Becca's right while Biggs moved in on her left.

"Put your hands behind your back…please." Biggs's voice was stern, but there was a note of discomfort in it.

"What are you…" Becca shook her head and began backing away from them.

"We're restraining you," Jason said. "Don't bother fighting us —you won't win."

She looked up at him. "But why?"

"Because we can't take the chance of you running away," Sanchez said from beside me, and when I glanced over, her face was completely unreadable.

"But I *want* to go back to the Colony. I *have* to. You do not need to tie me up." There was a hint of desperation in Becca's husky voice.

But Jason had finished tightening the rope around her wrists, and as she seemed to realize there was nothing she could do, her gaze shifted frantically around the room. Fear poured out of her. "You do not understand. I have to be ready for the escort when they return. If I fail…"

"Jason," I hissed. "We don't know for sure she's not Jake's sister."

Jason looked into Becca's eyes. "*Are* you Jake's sister?"

She slowly shook her head.

Jason's eyes shifted to mine. "If she doesn't believe she's his sister, that's good enough for me."

Pointing out toward the fire, Biggs nudged her outside. "Come on, let's go."

With pleading eyes, Becca urged me to help her, but I felt frozen in place, torn.

On his way out the door, Jason smacked Ky's knee. "Come on. Let's get you packed up. I'm sending you and Ben with Sarah."

Ky groaned and struggled to sit up. "Road trip?"

6

DANI

MARCH 15, 1AE

"There are a few things you should keep in mind," Gabe said as he unlocked the front door to my new home and let me in.

"Hmmm?" I was barely listening. *General Herodson is giving me my own house!* Gabe couldn't possibly have been saying anything that could compete with my excitement to explore. *My own home! Eeek!*

The house was in a neighborhood a little south of the building housing General Herodson's office, about a fifteen-minute walk. The exterior was painted a muted sienna with white trim, and it had been fashioned in a cookie-cutter, pseudo-craftsman style. From the outside it looked perfect, displaying its glaringly white two-car garage with evident pride. Momentarily, I wondered if a new car came with my new home. The whole thing felt surreal, like winning the lotto without buying a ticket.

"General Herodson keeps a strict order around here, but because of Project Eden—the reproduction program—some of the men think they can take liberties with any woman they want."

"Right," I said, hearing but not processing a single word he'd uttered. My attention was completely focused on the living room we'd entered. It was more luxurious than I'd expected for a house on a military base, with hardwood floors, huge, bright windows, and an open ceiling that allowed me to see the second-floor landing. There were two tasteful microsuede armchairs and a sofa in cream and sage green, with pillows, throws, and curtains in bolder reds and browns. "Does somebody already live here?" I asked, shifting my eyes from the furnishings to the ridiculously high vaulted ceiling. "You know, 'cause it looks like someone lives here…"

"Not anymore," Gabe said, and I heard him shut and lock the front door.

For some reason, his words resonated with me, and I suddenly had an overpowering sense of déjà vu. Except, in my head, it was someone else's voice uttering those words—*not anymore*—and I was in a completely different place. *What…?*

"Dani? Are you okay?" Gabe asked.

I could have sworn I was forgetting something important. Shaking my head, I looked up at his face and attempted a smile. "Yeah…just déjà vu."

Gabe sighed and continued on, guiding me further into the house. "The bedrooms are all upstairs," he said, pointing to the polished wooden staircase leading up to the second floor from the entryway as we passed by.

I followed him down the hallway parallel to the stairs. "This place is big," I said as a dining room came into view on the left. It was completely open to the hallway. Just like the living room, the dining room had been decorated by someone with elegant, if restrained, taste. A heavy, mission-style oak table was set up to provide seating for eight people. It was all so much more than one person needed.

"Um…shouldn't this place be used by a family or something?" I asked.

Gabe paused, and I nearly bumped into him. He didn't notice. Instead, he gestured with his hand toward a shorter hallway shooting off to the right. "This leads to the downstairs bathroom and the laundry room."

"You didn't answer my question," I told him, barely glancing down the hall.

Reluctantly, Gabe met my eyes. "I know." He took a deep breath, holding it for a second too long. "You see, Dani, General Herodson is hoping this *will* become a family's home…*your* family's home."

Baffled, I shook my head. "But I don't have any family left. How…?"

"You have a very desirable Ability, one the General would like to have passed on to the next generation," he said softly.

That made me raise my eyebrows. "What if I don't want to have kids? And"—my eyes widened as I remembered it took two people to make a child—"who would I even have kids with? Some soldier? A stranger? *You*?" I asked, pretending to be offended. Okay, I *was* a little offended. I liked the General, but I wasn't his possession to pass around as he saw fit.

Gabe started backing further down the main hallway, entering a large, open space. "Now, I never said—"

"Calm down, I know you're just the messenger," I said, swatting his arm. I swept past him and into the room, pausing to peer back at him. "Besides, you'd be a better choice than any military guy."

As the words left my mouth, they tasted wrong—untrue—but I had no idea why. It wasn't like the man standing several feet behind me couldn't have stepped out of most women's fantasies; he was handsome, put-together, charismatic, and kind. In his light gray slacks and white button-down shirt, he looked like the guy every parent wanted their daughter to bring home. I *knew* I was interested in him in a more-than-friends way—so what was with the weird part of my head screaming, *Wrong! This is all WRONG!*

Stop it! I told myself. I glanced around, taking in the open kitchen, with its earthy, tiled countertops and wide island, and the cozy family room adjoining it.

"Look! There's a fireplace!" I exclaimed, sounding like a little kid spotting a horse…or, well, *me* spotting a horse. But I liked fires; they were comfortable, familiar. After all, I'd spent the past few lonely months hopping from place to place, relying on campfires as my only source of heat during the cold, dark nights.

The second I thought about that—about sitting around campfires, isolated and alone—I felt the feeling of wrongness again. I couldn't picture a single place I'd camped, couldn't remember any of the houses I'd squatted in. I couldn't even remember the details of my journey to the Colony from…somewhere.

I squeezed my eyes shut, trying to think, to remember, but… "Gabe, I can't remember…I think something's wrong with me," I said, imploring him with my eyes. "I don't know how I got here… or where I came from. Did I come from Seattle? I must've, but I can't…I just don't know!"

On the verge of panic, I felt Gabe's arm settle over my shoulders, and several tentative steps later, I was sinking into the comfortable embrace of a couch. After only a moment of hesitation, Gabe seated himself beside me. I could see him out of the corner of my too-wide eye. He was watching me, his brow furrowed.

I opened my mouth, releasing a barrage of questions. "*Did* I come straight from Seattle? Why'd I leave? Did—oh God—did Cam…did everyone die? What about Callie? I just…I can't remember! Why didn't I go to Bodega Bay to check on Grams? Or Massachusetts to see if Zo survived? Why'd I come here? And why didn't I bring Jack? And how'd I meet you? I know I knew you before I got here, but how is that possible? And what about—"

Gabe captured my hands, halting my words. "Dani, calm down. You have a concussion. It's probably just short-term memory loss. Everything will be much clearer in the morning."

A concussion? I squeezed his hands, feeling like they were the only things tethering me to sanity. "Please tell me...how did we meet?"

"I found you when you were all alone," he said, not taking his eyes from mine. "I helped you learn to use your telepathy."

Right...that feels right. "Did we travel together?"

His eyes flicked down to our hands, then back up to my face, a plea evident in their pale blue depths. "Not exactly."

"Then how'd you find me?" My chin quivered as I said "me." I was trying to remember the details of the past four months, but I just...couldn't. *This is* not *good.*

Gabe looked away briefly and muttered, "He wouldn't have taken that, too, would he?" He shook his head. "Dani, I found you by using *my* Ability, remember? I can visit people's dreams."

The absurdity of the statement stopped my flow of tears before it even started. "You *do* realize how weird that sounds when you say it out loud, don't you?"

Releasing one of my hands, he wrapped his arm around me, pulling me against his side. "Yeah, I do."

A nervous laugh bubbled out of me. Being in such close proximity to him was making my stomach fluttery, in a really, *really* good way. "You should call it something grander; visiting people's dreams sounds a little lame. Maybe you should say"—I lowered my voice—"'I am a Dreamwalker.'"

Gabe's answering laugh was deep and melodious, and at the sound of it, my heart gave an enthusiastic thump. I peered up at him through my lashes. "So...should we explore upstairs? Check out the bedrooms?" *Check out the bed?* It had been months since I'd been this close to another person, let alone a man who made me feel so giddy.

He tensed up, clenched his jaw, and looked away. Abruptly, he stood, leaving me cold and alone where we'd been warm and cuddling only a moment before. "Of course. I'm sure you want to shower, hot water and all," he said dismissively.

At the words "hot water" I nearly drooled. All thoughts of

Gabe and beds evaporated as I imagined standing beneath a steaming stream of hot water. *Oh my God...or soaking in an oh-so-hot bath...*

Without another word, I stood and zipped past Gabe into the hallway and up the stairs, ignoring my aching head the entire time. It only took me a few seconds to find the master bedroom. Its oak furnishings were as tasteful as those on the ground floor, and there was a queen bed covered in a fluffy, bronze-colored down comforter and a wide window fitted with lowered bamboo blinds. The adjoining bathroom was spacious, including two sinks, an oversized tub, and a separate stall shower. *Definitely a bath*, I thought blissfully while I toed off my tennis shoes and peeled off my borrowed sweats. I left the door cracked open a few inches, wondering if Gabe would see it as an invitation. And yes, it *was* an invitation.

I fiddled with the hot and cold knobs on the edge of the tub, thankful that hot water poured from the faucet within seconds. Glorious steam floated up from the water's surface, enticing me to sink in even though the large tub was only a few inches full. I almost did, but after a quick glance around the ledge of the bathtub, I noticed an extreme lack of toiletries. Soap, at least, was a necessity.

Hopeful, I padded to the cupboards beneath the sinks on the opposite side of the bathroom, closed my eyes, and whispered, "Please have some shampoo and conditioner." I cracked my eyes open to peek into the far right cupboard and found only cleaning supplies.

"Damn."

The middle cupboard was jammed full of toilet paper and boxes of tissues. *Useful, but not what I'm looking for.* Crossing my fingers, I opened the left cupboard and sighed. Bottles of several types of shampoo, conditioner, and body wash fought for space with boxes of bar soap, cans of shaving cream, loofahs, and razors.

I was going to take a hot bath *and* shave my legs. “Oh God,” I groaned.

“What?” Gabe called from the other side of the door. Evidently, it hadn’t been a very quiet groan.

I frowned. He was in the adjoining bedroom, but apparently he wasn’t planning to cross the doorway and join me in the tub. My pride would have been wounded if the slight hadn’t been vastly overshadowed by my excitement about the gallons of hot water awaiting me.

“Nothing,” I replied. Glancing at the empty towel rack, I added, “Can you find me a towel? There aren’t any in here.”

“Sure.”

While I waited, I searched through the various bottles in the cupboard, finally settling on some herbal-scented hair products and a vanilla body wash. It wasn’t bubble bath, but that didn’t stop me from using it as such. I drizzled the thick, pearly liquid near the faucet, watching the water churn it into a frothy foam that smelled like vanilla icing. And then I stepped into heaven. *Oh God...*

The moment I sank into the sudsy water, I could have died from contentment. Closing my eyes, I savored the sensations, comparing the luxurious heat of the bath to the icy water I was used to…and then I sat bolt upright. Water splashed against the sides of the tub, spilling over the edge in a few places. I turned off the faucet. *When was the last time I bathed—and where?* I couldn’t remember, exactly, but I had the feeling it had been outside. I could almost feel the stinging sensation of water from a frigid mountain creek gliding down my bare skin, but I couldn’t actually remember. *What the hell?*

Taking a deep, soothing breath, I settled back into the hot water, rested my head against the porcelain edge, and closed my eyes.

“You decent?” Gabe called from the other side of the bathroom door, and my heart gave a startled extra pump.

I opened my eyes and glanced down at the layer of thick, white foam concealing my body. *Decent enough*, I supposed. "Yep."

Gabe pushed the door open further and poked his head through the crack. Seeing me in the tub, he smirked. "That wasn't exactly what I meant by 'decent.'"

I shrugged, making the layer of bubbles tremble and rearrange on the water's surface.

Gabe's smirk grew into a wicked grin. "I found the towels. They're in the closet near the stairs."

"Did you bring me one, or would you rather I get it myself?" I asked playfully.

His eyes narrowed as he pretended to consider his options, and then he laughed. "This time, I brought you one. Next time…we'll see."

I smiled and closed my eyes again. The pensive, concerned Gabe from downstairs was gone, replaced by the Gabe I was used to. "Come in and talk to me. It's lonely in here." *...and I'm tired of being alone.*

The hinges creaked as Gabe pushed the door the rest of the way open, letting some of the warm steam escape. "Feel better?" he asked from somewhere near the cupboards. Cracking open my left eyelid, I found him seated on the counter, a fluffy mauve towel beside him.

"You have no idea…but then, neither do I. Not really." I tapped my head. "Still nothing."

"Just don't panic for a few days. I have a feeling things will clear up sometime soon."

"Why?" I asked. "What makes you so sure I won't be stuck like this?" I felt broken, like a mirror that had been shattered and glued back together, but some of the pieces were missing.

Gabe shrugged. "Because that's how concussions work. I'm sure you'll get better."

I'd never had a concussion—I didn't even know how I'd ended up with one—so I didn't know if time healed all wounds and all that, but I figured it wouldn't hurt to trust Gabe for a few more days. And I *did* trust Gabe, even if I couldn't remember any specific reasons why.

I sighed. "I think I'm pruning."

"Hmmm…I wouldn't be able to tell without a closer look," Gabe teased.

Pinning him with my gaze, I said, "Then take a closer look," but he just chuckled and shook his head. *Suit yourself*, I thought, looking away.

Unfortunately, now I felt rejected…embarrassed. I needed a distraction. I snatched up the razor I'd snagged from the cupboard, raised one of my legs out of the water, and began lathering it with shaving cream. The tub was just deep enough that as I worked, the water still covered all of my important bits even though I was sitting up. I could see Gabe out of the corner of my eye and had to suppress a laugh. He seemed to be having an internal war with himself, alternating between looking at me and looking at the tile floor. I allowed myself a small smile.

"I'll, uh…wait outside," he said, slipping down from the counter and exiting the bathroom.

His timing was perfect; I was embarrassed, the water was cooling, and my fingertips resembled albino raisins. I rose from the tub, and dripping on the chilly floor tiles, I crossed the bathroom and stepped into the shower for a quick rinse.

Within five minutes I was done in the bathroom. I emerged with combed, wet hair, wearing only a towel. I was moderately surprised to find Gabe lounging on the foot of the bed, looking like he owned it. Based on his reactions in the bathroom, I was under the impression that he wasn't really interested in me, but based on the way he was lying on what was now *my* bed, he was sending an entirely different signal. *What does he want?* His hot and cold signals were confusing the crap out of me.

Regardless, an excited thrill flowed throughout my body. I'd spent so much time traveling alone, I was sure—pretty sure—that it felt amazing to be spending time with someone. I finally found somewhere I belonged. The Colony and General Herodson were great, but it was Gabe who made me feel like I'd finally found somewhere that could become my home.

When I crawled onto the bed beside him, his eyes locked on to me. They trailed from my curling, wet hair to my face to my bare shoulders and the place where the towel was knotted over my chest. I settled on my knees beside him and watched him study me.

"I like it here," I told him. "I like being here…with you."

Abruptly, Gabe sat up, bringing his face within inches of mine. He searched my eyes briefly, then looked away. "Dani, we shouldn't be…I don't know what he…your friends…"

"Friends?" I asked, confused. Shaking my head, I looked around the room. "I was alone—"

"No, you weren't," Gabe said, engulfing my left hand with both of his. "You've had people around you since the beginning. All of those people from the military…"

When he paused, I shook my head. "Who? What people?"

His jaw clenched. "I shouldn't be telling you this. It'll just upset you. I should wait until you remember."

"Who, Gabe?" My voice was too high. "Tell me! Who was I with?"

"Zoe…and Jason."

"What?" I screeched and scurried away from him to huddle on the edge of the bed. "I don't know what you're talking about!" Zoe was in Massachusetts and probably dead, and Jason…Jason was…I didn't know. *Why would I have been with Jason?* Nothing was making sense. Scrunching my eyes closed, I tried to remember, but the harder I tried, the more my head hurt. Panic churned within me, making me feel sick. My heart beat heavily, like my blood was too thick, and my lungs felt constricted.

"Dani," Gabe said, and I felt the mattress shift behind me. He scooted closer, joining me on the edge of the bed and draping his arm over my bare shoulders. “I’m sorry. I didn’t mean to upset you.”

Only when I looked up at him did I realize tears were streaking down my cheeks. “I don’t want to think about them…about any of it,” I told him. “If they’re gone…I just want to forget. I just want to be here, with you.”

“Dani, I think we should…”

I tilted my face up, leaning in closer to the safety and comfort of his body. “What?”

“Probably not be…”

“What?” I asked, raising my hand to his face. I brushed my thumb over his chin, feeling the rough stubble covering it, and angled his face lower.

“In here, doing this.” He breathed in jerkily when my thumb brushed across his full lower lip. It was soft and dry and begging to be kissed.

“I have no idea what you’re talking about,” I whispered, closing the distance between us.

When our lips touched, there was a moment of hesitancy on his part. He dropped his arm from my shoulders and remained immobile while I gently teased his lips with mine. And then he reacted.

Gabe’s hands were suddenly cradling my jaw, his fingers tangling in my wet curls. When his lips parted and our tongues tentatively touched, I sighed. His kiss was gentle, full of unspoken emotions. It didn’t stay that way. His grip on my face tightened and his tongue dove into my mouth with ferocity.

Wanting more—*needing* more—I slipped a leg over both of his, straddling him. With the bare skin of my thighs flush against the soft material of his slacks, I became very aware that the towel was the only thing covering me.

Gabe groaned as he slid his hands down from my face, running them over my shoulders, back, hips, and thighs until he reached the end of the towel. Slipping his hands under the soft, thick cotton, he teased the backs of my thighs, inching higher.

Wanting him to touch me everywhere, I groaned. "It's been so long. Please, MG…"

Instantly, he froze.

MG? Where the hell did that *come from? Who's MG?*

"Damn it…shit! Dani, I—I'm sorry. I can't…we can't," he panted, resting his forehead against the crook of my neck. Considering I'd just called him a name I didn't understand, I was okay with cutting things short.

"Why is this all so confusing?" I asked, my voice small and trembling.

Gabe shook his head and kissed my neck with all the tenderness he'd displayed earlier. "Tomorrow night," he breathed against my skin. "If you still want me tomorrow night, then we can do this." He smoothed the towel over my legs, covering me as much as possible, which wasn't very much considering I was still straddling him.

"You should get dressed," he said, dropping his hands to the bed. "There are clothes in the dresser that should fit you, and in the closet if you don't find what you need in the drawers."

Ungracefully, I crawled off his lap and moved to rummage through dresser drawers. Inside, I wanted to scream, but I wasn't sure why.

7

ZOE

MARCH 16, 1AE

"It's gonna be a cold trip heading west through the mountains," Sanchez warned, glancing between Grayson, Ky, and Harper, "but Jake said this dude ranch is the only place he knows of nearby that can house all the animals and a group our size. He said the lodge is big. It should be well-equipped for most of our needs." She leaned over a physical map of Colorado.

"If it's still there," Jason said tersely. Sanchez and I both glared at him. He'd been goading us all morning, upset that we hadn't departed immediately after we'd finished packing our things.

Chris scoffed. "Don't be a dick, Jason. It'll be there." She shrugged, seeming unconcerned. "And if it's not, that's why we have the secondary rendezvous point."

Sanchez nodded and leaned over to circle the location where the dude ranch, Colorado Trails, was supposed to be. "Assuming everything works out, the ranch should be somewhere between Mancos State Park and the city of Durango itself. Just follow Highway 161 southwest and pay attention to the signs. Apparently, you can't miss it."

Grayson and Ben nodded, Sarah bit her fingernails, a look of horror in her eyes as she worried endlessly, and Ky didn't do much of anything. He was still drunk, Jason and Chris not having the heart to take the booze away from him; it was the only thing alleviating any of the tumultuous feelings funneling into him.

"We should only be a few days behind you," Chris added as she sketched the relocation team's route on the map. "But if we're not there after a week or so, Biggs and Ky will decide what to do." Chris didn't linger long on the morose possibility that the retrieval group—the rest of us—might not make it to Colorado Trails at all. "Until you hear from us, I think it's wise to only unpack what you need, but have all the medical supplies handy when we get there, just in case. We'll have a limited supply with us."

Chris looked at me. "When we get into Cañon City, Harper and I are going with Jason and Sanchez to the Colony to offer the trade. Zoe, you and Jake are staying with our leverage to ensure she's watched at all times."

Even with mixed emotions, Jake had conceded to the plan, knowing he could do little to keep Becca out of the Colony since she wanted to go back so badly. His one request was that he be allowed to stay with her until the exchange, and even Jason hadn't objected to that.

I heard heavy footsteps behind me as Jake walked into the barn. He stopped a few feet from the workbench. I couldn't meet his eyes…I hadn't been able to since we'd tied up his sister.

"Zoe, once we leave Cañon City, I'll keep you updated on our progress as much as I can," Sanchez said, referring to her telepathy. "Now, there's an abandoned building in Cañon City you guys should hunker down in. It's on the edge of downtown, and it's got mirrored windows, so you can see out but no one should be able to see in."

Sanchez's words faded away as I focused all my attention on Jake, who was pacing behind me. Although he'd agreed to our plan, his reluctance was apparent. He'd begun to question our visitor's identity, not completely convinced she actually *was* Becca.

But if circumstances changed, and he felt she truly was his sister, I worried he might not follow through with our plan. *Why would he exchange his sister for Dani, a woman he barely knows?* He'd been up all night, dark emotions pouring out of him. When all was said and done, I knew Dani's life was contingent upon how important Becca was to the Colony. *If he changes his mind...*

"I know this isn't ideal," Sanchez said, "but Chris and I have identified three command buildings on base." She pointed to the diagram and continued speaking, but I stopped listening as I walked over to the doorway, feeling a strange sense of doom. My eyes locked on Becca's quivering body as she sat, arms tied behind her, on a hay bale by the fire.

Something was wrong. She was wincing, her eyes squeezed shut, her face flushed, and her breathing laborious. I ran toward her, watching her closely as I opened myself up to her emotions: fear and pain.

The brown-haired man—Father—stood proudly with his hands clasped behind his back and his stance wide. His eyes twinkled with some sort of twisted delight, and his mustache was upturned, a smile threatening to envelop his face.

With a flash, the image changed.

Bodies. A seemingly bottomless pit filled with dead people was all I could see. Becca was one of them—her body limp and broken and smeared with dirt and blood like the others. But her violet-gray eyes were open wide, filmed-over, and empty, and her once-thin lips were split and swollen. She was discarded like a busted toy that "Father" didn't want anymore. He was still standing there...smiling.

"She's having a vision," I said under my breath. *She really* is *Becca.*

"Goodbye, Zoe," Sarah said, flashing me a tiny, hopeful smile. Her eyes were red and filled with unshed tears. Biggs helped her mount the gray horse she would ride west through the snowy, southern Rockies to our rendezvous point in Durango, the look on Sarah's face almost heartbreaking. While I stayed behind, she would be riding far away, wondering if we would ever see each other again. *I hope so.*

After our brief, tormenting goodbyes—our faces brave and painted with false certainty—Grayson, Sarah, Biggs, Ben, and Ky rode away with most of our gear, all but one pack horse, and Dani's goats in tow. We all hoped getting them further away from the Colony would help ease Ky's Ability-inflicted angst and keep Sarah and her unborn baby safe.

In a somber haze, those of us remaining readied ourselves to head for Cañon City. Donning my thigh holster and pistol, I scoffed at my new dressing routine. I should have felt completely ridiculous, like I was pretending to be someone I wasn't, but I didn't really have a choice. *This is who I am now.*

Once we were geared up, we hurriedly secured the remaining supplies on our pack horse, climbed into our saddles—some of us doubling up—and rode for town, where Jake and I would stay behind with Becca, waiting for word from Sanchez.

When we finally arrived, our horses tired and our noses red from riding in the cold, Sanchez, Carlos, and I fenced the animals in a large backyard. The expansive lawn provided an afternoon snack, and there was a swimming pool the horses could drink out of. A block away and just north of downtown, Jason, Jake, Chris, and Harper were securing the inside of the abandoned, mirror-windowed store Jake, Becca, and I would be staying in for the next twenty-four hours.

"Will you be okay?" Sanchez asked as we watered the horses in the algae-infested pool.

I nodded absently, wondering how Jake was going to make it through the "hostage exchange" without losing his mind. "We just need to stick to the plan, right?" I glanced over at her, then at Wings and Jason's horse, who were sucking water into their mouths, almost pulling their reins from my grasp.

"If the plan works," she consented. "I honestly don't know what they're capable of up there."

We were silent for a moment, both of us lost in thought. *What if Sanchez can't make contact with us from that far away? What if the Colonists are somehow expecting this?* But I withheld my questions. Instead, I smiled, appreciating Sanchez's typical no-nonsense, no-mushy-shit goodbye.

I nudged her. "Let's just hope your claim will get you in. They *are* inviting any survivors to join their 'safe haven,' after all."

Sanchez practically snorted. "Getting in will be the easy part."

Hearing a dull thump on the grass behind me, I peered back at Carlos, who was walking toward us, Arrow clomping behind him. "The horses are ready," he said to Sanchez. "You want me to go get the others?"

Sanchez shook her head. "No, I'm on it. Make sure Chris's horse gets a little more water, and then we're ready to go."

Sanchez and I walked the horses over to the fence and tied them up so they didn't drink too much before the long, hurried ride to the Colony, and Sanchez marched through the gate and around the corner, out of sight. I stalled at the fence, realizing it might be the last time I would ever see Carlos, since he was riding away with the others.

"See you soon," I told him.

He nodded and flashed me a bright, cocky grin. "For sure."

I smiled back and turned away to follow after Sanchez. I caught up to her quickly, and we cautiously made our way down the sidewalk and into the alleyway behind the row of stores where Jake and I would be hiding. Entering through the back door, we joined Jake, Harper, and Chris, who appeared to have just finished securing the perimeter of the dilapidated building. Becca was sitting in a black, plastic folding chair in the center of the room, and Jake was stuffing our belongings into the cabinet beneath a broken display case.

The front door swung open, and Jason came in. "We're all clear on this row. The black-bands that were in the café are gone."

"Shit. Time to go," Sanchez said.

Harper walked over and gave me a kiss on the forehead before wrapping an arm around my shoulders. "See you later, Baby Girl." With a squeeze, he winked at me, making me smile, and then disappeared out the back door. Jason, Chris, and Sanchez followed, but Sanchez paused in the doorway. "If you don't hear from us within forty-eight hours, head to the ranch in Durango." She glanced between me and Jake, who was leaning against the wall, staring out the window. When her eyes found mine, they were sympathetic. *"Good luck,"* she said silently and strode out of the shop. Just like that, they were all gone.

But as soon as the door closed, it opened again, and my brother strode in, heading straight for me. Before I knew what was happening, his arms were wrapped around me in the fiercest hug he'd ever given me. I didn't have time to return the embrace before he pulled away and disappeared out the back door once more.

I stared at the door, stunned and wishing I'd been able to hug him back. *Will I ever see him again?* Exhaling, I crumpled the thought into an imaginary ball and tossed it into a lockbox that I planned to shove into the deepest chasms of my mind. I'd been tossing a lot of unwanted thoughts in there lately.

Feeling eyes on me, I glanced at Becca, and then at Jake. Both of them were watching me intently, but Jake averted his gaze almost immediately. He stood at the mirrored window, which stretched the entire length of the wall, again staring blankly outside.

This is gonna be a long wait. Taking a deep and concentrated breath, I sidestepped Becca and walked over to the window. I stood beside Jake and gazed out at the empty street.

Hiding out at the outskirts of downtown, we could barely see the old-fashioned buildings that were once quaint and rustic boutiques and restaurants—the raised flower beds that lined both sides of the street were unruly and overgrown, and the windows were still painted with holiday greetings and well-wishes.

It felt like an hour had passed since the others had left, since I'd been standing silently, wondering what to say to Jake, but it had only been a few minutes. Each second went by excruciatingly slowly, and Jake pacing from the front door to the window and back wasn't helping time lapse any quicker.

Feeling his overwhelming distress, I gazed back out the window and tried to focus on something else…anything other than his turmoil.

I watched the naked branches of the trees shudder in the breeze and the stray bits of garbage rolling down the deserted street like tumbleweeds. I contemplated giving in to the lethargy that was making my eyes heavy. It had been days since I'd *really* slept, but now wasn't the time.

I scanned the room, taking in every boring detail of my temporary cage. It had obviously been abandoned long before the outbreak. The plaster walls had fist-size holes in them, and clothing racks had been ripped from the walls and tossed into a pile in the back right corner of the store. There were a couple of crumbling boxes in another corner, stacks of magazines filling each of them. A woman bending over, ass bared, in a slutty French maid costume graced the top cover in one box, the other displaying a voluptuous cowgirl sitting precariously on a saddle. *An old porn shop?* I grinned. *Mirrored windows, just outside of downtown? Of course it is.*

As Jake continued to pace, memories of Becca flashed in his mind, and I saw their childhood play out like I was looking into a zoetrope. I wanted to watch each memory longer, to see more of what their lives had been like before, but the scenes flashed by regardless of my wishes.

A small boy—Jake—sitting on the edge of a tattered mattress. His sister sitting in front of him, her back to him and her little legs folded underneath her, barely raising her up enough for him to brush her hair and put it into a ponytail.

Jake, a little older, leaning against a yellow Formica countertop. The house was old and dirty. Piles of laundry and crumbling, old cardboard boxes were stacked against the wall behind him. Becca sitting on the counter nearby, eating an apple while he made her a peanut butter and jelly sandwich.

A teenage Becca stepping into a minimally decorated living room with a worn leather couch, a side table, a reading lamp, and a vintage green recliner in front of a small, boxy television sitting atop a wooden crate. Her brunette hair was curled into ringlets and piled atop her head, and a nervous smile inched across her face. She was wearing a strapless, crimson chiffon dress that hung just above her knees and simple black pumps. Jake handing her his old pocket knife, a familiar, severe look on his face. Her smile widening as she accepted the knife and placed it in her black velvet handbag.

Jake driving a black Jeep, Cooper sitting happily in the back, Becca hanging her bare feet out the passenger-side window. She was laughing and tossing popcorn at him, and I could tell he was trying not to smile. She rolled her eyes and pushed the play button on the stereo. Immediately dropping the bag of popcorn onto the floor, she wriggled and danced in her seat, letting the kernels fall all over the interior of the car. Jake pointed to the mess, trying to keep his eyes on the road, but she waved his anger away as she continued singing, shimmying her shoulders and flailing around.

"Please untie me, Jake." Becca's voice was almost booming in the silence.

I turned in time to see his eyes shoot to hers.

"Please? If I fail him again, he will be so angry. I do not want to make Father angry. *Please*."

Jake looked at me and then sat down on a plastic chair by the window, making it creak under his weight. He covered his face with his hands, and it looked like he was trying to rub away his own personal hell.

I glanced at Becca again, whose eyes were closed and chin was quivering slightly. "I have to get back," she rasped. "I have to warn them."

Warn them? I approached her, the rubber soles of my boots squeaking on the cement floor. "Warn who?" I asked her, but she didn't answer because Jake strode over. When he looked at me, his eyes were an inferno of rage, resentment, and despondency. My stomach dropped and my defenses flared.

"Jake," I said, reaching for him, but he pulled his arm away. "Please, talk to me." I reached for him again, and as soon as I touched him, my shoulders dropped; he was splintered inside, like wood being hacked into a thousand, unmendable pieces. "Jake…" His name was barely a whisper.

He tugged his arm out of my grasp. "Don't, Zoe," he said before he turned away from me.

"Don't wha—"

"I can't," he began, glaring back at me. "I can't do this. I can't send her back to that place…to that man."

"What?" Becca screeched. "Jake, I have—"

"I can't send her back, and I can't…you…"

"Me, what? You're scaring the shit out of me." My voice was trembling. "But she wants—"

"I can't breathe!" He stalked to the storefront window, his

broad chest heaving under his t-shirt. "I should've known. I should've—"

"Known *what*, exactly? That she wasn't really dead? Or that they'd somehow bring her back to life and brainwash her?"

"I am not—"

I continued to talk over Becca, my voice harsh and defensive. I couldn't help it. I'd never seen Jake so distraught, so…I didn't even know. "You couldn't have possibly known what she'd turn into or who she'd become."

With one palm pressed against the wall by the window, Jake bowed his head, drowning in the undertow of emotion. His jaw worked, his hand flexing and shaking against the plaster.

"I have to leave, to get her out of here," he said, adamant. "I can't just hand her over like she's not my sister."

"Jake," Becca tried again. "I need to go back. I *have* to go back."

He only shook his head, refusing to listen. "I won't let you go back there, Becca, no matter what you want. I'm getting you out of here."

I froze. *He's leaving.* I glared at his back, but feeling his misery, my anger quickly subsided. "We can figure something—"

"Stop!" He pulled his arm back and slammed his fist into the wall, denting it. "There's nothing to figure out. My sister will *not* be used as a pawn." His face fell. He leaned back and brought his hand up to pinch the bridge of his nose. "I wouldn't be able to live with myself."

He's already made up his mind. Instantly, I started to question everything about Jake and me…about us. My reservations from the first time I met him—the first time he saved me, opened his mouth, and pushed me away—flared to life, and I chided myself for being so naïve. *I knew something like this would happen.*

The questions jumped off my tongue before I could contain them. "What about Dani? What about me? You're just going to leave?"

When he didn't respond, reality burst overhead like a looming storm cloud, clearing away the fog that had settled in my heart and mind. *How could I have been so stupid?*

The conversation we'd had on the dock back in St. Louis resurfaced from under a month's worth of foolhardy emotions. Jake's words replayed in my mind.

"For whatever reason, I know you don't want to let me in...or maybe you just don't know how...what are you afraid of?"

This. This fucking feeling of inexplicable loss was what I'd been afraid of—the living lump of hysteria swelling in my throat, the desperation in my heart. I couldn't swallow it away.

Biting the inside of my cheek as hard as possible, I willed myself to calm down. *Keep it together, Zoe.*

Jake strode past me to Becca, pulling her up to her feet.

Lunging at him, I pushed against his chest as hard as I could. "You're leaving?" He stumbled away from Becca, and I pushed him again. "You're going to kill Dani!" I shoved against his shoulder. "You're going to kill us all if you take her!" I smacked his chest. "I won't let you ruin everything." *I won't let you break my heart!* I pushed, shoved, and slapped him again and again. "You son of a bitch!"

Jake gripped my arms, immobilizing me and forcing me to look up at him. His eyebrows lifted with sympathy...*or is it sorrow?* I was too upset to differentiate between his emotions and mine.

"Let go," I warbled.

As he opened his mouth to speak, a gunshot cracked through the air and Jake yanked me down to the floor.

8

DANI

MARCH 16, 1AE

Pine needles pricked my bare arms as I wandered through a shadowy forest. Towering redwoods and lodgepole pines shaded me from an unusually hot summer sun and saved my skin from burning. Luckily, the underbrush was sparse, consisting of scattered ferns and low, scraggly shrubs which didn't hinder my steps.

A sudden, loud rustle sounded off to my left. I paused mid-stride, wondering if I'd disturbed a rabbit, or possibly a deer, but when I peered in the direction of the noise, nothing moved between the thick, mossy trunks. I resumed my steady pace. The only noise was the crunching of twigs and dry pine needles underfoot…until I heard the sound again, closer and off to my right.

I snapped my head around, searching. I caught a glimpse of black near the ground before whoever—or whatever—had made the noise disappeared behind a redwood at least forty yards away.

"Hello?" I called. "Is someone there?" What if it's a bear? Oh God, I hope not! *I couldn't remember the rules for confronting a bear—was I supposed to stare it down, avoid eye contact, or make myself big and loud?* Fat chance there, *I thought. Loud I could do,*

but big was so far outside of my wheelhouse, it was in a different country.

For minutes I heard nothing but wind, the sounds of birds chirping, and small creatures scurrying through the branches overhead.

"Is someone there?" I called again, trying to keep my voice steady. Adrenaline flooded my body, doing its best to convince me to turn and flee.

From nowhere specific, a man whispered, "Dani." My name bounced around between the tree trunks, repeating and gaining strength. Not a bear...a person. Should I be relieved? *I wasn't.*

"Where are you?" I screeched, spinning around and frantically searching for the speaker among the trees. "Who *are you?"*

I spotted the black thing again and realized it was a boot. Before it disappeared behind a thick redwood twenty yards ahead of me, I glimpsed the rest of the man it was attached to. He was tall, and his jeans and black t-shirt did nothing to hide his powerful build. Too soon, he was gone, hidden by the trees.

"Hey! Where are you going? How do you know my name?" I tried to yell, though it came out strained and breathy. I jogged to the tree he'd disappeared behind, but by the time I rounded its monstrous girth, there was no one to find.

"Red," he called out from everywhere and nowhere. Again, the single word echoed off the endless forest of tree trunks. The rich sound of his voice made my heart swell in longing.

Hearing the rustle of dried sticks and pine needles directly behind me, I spun. For once, the man didn't hide.

He was larger than I'd first thought, about a foot taller than me. His dark hair was cropped close, and sapphire-blue eyes glowed in a handsome, angular face. Every plane and ridge was precise, almost severe, making him equally harsh and beautiful. Jason? *He wasn't alone.*

From behind the trunks on either side of him, a handful of people emerged. A slender, raven-haired woman whose jewel-blue eyes were almost identical to Jason's.

"Zo," I breathed.

I scanned the rest of the faces. A blonde woman with kind features. A teenage boy with dark hair, tan skin, and haunted eyes. A young Asian man whose lips were curled into a playful smirk. A middle-aged man sporting an impressive mountain-man beard. A beautiful young woman whose face was contorted by a haughty sneer. They all felt so familiar, like their names were on the tip of my tongue, but I didn't recognize any of them.

"Why are you following me?" I whispered.

One side of Jason's mouth quirked slightly upward, and a barely-there dimple appeared on his cheek. He laughed, the sound rough and baritone. "You need to remember."

"Remember," the others echoed in a ghostly chorus. It was more than a little creepy.

"I need you to come back to me, Red," Jason added.

"Why are you calling me that?"

He turned and began walking away. The others followed a step behind him.

"Wait!" I called after them. I didn't want to be left alone in the forest. I tried to follow, but shrubs appeared around my sneakers, tripping me with each attempted step. "Don't leave me! Jason! Zo!"

"Wake up, Dani," someone said. A hand was on my shoulder, shaking me gently.

"No," was my genius response. I rolled onto my side, away from the offending human alarm clock. Gabe.

He laughed softly. "You weren't supposed to fall asleep."

I flopped onto my back and glared up at him through sleep-swollen eyelids. "*You* weren't supposed to *let* me fall asleep."

Gabe sighed, a deep, mournful sound. It was very dramatic.

"True, but you were getting far too cranky." He didn't sound the least bit repentant.

I scowled. "What if I'd been hemorrhaging in my brain? What if I'd died in my sleep because you didn't want to deal with my crankiness? What if—"

His laugh was full and slightly booming. "Okay, okay! I'm sorry. I was far too careless with your life. I'm *so* sorry. Will you ever forgive me?"

"I'll think about it," I told him. "Now, let me go back to sleep. I'm obviously not going to slip into a coma." Turning my head away from him, I squeezed my eyes shut, willing myself to return to dreamland. I felt like I'd been having the strangest dream, and for some reason, I desperately wanted to return to it.

"Can't do that," Gabe said. "You're coming with me to work today."

Groaning into my pillow, I mumbled, "Can't you just let me go back to sleep instead?"

"No can do." The bed bounced as he stood. "If you get ready, I'll make you breakfast. You like pancakes?"

I stiffened, suddenly salivating. Pancakes. *How long has it been since I've had pancakes?* "Throw in some bacon and you've got deal," I said, sounding way too excited. If I was being honest with myself, he had me at "pancakes."

"I think I can manage that."

Entering Gabe's lab was like walking into Willy Wonka's chocolate factory, but for science fanatics, which I'm not. Thanks to my linguistics studies, I prefer tangling with syntax and semantics rather than compounds and cellular structures, but even so, the room was still awe-inspiring. Each consecutive counter in the long room was filled with more fantastical and majestic equipment, and each machine, with its shiny baubles and crystal-clear lenses, screamed of wonder and amazing discoveries. I brushed my fingertips over the scope of something that looked like the lovechild of a telescope and a machine gun.

"Please don't touch that," Gabe said.

Okay... "So, this is your lab," I noted as we passed by counters filled with meticulously arranged high-tech devices, glass containers, and yellow notepads.

"Yep."

"You're in charge of the whole thing?"

"Uh, yeah," he responded, smoothing his blond hair against his scalp—it was pulled back into his usual low ponytail, the few inches of gathered hair fanning neatly down the back of his neck.

"What exactly is it that you're in charge of?" Even if there were a gun held to my head, I couldn't have guessed the purpose of most of the obviously priceless equipment.

Gabe shot a quick look over his shoulder as he led the way down an aisle between two counters. "I'm in charge of the Ability Research Department."

"That sounds important."

"It is."

"Wow, you've really got that whole humility thing down, huh?" I said, shaking my head. As I scanned around the lab—the unoccupied lab—I frowned. There were three rows of work counters and dozens of stools, but no scientists. "Where are all of your worker bees? I mean, I'm assuming someone with such an 'important' job has a handful of science slaves, but this place is totally empty."

He unlocked a taupe fire door. "I told them to work on their other projects this morning." At my cocked head, he added, "We don't have enough scientifically-inclined people to devote a large number of them to one department alone...even if it is *the* most important department."

"Seriously, Gabe?" I asked, swatting his forearm. "Get over yourself already, you're not *that* amazing." Like a battering ram, the déjà vu hit me again, nearly knocking me breathless. I hunched over, gasping.

"Dani? What's wrong? Is it your head?" Gabe asked in a rush. He held my elbow in a gentle but strong grip and led me through the doorway to a worn couch in one corner of what could only be his office. The room was a mixture of neatness and clutter that was purely Gabe, and it held the faintest trace of his clean scent.

"I'm fine," I said, between slow, deep breaths. "I just need a second to rest."

"Are you sure?" His voice was filled with concern.

"Yeah, I'm fine."

"Okay. Well, while you rest, I need to run a quick errand. Will you be fine here?"

I glanced up at him through the stray crimson curls that had fallen in front of my eyes. "Oh, I'm sure I'll survive."

Gabe, who'd been backing toward the door, hesitated, and I offered him a faint reassuring smile. "Okay," he said. "I'll be back in about fifteen minutes."

"Gabe?" I called as he was shutting the door.

He poked his head back into the office. "Yeah?"

"Who's MG?" I asked, recalling the two letters that had brought our previous night's kiss to a screeching halt.

Gabe said nothing for several long seconds, simply blinked slowly and studied me. Finally, he said, "Someone you trusted… and he betrayed you."

"Did you know him?"

He nodded, the crease between his eyebrows reappearing. "I'll tell you all about him when I get back…if you want."

With a smile, I rested my head against the back of the couch and closed my eyes. "Yeah, I'd like that. Thanks."

He'd been gone for only a few minutes when I heard it: a scream. It was the kind of scream made by a mother giving birth, or by a torture victim being slowly flayed.

I rose from my comfortable, reclined position on the sofa and cracked open the door to the lab, listening. At first, silence greeted me, but it was closely followed by a second, nearly identical scream. *What the hell?*

As quietly as possible, I inched the door further open and slipped out into the empty lab. After a brief moment of deep-ish contemplation, I ghosted across the lab toward the door to the hallway. I snagged a smudged, white lab coat that had been draped over a nearby stool and shrugged into it.

After peeking from the lab doorway into the hallway and seeing nobody, I stepped all the way out, trying my hardest to look like I belonged there. I explored every hallway on the floor without hearing the scream again. I was about to give up and return to Gabe's office when another piercing howl emanated from a door to the stairwell.

My hand wanted to shake as it reached for the doorknob, but I wouldn't let it. Images of what could cause someone to make such a gut-wrenching noise overflowed in my imagination. Whatever the cause, I knew it couldn't be anything good.

I was inching the heavy metal door open, waiting for the scream to waylay me, when something touched my shoulder.

"Wha—" I shouted, spinning and backing away in a single motion. Of its own accord, my hand reached across my body for something at the side of my rib cage, but all it found was the bottom of my breast. I instantly lowered my hand, no idea why I'd raised it in the first place. "Holy crap, Gabe! Why'd you feel the need to scare the living bejeezus out of me?" I snapped.

Gabe, still standing before the stairwell door, held his hands out in front of him in a placating gesture. "Sorry," he said, taking a step toward me. "I thought you heard me."

"Obviously not," I grumbled, crossing my arms over my chest.

He looked from me to the door, then back. "Going somewhere?"

"I heard a scream…like a horror-movie, being-slashed-to-pieces scream."

"And you were, what—investigating?" Gabe's eyebrows shot up. "Because nothing's safer than searching out the cause of a being-slashed-to-pieces scream."

I shrugged, realizing that finding the screamer would also have brought me face-to-face with whoever—or whatever—was making them scream, which was more than a little stupid. "Not exactly," I mumbled.

Gabe sighed and turned away from me, walking briskly back toward his lab. "Good. That would be unwise." *Gee, you think?*

Scampering after him, which would have been embarrassing had he been looking at me, I followed Gabe back up the hall, through his lab, and into his office.

"No dry cleaning?" I asked, plopping back down on the couch. All that had changed between pre-errand and post-errand Gabe was the addition of the dictionary-sized, brushed metal case he was carrying.

"Huh?"

"Stamps?" I suggested.

"What?" He glanced at me, bafflement scrunching his brow.

I shrugged. "I swear, every time someone says they have to 'run errands,' it's to go pick up dry cleaning or get stamps. Maybe not lately, but you know what I mean."

"Right…uh, no then," Gabe said. Turning away from me, he placed the case on his desk and opened it, revealing two items encased in dark gray foam. One was a glass vial filled with neon blue liquid that looked like it might, if consumed, give its drinker either radiation sickness or a massive hangover. The other item resembled a shiny, steel gun, but I knew that wasn't what it was.

I watched as Gabe inserted the vial into an opening in the top of the inoculator and took a step away from his desk…toward me. I shot to my feet. "What are you doing?"

Gabe held his hands low, one gripping the inoculator, the other reaching for me. "It'll make you feel better, I promise. I'm just trying to help you, Dani."

"I don't need help," I said, backing toward the door. "I feel fine…great, actually. No more headache. All better," I lied.

Holding up the inoculator so I could see it better, Gabe said, "Dani, it'll barely even hurt. Just a little pinch, and then everything—the confusion and weird déjà vu moments—it'll all be gone."

"I know what that is." I backed into the door and slid my hands behind me to grip the doorknob. My chest was suddenly tight with terror. Even though I didn't remember why, some part of my brain *knew* I didn't want him injecting me with whatever was in the vial. "You want to hurt me. That's why you've been acting so strange toward me…why you wouldn't…why last night…"

Gabe shook his head, pleading with his eyes. It seemed genuine, but some visceral feeling inside me told me it was just… wrong. *This is all WRONG!*

"I want to help you, Dani. Please trust me."

I wanted him to stop saying my name. "I can't," I whispered, finding the door handle behind me and shoving the door open. I spun and dashed into the lab.

Unfortunately, Gabe's legs ate up about twice as much distance as mine with each stride; he overtook me in a matter of seconds. He tackled me, wrapping his arms around my body and trapping my arms at my sides. Turning our bodies, he cushioned my fall so that I landed on him instead of the unyielding linoleum floor.

"Why…are you…doing this?" I grunted, trying to wriggle out of his grasp.

"I'm trying to help you." After several deep breaths, Gabe whispered, "You'll understand soon."

He rolled until I was flat on my stomach on the cold, gray and white-speckled floor and he was straddling my back, holding my arms immobile against my sides with his knees. I could kick backward, a little, but it didn't do me any good.

"I'm sorry this had to be so difficult," Gabe said as he pressed the muzzle of the inoculator against the side of my neck. With the sound of compressed air being released, I felt a sharp pinch in my neck. It was quickly followed by a dull throb as the toxic-looking liquid entered my body.

"You're a bastard," I hissed.

"So much more than you realize." He sounded regretful.

"I'm going to…to…" I growled, floundering for an adequate form of violent, painful revenge, but Gabe cut off my train of thought by releasing me and standing.

I glared up at his towering form as I turned over and scooted backward until my shoulder rammed into a cabinet. I tried to stand, but fuzziness was filling my head and the floor seemed to be tilting like a carnival ride. "What'd you do to me?"

"Just wait," he said, crossing his arms and leaning his hip against the opposite counter. He was watching me, waiting for something.

"I—" Whatever words I'd intended to say died on my tongue.

An image of Callie, my roommate back in Seattle, burst into my head. She was curled in the fetal position on her bathroom floor, my dog beside her and the smell of vomit lingering in the air.

And then I was sitting on top of Cam, beating his lifeless body in an attempt to make him wake back up.

In another instant, a note from Grams appeared in my shaking hand. Her written words told me she was dying, but that she hoped I would survive.

"No. No! NO!" I wailed, clutching my head. *They're dead. They're all dead…how could I have forgotten?*

Hundreds of memories of Jason—of fighting with him, of watching him, of searching abandoned buildings with him, of feeling him lying beside me—overwhelmed all my senses. It had been Jason and Zoe, along with Chris, Ky, and the others I'd encountered since the outbreak, or my suppressed memory of them, who had come to me in my dreams, urging me to remember. "Oh God…"

And then I was with Zoe, hugging her and jumping up and down. She was alive…I'd found her. *Was that really only two days ago?*

General Herodson's voice—his words—were the final memory to return. "Oh my God," I whispered, suddenly recalling his exact words…words I hadn't really *heard* until now.

"I'm very sorry to hear that, Danielle. I had really hoped you would feel more at home here and that I wouldn't have to bend your mind like all the others. My most loyal are those who choose to follow me of their own accord. Oh, well. You will do exactly as I say. You will agree to stay in the Colony and be excited about moving into the house I'm providing for you. You will forget anyone and everything you experienced since you were infected with the Virus, up until you arrived here. You will forget any negative opinions you may have formed about the Colony or me. You will only remember that you traveled here alone—this has always been your destination—that Gabe is your friend, and, of course, how to use your remarkable Ability. You will always *tell me the truth. And, most importantly, you will work for me, doing whatever I wish you to do, and be happy about it. Does that sound acceptable?"*

General Herodson had manipulated my mind; he'd torn away my most valued memories and controlled my every decision. As his words replayed in my head, rage, hotter and more explosive than anything I'd ever felt, boiled within me. It rushed through my veins, flooding my muscles with adrenaline and white-hot fury.

I began to scream, channeling the single, concentrated emotion into the sound. I screamed until my throat was raw and my voice had faded to a rough rasp.

9

ZOE

MARCH 16, 1AE

Another set of gunshots cracked in the distance, and something clicked inside Jake. His fallen features transformed into something fierce and focused as he reached for my hand. All his chaotic emotions were shadowed by protective determination. *For me?* He looked at his sister. *No, for Becca.* I felt unsettled—an unpleasant mixture of hyperawareness and emotional numbness—and I was unsteady on my feet as he hauled me over to the display case and pulled out our duffel bag of weapons and ammunition.

There was more gunfire.

"Get your asses out here!" Sanchez's voice echoed in our heads.

They're still here? An unexpected sense of relief washed over me.

"We're by the movie theater, in the center of downtown. Chris and I are cornered in the ice cream shop, and Jason, Harper, and Carlos are holed up a few stores down. There's at least a half dozen black-bands scattered across the street. Come around the corner of Sixth and Main so they don't see you."

Jake lugged the bag out and opened it, tossing me extra ammunition before zipping it back up and heaving it over his shoulder. I slipped the two extra magazines for my pistol into the waist of my cargo pants, swallowed the bile rising in my throat, and tried to exhale the burning sensation in my stomach. I'd grown far too used to the taste of fear.

The touch of Jake's warm palm on my cheek startled me. "Stay down and stay focused." He raised his eyebrows, waiting for me to process his words.

I nodded back at him and offered a weak, but grateful smile. He kissed me. I didn't have time to overthink us, but I was confused.

"We'll come back for you," Jake told his sister, and before I really knew what was happening, he captured my hand again and we were running out the door.

We slinked around cars and buildings for a couple blocks, drawing closer to the mayhem. Approaching a drugstore at the corner of Sixth and Main, we sidled up to the cement wall to catch our breath. Jake peered around the corner of the building, his fingers still gripping mine.

A few gunshots cracked in the air and Jake pulled back, straightening. "There are three soldiers about two blocks down, and there are a couple of them making their way toward us. The ice cream shop is a couple stores down, and I think the rest of our people are in the restaurant and flower shop the next block over, but I can't be sure." He shoved our bag into a mass of juniper bushes lining the side of the drugstore. "We have to get closer. We'll use the flower beds for cover."

We rounded the corner of the drugstore and headed toward the firefight in the heart of downtown. "Stay low and keep quiet," Jake mouthed. Two black-bands, using abandoned cars as cover over a dozen yards away, were yelling at one another.

I wiped my sweaty palms on my pants, gripping the fabric like it was a stress ball. After another gunshot, I heard a pained shout, and my heart stopped momentarily. *Jason.*

"Over here," Jake said, tugging me down behind one of the raised cement flower beds. The pool table–sized beds lined both sides of the street, their contents dormant for the winter, aside from the garbage can–camouflaging shrubbery on one side; it was the only thing keeping Jake and me out of sight.

I heard my brother shout in pain again and Jake stiffened. "Stay here, keep your gun ready, and shoot anyone who even sees you," he whispered, releasing my hand.

I nodded and removed my pistol from my thigh holster.

"I'll come back for you. Don't come out unless I call your name. Okay?" He saw hesitation in my eyes. "They're military-trained, Zoe, not Crazies. If they shoot at you, they *won't* miss."

I nodded, feeling dumb while I watched Jake covertly crawl behind the cover of an abandoned Audi and disappear around a small, empty deli a few shops beyond the drugstore.

Upon hearing approaching footsteps, I froze. Multiple someones, probably the black-bands we'd seen arguing, stopped on the other side of the flower bed. I couldn't see them, but I could hear them and feel their emotions—an unnerving mix of exhilaration and determination—as they scuffled closer to my hiding place. When they opened fire on my friends across the street, my ears rang, my hands started trembling, and I broke out in a cold sweat.

A bullet hit the shop window just a couple yards behind me, and I watched as the glass spider webbed around the hole. Catching sight of myself in the broken window, I momentarily panicked. *I can see them.* The two black-bands were crouched beside a VW bus, their backs to me as they aimed their rifles through the vehicle's busted windows. *If I can see them, they could see me.* I couldn't risk idly waiting, hoping they wouldn't turn around.

Closing my eyes, I considered my options…but I already knew

what I needed to do. I needed to kill them, before *they* killed me. Briefly, I wondered if Jake's blood still coursed through my veins from the transfusion back at Fort Knox—blood which would help me to heal if I was wounded—but either way, I didn't have any other choice. *I have to kill them.*

I had shitty aim compared to the soldiers, but I had the element of surprise. Besides, they were *really* close…which was both a blessing and a curse. The shrubbery in front of me was tall and thick enough to obscure their view of me, allowing me the opportunity to shoot them before being seen. *If nothing else, I could at least slow them down…shoot them in the leg so they can't walk, or maybe the arm to wound them or ruin their aim…something…*

Jump-started by the sound of Jason swearing in agony across the street, I looked down at the gun in my shaking hand and took a few steadying breaths. As quietly as I could, I aimed through the bushes. The sound of gunshots continued to scream through the air.

The two black-bands moved, crouching only four or so feet from me on the other side of the flower bed as they reloaded their ammunition. I needed to act fast. I was so close I could see the sweat beading on their foreheads and above their upper lips, and the way their chests heaved under their gear. I ignored the fact the man nearest me had green eyes that reminded me of Dani's, and that he looked to be about my age. I ignored the fact that he had a tattoo on the skin between his thumb and forefinger. *It's probably his mom's name…or girlfriend's.*

I took a fortifying breath. *They're probably already dead*, I thought cynically and pulled the trigger. My entire body hummed with tension as my muscles absorbed the shock and recoil.

The green-eyed soldier fell to the ground, a bullet through the side of his neck. *It worked.* I blinked in disbelief before shifting my aim to the black-band beside him. As he leveled his assault rifle in my direction, I pulled the trigger again, missing once before shooting him in the chest. He dropped to the ground beside his comrade, still moving, but I could only focus on the man I'd shot in the neck. Blood was spurting from the wound. *I killed him.*

I pivoted and fell forward, dropping my gun and bracing myself on my palms while catching my breath. And then I heard footsteps beside me. I reached for my gun, but I was too slow.

Roughly, hands grabbed my hair, yanking me to my feet, and I shrieked. My scalp stung as my assailant tugged mercilessly at my hair, and the hot barrel of his handgun pressed into my temple.

"I thought I smelled a girl," he said. "You should've shot me in the head, you little bitch." He smelled of tobacco and sweat.

"Let her go!" a familiar voice demanded. Harper. The black-band spun, ripping me around with him and pinning my body against him with his arm. Harper's eyes traced down the curve of the man's arm, tight against my chest, and up to where his dirty hand gripped my throat. I winced as his exceptionally long fingernails dug into my skin.

A deadly glint flashed in Harper's narrowed green eyes. "I *will* kill you," he growled as he approached us, his steps steady and his rifle aimed directly at the man's head. "Let her go," he repeated without a hint of fear or hesitation in his voice.

"Fresh meat?" The man chuckled. "I don't think so."

Suddenly, I was being dragged behind a building. The man's hold on me loosened while we moved, enabling me to maneuver my arm so I could pull Jake's knife out of my pocket. My captor stumbled, making the knife difficult for me to unlatch, but as he caught himself against the building with his gun hand, I finally succeeded. I stabbed him in the side of his thigh.

The black-band howled in pain as I yanked the blade from his flesh. His grip loosened further, and I started to scramble away.

Seizing the opportunity, Harper pulled the trigger. Three gunshots sounded before the black-band started to fall, grabbing my hair and pulling me down with him. I struggled out of his grasp, but his hand latched on to my forearm.

I stabbed him again, this time in the neck. The muscles and

tendons were dense, making it difficult to drive the blade in, and I felt a sickening crunch as the blade hit something more solid. Almost instantly, I jerked my hand away. I stared at the man's body, wide-eyed and unable to move.

Everything after that happened so quickly, it was all a blur. More shots were fired, and Harper's arms were around me. I heard footsteps and shouting and more gunfire, and then there was silence. I looked around at a graveyard of dead bodies—almost a dozen of them littered the street and sidewalks. Blood splattered their faces and fatigues. Their vacant eyes seemed to bore into mine, accusing me. I couldn't look away.

Harper entwined his fingers with mine, tugging me with him as he headed back to the flower bed where I'd dropped my gun. Once I was rearmed, he checked me for wounds.

"I'm fine," I told him. "Promise." He swore softly, and I remembered my brother's agonized shout. "Shit! Where's Jason? Is he okay?"

Harper pointed his chin toward something behind me, and I spun around, seeking any sign of my brother.

Jake was striding toward us. "Sanchez and Chris are getting Becca and the horses," he explained. "And Jason needs medical attention." He pointed to another large flower bed across the street.

I followed the direction of his finger and found Carlos standing above my brother, reaching down to help him to his feet. Jason struggled to stand, favoring his right foot as he took a wobbling step over a dead soldier sprawled on the cement. Together, they limped toward us.

As Jake drew nearer and focused on me, his eyes widened. I glanced down at my clothes. They were covered in blood, and my face felt sticky and wet. *No wonder Harper was fussing over me.* When I glanced up again, Jason was closer. He had a deep gash spanning from his hairline down to his jaw and blood smeared pretty much everywhere.

"Jason! Are you okay?" I ran to him. "What happened?"

He waved me away. "I'm fine."

"You're not fine. You need stitches, and I've got to—"

Jason put his hand out, gripping my arm as he hobbled closer to sit down on the ledge of a flower bed. "Is any of that blood yours?" he asked.

I shook my head as horses clopped up the road. It was Sanchez and Chris. They stopped the five horses in front of us and jumped down, Sanchez walking with an evident limp. Behind them, I noticed Harper moving from dead black-band to dead black-band, collecting their weapons and searching their bodies for anything useful.

"Are you alright?" I asked Sanchez, searching her leg for blood.

"It's just a twisted ankle, I'm fine. Don't worry about me," she said. When her gaze landed on Jason, I felt a swelling of concern radiate from her. Taking a hobbling step closer to him, she began to ask, "Are you al—"

"I'm fine," Jason said dismissively, and Sanchez hesitated. Her face was almost expressionless, but I could feel her torment.

Shaking off Jason's apathy, she said, "Carlos, help Chris get Jason up on his horse. We need to get the hell out of here. This goddamn place is cursed." She glanced at Harper and Jake. "And Becca's gone." She shook her head and rested her hands on her hips. "There goes our leverage."

Harper joined us, carrying an armful of weapons. *Weapons... Oh! My knife.* I reached into my pocket, but my knife wasn't there.

Turning around, I looked at the man I'd stabbed. My knife was sticking out of his throat and covered in his blood. I hurried over to him, snatched it out of his neck without a second thought, and wiped it off on his sleeve. My eyes lingered on his black armband. I cut the band off both sleeves and stuffed them into my pocket along with my knife.

"We should collect all the armbands," I called. "They might come in handy."

Out of nowhere, my head started throbbing, and I grew dizzy in the thrall of the most intense storm of despair and fury I'd ever felt. My body tensed as the rushing swirl of frenzied emotions swept over me.

"Agh!" I screamed and fell to my knees, panting. I recognized the source of the emotions. "Dani…"

10

DANI

MARCH 16, 1AE

In a room filled with someone else's things, in a house given to me by one of the three people whose death would inspire me to dance a merry jig—Herodson, Clara, and Cece—I paced. I'd been walking from the window to the dresser and back for the past two hours, ever since I woke up in the bed…which led to the question of when and how I'd ended up in the bed in the first place. The last thing I remembered was screaming out my pain as all of the memories and heartache of the last four months burst to life in my mind. *It doesn't matter*, I told myself. *The only thing that matters is tearing apart the bastard who tried to control me.*

Each step solidified my hatred for General Herodson. Each step also brought to mind a new, more idiotic plan for destroying him, or at least allowed me to add some creative embellishments. As I approached the expansive oak dresser and envisioned acting out my most recent scheme in Operation: Kill General Dickhead—to march straight into his office with a butter knife hidden in my bra and shank him in the eye—I felt the urge to scream and punch something simultaneously. I'd been riding a nonstop wave of fury and adrenaline, and as a result, I couldn't stop shaking.

General Herodson's revolting charity surrounded me…taunted

me. I was in the Colony, comfortable and encased in luxury—not just because he allowed it, but because he wanted it. Sure, I might have been freed from his mental control, but I was still doing exactly what he wanted. I was still wearing the ridiculous yellow armbands he'd given me, like I'd been marked as *his* property. *Goddamn bastard.* Dead *goddamn bastard.*

I kicked the dresser, hard. It knocked against the wall, shuddered, and stilled. Just as I pivoted to march back toward the window, the bedroom door opened. I spun to face the intruder.

"Everything okay in here?" MG—or, rather, Gabe—asked. He'd poked his head through the gap in the doorway and was watching me, his eyes filled with some heavy emotion—worry, or possibly guilt. *Did he bring me back here? Did he put me to bed?*

I remembered being under the General's control. I remembered practically throwing myself at Gabe. I remembered him injecting me with the neon liquid, and I remembered screaming and screaming…and screaming. And then, nothing. *That liquid must've been the "neutralizer" he'd been talking to Dr. Wesley about. So…the "neutralizer" must do just that: neutralize the General's Ability. Gabe saved me from the General's mind control.* Finally, the doubt which had made me hesitant to trust Gabe, the doubt I'd felt ever since overhearing that conversation between him and the doctor, evaporated.

When I didn't say anything, instead opting to stand and do my best impersonation of a marble statue, Gabe entered the room the rest of the way.

"What do you remember?" he asked as he drew closer, shaking his head. "Christ, Dani…do you have any idea what you did?"

Huh? What I *did?* I shook my head slowly. "I didn't…you're the one who…what are you talking about?"

Gabe raised his hands like he was reaching for me, then pulled them back and shoved them into his pants pockets. "After I gave you the neutralizer and Herodson's hold wore off, you started to scream…do you remember that?"

I nodded.

He cleared his throat. "Well, when you screamed, you used your telepathy." He rubbed his hand over his smoothed-back hair. "From what I can tell, everyone in the damn building heard it…*felt* it. There were even a few bloody noses, and one person supposedly fainted." Taking a deep breath, he watched me, assessing. "Did you know you could do that…hurt people with your Ability?"

Eyes wide, I shook my head.

He rubbed the faint stubble on one side of his jaw. "I, uh, don't think *he* can track it back to the source, so you should be safe enough, but if he finds out you can do that…" He was shaking his head slowly. "Shit. He'll weaponize you in a heartbeat and use any means of motivation necessary."

Taking several dazed steps, I sank down onto the foot of the bed. "I didn't know I could…I've never…holy crap."

It was Gabe's turn to start pacing. "Use your Ability. Try to sense the minds around you."

"Right now? Why?"

He shot me the briefest possible glance. "Because—just do it. It's important."

Frowning, I did as he directed, focusing on the part of my brain that enabled me to speak in other minds. And there was nothing. "I…I can't."

Gabe was nodding. "Burnout. Interesting," he muttered.

I stood and placed myself in front of him on his way back to the window. "Burnout? What do you mean, *burnout*? Did I…oh God, did I destroy my Ability completely?" I reached for him and squeezed his arm. "What does that mean?" I was panicking. God, I was sick of panicking.

Gabe placed his hands on my elbows and bent down to meet my eyes. "I've seen burnout a few times, and it's never been permanent. But"—he hesitated—"each consecutive time the same person burned out their Ability, it took longer to return. You need to be more careful."

My voice was small when I said, “I didn’t mean to do it.” I looked away. There’d just been so much pain…too much to contain. And it was still there.

Gabe raised his hands to my face, gently turning it back to him. “What made you…was it the neutralizer?” There was no mistaking the guilt in his eyes.

“I suppose.” I stepped away from him, from his touch, and crossed to the window. Looking down at the neighborhood street from the second story of “my” house, I could almost imagine the world was normal…almost. “When *he* did what he did, he made me forget just about everything that’s happened to me since this whole nightmare began. And then you injected me with that…that stuff, and I remembered. Everything. It’s like it all just happened again—everyone dying, my trip here, Jason—everything.” I paused, taking a deep breath. “I killed people, Gabe.”

“It can be like that when his hold is broken, especially if he included a command to forget,” Gabe said, rambling. “It’s a lot to handle, I know, but—”

“You know? Really?” I retorted, spinning to face him. “You’ve been here—hiding from what’s really going on. So what could you possibly know?” I was fully aware that Gabe had done nothing but help me, but I *had* to lash out at something. I felt like a mindless, wounded animal. “Do you know about the man I killed with a shovel? Or the one I shot in the head? How about the cult freaks—the Prophets of the New World—do you know about them? Do you know about anything going on out there? How’d you even end up in here?”

Gabe shook his head. “Dani—”

I held up my hand, cutting him off. “The woman in charge of the cult, Mandy, she was like General Herodson with that mind control crap. She controlled hundreds of people—forced them to kill—raped them and made them think they liked it.” I thought back on everything Carlos had told me over our weeks of horseback travel, recalled all the twisted things that bitch had made her *flock* do.

My gaze was steady, locked on Gabe's pale blue eyes. "Mandy's dead, and I'm glad I was there when Jason put the bullet through her skull." *And I'll do everything possible to make General Herodson just as dead.*

Recognition filled Gabe's clear eyes. "Dani, with the General…you can't—"

"He's dead," I hissed, stalking toward Gabe. "He just doesn't know it yet."

Gabe scoffed. "And what are you going to do, just walk up to him and shoot him? Or maybe you're planning to stab him instead, hmmm? Make it a little more personal?"

Actually, yeah, that's the current plan. I said nothing.

"Listen to me!" he shouted. His hands were on my upper arms, his grip demanding. "Going after him like that…trying to assassinate him…that won't work. I agree—he needs to die—but he's too powerful for whatever you're planning to work. You can't do this alone, and you can't do it now. We need time…people…resources."

Unwilling to let his words permeate my thick skull, I shook my head.

"Damn it, Dani!" Gabe yelled, shaking me. "You don't believe me? Then I'll show you. If you still want to go all kamikaze after you see everything, I won't stop you."

I glared daggers—no, broadswords—at him until he let me go.

"Take a few minutes to get yourself together, then come down," he said as he stopped in the doorway. "There are only a few hours until curfew, and there's a lot to see."

Not quite slamming the door, Gabe left me alone with my unsettling thoughts. I would see what he had to show me, use it if I could—and *then* I would kill the General.

"There are people here now," I noted as Gabe and I walked through his lab to his office. Unlike this morning, the place was a veritable scientific anthill, teeming with efficient men and women in white lab coats with yellow bands around their upper arms. *What's the deal with the armbands?*

Gabe shot me a brief glance. "Yeah, well, I couldn't close the department down for very long."

"Why *did* you close it down? Because you've been with me? Can't they function without you?" I asked.

Gabe herded me quickly through the lab and into his office. When the door clicked shut, he explained, "They can, but sometimes they get a little too enthusiastic about their work and harm their test subjects. I try to be here as much as possible to keep them under control."

I lowered my eyebrows. "Harm people? Why would they want to—"

Gabe raised his eyebrows.

The General, I realized. *He probably commanded them all to get results using whatever means necessary.* "Oh…got it."

Gabe picked up a manila envelope that had been resting on his keyboard. He opened it and slid some colored plastic cards into his hand. They looked like hotel keycards attached to navy blue, nylon lanyards. Handing me a bright red card, he explained, "These are from Wes—Dr. Wesley. Red means you're still recovering—not healthy enough to work." He cut off my impending protest with a raised hand. "Think of it like a doctor's sick note. Keep it with you at all times. It'll keep people like them"—he nodded toward the door—"or that guard at headquarters, or anyone else wearing a yellow armband from getting ahold of you and doing something you're not okay with—like, um…hurting you." A flash of concern lit his eyes.

I glanced down at one of my own yellow armbands. "What do they mean—the armbands?"

"Different things based on the color. Yellow means mind-controlled. Black indicates someone who's following Herodson willingly." He held out his own arm, drawing my attention to the white armbands he was wearing. I hadn't noticed them during my first day here; they hadn't stood out against his white shirt. "White means the wearer has a leadership role—in charge of a department or is one of *his* advisors."

I watched him slip the other lanyard over his head. The attached card was plain white, like his armbands. "And a white *card* is like a free pass. It means I have an excuse not to work and can pretty much go anywhere on base—at least, anywhere that's not restricted."

"Not work? But what about them?" I asked, mimicking his earlier nod toward the door.

"Wes agreed to check in on them every half hour."

"She's going to walk all the way over here from the hospital every half hour just to check on your people?" I asked incredulously.

Shaking his head, Gabe said, "Her main office is downstairs. She only works in the hospital when her duties require it. Technically, she's more of a research doctor than a medical doctor."

"Oh." My thoughts drifted to the doctor in question as I settled the red card's cord around my neck. "Dr. Wesley's being very accommodating. How'd she end up with so much power here, anyway? *He* must really trust her."

Gabe shot me a sharp look. "It's a long story. What you need to know is that it's her blood that makes the neutralizer work. Her Ability blocks those of others. Probably a lot like your friend's."

My friend's…Jason's. Thinking of him made my heart hurt. *Oh, crap—I kissed Gabe.* It had been a melt-your-panties-off kiss… except I hadn't been wearing any. *Oh my God…kill me now.* If I told Jason about the kiss, he might kill Gabe, or at least maul him. Because, though my mind-controlled self had been the one to kiss Gabe, he'd kissed me back…and he'd been in full control of his mind.

Jason can never know.

"Anyway," Gabe continued, "while we're out in public, you need to pretend you're still under Herodson's control. Be *very* careful of what you say. You never know who might be listening… or how."

Frowning, I said, "I'll just talk in your head. Or, at least, I will once I stop being so burned out."

Gabe shook his aforementioned head. "Won't work—I use the neutralizer, too."

Damn. I hadn't thought about that. A light bulb was slowly turning on in my mind. "Gabe, does the neutralizer do anything else?"

"What do you mean?"

"Besides nulling—neutralizing—other people's Abilities, does it, say, give us a little power boost, too?"

Gabe froze in the process of zipping up his brown and tan ski coat. "Is your telepathy back online?"

"No."

"Then how the hell could you have possibly known that?"

Smiling mysteriously, I told him, "A girl can have a few secrets, can't she?"

He studied me suspiciously, but after a few heartbeats, nodded. "Just make sure they're the right secrets," he said, walking to the door. He opened it, motioned for me to follow him out, and secured the lock. "Time for the tour."

Two hours later, we were leaving a large cafeteria. It was part of the same university complex as Gabe's lab, which had once been an Air Force Academy. The room had been filled with several hundred Colonists, some in lab coats, some in sweats, and some in scrubs. Other than the people in scrubs, everyone was wearing either yellow or black armbands, and only those with black armbands were acting…normal. Everyone else seemed to speak only when necessary, and even then only in hushed tones. It wasn't that they were whispering schemes to overthrow the General or anything nefarious, unfortunately. They were just…quiet, subdued. Gabe and I had said nothing the entire time we'd been sitting across from one another at a small, square table, drinking a cup of coffee and sharing a turkey and cheddar sandwich and a blueberry scone.

He'd shown me enough of the base—including the perimeter, with its ever-moving patrols, the school, and the location of the warehouses storing food and weapons—that I realized how foolish my assassination plans had been. Seeing classrooms half-filled with perfectly cooperative and focused children of all ages had been the creepiest stop along the tour. It was unnatural. The kids were clearly under the General's mental influence. I feared that manipulating brains that were still developing would harm them permanently. *That man is all kinds of evil.*

I was uncomfortably aware of two *very* important things: everyone in the Colony had an Ability and was actively training to strengthen it, and nearly every single person was an emphatic follower of the General, either because of his mental manipulation or by choice. True free will was absent. Herodson's will was law.

I was resolved to contact Jason and Zoe once my telepathy returned, no matter how long it took me to actually find them. It wasn't just that I missed them like crazy—I did—but I needed to make sure they were okay. I *needed* them to be okay. And if they were, it was likely that they were planning some sort of prison break. I couldn't imagine Jason *not* planning such a thing, reckless as it might be. It was imperative that I pass on what I'd learned about the Colony.

"There's one thing that doesn't quite make sense," I said to Gabe as we walked from the cafeteria to a neighboring building. Wanting to make sure I passed as much relevant info on to my friends as possible, I intended to scour Gabe's mind for pretty much anything he could tell me.

"Which is?"

I moved closer to him, keeping my voice hushed. "Back in the cafeteria, most of those people were acting sort of zombie-ish—like they have no thoughts beyond what the General tasked them with. But everyone in your lab was busy and active, talking with their colleagues."

Gabe nodded but said nothing.

"Then there was that guard with the yellow armband who was getting all handsy at the entrance to the General's building," I explained. "He seemed to be operating outside the 'guard my building' parameters. It all just seems really inconsistent."

After several drawn-out breaths, Gabe said, "That guard was probably given multiple commands, one of them being to actively attempt to procreate."

The breeding program...Project Eden. I scrunched my face in disgust.

Ignoring my reaction, Gabe continued, "That's been a pretty standard order given to the men. The women are told the same... and that they should be open and willing to any man's advances."

I made a choking sound. "That's...that's...ugh!"

Gabe nodded.

"But...he didn't give *me* that command," I told him.

For once, it was Gabe who frowned. "I can only assume that's because he didn't want the pursuit of reproduction to interfere with your communication tasks." He was quiet for a moment. "That, and he likely wants to choose your future, uh, partner... someone with whom you could produce children who have *your* Ability."

"Hmmm," I murmured, processing his disturbing words. I was still processing as he led me into a squat, boxy gray building. The sign protruding from the overgrown grass proclaimed, *Humanities Building*.

Holding open a heavy glass door, Gabe said, "This is where you're intended to work once you're given a clean bill of health."

"And how will that work, exactly?" I asked, hoping I would be long gone before that could happen. I wasn't planning to stick around for much longer; I just had to figure out *how* to not stick around.

I followed Gabe down a bland hallway and through a second set of glass doors that led to some sort of reception office. I leaned in closer to him, acutely aware of the woman organizing papers at the front desk, and whispered harshly, "I'm supposed to just do his bidding, fully aware of my actions? What does he even need telepaths for, anyway?"

Gabe offered me a tight-lipped grin and murmured, "He uses them to spread the word…to draw people in. You remember what I said about the Colony being the new center of civilization?"

"He wants me to bring people here so he can control them?" Horrified, I stared into Gabe's cunning eyes as he towered over me. "I will *never* do that," I vowed.

Gabe shrugged. "You may not have a choice. When it's your life, or the life of someone you care about, versus a relative stranger…what'll you choose?" With one final, significant eyebrow-raise, Gabe left my side and approached the woman at the desk. She was pretty enough, in a perky, blonde, former-cheer-leader way, and the smile she offered Gabe contained more than a hint of "come hither."

"Emily, so lovely to see you again," Gabe said.

Emily giggled, sounding about ten years younger than she appeared. "Hi, Gabe."

It took an effort not to roll my eyes.

"I've brought someone in to meet you. She's your newest telepath." Gabe reached back, and closing his long fingers around my arm just above my elbow, he pulled me forward. "This is Dani. Dani, this is Emily—she'll be coordinating your schedule and assignments once you begin work."

When I said nothing, his grip tightened.

"So nice to meet you," I chirped.

Emily glanced at Gabe's hand, which was still on my arm, and her eyes narrowed almost imperceptibly before returning to my face. Jealousy, it seemed, was still ready and available through the lens of the General's commands.

"Welcome to the Colony," she said.

"Dani's the one General Herodson's been waiting for—the sender *and* receiver," Gabe explained.

Emily's face lit up with recognition. "Oh! How exciting!" she gushed, her enthusiasm genuine. She'd instantly transformed into my biggest fan. Apparently, like me, *her* commands included a directive about enthusiasm for her tasks. "We've got big plans for you!"

"Great," I said, trying as hard as possible to keep my smile from melting. "Can't wait."

"We have your office all ready and a huge list of communications to start you off," Emily explained excitedly. "We're going to draw in *so* many more new Colonists using you!"

Using me. "Awesome," I said with so much fake perkiness that I wanted to vomit. I was becoming used to my stomach being in a general state of nauseated discomfort. I needed to get the hell out of the Colony before I started luring in hapless survivors. I didn't care what Gabe said. I couldn't do it. I wouldn't.

As we left the building and returned to my house, I pondered the massive amounts of information I'd learned since leaving that afternoon. One fact kept bouncing around in my mind: the General had known about me and my Ability before I'd arrived. He'd been *expecting* me. He'd been waiting. The more I thought about the implications, the more pissed off I became.

Gabe.

A second after Gabe shut and locked my front door, I rounded on him. "When I was still brainwashed, you said MG was a guy I'd trusted and that he'd betrayed me."

"Dani—"

"What did you…I can't believe I've been so stupid!" I yelled as I stepped closer and slapped him as hard as I could.

"Dani, I can explain—"

I slapped him again and felt wicked satisfaction when he brought his hand up to his reddening cheek. "'You were attacked. Our patrol rescued you and brought you back for medical attention,'" I said, throwing his words back at him. "How could you? I asked for your help to find Zoe. You knew where we were. I—I *trusted* you!" I raised my hand to hit him again, but Gabe caught my wrist before I could land the blow. "It wasn't Crazies who attacked me, it was Colonists—because of *you.* I got knocked out and abducted because of *you,*" I hissed, yanking my wrist out of his grasp and spinning to stomp down the hall toward the family room. I had to get away from him.

"I'm sorry, Dani. It just—"

I stopped mid-step and spun to face him. "Oh, shut up! You're such a bastard! You…you…" Unable to find a word that adequately described how I felt about him at that moment, I growled in frustration. "Just tell me why. Why'd you do it? Why'd you set me up? Why'd you pretend to help me…to care?" He'd been my only human companion, even if it was only in my dreams, when I'd taken the sabbatical from my other companions several months back. He'd been the one to comfort me when I discovered that Grams was dead. I'd *cared* about him. I still did. The crushing betrayal weakened my voice to a sad whine as I asked, "Why did you let me kiss you?"

Gabe sighed, and having followed me into the family room, he lowered himself onto the couch. With his elbows on his knees, he clasped his hands together. "Herodson has people he calls Truth Guards—they're like human lie detectors. Their Ability allows them to hear truth and lies in what people say. He keeps them around at all times, just in case someone manages to break through his control." After a moment, he added, "And the neutralizer doesn't block that particular Ability; it doesn't block any that aren't directed at a person specifically."

So the neutralizer has limitations, and the General has people like Ben. Good to know. Stopping in front of Gabe, I crossed my arms and raised my eyebrows, silently telling him to continue.

"Every time I visit the dreams, I have to report back, and *he* or one of his seconds—they're called his Controllers—always asks me a series of questions in the presence of one of the Truth Guards. Did I find any people with Abilities I thought could be useful to Herodson? Who are they, and what are their Abilities? Where are they? And so on." Gabe paused, pleading with his eyes. "If I'd lied, he would have known I had a way to break his hold. He would have—"

It was an effort to unclench my jaw, but I managed it. "What? Killed you?" I wasn't some idealistic fool to believe that a man I'd never met in person would forfeit his own life to prevent me from being captured and mentally enslaved, but still, his betrayal hurt.

Staring at my boots, Gabe shook his head.

"Then what? What would he have done to you?"

"Not to me." He sighed. "There's a woman. I've known her most of my life. She's like a little sister to me, and…well, it's my fault he has her." His voice gained strength. "If I lie, or even if I simply fail to bring in people with the Abilities he's searching for, he'll hurt her. Badly. He won't kill her—she's too valuable to him—but he'll make her wish she was dead. He calls it 'extrinsic motivation.'"

Holy crap. "I understand," I said, my voice rough. I liked to pretend I was noble, to tell myself I wouldn't draw someone into the fire, but threatened with the safety of the people I loved, I wouldn't even hesitate.

"I'm really sorry," Gabe said softly, finally glancing up at me. "I didn't want to. Dani, I—"

"It's done. Apologizing doesn't fix anything."

"I know," he agreed, sounding defeated. "But I did leave something behind…something for your friends to find."

My eyebrows rose of their own accord. "You did? What?"

"One of the yellow armbands. I know you said some of the people you were with were in the military; they would've recognized them. I just wanted to leave them a sign. I didn't want them to give up, to stop looking for you." He shook his head in defeat. "I wish you'd never asked me to help you find your friends. I wish you hadn't trusted me."

I studied him for a long moment, took a deep breath, then sat on the sofa beside him. "We need to get out of here," I said. "You, me, the woman, and Dr. Wesley. We need to escape."

"But—"

"No buts," I interrupted. "You know what he wants me to do—to bring in who knows how many more survivors. Like what you're doing times a thousand, or however many people are left alive. They'll just become his mind slaves too, and then he'll be that much more powerful." Enunciating each word very clearly, I repeated, "We need to get out of here."

Gabe's eyes left mine, and he studied his hands. He seemed to be mentally warring with himself. Finally, he said, "Okay. I'll do whatever I can."

Exhaling, I reached for his forearm and gave it a squeeze. "Thank you. I don't think I can do it without you."

Standing, Gabe started making a circuit around the room. "We won't have long before you have to report to duty—a week at most. I can get Wes to extend your sick leave, but any longer than that and they'll become suspicious. Really suspicious. Herodson's been looking forward to obtaining you for a long time, and he wants to start using you as soon as possible."

God, that's disturbing. "Okay."

"Is your telepathy functioning yet? Can you get a message to your people? Tell them not to do anything stupid?" he asked.

I checked quickly and was incredibly relieved to find the telepathic portion of my brain alive and kicking. Nodding, I said, "I was planning to do that anyway, assuming the power boost from the neutralizer is strong enough for me to reach them and maintain contact. One question…"

"Yeah?"

"Define 'stupid.'"

Gabe threw his hands in the air as he continued his laps around the room. "Pretty much anything. They need to just sit tight. We'll need to coordinate with them…use them to set up a distraction or something, but we'll need time to study the perimeter guards. I haven't exactly had a need to pay much attention to their routes and Abilities in the past."

"Got it." I followed him around the room with my eyes. "I'm still mad at you, you know."

"I know."

Pursing my lips, I watched him stride into the kitchen and take a saucepan and skillet out of the cupboards beneath the stove. Apparently he was going to make dinner for me. *Where the heck does he live?* I was surprised I hadn't wondered about it earlier, since the only place I'd seen him sleep was on the couch I was currently sitting on. But I didn't ask; I had a far more pressing issue. I needed to make sure my friends were okay.

Closing my eyes, I opened myself to the millions of minds throbbing around me, and after spending a moment basking in the glory of the collective, I focused only on the human minds. I knew the general direction of my friends' camp, and that knowledge, along with its distance from my current location, should have been enough to guide my awareness to my friends' minds.

It wasn't. Or rather, they weren't where they were supposed to be.

*Oh God…*did *something happen? Crazies, or…or the General? But Dr. Wesley assured me they were fine…that if they'd been hurt, it would've been noted in my file.* I suddenly felt like there was a five-hundred-pound weight on my chest, suffocating me. *Had she* *been lying? Did his people attack them when they took me? Are they hurt...or dead? No, no, no, no, no...*

They're not dead! They can't be! I need them to not *be dead!*

There were other human minds in the area a few miles away, and I zeroed in on them. Relief flooded my body. It wasn't all of them, but I sensed Chris, Carlos, Zoe, and three others I was vaguely familiar with. *Where's Jason? And Ky and Ben? Mr. G? The rest of Zoe's people?* I fought the urge to curl into a ball under the sudden resurgence of anxiety. *Where are you, Jason?*

I took a deep, if shaky, breath and focused on Zoe. Each individual's mind had a certain feeling, almost like a signature or a fingerprint. As far as I could tell, I only had to touch a mind once in order to recognize it later. Zoe's felt hard and focused, similar to Jason's, but with fewer of the thorny briars that guarded his.

"Zo? Can you hear me?"

"Holy shit, D! Am I imagining this?" Zoe asked, sounding completely flabbergasted.

"Uh...no?" I felt giddy with relief at hearing her mind-voice.

"Damn it, D! I felt your pain. I thought you were dead. What was that? Are you okay?"

"I'm okay, I just—"

"We know you're in the Colony. We were coming to get you... but we ran into a few, um, issues. But we'll find another way."

I cringed and shook my head. *"No! Bad idea. Really,* really *bad idea. It's too dangerous for you guys to try to get me out right now."*

"What? Why? What the hell are we supposed to do? We're freaking out over here." She was starting to sound kind of pissed. It wasn't like I'd wanted to get abducted.

"It's just that going in blind would be a really great way to get yourselves killed. Everyone *here has an Ability, and they've all been honing them, so they're all super strong compared to us. And almost everyone's being mind-controlled.* I *was being mind-controlled at first, but I'm not anymore. Gabe said—"*

"Wait a second...who the hell is Gabe?" Zoe asked, cutting off my rambling explanation.

"Gabe is MG—that's his real name," I began to explain. *"And without him I'd still be one of Herodson's mind slaves...Herodson's the General who's doing the mind manipulation."*

"This is really bad. You do realize that this MG-Gabe guy is the reason you're there, right?"

I snorted. *"Yeah. We just had it out over that. It's sort of complicated, and he didn't really have a choice. But he's going to do whatever he can to help me escape."*

"But you're okay, right?" Zoe asked, sounding worried. God, I wanted to hug her.

"Yeah, I'm okay, more or less," I said.

"That's...good." I could tell Zoe had more questions, but thankfully, she let them go. *"So, what are we supposed to do in the meantime?"*

"I just need some more time to gather intel and stuff. Otherwise, anything we do is suicide, which sort of defeats the purpose. You guys need to think about how you can use your Abilities to attack and defend, and maybe create a distraction. Without using Abilities, there's no chance—not against these people."

"Okay, but Jason's not going to like this...just leaving you there," she said, stating the obvious.

"So he's okay?" I exhaled with relief. *"I thought...when I couldn't find him, or some of the others...I thought you'd been attacked or something."* When she said nothing, I added, *"He* is *okay, right?"*

I had the impression that she was sighing. *"He's nulling constantly, so I'm not exactly sure how he's doing, but I think he's better than he was."*

If he was surrounding himself with a nulling fog, it explained why I couldn't get through to him. It also meant he'd probably lost control of his emotions, since they tended to impact his Ability. *"Was he really* that *upset?"* I asked.

"Uh...yeah. He ran off to go after you, but came back before he got himself killed. He's calmed down some and is behaving a little *more rationally now."*

"Wow...that's just, wow. Can you, you know, let him know I'm trying to get through right now?" I asked, feeling desperate in my need to talk to him.

"It might be a while. He's a little...out of it." At her words, my heart seemed to pause for a few eternal seconds.

"What? Why?" I asked, clenching my fists. Something was wrong, I knew it. I could practically feel it in my bones.

"The bullet just grazed him—it's not that big of a deal," she explained. *"Harper already stitched the wound up...and the cut on his face."*

I had to take four deep, calming breaths before I could ask, *"He got shot? How?"*

"We were in Cañon City, and some bad shit went down...he'll tell you about it," Zoe said, sounding way less freaked out than I felt. *"But right now's probably not the best time. He's opted to dull the pain with whiskey instead of painkillers. But I promise, D, he's okay."*

I forced myself to stay calm, to not demand that she make him let down his stupid nulling shield right that instant. *"Okay...I'll try him in the morning. Can you at least tell him I'm okay and that I... I don't know...that I miss him."*

"Yes, of course I will. And I'll make sure he's sobered up to talk to you in the morning. I'm sure he'll do it if he knows you're trying to get through to him."

I smiled. *"Thanks, Zo...God, I miss you. I'm assuming you guys are moving camp...since you're somewhere else right now."*

"Yeah," she said. *"Some of the others went ahead and are already setting it up...far away."*

"Okay, good. Don't tell me where. If the General asks me, I need to be able to honestly say I don't know...he's got people like Ben."

"Of course he does," she said acerbically and then paused. *"I'm really worried about you, D."*

"Honestly, I'm a little worried about me, too, but that doesn't mean I'll let you guys risk your lives to get me out of here. Once we know more, we'll come up with a good, safe *plan,"* I said, feeling the first twinges of exhaustion. *"I hate to do this, but I gotta go. This is starting to wear me out. Love you, Zo."*

"Love you too. Be safe." She paused, and then added, *"And kick MG in the balls for me."*

"I'll do my best," I agreed before letting the connection go with an audible gasp of relief. Even with the power boost from Dr. Wesley's neutralizer, I was pooped.

11

ZOE

MARCH 16, 1AE

I was still covered in blood. It was just after nightfall, hours after our altercation with the contingent of Colony soldiers in Cañon City. We were finally miles away and clomping along toward shelter and safety…somewhere.

The day felt like it was never going to end. The wind was picking up, and the sun had already sunk behind the Rockies, creating a violet- and pink-hued watercolor that had faded all too quickly. I hoped we would find a sufficient camping spot soon. I was worried I might fall asleep atop Wings, and falling more than five feet to the ground wasn't how I wanted to end my day.

Harper had cleaned and stitched up Jason's wounds and given him a bottle of whiskey to help ease his pain somewhere near the suburbs of Cañon City. My brother's bullet wound was superficial, but there was no denying that the gash across his face would leave a nasty scar. More than anything, he needed rest; we all did. I just hoped the next shit pile didn't land on us before we found a safe place to stay.

After my mind-convo with Dani, we agreed we needed to keep moving—the further into the mountains and away from our old camp, the better. We rode in silence as our horses trudged across fields of tall grasses and between sparse, squat fir trees.

Jake watched me closely. I knew he wanted to talk about before, about what had happened in the abandoned shop, but I'd been trying to avoid that as much as possible. Instead, I focused on Chris as she fussed over Jason as we rode along. She checked his wounds and tried, unsuccessfully, to influence his emotional grid. He wasn't happy about Dani's advice to hold back, nor was he happy that he'd missed his opportunity to talk to her.

"Whoa," Harper said, bringing his chestnut, Delilah, to a stop.

"What the hell?" Sanchez said from her seat directly behind me on Wings. I pulled the horse to a stop beside Delilah.

Cooper and Jack continued trotting along, their fluffy tails wagging back and forth through the tall grass, but everyone else halted alongside us.

I followed Harper's line of sight and found the moonlit outlines of what looked like several buildings.

"Looks like a town," he said. "Jake, let's check it out. The rest of you…" He looked back at us, taking in our disheveled states: Jason drunk, Chris struggling to keep him upright, Sanchez massaging her twisted ankle, and me still a little shaky and covered in dried blood. "Um, the rest of you just stay put."

"I can come with you guys," Carlos said, and he nudged Arrow forward.

Harper nodded. "Let's do it." The three men coaxed their horses into a trot and made their way through the scattered trees. Before they reached the buildings, they dismounted, tied their horse's reins to a couple of scraggly branches, and readied their weapons—a pistol for Jake, an assault rifle for Harper, and Chris's shotgun for Carlos.

The three of them crept up to the side of the nearest building, a structure that appeared to be covered in wood shingles, before disappearing around a corner. I looked back at Chris, who just returned my stare, the embodiment of calm, but I could feel her anticipation. *This could be really bad, or really good,* I thought.

After a half hour, the horses were getting antsy, and I couldn't sit still in my saddle—especially not with Sanchez anxiously breathing down my neck, literally. *What's taking so long?*

"Should one of us go after them?" I asked.

"That would be stupid," Jason slurred as he emptied the last of the whiskey into his mouth.

I rolled my eyes. "How are you even staying on your horse?"

Whatever Jason's smart-ass retort was, I didn't hear it. I felt a sudden sense of apprehension, and my muscles tensed—but it wasn't my own fear that made me uneasy. Someone *else*—someone new—was frightened.

Scanning the darkness around me, I sought out the source of the fear. The moon was low and bright, providing a decent amount of light to see. *Is someone hiding in the shadows?*

"What is it?" Sanchez whispered, her head darting around anxiously. *"Do you feel something?"*

"Shhh," I said, trying to push everyone's growing concern away. "Someone's here." I struggled to dismount, Sanchez still straddling Wings behind me.

"Zoe—" But Jason's objection was lost in the flash of a memory belonging to a boy who felt uncertain and curious.

I saw the boy's mom being brutally raped and then murdered by Crazies in the alleyway behind their apartment. I watched his baby sister being hauled away for only God knew what fate. All the while, the boy writhed in pain, broken and bloody on the wet pavement, watching his family die horrible deaths while he could do nothing.

The memory faded in and out, and then a man was there, a gun shoved in his back pocket and a bow and quiver strapped to his back. He killed the Crazies somehow, but the boy could barely see, his vision waning along with his consciousness.

"It's alright, boy," the man said in a Australian accent. "What's your name?"

"Sam," the boy barely breathed.

"Sam, I'm Tavis. You'll be alright. I've got you now." He gathered the boy's limp body into his arms.

Unwilling to see another of the boy's memories, I closed my mind to his, wherever he was. "Sam?" I ignored the others' protests as I stepped away from Wings, focusing on the shadows around me. For some reason, I wasn't scared. I knew he was only a boy and posed no danger to us. "Hello?" I called out again. "Sam?"

Sanchez and Chris dismounted and readied their guns.

It was eerily silent for a moment before Wings's head shot up and I heard muffled footsteps in the grass a couple yards away.

"Who are you?" a small, distrusting voice asked. "And how do you know my name?" Sam appeared from the shadows, a drawn arrow aimed at my chest.

I raised my hands, palms out, in a placating gesture. "We won't hurt you." I bit the inside of my cheek for a moment, unsure how willing he was to listen. "My name is Zoe. These are my friends. That's my brother Jason," I said, pointing. "That's Chris, and this is Sanchez."

The boy stared at me for another moment. "Why are you covered in blood?" he asked, keeping his bow trained on me.

I examined my clothes, which appeared muddy in the moonlight. *How can he tell it's blood?* "There was an incident in town," I started. "We need a place to stay, to get cleaned up and rest for the night."

The man from Sam's memory, Tavis, stepped out from the shadows behind Sam, two rabbits hanging from a tether held between his fingers.

"Stop right there," Sanchez warned.

Like mine had, Tavis's hands rose in appeasement as he studied us. "Just a couple of dead rabbits," he said in an Australian accent.

After a few seconds, he lowered his hands and refocused his attention on me. "So, you got into a bit of trouble?"

"Soldiers from the Colony. They tried to kill us." I stood silently, waiting for his reaction.

"Did you kill any of them?" Sam asked, his voice flat.

I nodded, my mind eased by their growing sense of relief.

"How do you know my name?" Sam asked again, finally lowering his bow.

I eyed the boy, considering how much to tell him. "I saw one of your memories," I admitted.

"Zoe," Sanchez hissed. *"What the hell are you doing?"*

I peered over my shoulder at her. "It's okay…they're okay."

Sanchez scowled and took a deep breath. *"I hope you know what you're doing."*

Turning back to our new acquaintances, I sincerely hoped I did too.

"Where are your mates?" Tavis asked, pointing to the three horses tied up at the edge of the clearing.

"They're checking things out," I said. "Seeing if it's safe to stay here."

Sam looked back at Tavis, who gave him a nod, and the boy started to walk past us. "Come on then," he said.

I couldn't help but smile at the grown-up, matter-of-fact way Sam had about him.

Tavis stopped in front of me, outstretching his hand. "Tavis," he offered, and I shook it. "It's nice to meet people who aren't completely crazy." His eyes were heavy with exhaustion and gratitude, and I wondered how long it had been since he'd seen any sane, non-Colony survivors. "You heard the kid," he said with a smile to Chris and Sanchez. "Come on."

I glanced at Sanchez, who took a deep, steadying breath. "Shall we?" She motioned for the rest of us to follow them and headed over to gather our other three horses, while I collected Wings's reins.

"Are we sure about this?" Jason asked. I was surprised by the lack of criticism in his voice.

I met his eyes and then Chris's before nodding. "They're safe, unless Chris feels something I don't," I said quietly.

Chris shook her head, confirming my assessment, and led her horse to follow our hosts as they approached a stable. "Sanchez," she said as we drew closer. "Give the guys a heads-up so they don't accidently shoot us or the boy, would you?"

"So…what is this place?" I called to Tavis.

He chuckled. "A ghost town. Welcome home."

Unloading the last of our things, Sanchez, Harper, Carlos, Chris, and I dispersed inside an old boarding house—*Sackett House*, the faded, splintered sign above the door read. There were two parlor rooms we could hunker down in on the ground floor and three bedrooms upstairs. Tavis offered one of the bedrooms to Jason and Chris so he could rest comfortably and she could keep an eye on him, one to Sanchez, and the third to me.

"We like to sleep by the fire," Tavis had explained, but the look in his eyes and the feelings of sympathy and protectiveness that filled him at the thought told me there was more to the story. We didn't argue.

After bringing in wood from a stack Tavis showed me behind the house, I started a fire in the fireplace in the larger parlor and set a pot filled with chili over the flames. I figured feeding our hosts was the least we could do, since we'd encroached on their current home. Cleaning the blood off of my face was the next logical thing to do, but I lingered by the fire, unsure if I was ready to risk running into Jake outside in my search for water.

"Are you okay, Baby Girl?" Harper asked as he dropped his duffel bag in the corner of the room between a rickety rocking chair and a small reading table with a dusty oil lamp sitting on it.

I nodded and smiled. “Sure. I was just checking out our new digs,” I lied. Lending credence to my words, I walked slowly around the room, taking my time and studying the old federal-style furniture decorating the rectangular space. The fireplace was situated in the center of the wall furthest from the door, a bookcase on either side of it. The outer side of each bookcase was flanked by a narrow, single-pane window. Even in the candle and firelight, I could tell they were trimmed with cobwebs and adorned with yellow-stained, moth-eaten lace curtains. An antique, faded pink sofa and two matching chairs hugged a petite, water-stained table. A player piano was set against a wall to the right all by itself, and beneath it was an octagonal area rug that looked like it had been pulled straight out of a *Pottery Barn* magazine. *Right, because that fits.* Everything needed to be refinished or replaced, *except* the rug.

Tavis entered the room, stacking another heap of wood beside the fire. He had mussed, dirty blond hair, and when he smiled at me, his eyes bright in the firelight, I could see they were a vibrant blue.

“About a week back,” he said unexpectedly, “Sam and I were on our way to the Colony—just leaving Cañon City, actually—when we watched a group of soldiers kill three blokes.” He paused for a moment, stoking the fire. “I dunno why the patrol was in town or why they shot the poor bastards. Maybe the three of ‘em were trying to leave—they were running *away* from the uniforms—but…” He stared into the fire thoughtfully.

“I wouldn’t be surprised,” I conceded.

Tavis’s eyes found mine, and he offered a sympathetic smile. “If you want to get washed up, there’s a trough of fresh water out by the stable. That’s what Sam and I’ve been using.”

I shifted my gaze to Sam, who was watching Sanchez and Carlos intently. They were sitting on the worn wood floor, cleaning and inventorying the weapons we’d collected from the black-bands. The boy appeared to be around ten years old, with dark brown, disheveled hair that hung in his shrewd, pale eyes. Like

Carlos, Sam's expression wasn't that of a child, but of someone much older.

Since we'd arrived, Sam's excitement and Tavis's sense of relief had grown stronger, and I felt a stab of guilt. I had a group of companions and a semblance of safety. I'd never really considered what surviving would be like for the people who didn't have what I did, who were alone or without a means to protect themselves. While Sam and Tavis seemed to have adapted well enough, it wasn't without a price. I could see their struggles in the lines on their faces and the weariness in their eyes.

"Something wrong?" Tavis asked, and I wondered how long I'd been staring at the two of them.

I shook my head, offering a slightly embarrassed smile, and went in search of something to clean myself off with. I knew there had to be something I could use in place of the one towel and washcloth I'd brought with me. I didn't want to stain them with someone else's blood.

"There's linen napkins in the cupboard," Tavis offered, pointing to a door beneath the stairs.

"Thanks," I said before he exited out the front door. I opened the closet to find a propane lantern, along with spare propane, batteries, and flashlights. *Yahtzee!* Then, thinking of the cold trough water that awaited me, my excitement faded. I sighed, missing the luxury of a hot shower.

I stretched to pull a napkin down from the top shelf, just as an arm reached over my shoulder to grab one instead. I felt the heat of a body behind me. Jake. Steadying my nerves, I turned to face him.

He handed me the folded napkin and watched me, his expression once again unreadable.

"Thanks." I hated the way my gut twisted, remembering what had happened between us only a handful of hours earlier.

Reaching out, Jake brushed a scraggly strand of hair from my face and tucked it behind my ear. His fingers lingered there, and I fought the urge to lean into his hand. In the dim light of the lanterns set up throughout the house, his face appeared grief-stricken. *He was going to leave...* The thought made my heartbeat quicken with dread, and then with anger. No, fear.

"How are you doing?" I asked stupidly. "I mean, are you going to go after Becca now...or are you waiting until we go in to get Dani?"

Jake shook his head, and I could tell his mind was still a battlefield. "I'm sorry," he muttered and dropped his hand back to his side. "I know..." His eyes met mine. "I know I was acting crazy. I didn't mean to upset you." He searched my eyes, but didn't seem to find what he was looking for. "I didn't mean to scare you. I was—"

"Were you really gonna leave?" I blurted, wishing my mouth would just stay shut.

Jake's eyebrows lowered in uncertainty.

He was going to leave, we both knew it, and I was conflicted. I wasn't only upset with myself for trusting him, but with him for his willingness to risk Dani's life—to risk all our lives—even if it was unconsciously done. *But it* is *his sister.* Although I wanted to hold on to my anger, I could only justify holding on to the hurt.

In spite of Jake's silence, I put on a brave face, trying to convince myself that even if he would have left, he hadn't, and we still had one another...at least for a little while longer. "I understand," I said simply. "Things have been hard lately." I shut the closet door. "Besides, Becca's your sister. No matter what she says, we both know that. I wouldn't expect anything less." That much was true, no matter how painful.

I was about to sidestep him, to put some much-needed distance between us, when he leaned in, cupping my face in his large, burning palm. He was going to kiss me.

I shouldn't. My eyes closed of their own accord, and I wanted to melt. I was still covered in blood, but the feel of his rough thumb stroking my jaw made it nearly impossible to focus on anything other than his touch. He eased in for a kiss, giving me time to pull away, but I couldn't. I wouldn't. No matter how devastating, I needed this—the feeling of something other than the fear, anger, and determination that followed me like asphyxiating shadows.

Jake's lips were hot on mine, and the smell of wood smoke permeated his clothes; it was comforting, and I burned the sensations of his kiss, his scent, into my memory. Before I could comprehend, my body reacted and I rose to tiptoes and reached my arms around his neck, drawing him closer to me. His kiss deepened, excitement and contentment rushing through me like coalescing rivers, and I wanted to drown in them. My fingers explored his skin, my forefinger circling the soft hairs on the back of his neck as I savored the taste of his tongue.

The warmth of his body was euphoric, and I groaned. Though it had only been days, it felt like weeks since we'd been in each other's arms, since we'd laughed or wrestled or just sat quietly beside one another. I missed him.

Harper cleared his throat, reminding us there were others in the room, and Jake pulled back. His eyes were enlivened again, the flickering lantern light illuminating the red-amber of his irises, setting them aflame.

"That's something I've missed." The words formed naturally on my tongue, and I almost smiled.

Jake's brow furrowed. "The look in your eyes," he said quietly, severely.

"I'm just surprised," I started to say self-consciously, my eyes trailing down his perfectly imperfect nose to his full bottom lip. I wanted to lean in and take it between my teeth. I licked my lips.

"No, earlier." His voice was a low rumble.

Oh, right—that. "I told you, I understand." My voice was detached, despite my intentions, and I made my way to the door. "We'll get Becca out of there too, and once we have her and Dani back, everything'll be better." I struggled to believe my words as I reached out to turn the door handle.

"Where are you going?" he asked, and I heard him take a step forward.

I need space before you do *leave and break my fucking heart*, I didn't tell him. I couldn't bear it if I got closer just so he could leave. "I'm going to wash up," I said instead. "I feel disgusting. Chili's in the pot over the fire if you want some. I'll be back in a bit." I opened the door, letting Jack and Cooper go out ahead of me for added protection.

When I glanced back at Jake, he looked like he was considering accompanying me.

"I'll be fine," I told him. "Tavis is out there, and I have my pistol." I patted the gun on my thigh. I didn't give him time to reply before I escaped out the door and shut it tightly behind me. I hurried down rickety wood stairs that looked like they hadn't been replaced since the house was built, and headed to the stable where we'd put the horses—to the trough water I was going to bathe in. *Yay*.

"Easy, girl," I heard Tavis say, followed by a horse snorting. I took a few more steps, watching his form come into view around the side of the stable. He was talking to one of the horses that had already been here when we'd arrived. The trough was inside the paddock, but within easy enough reach for me to access.

Tavis was slumped, leaning against the nearly rotted log fence, his arm draped over the top and his fingers playing with the brown mare's mane as her head hung heavy with sleep. Propped atop one of the fence posts, a propane lantern burned bright, attracting moths to its steady glow.

Tavis's expression was thoughtful, his brow pinched almost into a scowl.

"Hey," I said, hoping I wasn't interrupting his reverie. "Is she your favorite?" The lilt in my voice sounded a little more jovial than I felt, but I was okay with that.

His head shot up, and his posture straightened. "Zoe."

I smiled, enjoying the way my name rolled off his tongue. "I figured I'd take you up on your offer," I said, pointing to the trough. "Dry blood isn't my color, you know?" Unzipping my filthy bomber jacket, I hung it over a fence post to clean later.

The mare's ears angled toward my voice, but she didn't stir from her sleeping trance.

After dipping the checkered cloth into the frigid water in the trough, I started scrubbing the exposed skin on my neck. "How long have you and Sam been staying here?"

"Since we saw those three blokes killed. I wasn't sure what to do afterward. I'd been so determined to get to the Colony that I didn't think about what we'd do if it didn't work out." He shook his head. "Until you all showed up, I was considering how long we could survive here."

"Well, you'll probably regret letting us stay," I teased. "We tend to have really shitty luck." I laughed bitterly.

"I like your laugh," he said, taking a step closer and leaning against the fence to face me.

"Yeah? Thanks. My friend always says that, too…though she also says she doesn't hear it enough."

"I haven't heard anyone laugh in a long time." He shoved his hands into the pockets of his jeans. "You should laugh more."

There was something intriguing about Tavis, and it wasn't just his accent. He was open and easy to talk to, like Harper, but not closed off and complicated like Jake and Jason. It was refreshing.

I flashed him a wistful smile. "Gladly," I said. "But it'd be easier to laugh more if things weren't so—"

"Fucked," he answered for me.

I chuckled and rinsed the napkin out in the water and started scrubbing my hands before moving to my face. "Exactly." I wrung the cloth out again. "How's Sam doing with all of this?"

Tavis shrugged and sighed. "I dunno. Better than I would've expected, to be honest. That kid's been through hell and somehow he's managed to use it to stay focused and to learn. I may be the adult, but we make our decisions together. We're a team."

"You're lucky to have each other," I mused.

He looked at me in surprise and nodded. "Yes, we are."

"Has it always been just the two of you?" I pulled my hair from its snare to gather it again and knot it into a bun atop my head so I could scrub behind my ears.

"No, there was another bloke I met by Vegas, but there was an accident right before I found Sam outside of Flagstaff, so now it's just the two of us." Tavis took another step toward me. "You missed a spot," he said, pointing to his jawline.

I scrubbed harder along the edge of my face and behind my ears and tilted my face to show him. "Better?"

He shook his head and took another step before he reached out to touch my cheek. "It's right here," he said quietly. The tip of his finger was cool and soft against my skin. "You want me to get it?"

Crunching gravel startled me, and I pulled away from Tavis's touch. Jake approached, stopping a few yards from me. He stood there silently, and my heart raced.

"We need you inside," he said coolly, and I couldn't help but feel his anger simmering beneath the surface.

I flashed him an innocent smile. "Okay." I rinsed and wrung out the linen once more before I grabbed my still-dirty jacket and headed for the house. I paused and glanced back at Tavis. "You coming?" I asked not wanting to abandon him outside…with Jake. When he nodded slightly, I shifted my attention to Jake, giving him a cautioning look before I continued on to the house.

Flinging the door open, I called, "Give me just a minute!" I ran upstairs to change out of my bloodied clothes. Falling clumsily multiple times, I struggled to pull on my pajamas. Finally warm and clean, I ran back downstairs and ladled some chili into a bowl. I curled up on the old, barely-padded sofa in front of the fire, welcoming the softness of my sweatpants and the comfort of the oversized Army hoodie I'd commandeered from Jason's bag when I was helping him into the room an hour or so before. He was too drunk to notice it was missing anyway. Pulling my hair out of its messy bun, I ran my fingers through it, letting it fall around my shoulders, and then scooped myself a hearty spoonful of chili.

Chris, Harper, Sam, Carlos, and Sanchez were resting lazily by the fireplace, empty chili bowls beside them.

I glanced around at them. “Am I too late?”

“For…?” Sanchez asked, looking up from her book.

“I thought…” I was confused. *I thought they needed me in here?* There were no maps lying around and everyone seemed barely able to keep their eyes open. “Did you need me for something?”

Chris looked at me askance. “No,” she said, shaking her head. “Um, your brother is passed out upstairs. Harper said he’s doing fine. That’s about it.”

“Jake said you needed me.”

A knowing grin spread across Harper’s face and he leaned back, sprawling on the floor with his arms folded behind his head. “We do. We need you and Chris to keep your feelers out, Baby Girl. Let us know if you feel anything strange. Just as an extra safety precaution.”

“I can help,” Sam added.

“Perfect,” Harper said with a warm smile and a wink at the boy.

The door opened and Jake strode inside, making a beeline for the pot of chili. Tavis entered after him and crossed the room to Sam, who was nestled on his pallet of blankets in the corner. Neither looked at me. In fact, it seemed they purposefully avoided my gaze.

“So, tell us about your friend inside the Colony,” Tavis said, sitting and leaning against the wall beside Sam. “What’s your plan?”

Chris shook her head. “We’re not sure yet. For now, the plan is for her to gather as much information as she can.”

“But she’s still in there all alone,” Carlos said. Like me, he clearly didn’t like the fact that she was still in the Colony.

I swallowed a bite of chili. "She said she's okay," I offered, trying to reassure him. It was senseless for both of us to worry. "She said that MG—I mean, *Gabe*"—I rolled my eyes—"is helping her, but I still don't—"

"What did you say?" Jake asked, his hand suddenly gripping my wrist. I looked from his white-knuckled grasp up to his scowling face. He emanated a ferocity that made my hands tremble. His chili bowl clacked against the small table beside the sofa as he set it down. "What did you just say?" he repeated, eerily calm.

"Um…that Dani said she's okay, and that Gabe is helping her?"

When recognition registered on Jake's face and his eyes flashed with rage, I suddenly understood. I instantly lost my appetite and lowered the bowl to my lap.

Jake shot to his feet and laced his fingers together behind his neck. He stalked away from us, his anger whipping around him wildly. We all stared at him, taken aback by the sudden, dangerous shift in his mood. None of us had ever seen Jake so angry, but between my killing someone for the first time, Dani sending me into a debilitating dizzy spell, being attacked by Colony soldiers, and pretty much everything else that had happened in the last twenty-four hours, the day had been filled with a lot of firsts.

He flung the front door open and stalked out into the darkness. Not even Cooper trotted after him. Jake's hatred and fear burrowed into my heart as he pictured Gabe at the Colony with his sister. When he pictured Gabe visiting me in my dreams, he could no longer contain his rage.

There was a loud crash outside, followed by another, and everyone turned to me, waiting.

It took me a moment to realize what they were waiting for. "Gabe's the one responsible for Becca's death…he's the guy who's with Dani."

My little-girl body was broken. The featureless woman who haunted my dreams stood, looming above me. Even without eyes she was watching me…waiting for me to die. I could feel hot blood covering me. My head felt dizzy, and my vision was blurring. Where am I? *The faceless woman reached for me and I squealed, trying to get away, but my body remained paralyzed and nothing but sobs escaped my little-girl lips.*

"There you are," a familiar voice said. The faceless woman was gone, but I knew I wasn't alone. "I was wondering when you'd die." My eyes were glued open, but my vision was blurred so I couldn't see who it was—but I didn't need to see her. I recognized the hair-raising lilt in her voice: Clara.

I gulped for air as my heart lurched. Grabbing at my throat, I tried to breathe, but I couldn't. "Finally," was all she said as I caught a flash of her blue eyes and blonde hair. But it was too late.

I started awake, snapping my eyes open. I was lying on my back, and I felt suffocated and disoriented. Nothing smelled familiar. Not the scent of fabric softener on my sheets or the comforting smell of leather and hay from the barn…*where am I?* I sat up. My eyes darted around in the darkness, gradually discerning my surroundings as I recalled the musty-smelling house we were staying in…and the feel of Jake's inferno-like body beside me. His presence eased my mind a little, and I exhaled. *It was just another stupid fucking dream.*

Rubbing my toes against the flannel lining of my sleeping bag I'd rolled out over the bed, I let the feel of the soft, well-worn fabric distract me from my rapid breathing and sweaty hands. Moonlight shone through the narrow windows on one wall, and Jake's long, deep breaths soothed me.

As my mind calmed, I could feel Jake's emotions churning: concern—regret—uncertainty. He was awake.

"I tried to wake you," he said in a quiet rumble.

"Jake," I breathed, looking down at his shadowed outline. I wanted things between us to be normal, comfortable, even if it was just for the night.

He seemed to know my question without me having to ask it. He raised his nearest arm, welcoming me to tuck myself in beside him. I lay back down, my head resting perfectly on his shoulder. Snuggling into him, I hoped the feel of his body would drive away the unsettling memories of my nightmare and make me feel like there was still something good in my life, still something worth holding on to.

I placed my palm on the t-shirt covering his chest, and the rhythmic thumping of his heart was all the reminder I needed to know I was safe…for now, at least. His arms tightened protectively around me, and I lifted my head to kiss the side of his mouth.

"Sorry I woke you," I whispered, letting the familiar sound of Cooper's tired sighs distract me.

"I wasn't asleep," he said hoarsely, and out of habit, I stroked his chest with my thumb. "Was it about your mom again?"

My feet found his at the foot of our joined sleeping bags. "Yeah." I was tired of wondering if the dreams would ever end.

Will I ever know what Mom really looked like? I hated not remembering anything about her, but I'd been too young when she'd died, and the hand-carved box Dani and Jason had brought from home was the only tie I had left to my parents. As frustrated as I'd always been with my dad for hiding it from me, I was also strangely relieved. I had something to look forward to now—potential answers. I needed to open the box, to find out what it contained.

A surprising flood of hope washed through me at the thought of opening it, and my eyelids slowly drooped closed as I drifted into unconsciousness.

12

DANI

MARCH 17, 1AE

I squeezed the doorknob and, not knowing what to expect inside the bedroom, felt my palm slick with sweat. Questions ran through my head. Will it smell like death? Will it smell like rotting meat? Has Cam been decomposing, melting into our bed?

Twisting my wrist, I let the door creak open. I instantly focused on the bed, on its unmoving occupant. Something was wrong.

The room didn't stink of death and decay, as it should have after holding my boyfriend's dead body for so long. And the body was covered by a sheet. I didn't cover him.

"What the…" I began in a hushed tone as I moved closer to the bed…to the body. I reached for the sheet and pulled it back from his face. The body was neither bloated nor decayed. It also wasn't Cam.

"Oh my God!" I wailed, falling to my knees beside the bed. "Jason! No! NO!"

I clutched on to his cold, motionless body, my fingers digging into him as I willed his life force to return. I reached out with my mind, searching for his, but there was nothing to find. As I stared at him, begging him to come back to me, dark splotches of blood began to leech through the front of his gray t-shirt.

"No, Jason! This can't be happening!" I cried, lifting the hem of his shirt to reveal that the smooth skin and hard muscle of his abdomen and chest was riddled with bullet wounds. I tried to stop the bleeding with my hands, but the viscous, red liquid welled relentlessly, forcing its way between my fingers.

"Jason! Please! I can't lose you, too...not after Cam. I can't lose you...can't lose you..."

With a gasp, I sat up in bed. *It was a dream*, I told myself. *Just a dream. Jason's fine.* I kept repeating it as I stared at the far wall of the bedroom. The sun had yet to rise, so the dull, pre-dawn light streaming through the window made the paint appear a sickly gray instead of off-white.

Jason usually rose with the sun; it was one of his quirks. I, on the other hand, was more of a night owl, preferring to loll in bed in a state of lazy half-sleep for hours each morning. The rigid travel schedule we'd stuck to over the last few months had been a lot easier on him than on me, especially since he'd practically functioned as our alarm clock. In my opinion, his morning perkiness was completely unnatural. Still, I would welcome it in a heartbeat if it meant I could be with him again.

Smiling at the thoughts of Jason, I stretched and lay back on the mattress, pulling the covers up to my chin. It was cold, sleeping without him beside me. After spending most of my life yearning for him and settling for unrequited love where he was concerned, it was odd that being separated from him hurt so much. But it did. My entire being ached for him—a dull, incessant pain centered in my chest that throbbed with each breath. I felt wrong...incomplete.

With that thought, I decided not to wait until the sun rose to try to contact him. I needed to hear his voice, so to speak, to reassure myself that he really was okay. I needed to know that he was out there, alive and waiting for me to return to him.

I closed my eyes, just as I'd done the previous evening when I'd contacted Zoe, and searched for the cluster of minds belonging to my friends. They'd moved again. I found them a little further to the west. Thankfully, unlike last night, Jason's mind blazed near the others.

When I reached out for his mind, something happened that I'd only experienced while talking in animals' minds.

"Red," he whispered, and then he stopped speaking to me with words. He showed me what he wanted more than anything at that moment, to hold me close against his body…to feel ourselves connected in that most intimate way…to know I was safe because he was touching me, shielding me from the rest of the world.

I could almost feel him, as if an ethereal version of Jason was with me, acting out what he was imagining. It made the pain from missing him—from needing him—increase to nearly unbearable levels. It also made me instantly and uncomfortably aroused.

"Oh God," I groaned. *"It was like you were here...how'd you do that?"*

"Really? I don't know, Red," Jason responded, melting my heart with the sound of his voice, even if it was only in my mind. *"I've been waiting for you for hours, thinking about you. I just...I don't know."*

Listening to him speak, I could almost imagine that he was lying beside me, holding me close. Tears welled in record time and streamed across my temples. *"I miss you so much,"* I told him, unable to keep a sorrowful wobble from my words.

"Fuck, Dani, I—I didn't mean to make you cry." He sounded utterly lost, desperate.

"It's fine," I told him. *"I'm just so happy to talk to you. I've been sort of...well, worried, but that doesn't quite cover it. Zo told me you got shot."*

"Barely," he grumbled.

"And that you got a bad cut on your face?"

"Can we not—"

If he didn't want to talk about it, that was fine, but I needed to know one thing. *"Are you going to be okay?"*

He didn't hesitate in answering. *"Not until you're back here."*

My tears increased. *"Oh, well...that's just...really, um, nice."*

"Zoe told me you were being mind-controlled by some General. What the fuck did he...tell me what he made you do," Jason demanded roughly. Though he didn't say it, I knew he was thinking of Mandy.

"Honestly, not much. But then, he didn't have control of me for very long. Mostly, he just made me forget things and want to obey him," I explained.

"So, nobody's touched you? Nobody's hurt you?" His voice was filled with barely controlled rage.

"No, no, I'm fine." I paused, unable to rid my mind of the images of him hurt...bleeding...dead. I frowned and blinked rapidly, annoyed at myself for being unable to restrain the sadness pouring from my eyes. *"Jason...if I lost you...I don't know what I'd do."*

"Red, I...me too," he said, making my heart flutter.

"I wish I could kiss you right now," I told him.

Jason chuckled, low and rough. *"I wish I could do more than that."*

I sighed, remembering the feel of his body against mine.

"How are you feeling? Are you tired? I don't want you to overwork yourself," he said, letting his overprotective colors show.

"I'm starting to feel it." I frowned, not wanting to say goodbye, but even with the power boost from the neutralizer, I was starting to strain to maintain the connection. *"I should probably go. Can we do this again tomorrow?"*

"Definitely," he agreed. *"Be careful, Red."*

"You too," I said before reluctantly letting the connection go.

It's going to be a long day.

As I wandered across the street in the late morning, kicking the stray rocks and pieces of garbage scattered on the asphalt, I thought about my mission for the day. I was heading for the cluster of buildings Gabe had pointed out as converted storage warehouses. I had a limited amount of time to gather as much information as possible on what we were up against, and that included doing a rough inventory of the Colony's supplies—weapons, medications, food, and otherwise.

Before leaving for his lab earlier in the morning, Gabe had drawn me a rough map of what he called the "warehouse district" and had labeled each building with a letter. As I approached the sprawling building marked with an "A" on the map, I folded up Gabe's sketch and stuffed it into the left pocket of my heavy, black raincoat. Luckily, the weather had remained too warm for snow, but that just meant the precipitation resulted in something I was far more familiar with—drizzling rain.

Glancing around to ensure that nobody was watching me, I reached for the door handle and twisted. It was locked. *Damn!*

Instead of standing in front of the door looking like I was trying to figure out how to break into the makeshift warehouse, I turned and walked away. I kept my pace even, neither rushed nor lagging, all the while glancing along the outer walls of the building, seeking a way in. There were dozens of windows, probably all locked.

I scouted the entire perimeter without luck. There were no convenient open windows, no doors accidentally left unlocked. Staring forlornly at the main doors from the sidewalk beside the building, I thought, *Come on, universe, toss me a bone here...*

He walked around the nearest corner of the building at that exact moment—the yellow-armbanded guard who'd propositioned me when I'd been on my way to meet with General Herodson. He was built thickly, and from the way he carried himself, I could tell his bulk was all muscle. I guessed he was around my age, maybe a few years younger. With his fairly attractive face and light brown hair, he looked like an all-American boy next door.

It only took him a few seconds to recognize me, but I knew the moment he did. He narrowed his eyes and grinned wickedly. As he prowled forward, I started to back away, shooting furtive glances around me as I searched for the best escape route.

"Well, well, well, little darlin'," he drawled. During our last encounter, I hadn't noticed his Texas twang through the haze of my concussion. "How about you and me have a little fun?" His eyes glinted predatorily.

"Thanks for the offer, but I can't right now," I said, impressing myself with the steadiness of my voice. "I'm a little busy with, uh…recuperating."

He kept coming, his pace increasing. His eyes scanned me from hood-covered head to sneakered toe. "You look just fine to me."

"No, I'm really not." I brought my hand up to my neck, searching for the cord carrying my red card. It wasn't there. *Oh no!* "I have a pass…from my doctor." I shoved my hands into my coat pockets, hoping I'd stuffed the card into one of them instead. All I found was Gabe's map. "I, um, guess I left it at home."

"Don't worry, darlin'. I'll do all the work, so you can just keep on recuperatin'," he told me, leering.

Without hesitating, I turned, intending to flee to Gabe's lab. It was only a few blocks away, and I was quick enough that I had a good chance of beating the guard there. Unfortunately, my toe caught on a portion of the sidewalk that had been pushed up by a tree root. I tripped over the crack and skidded to the concrete face-first. I barely noticed my stinging palms or my torn jeans and scraped knees because *he* was there, pulling me up and dragging me back toward the main doors of Warehouse A.

I wanted to scream, to fight, to claw out his eyeballs…but I was wearing yellow armbands, and struggling noticeably would alert the guard and any onlookers to my unusual, non-mind-controlled status. I was expected to go with the reproductive flow, as per the General's usual directives. My choices were death or pretending nonconsensual sex was consensual; it shouldn't have been a hard decision, but it was.

"Please…don't do this," I whispered.

He responded by wrapping his unyielding arms around me from behind, restraining both of my arms at my sides. He was just too goddamn strong.

"C'mon, darlin'," he said as he released one arm to unlock the warehouse door. "This can be fun. You're the one makin' it difficult. Why not just relax and enjoy it?"

If I get the chance, I'm so going to kill you! But, in the back of my mind, I wondered if the General's directive was the only reason he was behaving so aggressively toward me. Maybe he'd been a sweetheart prior to the have-sex-with-whoever-you-want compulsion. *So…can I kill him if he's little more than a puppet?* He wasn't like Mandy or Mr. Monk, or even like the Crazy I killed in the stable; his death wouldn't be justified. *There has to be another way…*

I stopped struggling, instead working on calming myself. I took slow, even breaths, hoping that doing so would steady my racing heart and bring rational thought back to the forefront of my mind. My captor's hold loosened as he registered my supposed compliance.

"There we go, sweet thang. That wasn't so hard, was it?" The way his arms were wrapped around me had transformed from aggressive and forceful to a mockery of tenderness, and he lowered his head to kiss my neck. I shivered involuntarily at the gentle contact, my skin crawling.

Pretend it's Jason, I told myself, thinking this stranger's touches would seem less repulsive that way. Jason might never forgive me for what I was about to do, but he definitely wouldn't be able to if I was dead.

Closing my eyes, I pictured him: his powerful body, intense

sapphire eyes, and short, jet-black hair. I imagined how safe I would feel if it was him embracing me in the warehouse, breathing against my hair and unzipping my coat to access what lay beneath.

Caught up in my fantasy, I whispered, “Let me see you. I need to see you.”

But when he turned me around to face him, I became all too aware that the man lowering his face to mine was *not* Jason.

And still, I let him kiss me.

13

MASE

MARCH 17, 1AE

"C'mon! We have to get closer!" Camille hissed and grabbed Mase's wrist as she stood. Her small hand didn't come close to encircling it completely, but that didn't stop her from tugging.

The two Re-gens were hiding between some bushes and a few trees to observe the tiny woman. Begrudgingly, Mase rose from his crouched position and let Camille drag him across the road toward the warehouse. He easily could have tossed her over his shoulder and carried her back to the chow hall, where they would finish their lunch hour pretending to be nice, obedient Re-gens. He thought he probably should have; it would've been safer. But Camille was determined, and Mase didn't have the heart to deny her.

She was his first memory. It had been her kind face smiling down at him when he first opened his eyes a few months ago, her soft, gray eyes gazing at him with nothing but affection. She'd watched over him, taught him how to be more like the normals and less like the other Re-gens, taught him how to *pretend* to be just like the other Re-gens. She was the center of Mase's universe, the only force holding him together when the fragmented images of someone else's life flashed through his mind.

The other Re-gens focused all their attention on Father, practically worshipping him. Camille and Mase pretended, did their jobs, and did whatever it took not to draw unwanted attention. But Camille had whispered the truth to Mase, telling him what Father had done to him, what he must have done to her, too. He killed them. He killed them and remade them into something else, something he thought he could control. He was wrong.

Every time Mase was near Father—the man the normals called General Herodson—he had to fight the urge to tear the man's head off and smash it against a wall. He could have, easily. But there were others like Father, others who controlled many of the normals' minds like Father did. He was just the strongest, largest, and evilest head on a many-headed monster. So, Mase bided his time, watched, and kept Camille safe.

"C'mon! Pick up your feet, Giant, or we'll miss it all."

Mase scowled, but inside he was smiling. "Giant" was Camille's nickname for him, and he loved it. At night, in the barracks they shared with the other Re-gens—vast rooms filled with row after row of bunks—she would often sneak over to his bed and let him hold her while she slept. She would call him her gentle giant and say he made her feel safe. Mase usually stayed up late watching her, avoiding the nightmares that haunted his sleep.

Camille had the nightmares too, as did some of the other Re-gens. Sometimes she would wake up crying, and the only way Mase could get her to stop would be to press his lips against hers. Eventually she would rest her head on his chest and fall back asleep. But he never slept after those moments. Mase would lie awake, hungry for something he didn't understand.

Camille looked back at him. Hair so dark it was almost black flew around her as she jogged, and her pale cheeks were flushed pink. "Faster, Giant, or I swear…"

Mase did smile then. "Calm down, Camille," he told her as

they neared the warehouse. He glared around at their potentially hostile surroundings. They were wearing jeans and sweatshirts instead of their usual uniforms—the scrubs worn by Re-gens—in an attempt to look like normals, but Mase was still wary. "If anyone sees us like this…if they recognize us, they'll report us."

"I know, but we can't miss it!" she said, her soft voice urgent.

"What makes you so sure she can help?" he asked, picking up the pace. He wanted to get out of sight.

Camille waited until they were crouched behind another bush, but their new cover was nearly flush against one of the warehouse's many windows. She wiped the glass with her sleeve to clear it of rain and grime and peered inside.

"I told you, I saw what happened in the science building when Dr. McLaughlin shot the glowing medicine into her neck. She screamed until she couldn't scream anymore, and her scream made my head feel like it was going to explode. She doesn't want to be here, Giant, and she's not under *his* control. She's perfect."

Mase looked through the window, finding the two normals a short way from the door in the shadowy interior. The tiny woman had stopped struggling, and her eyes were closed. The man was touching his lips to her neck and unzipping her coat. He ran his hands up and down the sides of her body. It felt wrong, but Mase wanted to watch it play out, to know what happened next. He ached to know what happened next.

The tiny woman said something, and the man turned her around, away from the Re-gens' view. Mase didn't understand why she wasn't fighting him anymore. She'd tried so hard to get away from him before. A sudden burst of anger surged through Mase as he imagined Camille in the woman's place. He didn't want the man to do whatever he was planning.

Mase felt Camille's eyes on him and glanced at her, unable to fully tear his attention from the scene inside. His face had transformed into a furious scowl. Sometimes, when rage overtook him, his strength emerged and he lost control.

"Calm down, Giant," Camille whispered, reaching for his hand. "This is not the time for that to come out."

"I don't understand." Mase's voice was hoarse and too deep. "Why isn't she fighting anymore? Why is she letting him…?"

Camille squeezed his hand. "I think she's pretending. Just watch. If it goes too far, you can go in, okay?"

Swallowing repeatedly, Mase nodded. He felt sick. He was no longer curious to see what happened next—not like that…not with the tiny woman who had no choice. "She's so small," he commented softly.

The tiny woman ran her hands down the man's back to his legs, and then Mase saw it. Her nimble fingers released the pistol from the man's thigh holster, and she pressed it against his groin. The man froze instantly, and she began backing away from him.

Camille's radiant smile caught Mase's attention. "Told you," she said proudly. "She *is* the one who can help us. You *have* to believe me now. Come on, let's go help. If she shoots that gun, it'll ruin everything."

Mase started to think that maybe, just maybe, Camille was right. Maybe the tiny red-haired woman *could* help them destroy this place from the inside, then get as far away as possible. Unlike Dr. Wesley, Dr. McLaughlin, and the few other normals covertly working against Father, *she* was from the outside. *They* couldn't be trusted, not completely, but maybe *she* could be.

Following Camille into the warehouse, Mase took control of his strength and speed. He felt it pumping throughout his body, making him an unstoppable force.

"Stop!" Camille cried out as Mase eased the door shut behind them. The tiny woman turned the gun on the Re-gens, and the second the man was no longer in her sights, he rushed her.

Mase got to him first. He slammed the man against a crate, and the wooden boards cracked behind him.

"Don't kill him, Mase," Camille said calmly.

Mase held the man up by the neck, but managed to restrain

himself from squeezing hard enough to crush his throat. “Don’t fucking move,” he growled.

The normal made a choking noise, and when Mase released him completely, he slumped to the floor.

“Are you alright?” Camille asked the tiny woman. Mase turned to watch them. Camille was holding her hands up, looking completely harmless. She *wasn’t* harmless. “Did he hurt you?” she asked.

The woman shook her head as she lowered the gun she’d been aiming at Camille.

“Who are you?” she asked, her voice shaking. She cocked her head as she studied Camille. “You feel…different.”

Camille smiled. “I’m Camille, and that’s Mase,” she said, pointing to him. “We won’t hurt you.”

“Whatever you say,” the woman said as she glanced at the other normal and then at Mase. When her eyes met his, he thought she suddenly seemed taller, less fragile. There was a fierceness in her eyes, and he truly began to believe that Camille was right about her. She *could* help them.

“We should take care of this,” Mase said, nodding at the normal groaning on the floor.

“Oh, right.” Camille fished a small vial out of the secret pocket she’d sewn inside her coat and handed it to him. It was the forgetting medicine she kept on her at all times, just in case someone witnessed them acting different from the other Re-gens. She refused to tell Mase where it came from, no matter how many times he asked, but he was pretty sure she got it from Dr. Wesley.

“Open your mouth,” Mase told the injured normal. When he didn’t respond, Mase kicked his side, and the normal cried out. It looked like he definitely had a few broken ribs. Mase grinned.

“Don’t hurt him!” the tiny woman shouted.

Astonished, Mase stared at her.

“It’s not his fault! He doesn’t know what he’s—” She clapped her hands over her mouth and started backing away, her eyes full of terror.

"We know," Camille told her. "We won't tell. We watched him bring you in here, and we wanted to help you."

"How do you…is it the neutralizer? Was it given to you, too?" the woman asked. Her iron-hard eyes were still wary, but she stopped backing away.

Camille shook her head. "Mase and I…like you said, we're a little different. Not like him." She motioned toward the normal at Mase's feet. "And, we're not like you, either. I guess you could say we're…special."

She was right about that. Mase and Camille had made sure of it, as had Dr. Wesley.

"Um, okay." The woman glanced around her. "It's a church," she muttered. "I almost get raped in a goddamn church? Isn't that effing poetic?"

Mase wasn't sure how to answer her question, so he looked at Camille, who shook her head, equally baffled. Sometimes normals said the strangest things.

"Well, thanks for, you know, helping me. I'm just going to, ah…go." The woman started for the door.

"Wait!" Camille called after her. "What's your name?"

Halfway out the door, the woman looked back at the Re-gens. The dull sunlight from outside glinted off her hair, turning it a coppery red. "Dani. My name's Dani." And then she was gone.

Mase watched the door for a few more seconds, then looked down at the injured normal. "I told you to open your fucking mouth."

That time, he did.

"Do you want me to move him?" Mase asked Camille after the man had lost consciousness, either from the medicine or from the pain. "To make sure someone finds him?"

"Yeah, but just somewhere else inside this place. We can't risk anyone seeing you carrying him."

Mase hauled the injured normal up and flung him over his shoulder, waiting for further direction.

"How about that platform up there?" she suggested, pointing toward the other end of the building. "There's even a nice long table you can rest him on. Someone's sure to find him, and then they'll be able to fix him up. Dani doesn't want him to be hurt anymore. She would probably be unhappy if he died."

Mase followed Camille up to the table and gently set the normal down. "You like her, don't you?"

Camille smiled shyly. "Yeah."

14

DANI

MARCH 17, 1AE

Though every cell in my body was urging me to sprint the two blocks to Gabe's lab, I forced myself to maintain a slow, steady pace. I kept my head down, my hood up, and I walked like my life depended on it.

Eventually, out of breath despite having only walked a few blocks, I pulled open the glass door leading into the building housing Gabe's lab. I rushed through the doorway and stepped to the side, out of sight from anyone outside. As far as I could tell, the building was empty. I leaned back against the wall, giving myself a moment to breathe.

What the hell just happened? And who were those people? Camille was little more than a teenager, delicate and still filling out, with brownish-black hair and a mixture of Asian and Caucasian features that lent her a doll-like appearance. And the big guy—Mase—had chocolate-brown skin and was scary as hell, and, well…huge. The man was built like a tank, and I thought he might've been able to give Jason a run for his money in the World's Deadliest Man competition. And then there was their minds; they were just…different.

A piercing scream shattered my inner monologue, and goose

bumps rose under my sleeves. It was the second time I'd heard such a terror-inducing scream inside this building. I knew the stupidest thing I could possibly do was investigate, but it was also what I *had* to do. I couldn't, in good conscience, just ignore the fact that somebody was apparently being tortured nearby.

The last time I heard it, I'd been on the second floor, and it had sounded like the scream was coming from the stairwell. This time, it sounded louder, closer. I figured the screamer must be somewhere on the ground floor with me.

Silently, I crossed to the right side of the empty, undecorated lobby and waited. And waited. And…waited.

After ten minutes had passed and I'd heard nothing other than the bumblebee hum of electricity, I decided to pick one of the hallways blind. There were only two options, so my odds could've been worse. I chose the one with a hard-to-miss *RESTRICTED* sign. According to the smaller print, only personnel with white cards and something called "Re-gens" were allowed access.

Taking painfully slow steps, I inched down the hallway. The walls were white and devoid of any hanging pictures or inspirational posters, with only blue-gray doors breaking up the monotony. The floor was composed of polished industrial floor tiles in various shades of off-white, and the air smelled faintly of ozone. I was thoroughly creeped out. *Dumb idea to investigate, Dani. Really dumb.*

Ahead of me, a door swung open. Before I could turn and bolt, a small man with thick glasses poked his head around the edge. I froze. *Crap.*

"Oh! You must be my ten-thirty. You Re-gens are so punctual. I can always count on you to be on time!" he exclaimed, rushing toward me and reaching for my arm.

What's he talking about? "Um…"

"My last subject crashed a bit earlier than planned, so we can go ahead and get you set up now," he said as he guided me toward the still-open doorway. The room beyond looked like a normal-sized classroom that had been converted into some sort of lab-meets-doctor's-office. There was only one door into the room. Three of the room's walls were covered in whiteboards filled with line after line of precise handwriting, while the fourth was a wall of windows, every single one shut.

"I'm not…I have a…" *…a nothing,* I thought, recalling that my red card was still at my house.

The small man led me toward what looked like a dentist's chair and situated me in it. Nothing fun ever happened in a chair like that.

"Is this your first time, er…" He picked up a clipboard from atop a nearby medical cart and glanced at the top sheet of paper, which appeared to be a schedule printout. "JD-two?"

First I was a "Re-gen" and then I was "JD-two"? *What the hell's going on?* The day was really starting to suck. How I'd managed to get myself into not one but *two* precarious situations so early in the day was beyond me. Not knowing how to respond, I nodded, fearing arguing with or disputing his assumptions would land me under the General's radar—the one place I *really* couldn't afford to be.

"I'm called Dr. Maxwell, but most of you just call me Dr. Max." Dr. Maxwell was talking to me like a young child. "It's very nice to meet you, JD-two. Are you familiar with your"—he glanced down at the clipboard again—"telekinesis? Have you noticed that you can move things without touching them?"

I stared at him, wide-eyed. If I was supposed to be telekinetic, then Dr. Maxwell was going to be mightily disappointed in my Ability, or lack thereof. "I, um…no?"

He sighed. "Fortunately for you, that's where I come in. I'm going to hook up some electrodes, and then we'll strap you into the chair…"

Wait, what? Strap me in? I glanced down and noticed padded straps dangling from the armrests and along the sides of the chair. *Oh, crap. Why does he need to strap me in?*

"The process is painful, but you'll find that it's very effective in strengthening your telekinesis," Dr. Maxwell told me.

I was getting the impression that it was time to make a run for it. I was pretty sure I'd discovered the source of the screams, and I really didn't want to be the next one to emit them.

While the doctor's back was turned to me, I quietly shifted so my legs dangled over the side of the chair. I was preparing to make like a tree and get the hell out of there, but as soon as my feet touched the floor, another, much larger man entered the room—Mase.

Unlike Dr. Maxwell, who was wearing a white lab coat, Mase had changed from his street clothes into light blue scrubs. Under the florescent lights, I could see that his irises were an unusual grayish-brown. He narrowed his eyes when he looked at me, and I knew he recognized me from our recent encounter in the church-warehouse. *Maybe he'll help me—or at least let me leave.*

But Mase seemed to read my intentions and, after flicking his eyes to the doctor and back, shook his head the barest amount. For whatever reason, he wouldn't let me go, or couldn't. And he was blocking my only exit. I was stuck with a new, awful decision—torture, or death. *First rape, then torture...damn it all to hell!* Internally, I screamed, being sure *not* to lace it with any telepathic power. If I let on now that I wasn't the telekinetic "Re-gen" Dr. Maxwell had been expecting—that I'd been pretending and therefore had been wandering around a restricted area of my own accord—the jig would be up. *Damn it! I can't believe I left that damn red card at the house!*

Dr. Maxwell shot the briefest glance at Mase. "Ah, there you are. MA-one will help you get situated," he told me without looking my way.

Optionless, I scooted back on the chair while the dark mountain otherwise known as Mase approached me. I sat quietly, watching his face as he strapped me in. He met my stare multiple times while he worked, his smoky-brown eyes intense and pitying.

Pitying was bad...*really* bad. Whatever was about to happen was going to hurt—a lot.

Then I had a realization that made me want to hit myself, except my arms were restrained. *Oh my God, I'm such an idiot! I can talk to him in his head!* I focused on Mase, on his not-quite-right mind. Camille's had felt the same, almost like it was somewhere on the scale between animal and human, but not belonging to either group.

"Please help me," I said to him silently.

He'd been focused on the restraints he was fastening just above my knees, but he froze for the briefest moment and glanced up at me.

"You can talk to me silently by thinking at *me."*

I had the impression that he was trying to respond, but no words were coming through the mental connection. Instead, I heard bursts of white noise and, in my mind's eye, saw something that reminded me of television snow.

Panic and frustration were doing a pretty good job of overwhelming me. *What about*...animals' communications always came through as images, not words. *"It's not working. I can't hear you. Try thinking in pictures,"* I told him. It was a long shot, but it was the only shot I had.

Mase resumed strapping my legs down, but images began to flash through my mind. Though they started out indiscernible and choppy, they quickly formed into recognizable scenes.

Me, sitting on the chair, strapped in and cooperating while Dr. Maxwell stood beside me.

Mase, running down the hallway.

Mase, talking to Camille.

Camille, talking to Dr. Wesley.

Did Mase and Camille know Dr. Wesley? *What the hell is going on?*

Mase tensed his face in concentration, and one last image appeared in my mind.

Me, smiling up at Mase and then hugging him tightly.

I pursed my lips, trying to understand his meaning. He was saying I would be happy with the result of what he had planned, that I would be grateful…assuming I was interpreting the final image correctly.

Mase looked up at me, raising his eyebrows and nodding. He wanted me to agree.

Happy and hugging him was determinedly better than whatever form of pain Dr. Maxwell was preparing to use to supposedly enhance my Ability. I locked eyes with Mase and nodded.

"I am finished. May I be excused for a few minutes, Dr. Max?" Mase asked. Unlike in the warehouse, his speech sounded odd, stilted.

"What?" Dr. Maxwell glanced at him. "You just had your lunch break."

"I feel wrong…here," Mase said, patting his abdomen.

Studying Mase, the doctor took a deep breath, then expelled it slowly. "Fine, but make sure you talk to your Domestication Officer about whatever pains you're feeling, okay?"

Mase nodded, maintaining eye contact with the doctor.

"Be quick about it," Dr. Maxwell said. "I'll need you once she starts to fight it."

That sounds really, really *bad.* Without sparing me another look, Mase left. I desperately hoped he found Camille quickly.

For once, my hopes were realized. Mase returned minutes later, before the doctor had paid any further attention to me. He met my eyes and nodded minutely, and I allowed myself a single, relieved breath.

"Alright, JD-two, let's begin. We'll start small and work up, so it's not too painful to begin with," Dr. Maxwell said, turning his attention to a small, high-tech switchboard. "MA-one—the bite protector?"

Mase moved to my side and gently tapped my chin. Fearful, I looked up at him. He nodded and tried to smile, but I could tell his heart wasn't in it; pity had filled his eyes again.

Pressing on my chin, Mase opened my mouth and inserted a rubber mouth guard. My fear quadrupled, and then multiplied exponentially when he secured one last strap over my forehead. I felt like I was in an electric chair.

Dr. Maxwell turned a dial on the switchboard. As an uncomfortable staticky sensation passed through my body and all of my hairs stood on end, I realized I hadn't been wrong about the electric chair. I shifted my focus back to Mase and implored him with my eyes. I tried to speak to him telepathically, but the moment I reached for my Ability, a searing pain ricocheted in my skull and singed outward to my nerve endings. Groaning, I bit down on the mouth guard.

"See, it's working already," Dr. Maxwell said.

I hated him. He turned another dial, the electrical current increased, and I hated him even more. I felt like I was floating in a bathtub filled with stinging jellyfish. When I whimpered, he turned it up again. My lungs seized, paralyzed by the electricity coursing through my body. I couldn't breathe.

"One of the straps is tearing, Dr. Max," I heard Mase say. His voice sounded far away and fuzzy. "Do you want me to hold her down?"

"Yes, yes—it would be counterproductive to stop now. Are you wearing your gloves?"

Though the doctor was fiddling with the dials on the switchboard, increasing the current further, my agony suddenly decreased and I was able to catch my breath. I glanced down to find Mase crouching beside the chair, one hand encased in a thick, black rubber glove and covering part of the strap holding down my hips, the other wedged between the chair and my lower back, the flesh of his palm pressed flush against my bare skin. As I stared into his grayish-brown eyes, I understood. He was absorbing the electrical current, sharing my pain by diffusing the current with his much larger body.

Holding his gaze, I screamed into the mouth guard, pretending my agony was so great that I couldn't possibly take any more. I hoped the show would finally convince the doctor that it was time to end the electroshock session. It didn't.

Instead, Dr. Maxwell made another increase, and I jerked and screamed again, no longer pretending. I couldn't believe Mase was holding still of his own accord, his clenched jaw his only sign of discomfort. Tears streamed from my eyes, and I shook my head back and forth as much as my restraints would allow. It wasn't his pain to bear, and I didn't want him to be hurting for me. *He doesn't even* know *me.*

The door opened and a tall, dark-haired woman in a white lab coat strode into the room.

"John, stop this at once!" she demanded. "This isn't JD-two! She's a special project of mine and you might be ruining her with your tests!" Through the white haze clouding my vision, it took me a few moments to identify her as Dr. Wesley.

The electrical current immediately vanished, and my entire body filled with the most intense pins-and-needles sensation I'd ever experienced. I felt Mase remove his hand from my back, but I couldn't tear my eyes away from Dr. Wesley.

"MA-one, release her restraints right now," she said. "Take her to my office and wait for me there."

Mase didn't seem to be having nearly as much trouble as I was with the aftereffects of the twisted electroshock therapy. He unstrapped me, slipped his powerful arms beneath my shoulders and knees, and picked me up effortlessly.

Once we were in the hallway and out of Dr. Maxwell's sight, I wrapped my arms around Mase's neck, buried my face in his scrubs, and began sobbing. "Thank you…thank you…thank you…" I repeated over and over again. He hadn't prevented the pain altogether, but he'd shared it and had done what he could to make it stop.

We walked for a short time, Mase carrying me and me crying uncontrollably, but eventually his steps ceased.

"Camille," he called. "Let me in. I have her."

But it wasn't Camille who responded. There was the sound of a door opening, quickly followed by Gabe's demanding voice. "Here, set her down over here. How far did he get in the process? What was the highest level he reached?"

When Mase tried to lower me onto a couch, I tightened my hold around his neck and whimpered. I wasn't ready to let go.

He made a low, rough sound—almost a growl—and turned, still cradling me in his arms as he seated himself on the couch. "Dr. Max just raised her to level six," Mase said. He started rubbing gentle circles on my back as I continued to cry against his shoulder.

"Level six! Her synapses must be fried!" Gabe exclaimed. "Dani? Can you hear me?" His voice was closer, more urgent. "Do you know who I am?"

Someone too small to be Gabe sat down beside Mase, lifting my feet and resting my legs on his or her lap. *It must be Camille.* She slipped slim fingers beneath the rolled cuff of my too-long jeans, wrapped her hand around my ankle, and started humming an unrecognizable lullaby. Her angelic song, or maybe it was her touch, was so soothing that I felt my body begin to calm, the pins and needles begin to fade.

"Dani?" Gabe repeated.

I felt hands on my hair, brushing it back and trying to turn my head. I tensed and pressed my face harder against Mase's scrubs. Twice he'd helped me in the past few hours. In such a foreign, friendless place, he'd proven himself to be an ally…to be safe. I wasn't ready to let go of that security. I missed my friends—my Jason—and being held by someone I could trust, at least for a little while, was like ice on a burn: it wouldn't fix the pain and loneliness forever, but it was a damn good temporary salve.

"Please, Dani," Gabe said, again trying to turn my head.

Mase's chest rumbled against my ear. "Let her be."

"I can't…I need to know if she's…if she's still…" Gabe made a choking sound, and his hands dropped away from my hair. "Oh God, what have I done? How could I have brought her here? It's just like before…it's always going to be like before. Forgive me. Please…forgive me." From the sound of his voice, I was pretty sure he was crying.

"She spoke earlier, when we first left the electrotherapy lab," Mase said quietly. "I don't think she's broken."

"But…how? Level six—" Gabe's voice was strained. "Even if it was only for a few seconds…"

"He starts me on ten. Level six is nothing to a Re-gen," Mase said.

"What are you saying?"

I felt Mase briefly raise his shoulders. "I shared it."

"You *shared* it?"

When Mase spoke, he sounded a little uncomfortable. "When she was at level three, I touched her here"—he ceased his back-rubbing for a moment to lift up the hem of my shirt and lightly touch my lower back; the patch of skin felt tender, almost like I had a bad sunburn—"and the electricity flowed through me, too."

"How did you know it would work?" Gabe asked.

"I didn't."

"I'm so proud of you, Giant," Camille said, pausing her hypnotizing song.

After a long moment filled only with Camille's humming, Gabe said, "You two aren't like the other Re-gens, are you?"

I jumped at the sound of the office door opening. "Camille, Mase, I need you both to get back to your usual duties. We can't have anyone asking questions about you two," Dr. Wesley said.

"But—" Mase said, raising me a little for emphasis.

"Thank you for what you did today, Mase, but Dr. McLaughlin and I will take it from here. She'll be safe with me, I promise." *Dr. McLaughlin...is that Gabe?* "Just set her on the couch and return to Dr. Maxwell's office. Camille, I believe General Herodson is expecting you for today's batch?"

"Yes," Camille said, and she and Mase shifted me around so they were no longer under me. I was suddenly alone on the couch.

I curled up on my side facing the back cushions and squeezed my eyes shut. How had the world turned into such a nightmare? *Will it ever get better?*

I heard two sets of footsteps, and then the sound of the door opening and closing again.

There was a heavy, female sigh. "Well?"

"Well, what?" Gabe asked.

"Just say it already. I'm too tired for these games, Gabriel." Dr. Wesley really did sound exhausted.

"You've been keeping secrets from me, Wes," Gabe said, his voice low and accusatory. All signs of his earlier grief had disappeared. Now he sounded pissed.

Dr. Wesley laughed, a sound that was equally rough and musical. "I keep many secrets from many people. Just part of the job, I suppose. But those two are a couple of my *best* secrets."

"You're playing with fire, Wes. If he discovers the truth about them, that the Re-gens aren't all under his absolute control—"

"I'm fully aware." Even more exhaustion laced the doctor's voice. "But what could he possibly do to me that he hasn't already?"

"Wes—"

"I'll give her a sedative," Dr. Wesley said, ignoring Gabe's single, plaintive word. I could hear her moving around behind me, opening a drawer, tearing open a plastic package, stepping closer to me. I didn't care. "She'll be out for a few hours, but when she wakes up, she should be back to normal, more or less. You'll have to inform her of the initial and long-term side effects of the electrotherapy."

I felt the prick of a needle in my upper arm, but didn't react.

"You can come back down here and take her home when your shift is over."

"I want to stay with—"

"No." Dr. Wesley's voice was soft, but firm. "You need to get back to work. You've missed too much lab time as it is. It doesn't do any of us any good if you get caught—especially not her." She paused, and I heard Gabe sigh. "You need to stay in control, Gabriel, otherwise…"

Their words faded out as I sank into unconsciousness's gentle embrace.

"Eat," Gabe said. He was sitting across from me at my kitchen table, watching me move unenticing food around on my plate. He'd hustled me home shortly after I woke up in Dr. Wesley's office, about an hour ago. He'd only left me for a moment to change out of his work clothes at his house, which turned out to be right next door. "Please, Dani. After what happened today, your body—you need to eat."

I dropped my fork, letting it clink loudly on the brown-speckled stoneware plate. The last thing I wanted was to take a single bite of the roasted chicken, mashed potatoes, gravy, and peas he'd brought from the cafeteria near his lab. In fact, I didn't want to eat another thing that had been prepared in the Colony. I didn't even want to breathe the air. Who knew if it held some repulsive mind-controlling agent, some failsafe in case the General's grasp slipped.

"After what happened today," I said, repeating his words. "Why don't we talk about *what happened today*." As I spoke, I speared him to his seat with an accusing glare. Based on what he'd said in Dr. Wesley's office, he obviously knew quite a bit about the ridiculously painful electroshock torture I'd been subjected to. I needed answers...an explanation...*something*.

"What do you mean?" Gabe asked, lowering his eyes to stare at the far corner of the table.

"What *did* happen today, exactly?" Before he opened his mouth, before I even knew if he would answer, I added, "What are Re-gens? How are Camille and Mase different? What secrets has Dr. Wesley been hiding from you? And why the hell is someone in *your* building electrocuting people?" It took an effort to keep myself from shouting. "Would a warning have been *so* difficult?"

Sighing and slouching in his chair, Gabe finally made eye contact with me. "Re-gens are...they're complicated." He shook his head. "I'll drop you by Wes's office first thing tomorrow. She can explain it a lot better than I can; after all, she's the one who created them. As for those two—Camille and Mase—all I know is that they're apparently different from other Re-gens." He frowned. "I don't know why, or how."

"And the electroshock crap? Is there some sort of purpose, or do you Colonists just get a sick kick out of torturing people?"

Gabe pulled the elastic band away from the base of his skull and let his golden hair fall around his face. "The electrotherapy—that's what we call it—is the quickest way we've found to strengthen a person's Ability. The effects are unprecedented." He paused, pain and regret filling his eyes. "But we've learned that it's too dangerous to use on humans."

I fought the urge to pick up my fork and throw it at him. "Then why the hell did that psycho Dr. Maxwell have a full schedule of people to electrotherapize?"

The corner of Gabe's mouth twitched. Apparently, my little tantrum was amusing him.

If he smiles, I'm throwing my plate at him.

"It's too dangerous for *humans*—not for Re-gens," he told me.

I scoffed. "Mase and Camille looked pretty human to me. If it walks like a duck, talks like a duck…"

Gabe said nothing, simply stared at me.

"Oh, come on. You're not saying they're not human!" I exclaimed. "That's ridiculous!" *Is it?* I recalled how different their minds had felt—closer to animal than human. *But they're people!*

A single, blond eyebrow rose over Gabe's eye.

"Fine," I said, sitting back and crossing my arms. "Say I *do* believe you and they're—I don't know, aliens or something…why doesn't the electrotherapy hurt them like it does humans?"

"It has to do with the process they go through when becoming Re-gens."

"Which is…?"

Gabe's mouth did quirk up at the corner that time. "Something you'll find out from Wes tomorrow…*if* she decides to explain it to you."

Sensing I wouldn't get any more information on the Re-gens out of him, I changed the subject. "So…I didn't die from the electrotherapy. Does that mean my Ability's going to be stronger?"

Too impatient to wait for Gabe's answer, I tried to use my telepathy—and hit a brain-numbing electrical wall. "Ahhhgggg!" I cried out, hunching over, clutching both sides of my head.

Large, gentle hands covered mine, and I looked up. Gabe was standing beside my chair, gazing down at me with sympathy-filled eyes. "Yes, you will…but not until the electrical charges fully integrate with your natural synapses. It usually takes about twenty-four hours. Until that happens, using your Ability will be impossible, and attempting to do so will be extremely painful. Also, your Ability may fluctuate—a lot—over the next few months. It might even change, to some degree."

Attempting to do so will be extremely painful. Through clenched teeth, I said, "Painful…you have no idea." Painful was an understatement.

He offered me a small smile. "Actually, I do," he said softly.

Stunned, I stared up at him. He was telling me that he'd gone through the whole process too, probably months ago. It explained why his dreamwalking Ability was so strong.

"Now, will you please eat?"

I shook my head and pushed my plate away, glaring at the food. "This…it's pretty much the product of slave labor. I—I just can't."

"And you wasting away during a hunger strike—what good would that do anyone?"

I shrugged.

Gabe reached out and placed his hand under my chin. Gently, he tilted my face up so I was looking at him. "How about if I make pancakes. Would you eat those?"

My stomach growled, and I failed to hide my eager grin.

Gabe laughed softly. "So it looks like you'll be living off a steady diet of pancakes and spaghetti until you get out of here, since that pretty much exhausts my culinary repertoire," he joked.

I chuckled until I fully comprehended what he'd said. *Until* you *get out of here.* "*We*," I clarified. "You meant, 'Until *we* get out of here,' right?"

"Dani…" Gabe turned away and started toward the kitchen, but not before I saw his pensive frown.

"No!" I jumped to my feet and followed him, snatching his wrist to stop his retreat. "You have to come with me, Gabe—you and the woman you told me about. Promise me," I urged. He'd been spending so much time with me, there was no way the General wouldn't catch onto his free state of mind once I escaped; I might as well have installed a neon sign inside his office blaring *GABE IS A TRAITOR!* I needed to get out of the Colony, but Gabe's life wasn't an acceptable price.

He shook his head, avoiding my eyes. "Dani, I—"

"You owe me," I practically growled. "Promise me you're coming with me when I leave."

The moment between my demand and his answer was tense, filled only with the sound of our breathing. "Fine," he eventually said.

"Promise me," I demanded quietly.

Finally, he met my eyes. "I promise I'll come with you when you leave."

"Thank you," I whispered, releasing his wrist and letting him go.

15

ZOE

MARCH 18, 1AE

Unable to wait idly by, wondering why Dani hadn't contacted Jason first thing this morning as planned, I needed to preoccupy myself. Since the box was fresh on my mind, I decided it was time to open the damn thing.

Jason seemed wound more tightly than usual, so I wasn't surprised by his absence in the house. Knowing he had the box and would want to open it with me, I was resolved to find him. Since my brother was still healing, I knew he couldn't have gone very far, so I could investigate the ghost town in the process of looking for him.

After I donned a fresh pair of cargo pants and a white tank top, I heard footsteps in the hallway.

"You look like you're on a mission," Jake said from the doorway.

I glanced up from tying my boots. "Sort of."

He leaned against the door frame and crossed his arms over his chest, waiting for me to explain.

"I'm going to find Jason. There's something we need to talk about." I didn't mean to be so vague, but I had enough on my mind.

"Sounds serious," he said lightly, and when I didn't answer he continued, "He's been in a bad mood lately. Are you sure—"

"Jason's always in a bad mood. I'll be fine." I smiled weakly and stood up. It was hard to ignore Jake's penetrating stare as he attempted to gauge my mood; he wanted to say more.

I snatched my leather jacket off the back of the chair.

"Zoe, we need to—"

"I can't really talk right now, Jake." I shrugged on my jacket. "Maybe later?" Giving him a pleading look, I strode past.

He reached out to stop me. "Zoe—"

"There's a lot going on right now, Jake." I knew the longer I stood there, the harder it would be to walk away. "We're both treading water, just trying to stay afloat, and I think we need to take a step back for a while. Get some clarity." The words tasted sour and wrong, but needed to be said all the same.

Without giving him a chance to respond, I patted the gun attached to my thigh, ensuring it was there, and hurried down the stairs, calling for Cooper to accompany me outside as added protection. We made our way out of the old house, and I took a much-needed, deep, calming breath.

Pulling my hair up into a ponytail, I plodded down the four wooden steps on the porch and stepped onto the dirt road that ran through the center of town. Main Street, I supposed…but then, as far as I could tell, it was the *only* street.

The weather was warmer than it had been in a while, but a little gusty, causing mini dust devils to whirl here and there along the abandoned street and the hanging signs to clack and clang against the Old West storefronts. The smell of wood and dust reminded me a little of the barn at our old camp. I liked it.

Standing in front of the Sackett House afforded me a decent view of the town. Two surprisingly well-maintained rows of antique buildings stretched out before me. Upon noticing the saloon sign at the end of the road advertising "a good time," I smiled. The church to the left of it resembled a log cabin, and the general store to the right was rickety enough to believe it might have been completely authentic.

If I were Jason, where would I be? I figured he wasn't morbid enough to hang out at the undertaker's, so I continued on and headed quickly toward a log structure quite a bit smaller than the church—the sheriff's office a few buildings down from the boarding house. *That* seemed a little more like a spot Jason would choose to hang out in. Pausing on the road in front of the sheriff's, I studied the building. It looked like the door hadn't been opened in a while, but I assumed there was a back entrance, so that didn't necessarily mean anything.

Quietly, I walked up onto the front porch to the door and stilled, listening closely. I could hear a muted scraping sound—like metal on wood, a sound that reminded me of my woodsmith dad—and I placed my hand on the hilt of my pistol. The repetitive scratching continued, broken only by the sound of someone clearing their throat behind the sun-bleached wooden door.

I crept toward the window set off to the right, careful not to alert whoever was inside in case it wasn't one of my companions, and peered through the dusty glass. I let out a relieved breath; it was Jason. He was sitting near the window in an old wooden chair by a simple oak desk, hunched over, with his back to me.

I moved back to the door and opened it.

Jason jumped in his seat, then turned his head to glare at me. Even Jack started from his curled position in a patch of sunlight streaming through the window.

"Sorry," I said, trying not to enjoy his surprise too much. "What are you doing in here?" I glanced over at the single jail cell and the sign above it that read, *Take Your Picture Here!*

"Nothing."

My eyebrow rose in question, but I didn't push the issue. Jason wasn't one for sharing, and like me, he had a lot to deal with, so I tried to respect his privacy by pretending I didn't care. I approached the chair on the other side of the desk and plopped down, slouching like I was back in high school and had *so* many better places to be.

"What do you want?" He shifted in his seat, hunching his shoulders even more. His combat knife was in his hand, and it made me think of the rolled-up carving tool kit I'd spotted when I'd been rummaging through his bag in search of a sweatshirt. "You're carving again?"

Jason looked down at the desk, where an "R" and an "E" were carved into its surface. He covered the letters with his palm.

"Not that," I said, rolling my eyes. "The kit. I saw it in your bag. I also stole one of your sweatshirts," I added in case he cared.

I couldn't remember the last time I'd seen Jason work with wood. For years, he and Dad had been nearly inseparable, spending hours upon hours out in Dad's workshop. But that changed when Jason left for the Army. He'd left his tools behind, and everything fell apart after that. Dad hadn't worked in the shop as much, and his constant state of distraction had worsened, especially when Jason stopped calling or coming home when he was on leave.

Like Jason, my dad was the epitome of "emotionally unavailable." When I was younger it hadn't seemed so bad, but as I grew older they both became more withdrawn. If it hadn't been for Dani, I would have been utterly alone. It was like Jason had been the glue keeping our fractured family together.

"I miss the smell of his shop," I said absently. Jason only stared at me. I also missed the smell of Dad's aftershave and the smoky barbeque scent that clung to the house whenever Jason was making dinner.

"Why can't I remember things like that more often instead of having those stupid dreams all the time?" I asked, not expecting him to answer.

"Of Mom? You're still having them?" He set down his knife and leaned back in his chair.

Surprised by his interest, I nodded. Jason hadn't seemed interested in my dreams of the faceless woman since I was a little girl. When I was five years old, I'd run crying into his room across the hall after one of my nightmares, as I'd done countless times before. But *unlike* all the times before, he'd refused to let me crawl into bed beside him. "Grow up, Zoe," he'd said. *Was that the night everything changed between us?* I couldn't help but wonder *what* had caused the change. *Was it Dad? Was it something I did?* Maybe it had nothing to do with me at all.

"I stopped having them for a while, before the shit hit the fan, but they're back. They've changed a little, but they're the same basic thing as before."

Jason glanced out the window, and I wished I knew what he was thinking.

"I'm tired of it, Jason." I fiddled with my fingers, nervous what his reaction might be. "I want the dreams to stop."

He looked back at me expectantly.

"Dani told me you have the box…and the key."

Jason said nothing, simply reclaiming his knife and twisting it point-first on the desk.

"I want to open it," I said without hesitation. I wanted to open our dad's box to rid myself of the looming burden of the unknown. "What if whatever's in it could fix…could stop the dreams?"

My brother's eyes met mine—really met them for the first time in days—and for an instant I saw a reflection of my own curiosity flicker in their blue depths. It only lasted a moment. Jason narrowed his eyes and shook his head, disappointed. "Dani's still with *them,* and you're worried about the fucking box?" His voice was cold, everything I should've expected but hadn't been prepared for.

I stood up, resentment surmounting my weariness. "Like I could forget," I snapped. "Opening the box isn't only up to *you,* Jason."

While my brother was currently living in a world devoid of any emotions other than anger and despair, I was haunted by fear and an acute loneliness that I didn't understand. I wanted to open the damn box and finally gain some resolution.

"I'm the one who has nightmares almost every night. I'm the one who can't remember Mom. Jesus, Jason, I've never even *seen* a picture of her," I screeched. Desperation bubbled in my voice. "I'm sick of being in the dark!" *I'm sick of feeling like an outcast in my own family!*

My brother just watched me, emotionless, still twirling the knife on its point.

"I don't know why I expected you to care. You never have before," I spit out and rushed to the door. I needed to distance myself from him before I said something worse, something I would regret.

Sensing no alarming emotions, I fled, Cooper trotting beside me. I cared little where my feet landed as I tromped across the dirt road, between two unmarked buildings, and into the woods beyond. *Why does he have to make everything so damn difficult?* Ever since Dani's kidnapping, all Jason did was rage and brood and act like he'd lost everything. Part of me understood him, could relate to the anger and turmoil that blazed in his eyes. But he wasn't the only one hurting. I'd lost Dani, too. And our dad. I'd lost my friends and family, and I was somehow coping with it.

Stumbling out into a clearing of moss-covered boulders and fallen trees, I sat down on the thick trunk of a pine that had toppled over long ago. It was smothered in lichen, and I began adamantly picking the orange and green fungus from its defenseless host, each pick and gouge of my thumb and index finger more determined than the last. I barely noticed Cooper loping off to explore the surrounding woods.

After all that's changed...after everything, Jason is still... Jason. His stubborn, closed-off attitude seemed like the only thing in the world that hadn't changed. It had been too much to hope that he would *really* talk to me. For the first time in...ever, I felt like we actually had *something* to talk about—the end of the world, him sleeping with my best friend, him knowing Sanchez from before—but he clearly didn't agree.

I'm opening that fucking box.

You're frowning again, Zo, Dani's voice echoed in my head. *It's not pretty. You should really stop.* It wasn't really her, but the imaginary version of her I'd come to rely on over the past few months. Sometimes I wondered if I might be going a little bit crazy.

I leaned forward, my elbows resting on my knees as my fingertips found their way to my temples, massaging in an attempt to loosen the pressure wrapping itself around my brain. I thought about never finding Dani and of my brother's infuriating…everything. I thought about Jake and his sister and losing him for good.

"Nothing is okay anymore," I whispered as I let out a much-needed breath. I exhaled again, my eyes stinging.

"One day at a time, Zo," I said after exhaling another deep breath.

A gray squirrel scurried from boulder to boulder, stopping momentarily to sniff the air. His beady eyes met mine before he bounded away, his scraggly tail undulating behind him.

Slow, heavy footsteps interrupted my musings. I didn't bother looking back. The complete void of any emotion settling in my mind told me it was Jason.

He stopped behind me but said nothing.

I didn't turn around. "What do you want?"

I heard a long, deep exhale. "Once we open the box, there'll be nothing left," he said. He'd obviously *thought* about opening it, even if he was opposed to doing it at the moment. I understood his hesitancy. Part of me was nervous to discover what was inside, to open it and examine the last remaining pieces we had left of our parents. But the burden of not knowing what was in the box outweighed my reluctance.

"I *need* to know, Jason." My voice was only a whisper among the sound of chirping finches jumping from branch to branch and woodpeckers hammering on a nearby tree.

"Know what? What the hell do you think's in there? Mom and Dad won't come back to life just because you—"

"Answers!" I shouted and stood to face him. "I think there'll be answers!"

Jason looked at me like I was nuts. "Answers to *what*?"

"Umm, I don't know. Let me think—what happened to *us*, maybe," I said, laying on sarcasm as thickly as possible. "Or what the hell is so damn secret that Dad would hide the box in the first place."

"What do you mean, 'what happened to us'?" he asked, and his obliviousness pissed me off even more.

"This…" I gestured between us.

He rolled his eyes. "Oh, come on."

"This isn't normal, Jason. We can barely stand to be around each other, and half the time I don't even know why."

He scowled.

"Look, it doesn't even matter. You don't have to look in the box, okay? But I deserve to know what's in it. Dad left us the key; he must've wanted us to know what's inside. I have so many questions, and there could be answers in there—"

"Or not," he said calmly.

I turned away from him and started pacing. "Isn't it weird that I don't know anything about Mom? Would it really hurt to know who the hell she was or what she even looked like? Why wouldn't Dad ever talk about her? Shouldn't he have gotten over her death—"

"Gotten over it?" Jason sounded offended.

"You know what I mean. Don't you think she'd want her own daughter to know who she was? I *am* her daughter, right? Or is that the big secret? Are we not really siblings? Is that why you hate me?" My voice was more scornful than I'd meant it to be, but letting out my frustration felt like finally taking a breath after holding it for years.

"Don't be stupid—"

"Stupid? You and Dad have always walked on eggshells around me, and neither of you ever tell me *anything*. Dad always looked at me with sadness and I have no idea why. *You* can barely stand the sight of me!" Saying the last bit out loud hurt more than I'd expected.

Confusion flashed across Jason's face, but he said nothing.

"I'm tired of being in the dark just because I was too fucking young to remember anything. I'm tired of you looking at me like I did something wrong."

"Knock it off, Zoe. You don't know what the fuck you're talking about." His tone was cold and flat, which only ignited my anger more.

"Would you stop being an asshole for once in your life? I barely know you because you always stop a conversation before it starts or you're too busy or you're in a bad mood or you're off with some girl…take your pick! The way you glare at me all the time, like you're judging me, is getting old. You've never been around or cared what the hell happened to me. There has to be a reason. It's the end of the fucking world and you still can't stand the sight of me—or is that just second nature from all the years of practice?"

"God, you can be such a bitch," he replied, shaking his head in disbelief.

I glared at him, using my frustration to keep the tears at bay. "Yeah, maybe, but you know what I'm talking about. I'm not blind, and it hurts. I—"

"You want to know why I hate looking at you?" he interrupted, taking a step closer to me. His intense eyes fixed on mine.

You want to know why I hate looking at you? Hearing him say it stung, and I took a cowering step back.

"You look *exactly* like her. The older you get…" He shook his head. "You think I want to remember Mom every time I look at you? Remember her accident…that she's dead?" His eyes searched mine, hostility burning in their blue depths, and resentment dripped from his tone. But in an instant, his expression blanked. I wasn't sure if I'd really seen remorse flicker across his face, or if he was even capable of remorse. Either way, the truth was finally out.

I felt my face fall, and another lump swelled in my throat. "Oh," was all I could manage to say. Jason's eyes thawed momentarily, considering something, but I turned away from him. In a strange way, I understood him…empathized with him.

My mind was reeling. I was embarrassed but also relieved. I finally knew the cause of Jason's distance—I looked like our mom. The fact that I resembled her filled me with joy, but it was a bittersweet joy. Jason had known our mom, had been nurtured by her most of his childhood. He remembered what it felt like to be around her every day—and what it felt like when she was suddenly torn away.

I heard Jason walk away behind me, leaving me alone with my thoughts. A sense of helplessness settled over me. Even though I understood why Jason distanced himself, there was nothing I could do about it, about the way I looked. I sat back down on the log. There were still unanswered questions. *Why didn't Dad ever talk to me about her?*

Only a few moments passed before, again, I heard footsteps approaching. I turned around to find Jason standing there with Dad's small, cedar box gripped in his hands. The key swung from a chain wrapped around his thumb.

My heart sputtered to a halt as he stepped over the fallen log to sit down beside me, setting the box between us. We looked at each other with silent understanding, and then he handed me the old-fashioned iron key. *The moment we've both been waiting for…and dreading.* We were finally going to know what was in the stupid box. For a long time, all I could do was stare at it.

"Just open the damn thing, Zoe," Jason said impatiently.

Biting the inside of my cheek to avoid smiling at his mounting curiosity, I placed the tiny, ornate key into the lock. With a click, the box was unlocked. I scooted closer to Jason, still balancing the box on the log between us. Running my fingers over the intricately carved scrollwork on the lid, I slowly lifted it open.

A cedar scent escaped its stuffy confines, and I wondered when it had last been opened. The wood's grain was rainbowed with coppers, reds, and browns, and the initials "TJC" were etched in the bottom right corner on the inside of the lid—confirmation that the box had been handcrafted by my dad.

Peering inside, I examined its contents. A folded newspaper clipping lay on top. I carefully lifted it out, revealing what I assumed was my mom's gold wedding band resting on the box's black velvet lining. Beside it lay a lock of long, black hair tied with a white lace ribbon. Beneath that was a small envelope.

My eyes flicked to Jason's, and when I realized his attention was focused solely on the items inside, I painstakingly picked up the gold ring and studied it. It was delicate and dainty. I checked the inside of the band for an inscription before slipping it onto my left ring finger, imagining what it might have looked like on my mom's hand. It fit perfectly. I glanced at Jason again, and his eyes darted to mine. He nodded for me to continue.

I turned my attention to the lock of hair. Picking it up, I examined the long, thick black strands, wondering how old our mom had been when she'd given it to our dad. It made sense that she had black hair like us—our dad's was much lighter, though it had been mostly gray all my life. I let the silky wisps fan across my fingers before setting the black tresses back inside the box. I lifted out the folded newspaper clipping. It was yellowed, and the black print was so faded I struggled to read it.

"It's their wedding announcement," I mumbled. "Do you want me to read it?"

Jason closed his eyes and took a deep breath, giving me a hesitant nod.

"San Diego—California. Miss Annabel Elizabeth and Mr.

Thomas Cartwright of this city were privately joined on Tuesday night, January 3, at City Hall. Directly after exchanging vows, Mr. and Mrs. Cartwright left for their honeymoon in Mexico."

I was disappointed by the absence of any photos or interesting details about them. I handed the clipping to Jason and reached for the last item in the box—the envelope. Opening the flap, I was careful not to tear the well-worn paper.

My fingers fumbled with the page as I pulled it free. Glancing to the bottom of the letter, I saw her name, *Anna*, written in a slanted script. I looked at Jason. He folded the wedding announcement he'd been rereading and placed it in the lid of the box.

"It's from her," I clarified, making sure he realized the significance of the letter. "You want me to read it out loud?" My voice cracked. I was both scared and ecstatic to read our mom's words.

Again, Jason hesitated before nodding.

Clearing my throat, I began to speak. My voice sounded foreign, and my mounting anxiety made me feel nauseated. "'Tom,'" I said, trying to ignore the strangeness I felt in reading our mom's private words to our dad. "'Please know that I love you very much. I've loved you since the first time I saw you. The sight of you completely crumbled my resolve to never date a…'" The next word caught in my throat. *Holy shit.* I tried not to wrinkle the paper in my clenched, frozen fingers.

"What? Why'd you stop?"

I took a weary breath, knowing Jason wasn't going to like what he heard next, and continued. "'…crumbled my resolve to never date a military man…'"

Out of the corner of my eye, I saw Jason stiffen. Like me, he'd apparently had no idea Dad was ever in the service. But for Jason, that omission was a far greater insult than it was for me. Not wanting to see his expression, I read on. "'…but your smile alone dulled every rational part of me. I'm glad it did. I'm sorry I had to leave, but please remember that it wasn't by choice.'"

This time I couldn't help glancing at Jason. He was frowning.

"Maybe they were having problems and she left for a while," I suggested, grasping for a shred of understanding. But reading the date on the top of the page, I realized something was wrong. "It's dated two days after she died," I told him, pointing at the date to make sure I hadn't misread it. "Right?"

The crease between his eyebrows deepened, and he nodded.

"But the accident…and Dad practically disowned you when you joined the Army," I said dumbly. "He hated the military. I don't understand." I tried to push away the crushing realization that, for whatever reason, Dad had lied to us. "Does any of this make sense to you?" I asked, hopeful.

"Keep reading," Jason ordered, unblinking as he stared ahead. He wasn't showing any outward reaction, and I couldn't feel his emotions, but somehow, deep down, I knew he was filled with a violent maelstrom of confusion, disbelief, betrayal, and anger that easily rivaled mine.

I refocused on the letter. "'It's best if the kids never know the truth,'" I read hollowly. "'Tell them whatever they need to hear so they never come looking for me. It's safer for them that way. We both know this.'" I hesitated, trying to rein in the sudden suffocating pain I felt in my chest. "'Remember, every scar makes us stronger. We have to be strong…for them. This is for the best. Love them, Tom, for the both of us, and take care of our family. I love you, all of you, always. Yours forever, Anna.'"

The letter fell from between my fingers. "She left us," I whispered.

Abruptly, Jason stood. He said nothing, just stalked back toward the ghost town, while I stayed behind, motionless…heart-broken…betrayed. I didn't doubt that the same emotions fueled his actions as he disappeared through the trees.

I looked down into my lap. The thin, worn letter still rested between my fingertips. It seemed impossible that our dad had lied to us for so long, that he'd kept so many secrets. As I stared blankly at my mom's words, my eyes began to sting and the writing turned blurry.

It wasn't long until Jason reemerged through the trees, a giant ax gripped in his right hand. He passed by me without even sparing a glance in my direction. I watched him stalk away, his steps determined, until he was out of sight again, deeper in the scrubby woods. In the distance, I could hear the sound of the ax blade splintering wood.

I'd never pretended to know my brother well, but his eyes tended to deceive him—they always had. When Dad cursed him for joining the Army, his eyes had filled with sadness. And seven years ago, when Dani and I had wandered home after a day basking in the sun on the beach, a look of wonder had filled his eyes as he looked at her—like he'd discovered something hidden, something pure. So the emptiness I saw in his eyes when he walked past me with the ax told me how much our dad had hurt him. How much our mom had. *Why'd they do it? Why'd they lie?*

As I slipped the note back in its envelope, I noticed something else inside—a photo. The back was discolored and the edges were torn, but the moment I saw the cursive name written in faded black ink on the back, my heartbeat quickened. *Anna*.

I slowly flipped the photo over to find the image of a woman who could only be my mom staring back at me. Her hair was straight and black like mine, some of it hanging past her shoulders while stray wisps were suspended on a breeze, frozen in time. Her eyes were like Jason's and mine, as bright and vivid as gemstones; they could've been green or blue or maybe both, and they were surrounded by dark, thick lashes. Though her gaze was shrewd, she looked happy. Her full, pink lips were pulled into a broad smile that revealed perfectly white, straight teeth. She was wearing a white eyelet skirt and a purple tank top that exposed her pale skin and slender frame. Beside her, a resplendent collection of driftwood and green and white sea glass rested on the sand. Her bare legs were folded under her, her yellow painted toes peeking out.

Although her right arm was raised as though it was draped around someone, the photo was torn in their place. All I could see was a child's hand resting on her skirt. *Jason's hand. Does he remember taking this picture?* She, Anna, my mom…was real. She was stunning, and seeing her for the first time sent silent tears streaking down my cheeks.

I wasn't sure which feelings made it so difficult to breathe: desperation—grief—resentment—curiosity—maybe love? Did I love my mom? I didn't know if I could. I loved her for existing, for being alive and so vibrant, even if it was only in a picture. But she'd left me…us. Part of me hated her for that, and hated my dad for lying to us. He'd cheated us out of ever knowing the truth, and his death had cheated us out of ever knowing the reason for the lies. I wanted to scream…but instead I just cried.

16

DANI

MARCH 18, 1AE

Dr. Wesley studied me, her gaze sharp and unwavering. I was in her office, again, sitting on her small, unyielding sofa, again—but unlike the last time, I wasn't lost in a haze of pain. I was paying attention. The décor was as stark and no-nonsense as the doctor herself, lacking any embellishments or personal touches.

Dr. Wesley sat behind her wide, wooden desk, looking as exhausted as she'd sounded the previous day, and I felt a little guilty about the arsenal of questions I'd just launched at her. Anything and everything I could think to ask about the Re-gens, her work in the Colony, and the Colony in general had erupted from my mouth.

"I'll answer your questions," she finally conceded, and I squirmed under the intensity of her stare. "But nothing I tell you gets written down." She made a shooing motion in my direction. "Put that away."

I glanced down at the small notebook on my lap. Later, when my Ability finally came back online, I was planning to relay everything I'd learned over the past day and a half to Zoe, Jason, and the others, and it would be a whole lot easier if I was able to take notes. But, once the doctor pointed it out, I realized it was one of the dumbest ideas I'd had in a long time—and dumb ideas seemed to have become my specialty lately. Absently, I hoped Jason wasn't too worried about the fact that I hadn't checked in with him this morning. *Fat chance...*

Tucking the book into the blue- and green-striped canvas tote bag I'd found in my coat closet earlier that morning, I crossed my legs and nodded. "I just need answers, Dr. Wesley. This place is so..." I shook my head. "I feel like I'm losing it, and—"

The doctor's wan face transformed as she laughed halfheartedly. I thought it might have been the saddest laugh I'd ever heard. "I understand," she told me. "You feel like you need to be doing something, taking a stand, because everything around here is too unbelievably"—she raised her eyebrows—"awful...at least, under the surface. And you need more information to do whatever it is you're thinking of doing." After a short, contemplative pause, she added, "You and I...we're not so different, Danielle. I bet you'd do anything—whatever it took—for the people you love. You'd pay any price, or exact it from others, just so long as it meant *they* would survive."

I moved my head in a single, protracted nod. I suddenly felt an odd connection to her...an unexplainable familiarity.

"Just remember that you can't fight if you're dead. If you're dead, you can't do anything."

Again, I nodded.

"Very well." She took a long, deep breath. "The Re-gens are, for the most part, my greatest creation. Giving life to a being that has passed—there's no greater form of redemption."

"Wait..." I shook my head, utterly confused. "Are you saying...you can't mean that the Re-gens *died*, and you brought them back to life? That's—"

"Crazy? Impossible? *Noli, si quid tibi effectu difficile, opinari, hominem id non posse praestare*."

"'Because a thing seems difficult for you, do not think it

impossible for anyone to accomplish,'" I said. It was a quote I'd translated repeatedly during my graduate studies in linguistics. "Marcus Aurelius was a wise man."

Surprise flashed across Dr. Wesley's face, but was quickly hidden behind a mask of disinterest.

In a twisted way, I was actually enjoying myself. It was like playing conversational chess, and I hadn't played a good game of chess in a really long time. I bit my bottom lip to keep from smiling. "So, you really did bring people back to life. But as they say, they didn't come back the same. They came back different…wrong."

"Not wrong, exactly," Dr. Wesley countered. "Just different. They're…well, they're *changed* by the process in ways that even I don't entirely understand, and *I* created the process." She laughed bitterly and shook her head, making her black, chin-length bob sway. "They don't remember anything of their former lives, though some report having disturbing dreams. Camille and I believe these are memories from their pasts attempting to resurface. And it would seem that, among other factors, those who are nurtured more fully upon waking the first time are more open to such dream recollections."

I tapped my pointer finger against my lips, thinking. "So… Camille and Mase, they were nurtured more than other Re-gens?"

Dr. Wesley nodded. "In a manner of speaking. With every Re-gen—Camille and Mase excluded, though nobody but a select few knows that—as soon as they wake up, they're programmed with General Herodson's commands and teachings, but they're not shown much in the way of genuine care. They're extraordinarily impressionable during their first few hours of rebirth, and they learn remarkably quickly. This impressionability is the reason why Herodson likes them so much—he acquires devoted followers without ever having to use his Ability." She took a deep breath and frowned. "It does seem that some remnants of their former personalities and preferences remain, though again, that effect is greatly enhanced in Camille and Mase." Her lips curved into the first genuine smile I'd seen on her since entering her office. "You may or may not have noticed Mase's penchant for a certain word that starts with 'F'—that's spillover from who he was before. Camille took very good care of him when he first woke."

Fiddling with my hands, I said, "This is going to sound completely ridiculous, I know, but…are they zombies?"

Her genuine smile evolved into a genuine laugh. The sound was musical and heartwarming. "For goodness' sake, no! They're *alive*. They breathe, their hearts beat, and so far as we can tell, they age normally. They were the recently deceased, made into Re-gens before too much cellular deterioration made them impossible to revive."

Cellular deterioration. Recently deceased. Re-gen. Pieces were starting to fit together, and the image they created was unsettling. I pictured rows of hospital beds, the people lying in them being drained of blood day and night. "Let me guess…you use the blood of someone with the Ability to regenerate."

"How could you possibly—"

"A friend of mine almost died—well, actually, she did die for a few seconds—but they brought her back by transfusing her blood with that of someone who could regenerate," I explained.

The doctor looked pensive. "Hmmm…would this be one of the friends you mentioned the other day?"

Glancing down at my hands, I frowned. *How much should I tell her? How much can I really trust her?* "Yeah…it was my best friend, actually, though I didn't know about it at the time. Someone poisoned her, and she died." I shook my head, swallowing repeatedly and blinking away tears. "I can't believe she actually died." As terror filled me, my eyes flashed to the doctor. "Oh my God…is she a Re-gen?"

Dr. Wesley took a long time to answer. "No," she finally said. "The process is very specific and requires the delivery of precise electrical pulses, several chemical compounds, and an infusion of a substance derived from the blood of someone with hyper-regenerative abilities. Your friend's body probably just shut down for a few seconds before the regenerative properties of the donor's blood could take effect." After a pause, she added, "Danielle, I'm so sorry for what your friend went through…so unbelievably sorry." She sounded on the verge of tears.

"Thanks, Dr. Wesley, but it's not your fault." But a nauseating feeling was settling in the pit of my stomach. *Why is she sorry?* I replayed several other things I'd heard Dr. Wesley say over the past two days…*no greater form of redemption...you'd pay any price, or exact it from others...I don't deserve...* "Can I ask you a personal question?"

She sat up straighter and, hesitating for only a moment, nodded.

"Why are you here?" I asked.

Dr. Wesley looked down, lowering her chin, then glanced up at me through her lashes. "I guess you could say I made my bed… this is me lying in it."

Does that mean... I threaded my fingers together, straining to hold my hands in place. "Did you create the Virus?"

Without lowering her eyes, Dr. Wesley said, "Yes."

17

ZOE

MARCH 19, 1AE

The morning after Jason and I opened the box, Jake, Carlos, and I ventured over to the other side of the Arkansas River, which was about a mile south of our new camp. We brought the dogs with us, while the others stayed in our ghost town home. I was glad to be away from Jason. Every time I looked at him, I thought about what we'd found in the box, and I was *tired* of thinking about the box.

The night before, while we'd all been eating dinner around the fireplace in the larger parlor, Carlos had reached for a metal skewer sticking out of the fire, evidently forgetting that it would be searingly hot.

There'd been a soft sizzling sound as his skin burned, and he'd yelped a curse. At the same time, a dust-covered radio sitting atop one of the antique cherry bookshelves had turned on. Carlos had dropped the scorching metal skewer back into the fire and shook his hand vigorously.

I'd risen and dunked a napkin in one of the buckets of water we kept near the fire. "Here," I'd said, handing the wet cloth to Carlos before running to get burn cream. The instant the cloth had been wrapped around his hand, soothing his burn, the radio had shut off.

The others anxiously glanced around at one another. The static of the radio had been the first electronic sound we'd heard in months, and it had been strange how creepy the noise was.

Chris had been the first of us to connect the dots. "Was that…" She'd glanced back and forth between Carlos and the radio. "Did *you* do that, Carlos?"

"I—I don't know," Carlos had said. His eyes had been filled with pain and confusion, making him look a little wild-eyed.

It hadn't taken us long to come to the conclusion that Carlos's previously unseen Ability was directly connected to energy. It turned out it wasn't just pain that enabled him to channel energy into electronic devices, but concentration and control. If he really focused, he could even send out an electromagnetic pulse that would shut down everything nearby. He'd done so with our flashlights…repeatedly.

We didn't know how far his Ability would reach, but we thought it could be useful in retrieving Dani, so it merited more exploration. We needed to test how far it could reach, which was why we were heading to the other side of the river. Our horses trekked effortlessly over the mountain trails toward Royal Gorge. The considerable amount of traveling they'd been doing was turning them into oversized mountain goats.

Once we reached the mile-long pedestrian suspension bridge, the horses were reluctant to step onto it. Eventually, after much coaxing, they did, falling into an easy pace.

As we crossed, Jake's horse leading the way, Wings fell into step beside Arrow. Peering down at the rushing water of the Arkansas River far below, I realized the river had been the only constant part of my journey since leaving Fort Knox months before, following us as we made our way through Kansas and into Colorado. I'd come to rely on the sight and sound of the water to calm my nerves. The clomping of hooves on the wooden planks resounded throughout the canyon, and I closed my eyes in momentary contentment.

Jake and Cooper plodded ahead of us, while Jack trailed behind, sniffing and exploring the unfamiliar wooden slats beneath his feet. His tail wagged happily, and his nose found its way back to the ground every few strides.

"Holy shit," Carlos gasped beside me. His arms were tense. His knuckles whitened as he gripped the reins more tightly, and his eyes were opened wide like those of a frightened child. I could see the sweat beading on his brow.

"What's wrong?" I asked.

"I don't like heights." Carlos cleared his throat and looked straight ahead, refusing to let his eyes wander.

I'd never seen him afraid of something so normal. In an odd way, it felt good to know I wasn't the frightened one for once.

As Arrow and Wings stepped onto solid ground, Carlos drew in a deep, calming breath.

Barren, rocky bluffs quickly gave way to dense shrubbery as we drew closer to the wooded hills. We searched for a shady spot within the trees that was large enough for all of us to dismount and concentrate on Carlos and his Ability.

"Over here," Jake said quietly. He'd stopped his horse beside a squat fir. He pointed through the trees to a farmhouse down in a narrow dell, letting his reins slacken momentarily while his horse gnawed on the bit.

The single-story farmhouse was old, and junk was strewn all over the yard surrounding it. An overgrown, surprisingly bountiful vegetable garden filled multiple raised beds on one side of the house, and a few laundry lines were strung between trees on the other, a handful of chickens pecking at the ground and clucking between them.

"Should we check it out?" Carlos asked.

The place looked abandoned—the gardens were unkempt, there was no laundry hanging from the lines, and the chickens were running around freely.

I nodded, having the same interest in the property that Cooper and Jack displayed with their excitedly wagging tails and anticipative whines. They were eyeing a rickety chicken coop beside a small stable. There were another handful of chickens clucking around inside the coop.

"No," Jake told the dogs sternly, a smile curving his lips. "You'll scare them off," he said, like the dogs might understand. "Stay."

I leaned down and patted Wings's neck. "We should check the garden and the stable, too. It couldn't hurt."

Jake nodded and we dismounted on the side of the road, tied the horses to a couple of firs atop the hill, and headed down into the shallow valley to catch some dinner.

Unsure what to expect, we held our weapons at the ready—Jake and I with our pistols, and Carlos with Chris's shotgun—moving silently and swiftly toward what appeared to be the back of the house.

The place looked like a junkyard. We passed a few rusted tractors and a mound of bowling balls that had been there so long weeds had grown up out of the finger holes of each ball. Old, splintered doors were piled up in what might have been a burn pile at one time, and a pale pink bathtub from the fifties sat inside an upside-down truck hood, broken in half.

I began to feel uneasy as we approached the garden. Letting my mind find the offending sensations, I realized there was someone inside the stable. Someone…wrong.

Without hesitating, I grabbed Jake's arm and pointed to the dilapidated structure. "There's someone in there," I mouthed. My index finger drew a few invisible circles beside my ear to indicate it was probably a Crazy. I looked back at Carlos to make sure he understood, but he was gone. *Shit.*

"Stay here," Jake mouthed, and I knew he was going to find Carlos.

I shook my head and raised my pistol back up in front of me. I was going with him. I didn't have the best aim, nor was I a strong fighter, but I wasn't going to keep waiting behind the scenes to get attacked, or worse. I preferred to be with him, knowing what was going on, instead of guessing and hoping for the best.

Jake gave me an exasperated look, but I ignored it and followed him. I could feel the emotions of whoever was inside the stable shift between blissfulness and anger before settling on excitement.

Without warning, the person stepped out of the stable, and Jake and I crouched down behind a mound of stacked firewood a few yards away, watching the stranger through the cracks between the logs.

It was a slender, young woman in a floral nightgown that looked like it was meant for a woman three times her age. Her golden hair was gathered on top of her head in a messy bun, and her nightgown was covered in brown smears. She was wearing a gas mask and carrying something at her side as she glided closer to us. I strained to see what it was—some sort of dark, fringey mass hanging from her fingers. I glanced at Jake, finding his eyes wide with disbelief.

Looking back at the woman, I watched as she dropped the mass onto a pile of*...are those...shoes...and hooves?* Bile rose in my throat. *And hair?* The woman took a few steps to a nearby stump and struggled to pull out an ax that was wedged in its surface. Her arms shook and strained as she tried to manhandle the ax, but eventually her efforts paid off. She heaved it up to her shoulder and walked back into the stable.

Jake and I exchanged glances, and his eyebrows lifted in curiosity. We continued creeping toward the house, hoping Carlos was inside.

"Carolann!" a woman called from the far side of the house.

Instantly, Jake and I crouched down again.

"Carolann, I've got somethin' fer ya!" she yelled and finally came into view.

Carlos stumbled ahead of her, the barrel of a shotgun pressed between his shoulder blades. They were on the far side of the garden beds, their forms coming in and out of sight as they walked between cornstalks. It was difficult to see Carlos's face, but I could feel his fear. As they passed the last cornstalk, I could see his right hand twitching to grab the knife stowed in one of his cargo pockets.

"Shit," I breathed, looking at Jake.

He nodded and brought his index finger to his lips.

I returned my attention to Carlos and the woman holding the gun. She was old, in her seventies or maybe even her eighties. Her hair was long and matted and appeared to have been white at some point, but was streaked with brown and deep red. She was only wearing a bra, a long denim skirt, and a pair of mud-stained slippers. *Jesus.*

"Carol—"

"Stop hollerin'!" the woman who must've been Carolann yelled as she came out of the stable. She pulled off the gas mask and set it on the stump, then wiped thick, brownish-red gunk from the ax blade onto her nightgown. Her pretty features brightened with excitement. "Oooh…where'd you find him?" she asked, her voice suddenly heady, like he was fresh meat and she was completely starved.

"I was buryin' the bones from this mornin' for mulch in my garden, and he crawled right past me, just like one of them damn ground squirrels. I hate 'em, Carolann. You know I do."

Carolann waved them over to her. "Come on," she said.

When Carlos hesitated, the older woman urged him forward with the barrel of the shotgun. "Move it!"

Carlos still resisted.

In the blink of an eye, the woman flipped the gun, ramming the butt of it into the back of his skull as hard as she could, and he fell to the ground. "I told you to move, boy," she grumbled.

My stomach dropped at the sight of Carlos's limp body. I felt the old woman's joy, her sheer excitement that verged on lust.

"Get the rope, Carolann."

The gaiety they felt made me livid. We couldn't let them hurt Carlos. I nodded to Jake, and without hesitation, we both stood up and opened fire.

Following two misses, I landed a shot in the old woman's chest. She dropped to the ground before she could even get her shotgun aimed in our direction. As Carolann was trying to escape back into the stable, Jake took her out with a single shot to head.

While our hearts still hammered, pumping adrenaline-rich blood, Jake turned to me. "I'm gonna check the house for anyone else."

I nodded. "Be careful."

Once he was gone, I approached the stable. I was petrified of what might await me inside. *More Crazies? Dead bodies?* I didn't feel any other twisted emotions, but I knew I needed to clear the structure…just in case.

Hands shaking, I held the gun against my chest as I sidled up to the splintered wall. The putrid smell of rotting meat permeated the air, sending my stomach into somersaults. My gag reflex kicked into overdrive. Covering my nose with the crook of my arm, I took a deep breath through my mouth and held it. *Hurry up!*

I aimed my gun in front of me and stepped inside with my finger on the trigger just like Jake had taught me. I didn't sense anyone. Weak sunlight shone through the windows and the cracks in the siding. Riding gear, hay picks, and rakes hung on the walls and from the rafters, but there was no sound to alert me of anyone's presence. I tried to read the shadows for anything that might prove dangerous, but again there was nothing.

I moved quickly, still holding my breath. The gun was slippery in my sweating hand as I swept my aim across the four stalls. When my eyes settled on the origin of the stench—the decaying pile of human and animal body parts in the far-right stall—I turned and ran out of the stable as fast as I could. My eyes burned from the foulness, and I stumbled out into the open, into Jake's arms.

His eyes were wide, and his grip on my shoulders was firm and protective.

"I'm okay," I panted and spat, the disgusting smell making me salivate profusely. "There's no one in there."

On the ground a few yards away, Carlos moaned.

I pulled out of Jake's hold and stumbled over to Carlos, falling to my knees and rolling him onto his back. "Are you okay?"

He squinted in the sunlight. "Stupid crazy bitch came out of nowhere," he mumbled. He brought his hand up to the back of his head and cringed.

"They're dead," I said. "But we should get out of here. I don't know if—" At the sound of footsteps behind me, I turned on my knees and reached for my gun. It was Jake.

"You guys should see this," he said, nodding toward the back of the stable.

Fighting the urge to ask if I absolutely had to, I helped Carlos up to his feet, and we followed Jake around the stable to a muddy paddock stall. A thick, red rope was tied around the metal fencing. I followed the line of it toward the ground and spotted a white mass surrounded by tall, wild grasses. When I took a few, uncertain steps closer, Jake's hand gently touched my arm, warning me. I glanced back at him, raising my eyebrows in question. He peered past me again, at the rope. I shifted my gaze back to it. The red rope was attached to a white horse…a bony, dead horse.

"They starved it." My voice was barely audible as I took a horrified step forward. The body was so emaciated its backbone protruded from its form, and the skin between its ribs was concave. I wondered how much of its condition was the result of starvation and how much was the result of the onset of decomposition. "If it was tied up, it couldn't graze or…" *How cruel.* I looked back at Jake, wondering why he would've wanted me to see something so unsettling.

He stepped up closer behind me and pointed into the next paddock stall. "Over there."

At first, I saw nothing but shadows in the sheltered portion near the back of the paddock. But then a yellow and black striped lead rope tied to one of the metal crossbeams of the fence grabbed my attention. In the shadows, I saw the whip of a tail, which was quickly followed by a soft snorting. It was another, living horse.

The taut rope slackened and a large black body hesitated in the shade before stepping partially out. Although it wasn't tied as close to the fence as the dead horse had been, it was still thinner than it should have been, and its face was raw from trying to tug free from its halter.

I peeked over at Carlos, who was still rubbing the back of his head, looking disoriented, and then at Jake, who was staring at the horse, unsure what we should do.

"We have to at least untie the poor thing so it can move around," I said. The horse had eaten everything within reach, and it was only a matter of time before it either starved or died of dehydration.

I walked over to a patch of tall grass growing beside the stable and pulled a hefty bunch from the ground, roots, dirt clods, and all, and took slow, timid steps toward the horse. As I opened the gate, I watched the way its ears moved and its pensive, sinewy muscles shifted anxiously.

"Easy," I cooed quietly, trying not to startle the starved beast. "Easy." I took a step closer and gingerly tossed the grass toward the horse as a sign of goodwill.

It eyed the offering hungrily. From so close, I could tell it was male. His mane was long, hanging in his eyes and matted into clumps against his forehead, temples, and down his neck.

I looked around for water, but found no trough or puddles. There were a few bushes he'd nibbled down to twigs, and I assumed the only sustenance he'd received in a while was from their leaves.

The horse's head bobbed with anticipation as he inched toward the food. Getting as close as he could, he lowered his head and strained his lips to pull the blades of grass into his mouth.

I took a few more steps toward him and stopped just within reach of the rope. Slowly, I extended my hand forward to untie it. The horse's head reared back in panic, causing the fence to shake with each forceful tug and the rope to creak and groan as it tightened. His eyes were filled with fear, and he whinnied and snorted as he relentlessly tried to break away.

"Shhhh," I murmured, attempting to calm him. "Easy, boy." But the horse continued thrashing, the rope rubbing against his already exposed flesh.

Knowing he wouldn't calm any time soon, I stepped closer and untied the rope as quickly as I could. I struggled to loosen it against his pull. As he seemed to realize I was trying to help him, he calmed, but I didn't know how long his quietness would last.

After a few seconds, he began pawing at the dirt and looking between me and the remaining grass on the ground. He quickly gave in to his hunger and went back to eating what he could reach. The slack in the rope enabled me to untie him, and the lead fell to the ground. I wanted to remove the halter from his head, but I knew he didn't trust me enough to get anywhere close…and I wasn't brave enough to try.

His head flew up. "Easy," I said softly and began to back away. He regarded me for a moment before deciding I wasn't a threat and returning his attention to the grass; he couldn't seem to consume it fast enough.

I continued to back away, one steady step at a time, until I was standing beside Jake again. When the pile of grass I'd left the horse was gone, he took two strides to the nearest plants and began tearing the long strands free, his lips maneuvering each clump of nutrients into his mouth and letting the dirt and roots fall to the ground.

"We should go," Jake said softly, and I felt the warmth of his palm on my lower back.

I nodded, again wishing I could remove the halter so the horse would be uninhibited, but I decided I'd taken enough chances for the day. Taking Jake's hand, I started back up the hill toward Wings and the other horses. Before we were too deep into the cover of the trees to see, I glanced back down at the farmhouse. The shadow horse was still down there. He was no longer grazing, but was standing over the dead horse, nudging it as he stepped restlessly around its remains.

"He'll be okay, Zoe," Carlos said. "He can take care of himself."

I hoped he was right.

We hiked back up the hill, leaving our hope of a chicken dinner and fresh vegetables behind. Though we were tempted to collect the chickens, eating anything from that sick-infested place was enough to make our stomachs churn. We had no idea what the chickens had been fed, not to mention what had been used as fertilizer.

Upon reaching the top of the hill, the animals excited to see us, we anxiously climbed into our saddles and trotted back toward the bridge. Although we still needed to practice Carlos's EMP Ability before we returned to the ghost town, he was having a difficult time concentrating. Giving up, we headed back to camp, worried he might have a slight concussion and determined to test his Ability another, less eventful day.

We stepped onto the suspension bridge, and we'd made it almost halfway when a miserable groan came from behind me. I smiled back at Carlos. "You're doing fi—"

Beyond him, where the road ended and the bridge began, stood the black horse. He tapped his front left hoof on the wooden planks like a cat might do before walking over wet grass. His head sank low as he scented the planks. I could hear him breathing as he hesitated. His eyes were wide and his ears alert as he stepped out onto the bridge behind us.

18

DANI

MARCH 20, 1AE

D*r. Wesley was holding out her hand, her fingers crooked. "Come here, Danielle. I want to show you something." She was standing in the shadowed doorway leading into my closet...at Grams's house.* Why is she at Grams's house? Why am *I* at Grams's house? *And then it came to me:* It's a dream.

The doctor turned and disappeared into the oppressive darkness, and tentatively, I followed. Like the small walk-in was actually a magical wardrobe into another world, I pushed through hanging sweaters and dresses—except instead of finding myself in a frozen, winter forest, I emerged into an enormous laboratory filled with a meticulously arranged sea of antique, metal-framed medical beds that stretched as far as the eye could see. It was as though an infirmary from the First World War had been transplanted into an infinitely expansive, modern laboratory.

"Come," Dr. Wesley said, walking away from me.

"What...where...what...?"

"Come." Her voice surrounded me, a whirlwind of sound pressed into the single word.

She stopped by one of the beds. It was empty, with crisp, white sheets pulled tight over the mattress. "You must choose. We can only make two more Re-gens, but we have three recently deceased to choose from. You *must choose."*

"What are you talking about?" I asked, looking away from her and back down at the bed. It wasn't empty anymore. A body—a person—lay under the covers, the top sheet a shroud hiding his or her identity. When confusion drove me to raise my eyes, I found that all but three of the beds had disappeared and the walls had closed in around us.

"Choose."

I shook my head and backed away, but a wall sprouted up behind me, preventing my retreat. "Why do you want me to do this? You're the one who creates them. You *choose!" I didn't want to see the face of whoever was under the makeshift shroud.*

My stomach lurched as Dr. Wesley pulled the sheet back, revealing the face of the nearest bed's occupant.

Zoe.

She looked serene, like she was merely sleeping, but I knew better. She was too pale, too still. No, no, no, no, no… *I couldn't tear my gaze away from her face. "Her, I choose her!" I whispered fiercely.*

"Are you so sure?" Dr. Wesley asked. She hadn't moved away from the side of the bed, and when I raised my eyes to meet hers, to tell her—to beg her—to make Zoe a Re-gen, to bring my best friend back to life, the breath whooshed from my lungs.

Dr. Wesley's jewel-blue eyes, her black hair, her bone structure —here, next to Zoe, the resemblance was impossible to miss. Dr. Wesley looked like an older version of my best friend, how I imagined Zoe would look in thirty years. "Oh my God," I whispered. If I hadn't known Zoe's mom was dead, I would've bet my life that I was staring at her.

Oblivious to my shock, or possibly uncaring, Dr. Wesley strode to the next bed and drew back the sheet. I wasn't surprised when she revealed Jason's blank face. I didn't have room for surprise. All I felt was near-fatal heartbreak.

"Both of them," I said, my voice rough. "I choose both of them." Even if the third body were Ky or Chris, I would still choose to bring back Zoe and Jason. Living in a world without Ky or Chris would be difficult and painful, but doing so without Zoe or Jason would be unbearable. They were my weakness, and I didn't feel the least bit of shame about it.

Dr. Wesley rounded Jason's bed to the final of the three, and again, she drew back the sheet.

"Oh God!" I howled, lunging toward the third bed and falling on my knees beside it.

Cam. He was lying on the mattress, his face expressionless... peaceful, even. I glared up at the doctor, hating her for forcing me to make a choice that would stomp my heart into a bloody, meaty pulp. "Why?" I whispered, then repeated, louder, "Why? Why are you doing this? Tell me WHY!"

"I can't choose...you have to," she said, her voice devoid of emotion.

I gazed at Cam, memorizing the lines of his face. It had been so long since I'd seen those lips curved into a joyous smile, those eyes sparkling with laughter. I could see those things again...I only had to choose him. But to do that, I had to give up Zoe...or Jason. "I can't," I said hollowly.

"You must."

"Why? Why can't you do it?"

She waited for me to look up before she spoke. "Because it wouldn't be fair. Because I killed them."

My eyelids snapped open, and I gasped. Despite the chill pervading the house, I was covered in a sticky layer of cold sweat. I kicked off the sheets and growled. *Can I hurt her? Can I make her pay? Can I* kill *her?* For everything she'd done, it would be justice. That was undeniable. She was Kali, the destroyer of worlds…the destroyer of *my* world. Somehow, for some reason unknown to me, she'd created the Virus that had killed billions, including some of the people I cared about the most in the world—Callie, Cam, and Grams. *Why?*

The sun had yet to show any intention of rising, so I peeked at the clock on the bedside table. It was 3:34. With the adrenaline coursing through my veins, sleeping was a non-option, and though I felt awful about making him worry, I couldn't have an early-morning mind-convo with Jason—my Ability was still out of commission, courtesy of the electrotherapy. It was taking longer to return than Gabe had predicted.

What if it never comes back? What if it's weaker…broken? What if…

I sighed as I rose from the bed, thinking darkness was the perfect cover to continue my failed explorations of three days past. Searching through the warehouses, inventorying the Colony's supplies, would distract me from my murderous thoughts and useless fretting, at least for a little while.

After a quick shower, I searched through the dresser and closet until I'd assembled the perfect nocturnal stealth outfit: black leggings, a black, long-sleeved t-shirt, a snug black hoodie, black socks, and black combat boots. I dressed and assessed myself in the full-length mirror hanging on the closet door, and smiled. I looked like a cat burglar. *Perfect.* As an afterthought, I slipped the red card's cord over my head and tucked it beneath my sweatshirt. I didn't like relying on something the world destroyer had given me, but I wasn't stupid. A gift horse and all that. Plus, it carried the other item I would need—my would-be molester's key to the warehouses. I'd stolen it before securing his sidearm; obtaining it had been half the reason I'd let him get so handsy with me in the first place.

I considered stopping by Gabe's house before heading over to the warehouse district, but I figured he would just try to stop me… or bribe me with pancakes. My mouth started watering and my stomach growled. *Damn it!* I'd forgotten to eat, and my stomach roaring like that would alert any passersby or guards to my presence as easily as me stepping in front of them, waving, and saying, "Howdy, I'm a spy!"

Quickly, I doubled back to my house, snatched a granola bar out of the pantry, inhaled it, and then continued on my mission.

The church that had been converted into Warehouse A was completely devoid of light as I approached. Thinking about what had almost happened in that building—as well as the kisses and touches that *had* happened—I felt sick to my stomach. I wanted to forget.

Hands shaking with disgust, I yanked the key out from the neck of my sweatshirt and leaned closer to the warehouse door to unlock it. I crossed my fingers, hoping the General had changed all of the warehouse locks so that one universal key would work; with almost all of his little Colonists under his mental control, I was betting on him leaning toward uniformity and ease. After all, it wouldn't do to have his patrols jingling along like prison wardens. I was in luck.

I opened the door as quietly as possible, then quickly slipped inside and eased it shut, making sure to relock it. Compared to outside, the interior of the warehouse was night incarnate. Outside, the moon shone, bloated and silvery, but inside, the narrow windows admitted only long slits of light and the surrounding darkness was practically tangible. It was good for me, because my outfit blended better with the unrelenting blackness than the washed out grays of the moonlit base, but it was also annoying because my eyes required another twenty minutes to adjust to the deeper darkness.

Sitting down beside the door, I waited…and listened…and thought.

What am I going to do about the "world destroyer"? Should I kill her? Can I even do it? Sure, she killed my loved ones—but she also freed me from the mental hold the General had over me at great risk to herself. *Gabe trusts her. He probably won't forgive me if I hurt her. And what about Mase and Camille? What about all of the Re-gens?* She'd been bringing people back to life. True, most of them were under the General's *absolute* control and most of them were clueless as to their former lives, but she'd taken another huge risk with Mase and Camille. *What's her endgame?* And, of course, my mind dwelled on the same question it had been turning over and over...and over. *Why'd she create the Virus to begin with? Why'd she destroy the world? Why'd she kill my family...my Cam? Why?*

Amidst those troubling thoughts, I looked around and was relieved to find that my eyes had adjusted. The warehouse was still overwhelmingly dark, but my surroundings were painted in a pallet of grays and blues instead of relentless black.

I rose and began creeping toward the first aisle of stacked crates and plastic-wrapped pallets. Nonperishables—canned goods, boxed foods, and the like—went on for four aisles. The fifth aisle contained hygiene items, as did the next three, and then I reached the back of the cavernous room. I estimated that the supplies could last the several thousand Colonists a few weeks, maybe.

Moving to the nearest window, I removed Gabe's map from my sweatshirt pocket, angled it so the moonlight made it legible, and searched for my next target. I opted for Warehouse B, which was the closest and therefore safest route, and I was all about not getting caught...or ending up dead.

Squeezing my right eye shut to preserve half of my night vision in the moonlight, I snuck back out into the night. The short, cautious trek to Warehouse B went down without running into any patrolling guards, as did the one to Warehouse C. The first contained more packaged and preserved food, and the second housed both food and medical supplies.

As I finished up in Warehouse C, it was still full darkness, but my time was running out. I guessed I could only fit in one more stop before I had to sneak back to my house. With another moonlit glance at Gabe's map, I decided to bypass Warehouses D and E and head straight for Warehouse F. It was the largest of the three, and also the closest to my house.

I stuck to the cover of the bushes and trees surrounding the buildings as I made my way toward Warehouse F, doing my best to blend in with my surroundings. There was a heart-pounding moment when a patrol of four soldiers wearing yellow armbands rounded the corner of the nearest building. I had to become one with the trunk of an evergreen tree, slowly inching around it to avoid their view as they approached. Luckily, they passed without noticing me and eventually disappeared around the next corner.

No other obstacles hindered my path, and I reached Warehouse F safely, ducking inside, easing the door shut, and heaving a huge sigh of relief. *It is seriously my lucky day.*

As I stood just inside the entrance to the dark warehouse, focusing on taking slow, even breaths to calm my hyperactive nerves, I studied my new surroundings. Warehouse F looked as though it had actually been created for the function of being a warehouse—it was filled with row upon row of towering shelving units constructed of heavy steel, and each was filled with a variety of paper goods.

A hushed noise broke the silence. Someone else was inside with me. I could just barely hear two whispering voices. There was the sound of a footstep. Too close. I reached for the doorknob, thinking I could escape and dash into some nearby shrubs before they exited after me, but they were closer than I'd anticipated.

A monstrous figure clothed in camouflage rounded the end of the nearest aisle, and I glided into the shadows, plastering my body against the wall beside the door. If I didn't move, if I barely breathed, whoever it was might not notice me.

"I know what I heard, and the patrol is due any minute. Let's get out of here," one of them whispered.

"No!" another hissed. "Not until you remember!"

A second, much smaller figure emerged from the aisle in the

wake of the other. It pointed, and barely audibly, it said, "I hid there, and you crouched down and spoke to me. You were so sweet, Giant."

Giant? Isn't that what Camille calls Mase?

"I don't remember," the other whispered.

After a heavy sigh, there was a resigned, "Fine. What did you hear?"

"Something. We just need to go."

Swallowing the baseball-sized lump in my throat, I opened my mouth and whispered, "Camille? Mase?"

Both froze, and as one, they turned to face me.

I took a step forward. "It's Dani," I said softly, then held my breath. *I hope I'm right.*

The smaller figure rushed toward me on silent feet, and once it was close enough, I confirmed it really was Camille. Shakily, I exhaled and closed my eyes for a long moment.

"What are you doing here?" she hissed. "The patrol…it'll be here soon. Do you have any idea what they'll do to you if they catch you in here?"

Probably the same thing they'll do to you.

Mase was suddenly behind her, towering over her small form. "We have to get away from the door…they'll be here in a few minutes."

"Is there another way out?" I asked.

"No."

On cue, there was a clang on the other side of the door—a key being fitted into the lock.

"Fuck! They're early," Mase hissed. Stealing my breath, he picked up both Camille and me.

What the—

He slung us over his shoulders, and jumped. We landed on one of the oversized shelving units…on the top shelf.

Thunder resounded throughout the cavernous space and the metal shelf vibrated beneath us. *Holy shit!* Mase set both of us down right before the door opened and the four soldiers I'd seen earlier stepped inside. The three of us lay side by side, watching with bated breath.

"What the hell was that?" one of the soldiers asked. When nobody responded, he commanded, "Do a sweep. Check all the back rooms. If someone's here, I want them found."

As the three other soldiers fanned out, deftly waving their rifles and lights around in search of whoever had caused the noise, the leader waited by the door.

Careful not to make a sound, Mase raised his hand to his head and tapped his fingers against his temple, and then did the same against mine. *He wants me to use my telepathy?* Doubtful, I concentrated, fully expecting to run into the electrified wall that had been erected in my brain and had been blocking my Ability for the past day and a half. It wasn't there. *Oh, thank God!*

"You got a plan, big guy?" I asked, astounded at the ease with which I connected to his mind. It was unlike anything I'd ever experienced, even with Jason or Dr. Wesley's neutralizer boosting my Ability.

He nodded minutely, and several images flashed through my mind.

Mase leaping down to the floor like a panther and snapping a soldier's neck before the other man could cry out.

Camille and me quickly climbing down from the top of the shelving unit.

The three of us sneaking through the door and running far away.

"Can we do it without killing him?" I flicked my eyes toward the guard below.

Mase frowned, and three more images appeared in my

mind's eye.

Mase leaping down to the floor and putting the soldier in a choke hold until he passed out.

The other three soldiers coming in search of the cause of their leader's struggle.

The soldiers finding Camille and me, and...

I blocked the rest of his communication, not needing to see myself being killed. *"Okay, I understand,"* I said, resigned.

Without waiting for further confirmation, Mase silently launched his massive body off the shelf and dropped to the floor, his landing unbelievably quiet despite the twenty-foot drop. He landed directly in front of the patrol leader and snapped his neck before the other man even knew he was in danger. *Holy crap... how's that even possible?*

As Mase eased the limp body to the floor, I couldn't help but replay what had just happened. It had taken only a few seconds, and Mase's unexpected grace had made the attack appear unnaturally easy. I wasn't sure what his Ability was, exactly, but it was obviously very physical...far more so than any other I'd witnessed.

Camille tugged on my sleeve before easing over the edge and beginning her climb down the oversized shelves. It wasn't easy, but I followed, descending beside her. My legs and arms shook, my hands felt cramped, and my heart pounded. I beat Camille down, and as soon as Mase could reach her, watched him take hold of her hips and lower her the rest of the way to the floor. The motion was so protective, his hold so tender, that watching made my heart ache. *I miss Jason.*

Mase led Camille to the door and motioned for me to follow. Shoving my loneliness away, I slipped outside behind Camille and held my breath as Mase soundlessly eased the door shut.

19

DANI

MARCH 20, 1AE

Before she and Mase had run off in the gray morning light, I'd convinced Camille to pay me a visit later that day. As I puttered around the kitchen that afternoon, making one of the two things I could actually cook—tea—I attempted to focus on the questions I wanted to ask Camille when she arrived. It was better than replaying the memory of Mase snapping the patrol leader's neck and him falling to the cement floor, limp as a rag doll. I wasn't being very successful. There were so few sane people left alive; I felt like we'd done something unforgivable in snuffing out his life.

You did what you had to do to survive, D, Zoe's imaginary voice said. *Suck it up and move on. It's done.*

I shook my head and laughed bitterly. My hatred for General Herodson was reaching a critical level. His mind-controlled Colony was making me do things, terrible things, and turning me into someone I didn't want to be. Right and wrong had been blurred for a long time, but the false utopian prison was flipping them upside down. If I didn't get out soon, I would lose it and either make a poorly planned run for freedom—and get shot—or attempt to carry out a poorly planned hit on the General…and get shot. I wasn't a big fan of getting shot.

A high-pitched whistle started quietly, quickly building up to a steamy scream. I let it continue, appreciating the ear-piercing distraction. At a knock at the front door, I switched off the electric burner and let the teakettle slowly return to a mostly silent state.

"After the way you both ran off this morning, I wasn't sure you'd really come," I told Camille once I'd opened the door for her to come inside.

She was standing on the welcome mat, alone, smiling a small, secret smile. Her eyes were an odd grayish color, like they'd once been hazel but had faded along with her first life.

"Please, come in," I said hurriedly, opening the door further. I didn't want her to stand on the porch long enough to draw the attention of some nosy, mind-controlled neighbor.

Camille stepped inside and looked around the entryway. She seemed eager, of all things, her eyes hungrily devouring the furnishings, decor, and layout of the house.

"So…er…this is my house," I said as I led the way down the hall into the kitchen.

She followed, if a bit slowly.

"I made tea…do you like tea? I think I have some cookies too, somewhere…" I disappeared into the pantry that was in one corner of the kitchen, searching for the box of chocolate chip cookies I'd spotted the other day. When I reemerged, cookies in hand, I found Camille leaning over the stove and fiddling with the nobs that controlled the burners…which didn't bode well, because the ends of her hair were brushing over one of the burners. One that she'd turned on.

"Camille!" I rushed to her, pulling her away from the stove just as the thick, coiled metal started to glow orange. "What are you doing? Are you trying to set yourself on fire?" Standing between her and the stove, I looked into her eyes, making sure she was still the young woman I knew and hadn't gone through some weird body-snatching process. *I wouldn't be overly surprised*, I thought, considering everything I'd seen within the Colony's walls.

Camille stared back at me, her eyes wide. Until that moment, all I'd seen from her had been a young woman with an iron backbone and balls of steel. But looking into her frightened eyes, I found a girl—a scared girl. Her bottom lip trembled.

Mentally kicking myself for my harsh reaction, I wrapped my arm around her narrow shoulders and guided her to the sofa in the adjoining family room. She sat woodenly and stared ahead. Tears streaked down her pale cheeks.

"I'm sorry for yelling at you, but I didn't want your hair to catch fire," I told her softly, sitting down beside her. I brushed her hair out of her face with my fingers. "You have such pretty hair; it would be a shame."

She shook her head, and her voice was wobbly when she finally spoke. "I live in—I've never been in a real house before… at least, not that I can remember." Her eyes seemed to be searching the wall across the room. "Sometimes I have dreams about a place a lot like this, and there's one about a burning metal machine like that—"

"A stove," I told her.

"About a stove, except real flames come out of the top," she said, finally meeting my eyes. "There's always a woman standing beside me in those dreams, laughing. She makes me feel safe and happy. And then, when I'm laughing with her, she turns on the stove and starts to burn. Flames cover her, and she blackens and dissolves into a pile of ashes and bones. When I wake up, I'm crying." Camille paused for a moment. "I don't know who she is. Why does it make me sad that she burns?"

Because you're only human, I thought, but then I remembered that she wasn't, exactly. With a gentle smile, I again wrapped my arm around her and pulled her close. Only when she could no longer see my face did I let myself frown. *What happened in her past? What's she remembering?* "Do you think—is it possible she's your mom, or maybe your sister?"

"I know what those are from a book I read, but I don't have any of those. I only have Father."

"No, I mean, from before you di—from before you became a *Re-gen*." I said the word stiffly, trying not to load it with the disgust I felt for Dr. Wesley and her unnatural science projects. *Dead is dead…or at least it used to be.* I had no idea what it was like to be a Re-gen, to have died and been brought back to life with fractured memories at best, but it was just…wrong. *Did any of them even have a choice, or were their bodies stolen and used without their permission? What happened to letting the dead rest in peace? What about souls, if there is such a thing?* I shivered, terrified by the possibilities. *What if—*

"Dr. Wesley told me most of us don't dream," Camille said, drawing my attention back to her, "but that if we do, it might be our memories trying to resurface—so maybe you're right. But she also said our memories shouldn't have been able to survive the process. She said those synapses are too fragile and they die too quickly." She paused. "Synapses…I don't know what that means."

"Synapses are…" I searched for a simplified way to explain the complex processes that occurred within our brains every millisecond—processes I didn't hold a firm grasp on myself. Talk about the blind leading the blind. "Synapses are what happens inside our heads that make us do and think things. There are different synapses that do different things, like store memories or make our mouths open so we can speak." I was pretty sure I was botching the explanation…royally. "They're electrical, so—"

"They're electrical?" Camille asked, pulling away and straightening. She looked at me curiously. "Like, electrotherapy?"

I eyed her. "Yeah…"

"Do you think that, maybe, electrotherapy might bring the memory synapses back to life?" Her pupils expanded with her excitement, drowning out the lighter gray in her eyes.

"I—I don't know. But if it did, wouldn't it affect all of the Re-gens, not just you?"

"Well…" Camille raised her eyebrows and pursed her lips, looking like she was deciding whether or not to hold in a secret.

I mirrored her eyebrow-raise. "Well…?"

"You know how Mase works with Dr. Max a lot of the time?"

I nodded, suspicion sneaking around in my mind.

"Well, he has keys for that electrotherapy lab—"

"Wait," I said, holding up a hand. "*That* electrotherapy lab? As in, it's not the only one?"

She nodded and continued. "Some nights, after all the other Re-gens are asleep, we sneak into Dr. Max's lab and do it to each other."

"Do *what* to each other?" I squeaked, dreading the answer. I had a sinking feeling she wasn't about to tell me they spent the wee hours of the night playing doctor.

"Electrotherapy," Camille said. She was practically bouncing on the couch cushions.

Again, I paused her with an upraised hand. "Let me get this straight. You and Mase sneak into one of the electrotherapy labs and *electrocute* each other? *Why*? 'Cause it's so damn fun?"

She swatted my leg and giggled. "No, silly. So we can be more powerful than everyone else."

Uh…that's not creepy or anything…

"When we first wake up as Re-gens, we're a lot weaker than normals—regular humans, like you—and it takes a lot of electrotherapy to bring our Abilities back up to whatever strength they were at before. But we can also become stronger than normals by doing more electrotherapy, because it's too dangerous for them. But I heard Father tell one of his Controllers that he doesn't want us to be *too* powerful, because he wants to make sure they can avoid any 'Spartacus situations' before they have a chance to turn everyone into Re-gens or T-Rs." She cocked her head, looking at me quizzically. "What does that mean, a 'Spartacus situation'?"

I couldn't tear my eyes away from the young woman sitting beside me. *How does she know all this? And why is she telling me?* "A...uh...'Spartacus situation' would be a rebellion—a *slave* rebellion," I told her, then whispered, "So he *does* consider us all his slaves." Biting my lip, I studied the diminutive Re-gen. "Camille, what's a T-R? Is it like a Re-gen?" *Holy crap—does the General want to kill everyone and make them into perfect little Frankenstein slaves?*

From his perspective, the plan was genius. Re-gens, if they were initially trained to follow his every command—and didn't electrotherapize themselves at every possible opportunity, like Camille and Mase—they wouldn't require the use of his mind-manipulation Ability at all. *But why? Why is he doing any of this? For power?* Could anyone be so power-hungry...so truly, unequivocally evil?

Camille pursed her lips again and shook her head. "I don't know exactly what T-Rs are, but it stands for 'Tabula Rasa,' and it has something to do with the Ability of this new normal who arrived a few weeks ago."

*Tabula rasa...*blank slate. *Oh my God, does he have someone who can wipe our minds completely clean? Oh no...*

I'd been betting on the dwindling resources left over by civilization to limit his expansion, but if I was right about T-Rs—about the new "normal" who'd arrived—all bets were off. General Herodson wouldn't need to rely on Dr. Wesley or scientific equipment or electricity to make his perfect, obedient slave army; he would just need one person with the Ability to wipe a mind free of memories.

Shakily, I stood and walked back into the kitchen. "Do you want some tea?" I'd been planning on drinking English breakfast tea—hearty and full of caffeine—but I searched the little combo box for a packet of chamomile instead. I definitely needed something to calm my nerves, not excite them.

"I've never had tea," Camille said, sitting on a stool on the other side of the counter. "Is it good?"

I picked out a packet of Strawberry Fields for her, tore it open, plunked the teabag in a mug, added a spoonful of sugar, and filled the mug with steaming water. "I like it," I told her as I slid the mug across the counter to her and began preparing my own. "It's hot, so I'd wait a few minutes."

Camille leaned down and sniffed…and giggled. "It smells sweet…and pink!"

I couldn't help but laugh at her innocence. *Not innocence*, I reminded myself, *just a weird form of amnesia unique to Re-gens.*

When I didn't say anything for a few minutes, Camille asked, "Are you mad at me?"

"What?" I blurted. "No, of course not." I opened the box of unbelievably hard chocolate chip cookies and nibbled on one, more wanting something to occupy my hands than wanting to eat a stale, processed cookie. "It's just…once I think I understand how horrible *he* is, I learn something else about this place, and—" I cut my words off abruptly and closed my eyes. I was revealing too much.

"You mean Father?" Camille asked.

Opening my eyes, I watched her warily. I liked her, despite her moments of creepiness, and I owed Mase—big-time—but I still didn't know how much I could trust them.

Camille stared at me point-blank and said, "I want a 'Spartacus situation.' That's why Mase and I sneak into Dr. Max's lab to do electrotherapy on each other—so we can be stronger than everyone, strong enough to create a rebellion. But…" She paused, chewing on her bottom lip and testing her tea with the tip of her finger. "This Spartacus situation has to be big enough to get rid of Father *and* the Controllers."

"The 'Controllers'?" I asked, hoping to get more information about the General's mind-controlling lackeys than Gabe had given me.

Nodding, Camille clarified, "The others like Father, who make the normals do what they want. They control all of the people wearing those." She motioned to my yellow armbands with a wave of her hand.

I took a deep breath. I'd suspected that taking the General out wouldn't solve the problem; it would just give the problem a new face…an unknown face. *Better the devil you know, and all that.*

I munched on the cookie and sipped my tea, thinking. "Do you know who these Controllers are?"

Camille shook her head. "The only people who have direct contact with them are Father and the people they're controlling, and they won't reveal their identities because they're mind-controlled, so…"

Damn! If I'd known who they were, then I could've made some sort of insane sleeper cell assassination attempt. *And probably gotten myself killed,* I thought. *But still…*

After a long moment, Camille asked, "What was it like before?" I watched her as she raised her mug to her lips, took a sip, and smiled blissfully. Apparently, she liked strawberry tea.

"What do you mean?"

"Everything—the world, people, life—what was it like?"

I tapped my lips with my index finger as I pondered her question. *What* was *it like?* It was a question that should've been easy to answer, but it wasn't. "I guess it was kind of like it is in here, except way more chaotic and *way* less mind-controlled. And it was louder…more energetic. People would get angry or laugh or cry a lot more than Colonists do. Many people spent hours sitting in front of TVs or their computers just surfing the Internet. We worried about making enough money to pay for the things we needed, even though we spent money we didn't have on things we didn't need. And there were too many of us." I frowned. "Most scientists agreed that we were killing the planet, slowly, and that if we continued, we'd destroy our own species eventually just by running out of resources. And, um…" *Why is it so hard to explain? Why can't I think of anything positive?*

Camille took another sip of her tea. When she set her mug down, she opened her mouth, and then closed it before saying anything.

"What?" I asked.

She shook her head, staring shyly down at her tea. "You'll laugh," she said softly.

At that, I did laugh, but not unkindly. "I might. I can't promise you I won't, but I don't think I'll be laughing *at* you. Some things are just funny."

Camille raised her eyes to meet mine, their gray depths twinkling mischievously. "What was it like between men and women?"

I smiled, not laughing. "What do you mean, exactly?"

Camille frowned, searching for the right words. "Was it always like it is here…like with you and that guard in the warehouse? Did men always treat women like that? I've seen…did they make them do things with their bodies? Did women have a choice? Or did they like it? And why do the men want to do that with so many different women? I wouldn't want to do that with anyone but—" She caught herself mid-sentence, blushing.

"Anyone but Mase?" I finished for her. When she nodded, looking down at her half-empty mug, I said, "I have someone like that, someone who's the only person I want to, um…be with. His name is Jason." I smiled fondly, forcing myself not to dwell on the possibility of never seeing him again.

Camille met my eyes. "Once, in the middle of the night, I got out of bed to go to the bathroom and two of the Domestication Officers were in there, and—"

"What's a 'Domestication Officer'?" I interrupted. It was a term I'd heard several times, but I still didn't know what it meant.

"The people who watch over Re-gens," she said, dismissing them with a wave of her hand. "They're not always very attentive. Anyway, when I opened the bathroom door and saw they were in there, I stepped back and watched through the crack in the door. They were, um…" Her already-pink cheeks flushed a bright red.

"At first I thought the man was hurting her—she was making these noises—but then I saw her face. She was—I've never seen anyone look so happy." Her eyebrows drew together and she shook her head. "I don't—I thought maybe Mase and I…have you ever, um…*what* were they doing?"

Though I tried, I couldn't hold in my nervous laugh. "Uh…yes, I have ever, and I'm pretty sure the Domestication Officers were having sex."

Camille's eyes widened in horror. "Sex is forbidden! Re-gens can't do that!" Slowly, her eyelids narrowed. "But…what is it, exactly?"

I sighed, figuring the apparent Re-gen antisex rule was just another way to control them. Pity for her stunted understanding of life overshadowed my embarrassment at the topic. After explaining the mechanics of the act and emphasizing the emotional connection and how important it was—I really didn't want Camille to go off and start sleeping around like crazy—I refilled Camille's mug and sat down on the stool beside hers. Though she'd listened to my explanation eagerly, she turned suddenly glum.

"What's wrong?"

She took a deep breath, and exhaled in a long, despondent sigh. "It's not fair. I can never do that with Mase."

"Uh…why not?" *Are they physically incapable? Is that one of the differences caused by the Re-gen process?*

"If someone saw us, they'd know we were different and we'd be destroyed."

Oh, right. "You know, I have other rooms here," I said. A plan was forming in my mind, and Camille had just given me the currency to buy what I needed.

Camille's eyes lit up, and a purely devilish smile spread across her face.

"I'll let you and Mase have the house all to yourselves whenever you want, but…I'd like something in return."

Camille cocked her head, silently asking.

"Can you both meet up with me tonight? I have some more reconnaissance to do." At her blank look, I clarified, "Scouting... looking around...gathering information..."

Camille hopped in her seat happily. "Oh—yeah! What are you looking for?"

"Anything that'll help me get out of here and back to my friends," I told her.

"You're leaving?" Her eyebrows drew down and she looked like she was on the verge of tears. I hadn't expected such a strong reaction.

Reaching for her hand, I squeezed gently. "Yes, but maybe you can come with me. You and Mase." She looked unsure, so I added, "I'm going to find a way to stop him—General Herodson *and* the Controllers. I just can't do it from *inside* the Colony, at least not right now. He's too close, and we don't know who the Controllers are, and it's too dangerous, and...I just need to get out of here."

After a long moment of thought, Camille smiled. "We'll help you, but it'll have to be tomorrow night. I can think of lots of places for us to do this, um...reconnaissancing."

I let out a sigh of relief. Camille and Mase knew their way around and seemed to be really good at staying under the radar. I'd been planning to ask Gabe to join me, but it wouldn't hurt to have more eyes—and Abilities.

"There's one thing you might want to try to get first," Camille said. Her eyes were narrowed into conspiratorial slits.

"What's that?"

"Dr. Wesley's master key. With it we can get into most of the restricted areas."

I frowned. "I don't know how I could get—" But the solution popped into my head. *Blackmail.* I didn't owe Dr. Wesley anything, not after discovering her role in killing nearly everyone I loved, so I didn't feel an inkling of remorse at the thought of potentially hurting her. Plus, I had one hell of a blackmail item.

The neutralizer—it was made from *her* blood.

20

ZOE

MARCH 20, 1AE

"I can't wait to actually *bathe*," I said, groaning with anticipation. We'd decided to take a field trip down a deer trail to the river for some much-needed scrubbing—with the exception of Jason, who'd opted to remain back at camp just in case Dani tried to contact him again.

Carlos barked a laugh and gently tugged Arrow's head back up; his horse, along with most of the others, had become increasingly distracted by the wild green grasses emerging from the ground for spring. I shared in their joy, reveling in the smell of alfalfa and grass and basking in the periodic rays of sunshine. We'd had a lot of rain off and on over the past few evenings, and mixed with the sunlight, it was encouraging everything to sprout. *One month closer to summer.* I sighed contentedly.

"Laugh all you want to, Carlos." I looked at him askance, barely able to contain my growing anticipation. "I've been waiting for this moment for days."

Carlos nudged Arrow toward the river. "I've been meaning to tell you…you stink," he teased.

Sam giggled from atop his smaller palomino, Buck.

"Really?" I turned in my saddle to face them both, tapping my index finger against my lips in mock forgetfulness. "You'll have to remind me, Carlos, when was the last time *you* bathed?"

He shook his head, not sparing me a glance as he tried to contain how entertained he really was.

"At least *I* took a sponge bath the other day." I wrinkled my nose playfully.

Harper and Chris paused their easy conversation beside us and snickered. Everyone seemed amused, and I even thought I saw Jake's lips curve into a slight smile as he rode past me. As usual, Cooper and Jack trotted behind him, blissfully unaware that the world had been turned upside down and that we all smelled like dirty pond water.

Tavis's brow furrowed, and his horse, a tall, coffee-colored mare named Mini, stopped momentarily to pull up another mouthful of grass. "What's that even mean—'sponge bath'? I watched you—it's not like you actually used a sponge. People always use a rag or a towel or piece of cloth or something." He seemed deeply perplexed, and I chuckled softly.

"You're funny, Tavis," I said, shaking my head.

"How many people have you seen take a sponge bath, anyway?" Sanchez called, looking back at us. Her tone was light, but as usual, her expression was blank. "Should we be worried?"

Tavis grinned and rested his fist on his hip. "Alright, I surrender."

Up ahead, the dogs started barking, and I could hear splashing as they lunged into the water. "Finally," I practically sang and pressed Wings on, the anticipation nearly too much to bear.

When we reached the edge of the river, we let the horses drink before tying them up in a clearing a few yards away.

"How's Shadow doing?" Harper asked as I untied my bag from Wings's saddle and carried it over to a large, lichen-covered boulder beside the water.

"He's okay, I guess. I wish you knew more about horses so you'd know if I'm treating his wounds the right way."

"You're doing fine." He nudged my shoulder. "And Carlos is a big help, right?"

"Yeah, he is. In fact, Shadow's not in as bad of shape as I thought. I washed off about seven layers of muck. Mostly he's just scared, tired, and needs to be fattened up a bit. He *finally* let Carlos and me get the halter off him, and since he followed us all the way back to the ranch, I think it's safe to say he wants to trust us."

"I don't blame him for being scared." Harper squeezed the bill of a baseball cap in his hands to shape it better before putting it on. "Who knows what they did to him."

"If Dani were here," I said wistfully, "it'd be a whole lot easier."

"Is that what's been bothering you, Baby Girl? You haven't been yourself lately." Harper quickly removed his hat and tugged off his shirt, draping it over a low-hanging branch.

I sighed and sagged against the side of his horse. "Yeah, it's Dani, but it's everything else, too. Things just keep getting more complicated."

"Things with Jake?"

I scoffed. "With Jake, with Jason—and then there's my lying, deceitful family." I groaned. "And I've been dreaming about Clara the last couple of nights," I said, the discomfort in my voice too deep-seated to hide. "Why is she in my head suddenly, H? It's weirding me out."

He shook his head, looking equally discomfited. "Stop dwelling on Clara. She's long gone. Besides, your Ability's getting stronger, so if she's really around, you'll know." He snapped me with his towel. "Come on, Baby Girl. Let's get you cleaned up. You look like a ragamuffin." Harper winked at me, making me smile, and headed to the water toward Chris and Sanchez.

After digging out my wash cloth, body soap, and shampoo and setting them on the waist-high boulder I was using as a vanity by the edge of the river, I stripped down to my bikini and tossed my clothes on top of the boulder as well. Slipping on my red rubber flip-flops, I crept over to the riverbank and dipped my right foot in. Big mistake. It was ice cold. I shook my head, taking a deep breath. *You've been attacked by Crazies, almost died—more than once—and lost Dani twice. You've suffered worse than this, Zoe,* I told myself and glared at the water.

Cooper and Jack splashed by me, interrupting my internal pep talk.

"Oh my God!" I cried when the water sprayed all over my already chilled skin. The brisk March air bit at my bikini-clad body, but I was determined to deal with it…as long as I could clean the lingering blood and weeks' worth of grime off me.

"Green togs?" Tavis remarked, wading up to the riverbank.

I peered over at him. "Togs?"

He gestured to my bathing suit, his eyes wide and approving.

Unable to prevent my gaze from wandering, I appraised his disheveled hair and sinewy muscles covered by tanned skin. He wore nothing but plaid boxers, a towel draped around his neck, and a big-ass grin on his face.

Looking around at the rest of the group, I realized I was the only one with an actual bathing suit on. Harper was shirtless, laying on his back in the sunshine, his arm beneath his head and the shade of his ball cap covering his eyes. Chris and Sanchez were playing fetch with the dogs in the water downriver, both of them wearing sports bras and gym shorts. Carlos and Sam, wearing only boxers, were skipping stones on the river's surface. And then there was me.

I suddenly felt self-conscious. "I guess I'm the only one who planned ahead," I said lightly, then looked pointedly at Tavis. "At least I'm not standing around in my underwear."

At the sound of crunching footsteps, I glanced over my shoulder. Jake stopped a few feet behind me and started undressing.

My heartbeat picked up, and I unintentionally held my breath. I watched as he pulled his black t-shirt off over his head, revealing the broad, sculpted chest I'd traced with my fingertips so many nights. I'd seen him shirtless in the dimly lit locker room back in Fort Knox, and I'd memorized the contours of his abs with my hands, but I'd never appreciated Jake's mostly bare body in the sunlight—the dusting of light brown hair between his pecs and the hard muscle beneath his flawless skin…*no scars.* I thought back to the first time I met him, the night he'd been shot in the shoulder, but there was no mark. There were no burn scars from the fire, either.

As he stood there, wearing only his gunmetal-gray boxer briefs, I couldn't look away. Things had happened so fast since we'd met, and time seemed to be passing so achingly slowly, that I hadn't realized how little we'd really *seen* of each other; we were always layered in clothes. I suddenly wished we'd spent more time together…alone.

The thought of his life before I met him seemed more intriguing than ever. Although I couldn't picture him without his reserved veneer, I assumed he hadn't always been so impervious. He must've laughed and gone drinking with friends and made love to women. He must've lived. *What would it have been like to go on a date with you, Mr. Vaughn?* I couldn't help but wonder what his type of woman was back when he actually had options. *Is that all that we are? Convenient?*

Jake sauntered toward me, oblivious to my mind-wanderings, and his eyes raked over me. Narrowing, they shifted to Tavis. I blinked out of my intrigued haze and forced myself to look away. Groaning inwardly, I took a long, deep breath, inhaling the crisp, mountain air and welcoming the taunting breeze. It kept my mind from wandering…again.

Jake cleared his throat. I was too busy *not* looking at him to notice what had passed between him and Tavis, but Tavis walked away toward Sanchez and Chris while I crouched down to submerge my washcloth in the frigid water. When Jake continued to stand there, saying nothing, I peered up at him. I was greeted by a raised eyebrow.

"Nice suit," he said casually as he bent down to snatch the plastic bottle of body wash I'd brought.

I held my wash cloth out and he squeezed orange-scented soap onto the wet terrycloth. I gave him a rueful smile. "I like yours, too." I shifted my eyes to his tight underwear. His toned thighs alone made my mouth dry out, and I forced myself to swallow.

I brought the sudsy, dripping washcloth to the nape of my neck and cringed as I began scrubbing away the grime…and the heat from Jake's gaze.

He crossed his arms as he watched me, which was apparently the most entertaining thing he'd ever seen.

I continued scrubbing, first around my face and then under my arms. "You seem to be enjoying this," I said, glowering at him.

"Why aren't you doing that in the water?"

I tilted my head. "Seriously? Do you know how cold that water is?"

He nodded and glanced over at the rest of our group, who were bathing several dozen feet downriver. "They're handling it fine," he offered.

"Harper isn't in the water," I retorted.

"I washed up yesterday while you guys were being assaulted by half-naked Crazies," Harper interjected. I'd forgotten he was lounging in the patches of sun behind me.

"Well, then I'm a wimp, and I'm okay with that." I submerged my washcloth in the water for a rinse.

Jake just shook his head, his sexy grin warming my insides. "You're only prolonging it," he said with a deep chuckle. "Just jump in, scrub, and get out."

"Ha! That's easy for you to say. You have, like, no hair, and you like to pretend nothing fazes you. I, on the other hand, pretend no such thing. Lots of things faze me…like cold water." My teeth chattered as the water ran down my body, trickling suds down my chest and stomach. I had yet to wash my hair and dreaded dunking my head into the water.

I hadn't noticed Carlos wade up to us. Without warning, he splashed me, and I shrieked like a little girl. "Stop it, Carlos, or I swear—"

"You'll do what?" He splashed me again, and I instinctively tried to block the spray with my hands.

I gave him the evil eye, and he shrugged. "You're no fun," he said and called for Jack, who was drying off in the sunshine, to come back and play with him in the water.

I returned to my diligent scrubbing. "Did I get all the dirt off? And the blood?" I asked, pointing to my face and neck. Jake nodded, and I looked down, taking inventory of my sudsy body. "I just need to wash my hair and rinse off, then I'm done," I said, running through my list of cleansing to-dos.

"That's the worst part," Jake remarked.

I flashed him an insincere smile. "Thanks." When he only nodded, I continued, "Are you planning on watching me the whole time, or are you washing up at some point, too?" He didn't answer, only eyed me, a scheme clearly forming in his mind. I froze with fear and scowled at him. "What are you thinking?"

"I'm thinking I'm just gonna pick you up and dunk you in the water…just get it over with."

"Don't even think about it, Jake." The predatory look in his eyes made me giggle. "No, seriously, don't. Don't!" I tried to make my voice as stern as possible.

Despite my protests, he bent over, picked me up, and tossed me over his shoulder.

"Seriously," I squeaked. "I'll never speak to you again!"

Jake said nothing, but walked into the water, his arms tightening around my legs to hold me in place.

"Let me go, Jake! Please!"

I heard his rumbling laughter. "Oh, you're still speaking to me?"

I squealed and laughed again, part thrilled and part panicked as he stepped further into the river. "Please, Jake, I'll do whatever you want, just don't dunk me." I screamed and squeezed my eyes shut as I clasped on to the back of his arm, bracing myself for the imminent cold.

"People are going to think you're being attacked if you keep screaming like that," he said ruefully.

"I am!"

I heard the water splashing at his feet as he faltered down the rocky decline, deeper into the river. "Do you want me to put you down?" he asked. I could tell he wore a mischievous grin.

I looked down to see the water swirling at the backs of his knees. "No!"

With little effort, Jake repositioned me so that I was against his chest, his arms wrapped around me as I held on for dear life. At first, I considered wriggling free, but I wanted to stay in his arms a little longer. So instead, I wrapped my arms around his neck, pulling myself closer to his body. Although I shrieked and screamed a little more, my rigidity dissipated and instead I felt alive, adrenaline coursing through my body as he held me against him.

His hold loosened a little.

"No…no!"

Jake stepped further in, the water rising to his waist.

"Please take me back to the riverbank, Jake. Please?" I gazed into his eyes, a desperate, innocent expression on my face. I felt a thrill of excitement as he eyed me. I lifted my eyebrows, hopeful.

Jake shook his head, and a genuine, make-my-heart-flutter smile spread across his face. "You're always doing things the hard way." He took two more steps, holding me tighter against him.

"Okay, okay! Wait!" I peered into his eyes. "Wait until I say, okay? Let me just think for a sec."

"You can't think about it. It only makes it worse…like tearing off a Band-Aid. You're horrible at this."

The gang was cracking up behind me, and I wanted to flip

them off and laugh with them at the same time. I smiled at Jake instead, taking a deep breath, and then nodded.

I let out an exhilarated scream and felt the icy water sting my body as he submerged us both in the river. The moment he let me go, I bobbed back up to the surface. The cold water felt like razor blades cutting my skin. I gasped and cursed as I struggled to stand.

Jake emerged beside me, wiping the water off his face, and then wrapped his fingers around my wrist to pull me back underwater.

I screamed again, invigorated and awakened in a way I hadn't felt in a long time. Laughing, I splashed him. The water was so cold that I began to feel numb.

He splashed me back before he stood up. "Sanchez," he called, and a bottle of shampoo was flung into the air. Jake caught it with his left hand and looked down at me. "Come here," he said huskily. "Let's get your hair washed so you don't die of hypothermia."

I stepped closer to him in the chest-deep water and steadied my feet on the rocks at the bottom. Jake's fingers hurriedly kneaded my prickling scalp, and I couldn't let it go unnoticed that he was shaking too.

"I thought you could handle the cold water?" I asked, unable to resist a smug smile.

"I *can*. Notice I'm not whining, like you." He gently tugged my head back down into the water to rinse again. He twisted the water from my dripping hair, and as I clumsily made my way up to shore, he swatted me on the butt. "You can shoot and stab people, cuss like a sailor, and knee a man in the groin like it's nothing, but water horrifies you?"

"*Cold* water, Jake. And it doesn't horrify me. I just—I hate it. I wish it was summer all year long," I said through chattering teeth. Forcing my feet to work, I scrambled for my towel.

Jake finished bathing quickly and joined me on dry land. He picked up his towel, which had been draped beside my dry clothes, and began wiping the droplets of water off his body.

I dried my feet and slipped them back into my flip-flops. "I can't believe you did that to me," I muttered. "Traitor."

Jake took a step toward me, and his body was suddenly so close that his heat enveloped me, warming me more than the damp towel I'd wrapped around my waist. He glanced around before he reached behind me and untied the back of my bikini top.

"Hey!" I screeched, my hands flying up to my chest.

He said nothing, just stared into my eyes, letting his hand linger on the skin of my back.

"You should probably get changed," he said, his voice thick with desire.

I nodded dumbly. "Hold the towel up for me?"

Jake unwrapped the towel from around my waist and held it up, blocking me from everyone's view, never taking his eyes off mine.

I removed my hands, untying the final tie around my neck, allowing my green bikini top to fall with a soggy splat onto the rocks at my feet. Jake's eyes flicked to my chest for only an instant, but I could feel his increasing arousal infuse with my own.

I was too busy battling our mutual desire to feel the least bit self-conscious as I stood in front of him—in only my bikini bottoms and a mess of scraggly hair hanging over my shoulders. He handed me the white tank top I'd tossed on the tall boulder beside him.

"You should probably put this on."

By late afternoon, we were approaching camp. I spotted Jason in the distance, pacing back and forth in a clearing behind the stable. Each step was deliberate and intense. *What the hell?*

"What's he…?" Carlos started to ask.

I peeked back at Chris, who looked as clueless as I felt. Suddenly fearful something horrible had happened in our absence, we urged our horses forward. An endless cycle of what-ifs looped through my mind.

I drew Wings to a halt mere feet from the matted line of weeds Jason had trampled before I dismounted. "What's wrong?" My eyes shifted over his body, taking in the bandages crossing his face. *He looks okay...*

His eyes shifted to me, a wistful smile on his face, but it instantly hardened into a scowl.

"Are you...okay?" *I can't tell anymore.* Jason's mood was constantly changing, and I couldn't keep up with him.

"Just that Dani and I've been waiting for you." His words startled me far more than his accusing glare.

"Dani?" I looked around like I might find her walking over from the fallen log, where Jason and I had opened the box, or sitting on the wooden pasture fence, although I knew she was miles away.

"Hey, Zo. Did you get all clean?" Dani asked, and the sound of her voice in my head eased the usual tension in my shoulders.

"Where've you been, Dani? You were supposed to check in yesterday. We've been a little"—I glanced at Jason—*"on edge waiting to hear from you."*

Jason resumed his pacing.

"Yeah, um...I was just starting to tell Jason about that..."

Under his breath, Jason muttered to me, "If you don't talk out loud, I can't hear what you're saying to her."

I rolled my eyes...even though he had a point.

"Long story short, I accidentally got this electroshock therapy that—"

"What?" Jason and I both shouted at the same time.

"Can you two be quiet so I can explain?"

Jason stopped his pacing long enough to shoot me a sideways glance.

"Sorry," I grumbled for the both of us.

"Anyway, they call it 'electrotherapy' and it's specially

designed to increase the power of Abilities, but a side effect is that the recipient of the treatment can't use their Ability for a while. It was an accident, mostly, but if it hadn't been for two Re-gens, I would've been brain-fried, extra crispy. But I wasn't, so...yay..."

"Fucking...damn it all to fucking hell!" Jason was stalking around, apparently looking for something to hit.

Trying not to picture Dani being electrocuted or brain-fried, I frantically asked one of my many questions. "What's a Re-gen, D?"

"Oh, right. I've made a few discoveries since I've been out of commission. It worked, by the way—the electrotherapy, I mean. My telepathy is way stronger than it was before. I'm not sure if it's permanent, or what, but anyway: Re-gens are people who died and have been brought back to life."

"Oh, shit," I breathed. *Becca. That has to be what happened to her.* This time I was the one who started pacing, periodically looking over at Jake, who was standing a few yards away with the others. He was completely oblivious to my realization.

"Really, it all boils down to Abilities and being able to control people. Re-gens are still people, but their minds work differently, and they don't remember who they used to be. But two of them are different. They're helping me. They helped me when a guard—I mean, when the doctor snagged me and started the electrotherapy."

I peered over at Jason, wondering if he'd noticed Dani's hesitation.

"And, oh my God, you guys are never going to believe this—Chris was right. Someone did *orchestrate everything. I don't know all the details, but I do know who created the Virus. And, I gotta admit, I'm kind of having a hard time not beating her face in..."*

"Don't do anything stupid," Jason practically growled.

"Of course not."

I pictured Dani smiling impishly. "I'm not surprised about the

Re-gens. I'm almost positive we had one of them with us a few days ago."

"What? Really?" Dani seemed almost afraid to ask.

"It was Becca." I paused. "Jake's sister. We didn't know *what* she was. We just knew she was…wrong." Dying and coming back to life definitely *wasn't* normal. "We have to at least try to get her out too, Dani. She's back in the Colony now, but she may not be willing to leave."

"Okay, wow. That's crazy. But, yeah, I'll see what I can find out about her. What else has been going on down there?"

Jason crouched on the ground, seeming to focus on controlling his anger. "Not a fucking thing," he grumbled.

I hesitated, wondering how much to tell her, but I knew Dani would be hurt if she found out I was keeping things from her, especially when it came to the box. "Well, we had a few run-ins with some Crazies…and we opened the box. But mostly—"

"You opened it? What's in it?"

I was reluctant to answer her. Jason and I hadn't spoken about the box since that day. Beyond that, I wasn't sure how much I *could* tell Dani without breaking down. I gazed over at the rest of my friends. They were leaning against their horses casually as they waited for our conversation with Dani to come to an end. Jake picked a piece of grass from his horse's mane and looked at me questioningly. His idle expression transformed to one of deep concern.

Jason cleared his throat, capturing my attention. He glanced up at me, his eyes full of caution. "Are you getting tired, Red? Do you need to go? I don't want you to get worn out, and—"

"No, I'm fine—better than fine. It's easy now."

Jason ran his fingers through his hair. It was nearly as dark as mine and longer than I'd seen it in over a decade. He said nothing.

"Um, guys…the question about what was in the box wasn't supposed to be a stumper…"

Oh, right. "We found out our dad was a liar," I blurted. "And that our mom's alive. Or, at least, she was. There was a letter from her explaining…well, not much."

"Holy crap."

"And there was a picture of her." My voice was cold, but it was better than crying about it.

"What did she look like?" Dani asked. She sounded nervous.

My eyes shifted to Jason's once more, and I recalled the argument we'd had before opening the box. "Like me," I said. I wasn't sure if the quietness of my voice was a result of guilt, sadness, or anger. It was probably all three.

A long moment passed, and when Dani didn't respond, Jason said, "Red? Are you okay? Are you sure this isn't too much?"

"No, I'm fine, I promise. I just…that's a huge thing. I'm trying to wrap my mind around it." She paused, then added, *"Did you learn anything else?"*

"Umm, that our dad was in the military, and that's how they…"

Jason stood, his head lowered and hands clenched into fists.

"It doesn't really matter anymore," I muttered, hoping to spare Jason further pain.

"Oh, I…I can't believe he hid all that for so long. But don't you think he must've had a reason? Do you have any clue as to why he kept all that from you?"

I shook my head, lazily stroking Wings's velvety nose before I realized Dani couldn't see me. "It doesn't matter," I said bitterly, not wanting to spend another second thinking about my parents and their lies. "They're dead now, so we'll never know. We need to focus on getting you out of there."

"I know. I've only got a few days left until General Douchebag starts using me to draw in more people…which would be bad. Really, really *bad. The Re-gens aren't the worst of his science experiments."*

Re-gens…Becca…"Father"…the General. It was all starting to make sense.

Jason looked at me sharply. "What do you mean?"

"I don't know much, but there's apparently another program being developed here that creates mind-slaves without the need for mind manipulation or labs and electricity. They're not Re-gens—they're something else. They call them T-Rs."

"Jesus, this guy is taking over the world one brain-dead person at a time. I repeat: we've *got* to get you out of there, D," I said, gesturing emphatically.

Jason started pacing again. "Exactly how long until you need to get out?"

"I start at the comm center in three days."

"Then we'll get you out the night before you're supposed to start. That gives you a couple more days to gather intel. What do you already know?"

"Um...what do you want *to know?"*

"We need guard numbers and patterns, the General's schedule throughout the day, even at night, and anything else you think might help us plan the extraction."

"Gosh, you guys don't want much, do you?" Dani joked.

"It's not funny, D," I said, and Jason growled, "We just want you back."

There was a long pause. *"I know, sorry. Bad joke."*

"Is there anyone you can trust?" I asked. "Anyone who can help you?"

"Um, yeah, there are a few people I can trust. Gabe, and those two Re-gens I told you about. I'll scout around tomorrow night with Camille and Mase—they're the Re-gens. They know a lot about this place and have some ideas about where to look."

"Be careful," I pleaded.

"Promise. As for the info about the guards and stuff, and the General's schedule, I'll ask Gabe tomorrow at dinner—"

Oh shit, I thought, closing my eyes.

"What do you mean, 'dinner'?" Jason asked, his voice low and cold.

I had the impression that Dani was smiling. *"Calm down,*

Jason. I'm having dinner with Gabe to interrogate him for more information that'll help you guys plan the breakout. Crap, you'd think it was a date or something..."

"Is he coming with you when you leave?" Jason asked quietly.

Dani didn't say anything, and I scoured Jason's face for signs of boiling emotions. There was only a glint in his eyes, a dangerous glint.

"Dani…?" Though Jason's voice was soft, it was filled with warning.

"Yes, he's coming with me. But—"

"Good. I've got a few words for him."

"Jason, it's not like—"

"After what he did, it doesn't matter what it's—"

"Alright you guys, this isn't helping." I glared at Jason, willing him to calm down. "You can argue about this later when we've got her back," I reassured him. "…and when Gabe is within punching distance," I muttered.

Jason grunted.

Dani sighed mentally. *"Fine. But you should know, Camille and Mase might be coming, too."*

"Anyone else tagging along?" Jason asked. "Maybe you should make a Colony-wide announcement."

"No," Dani said tartly. *"But if you think it's a good idea, maybe I will."*

Jason closed his eyes, but the hint of a smile tugged at the corners of his mouth. "Sorry," he said.

There was a pause, then Dani said, *"Me too. I just...I miss you, Jason. I miss everything...I miss—"*

"Okay guys," I blurted, unable to handle their love-ness. "I'm gonna go. Dani, please be safe and promise me you'll let us know if plans change and we need to get you out sooner."

"I promise," she said.

Jason didn't even glance at me before wandering off into the sparse woods beyond the stable to continue his conversation with Dani in private.

I turned to face the group, all of their curious, concerned eyes on me. “Come on,” I said, snatching Wings’s reins and leading her toward the stable. “I’ll fill you guys in.”

As I ran through everything with them, answering the few questions I could, I couldn’t stop my mind from wandering to thoughts about Dani and Jason and how obscenely much they cared about one another.

Jake had proven he cared about me many times. I knew that if it was in his power, like Jason with Dani, he would never let any physical harm come to me. He could protect me from bullets and transfuse his blood with mine when I needed it. He could wash my hair and help keep me from freezing at night—but he couldn’t protect me from the tension that tightened my neck and shoulders or the dull, incessant ache that pulsed inside me at the thought of him leaving, like he’d almost done.

I didn’t have a choice with Mom—she was gone before I could even get to know her. Jason had been gone since we were little kids, leaving me alone with our broken dad, who was always distant and preoccupied. But it was different with Jake. He’d never made me any promises. *He’s not tied to me like my family was supposed to be.* I rolled my eyes. The frequent conversations I was having with myself hadn’t escaped my attention.

After I unsaddled and brushed Wings in her stall, I moved to the next stall over to check on Shadow. He was standing in the shade of his paddock, his head drooping as he snoozed. His ears perked when he heard my footsteps, and his head shot up. Without the halter, his wounds were able to heal, and the raw flesh lining his forehead and jaw was already scabbing over.

I leaned against the fence, crossing my arms on the top slat. “Hey, fella. How you feeling?” I asked him softly. He looked better. Although his muscles were wasted, his chest was broad and his legs were long. He was a good five and a half feet tall. His onyx coat had blue undertones in the dying light. He walked toward me, his ears never moving from my direction.

"Are you going to let me pet you again?" I asked, holding out the back of my hand.

He stopped at the railing and bent his head down to hang languorously, waiting to be touched.

"Well, that was easier than I expected." I smiled and reached out to brush his nose with the back of my hand.

He took a step closer, making me lean back to allow him into my space.

"You're affectionate today." Being careful of his wounds, I stroked his face, moving his long bangs to the side so I could rub his forehead and velvety ears.

I stayed with him until the sun started to set behind the hills. The clouds were soft and airy, giving the appearance that pink frosting had been spread throughout the pale purple backdrop of the sky.

"How's he doing?" Jake's voice was low and soft as he sidled up beside me.

I tensed, my insides both warmed and nauseated by his presence. He smelled so good, like leather and soap and hay, but the uncertain tone of his voice was unfamiliar. I shook all pesky, lustful thoughts from my head.

"He's doing really well." I examined the dwindling amount of grass in the pasture before shifting my eyes to a cut on my finger. I wondered how I'd injured myself as I looked everywhere but at the formidable man standing directly beside me.

"Bet you'll be riding him sooner than you think." Jake's attempt to be normal was admirable, but I cringed inwardly. I couldn't bear the awkward small talk. I shrugged, looking at Shadow, not sure if he'd ever let me onto his back. But then he nudged my shoulder, wanting more attention. "Yeah, maybe."

There was a pause, a breath that turned into three, and then four.

"What's going on, Zoe?" Jake asked, suddenly closer to me. His body heat seared through my clothes and into my skin. I wanted to melt into him, but I didn't want to feel the vulnerability that always came with being alone with him…not anymore. I stepped away.

"Why are you—are you still upset with me about what happened in town? Back at the river, I thought…"

I shook my head, not sure if I was lying. "I'm just tired, and I've got a lot on my mind. There's a lot going on, and…I think I'm just going to call it an early night." I turned toward the house.

Jake reached out and gripped my upper arm. "Please stop walking away from me." He paused. "Is it Dani?"

I shook my head again.

He let go of me, both of our arms dropping to our sides in exasperation. "You're not like Jason," he said bitterly.

I glared at him. "What's that supposed to mean?"

"You can't hold everything inside like he does." I could tell Jake felt slighted. "You tried that before and it didn't work, remember?" I could feel his anger rising, and I saw an image of me in his mind—the memory of my breakdown at Fort Knox, the night reality had crashed into me and I'd crumpled to the floor in the cafeteria, sobbing.

"Thanks for the reminder," I quipped quietly.

"Tell me what it is." The injured look in his imploring brown eyes made it impossible not to say something.

"I can't—"

"Why not?" He took a step closer, and I remembered how his arms had felt wrapped around me down at the river.

"Because—"

"Because why?"

"Because you're just going to leave!" I blurted. "That's why I never…I can't keep letting you in, Jake. I know that's how this thing between us ends."

"Oh, really?"

"Yes! And I don't have the strength for that. Not right now." My voice was unsteady and quiet. "Besides, with Becca and everything…things are changing."

His eyes widened.

I was floundering, losing my grasp on reason, wanting to give in to instant gratification, to just fall into his arms. But I couldn't allow myself to, so I tried again. "Things are already—"

"Things are already what?" He braced his hands against the fence, pinning me in place.

"—hard enough!" I straightened. "I can't—"

"Can't or don't want to? There's a difference. You have no idea—"

I pushed past him, on the verge of unrelenting tears. "I'm sorry, Jake, but I can't do this. Please. Just let me go."

Overwhelmed, I hurried into the house, relieved there was no one around to ask me any more questions. I passed the parlor and ran up the stairs to my room. Jake's room. *Our* room. I looked at the double bed, the old patchwork quilt covered by our conjoined, nylon sleeping bags. Just looking at our bed—the one that felt like it changed form weekly, but always felt the same with us in it together—the tears I'd been holding back began streaming down my cheeks. Taking a resolute step forward, I unzipped the sleeping bags, leaving them separated on top of the mattress. I was too exhausted to think anymore.

Leaving the door open, I hoped the heat from the fire downstairs would find its way in during the later hours of the night, since I wouldn't have Jake's body to warm me. I was too focused on the growing emptiness I felt to pay much attention to the whispers and movement in the parlor below. *I just need some sleep*, I told myself. *I'll pull myself together in the morning.*

I pulled my sweatshirt over my head, then wrestled to get out of my boots, eventually flinging them across the floor in frustration. My patience was wearing thin, and my bones were still cold from the river. I pulled off my pants, too exhausted to worry about finding and donning my pajamas, and crawled into the soft flannel lining of the sleeping bag. I exhaled a long, deep breath and nestled into its warmth.

The sound of the wooden floorboards creaking jarred me from the brink of sobs. My back was to the door, but I heard heavy footsteps entering the room and then boots falling to the floor. I heard the muted sound of metal being set on the wooden vanity and then the click-clack of Cooper's nails as he padded into the room to sleep on the floor on Jake's side of the bed.

The mattress depressed behind me as Jake lay down. He turned to me, curling his warm body around mine outside of my sleeping bag. His arm came around my middle, pulling me against him, and his worry and sadness enshrouded me.

I held my uneven breaths, hoping I could suffocate my sobs.

Jake said nothing. He whispered no reassurances, nor did he ask me to confide in him again. But he held me, and I clutched on to his strong, comforting arms as they tightened around me. I sobbed silently, thankful the room was dark.

21

DANI

MARCH 21, 1AE

Part of me wanted to stand up and pace, and part of me craved to reach out with my telepathy to tell Zoe and Jason that I'd found their mom…but I couldn't do either. The latter was off-limits because, though I was certain Dr. Wesley *was* their mother, she was also the one who created the Virus, killing almost every person my friends and I loved. Knowing what she'd done would hurt them more than her abandonment. They were better off thinking the Virus killed her.

As for the standing, I couldn't do that because I was in Dr. Wesley's office with her, trying to keep myself from attacking her. I had to sit on my hands to keep from scratching out her eyeballs.

Only a few words had been exchanged since I'd stormed into her office, and at least a quarter of an hour had passed in verbal silence. Staring into her jewel-blue eyes, I despised her, even more so for her striking resemblance to my two favorite people, and for what she'd done to them…abandoning them. *How did I* not *see it before? I can't believe I was so blind!*

Finally, my voice low and cold, I managed to ask, "Why?" When she didn't respond, I jumped to my feet and stalked to her desk, planted my hands on the surface, and leaned in. "Tell me why you did it. Tell me why you killed everyone."

She blinked, slowly, the rest of her body going completely still. "For my family. For my children. I had no choice." *Does she know that I know who she is?*

"There's always a choice," I snapped, but the words didn't sound as harsh as I'd intended. She was talking about Zoe and Jason—*my* Zoe and Jason—and, unwillingly, some of my fiery hatred for this woman dampened. *But I* want *to hate her...* "Explain," I demanded.

Dr. Wesley sighed, and her strength of will seemed to deflate, like she was letting go of a burden she'd carried all her life. She suddenly appeared an older, more haggard woman than she'd been a few seconds earlier. "Before my children were born," she said softly, "before my husband and I were married, I worked for a civilian company contracted by the Department of Defense. I made a breakthrough that landed our little lab on the DOD's radar, and the opportunity to receive their funding was one we couldn't turn down, so we relocated from our small Maryland town to a military base." She laughed softly, a sound devoid of humor, and shook her head. "Shortly after my team and I moved, I met my husband."

As I watched Dr. Wesley—Dr. Cartwright, in all reality—lose herself in memory, I lowered myself into one of the worn, padded chairs in front of her desk. I didn't think her story was going to be short, but if it contained the answers I sought, an explanation for why any person would do what she'd done, I could sit and listen and be patient. Why she was telling me her story, I didn't know, and honestly, I didn't care, just so long as she gave me answers... information...ammo. *Assuming she's telling the truth...*

"He was a soldier, one of the men in the unit assigned to guard us, which really meant keep an eye on us so we didn't hand potentially dangerous technology over to 'the enemy.'" She smiled wistfully, the past filling her eyes. "I hated him for months, but that was really just because I'd fallen for him almost the first moment I saw him, and I refused to give up my career for a man." She was quiet for a moment. "When I discovered what the military intended to do with my research, he was the one who helped me escape."

So she didn't want *to hurt anyone...but she still ended up killing everyone.* I tried to imagine Tom Cartwright, my best friend's scatterbrained, hardworking craftsman father, as Dr. Wesley's knight in camouflage armor. But I'd only known him as a troubled, middle-aged man, and picturing him as a soldier was impossible.

Quietly, I asked, "What were you researching?"

The doctor's hint of a smile disintegrated. "A base pair on a specific strand of DNA estimated to be present in a little over 10 percent of the human population. It held the genetic key to accessing never-before-seen mental and physical abilities."

"Like what we're experiencing now?" I asked.

She nodded. "One of my colleagues hypothesized that—" She halted, her gaze sharp, assessing. "How familiar are you with genetics?"

I shrugged. "Not very. I took a biological anthropology class as an undergrad, so I understand Darwinism, natural selection, and all that good stuff, but being able to picture a pretty, multicolored double helix is about as far as my DNA comprehension goes."

With a frown, Dr. Wesley nodded. "I'll keep it simple, then. Basically, we discovered the strand of DNA that, among other things, controls our genetic potential to exhibit an Ability. I discovered the base pair on the strand that inhibits—or used to inhibit—that potential. All we had to do was determine a way to delete the inhibiting pair, and then we could really see what the strand could do."

I held up a hand to interrupt. "Can you even do that—delete a gene?"

Shaking her head, Dr. Wesley corrected, "A base pair, not a gene, and nature does it every day. You have some understanding of evolution, so you know that genetic mutation, one of the driving forces behind evolution, is random, correct?" Whatever my personal feelings for the doctor were, I couldn't deny her genius. Her eyes practically glowed with it.

I nodded.

"Those natural, completely random mutations generally take place in three ways: substitution, when one base pair is substituted with another; deletion, when a base pair is left out; and insertion, when an entirely new base pair appears. Unfortunately, such mutations are completely unpredictable, usually harmful, and, for the most part, uncontrollable, not to mention limited by the reproductive rate of a species."

Raising my eyebrows, I said, "But…" The genetic changes caused by the Virus hadn't been limited to the next generation of humans; they'd impacted us all, changing everyone who survived.

"But," Dr. Wesley agreed. "Over two decades ago, a few months before my husband-to-be helped me flee from the military, I read an article by a brilliant young microbiologist on something he called 'gene therapy.' Have you ever heard of it?"

Entranced by her story, I shook my head. It was mind-boggling that the moves leading to the destruction of mankind had been set in play so long ago, before I was even born. Had anyone known the consequences of their actions? Had the demolition of civilization been the goal even then? Or were the key players just looking to make a new, stronger breed of people?

"Essentially, gene therapy is a way to *force* spontaneous genetic mutation, even in a fully grown subject."

Subject. I snorted and clarified, "Person."

"Person, cat, apple tree—anything with DNA," Dr. Wesley explained. "In gene therapy, a virus is the delivery method for the mutation—either to transport a new base pair for substitution or insertion, or to delete an existing base pair." Dr. Wesley dropped her eyes, looking at her hands instead of at me. "Unfortunately, though the virus we initially used was mostly harmless on its own, our trials proved that the gene therapy was too dangerous to continue researching and experimenting with."

"Trials? As in, *human* trials?"

"Well, we couldn't exactly use a bird, could we? And unless you know of a secret preserve of Homo sapiens neanderthalensis, our only route to test the procedure was to try it on our fellow humans." At seeing the appall warping my face, she added, "They were all volunteers."

I snorted again. "I'm sure. So what happened? You said it was too dangerous. Did the government shut the program down?"

Dr. Wesley shook her head. "If only. The gene therapy had an unfortunate side effect for most of the test subjects. During the first round, we only chose subjects who were confirmed carriers of the P-strand."

"P-strand?"

"Pandora strand." She laughed bitterly. "One of my lab assistants came up with it as a joke. She had no idea how appropriate the name was." There was a long pause before Dr. Wesley resumed her explanation. "We only chose people whose genetic makeup contained the P-strand, but we didn't notice the variation among different test subjects. The gene therapy was designed to take out the final base pair in that strand, which we'd identified as the Ability-inhibiting pair. But"—she took a heavy breath—"eighty percent of the test subjects in that first group had an additional base pair, which inhibited something else entirely, and in those subjects, *that* was the base pair that was deleted. We hadn't been looking for it, so we just…missed it," she said, an air of defeat in her voice.

So…what does that mean? I thought about my experiences in the post-Virus world over the past few months, and I was pretty sure I'd puzzled out what that additional base pair inhibited. "Let me guess—it inhibited insanity, and once it was deleted, those people lost it?"

Eyebrows raised, Dr. Wesley nodded. Apparently, I'd impressed her. *Go me.*

"It wasn't obvious at first," she explained, "just like the Abilities didn't develop immediately. But in time, it became clear. I begged my superiors to set the project aside. I told them it was far too dangerous, but they ordered another trial, this time with a random sampling of people who weren't preselected based on their genetic makeup. I hated myself for doing it, but I followed orders, carried out the trial, and cried myself to sleep every night. Tom was all that got me through it."

Looking into my eyes, imploring me to understand, she said, "There were one hundred people in that test group, and ninety-one of them died within a month of treatment. Not from the gene therapy, exactly, but from colds, allergies, blood infections caused by minor wounds, you name it. You see, unlike in the first trial, where we made sure *everyone* carried the P-strand, we didn't do so with the second trial group. Ninety-one of them didn't carry the P-strand. The strand that was in the place of the P-strand for *those* test subjects"—at my sudden scowl, she amended what she'd said—"for those *people* related directly to the immune system. Deleting the final base pair did something that almost completely destroyed their bodies' ability to heal. It was irreversible, and no matter how—" An uncontrollable sob choked off her words.

Sympathy welled inside me, but I shoved it away. She deserved her pain. *She killed Grams…Cam…Callie…her own husband…*

Voice cracking under the weight of her sorrow, she said, "No matter how many hours I spent in the lab, trying to find a cure, they all died. My superiors wouldn't even let us contact their families so they could speak to their loved ones one last time." After another choking sob, she regained her composure. "Tom said he would take me away…that we could start a new life somewhere else, where we would become other people—normal people—and hide from the horrors of what I'd done. We developed a plan that protected us, and once we were married and had children, protected our family, for almost ten years."

Tilting my head to the side, I said, "You disappeared?"

Dr. Wesley's answering grin was sly. "Better than you can imagine. Tom and I—we both carried the P-strand, and by some glorious twist of fate, neither of us had the extra base pair. It seemed like destiny at the time, like some higher power was guiding us, telling us we were doing the right thing. So, we gave ourselves the gene therapy treatment and waited for our Abilities to develop, hoping they would be in some way beneficial to our escape. You know mine—nulling others' Abilities—"

"And amplifying," I said, interrupting her. "The General only knows about *that* side of your Ability, doesn't he? I'd imagine he'd be pretty upset if he found out you could block other people's Abilities as well."

Her eyes narrowed, but she agreed with a stiff nod. She'd heard my not-so-subtle threat, and it seemed she would continue to cooperate. "Tom's Ability proved equally useful. He could alter people's memories, making them forget they'd ever seen us. It was the next best thing to being invisible."

I stared at her, flabbergasted. Overloaded on insane information, I'd yet to process the fact that Tom—Zoe and Jason's dad—had an Ability, or at least, he'd *had* one before he died of the Virus. *He died of the Virus.* Suddenly, several things clicked. "The Virus—it was different this time, wasn't it?"

"It was," she said. "It was a modified influenza virus, nearly universally contagious and designed to take advantage of the weakened immune systems of the non-P-strand carriers."

"And *you* created it that way, didn't you? You created it to kill everyone." Too angry to wait for an answer, I repeated my initial question, "Why?" *Why'd you create it? Why'd you leave your family? Why'd you kill everyone? Why?*

Dr. Wesley met my eyes, then immediately looked away. "Gregory—General Herodson—had been one of the lower officers overseeing my project in the beginning. He and I had gone on a few dates before I realized my feelings for Tom, and he convinced me to check his DNA for the P-strand. Like Tom and me, he was a viable candidate for the gene therapy. He convinced me to include him in the second trial, which I shouldn't have done because it invalidated the random selection process, but I did it anyway, hoping it would make him more amenable to letting me leave."

Raising her furious gaze to mine, she said, "It didn't. Tom and I escaped before Gregory's Ability was strong enough to really control anyone's minds, but once we were gone, he had several decades to strengthen and perfect his control...to plant people where he needed them. And for the past twenty-four years he's used *my* Ability—or half of it—to make his even stronger." From the fury in her voice, I could tell how much she hated him. *Good. At least we agree on that.*

Dr. Wesley took a few deep breaths, then said, "During the ten years Tom and I were gone, Gregory built up his own mind-controlled army within the military, and eventually he found us." She sounded utterly despondent. Broken.

Oh God...I can't *hate her.* I wanted to scream.

"We'd gotten married and had two children at that point—a young boy and a girl little more than a baby—and he threatened to kill them if I didn't join him...work for him...be his *plaything*." She spat out the final word, and for once, I didn't squash my sympathy. "He told me he loved me and needed me, and that if I attempted anything to be free of him—end my own life...try to end his—he would kill my children and husband. He had people ready to destroy my family if I hurt him or his plans in any way. He called it his 'contingency plan.'" With liquid blue eyes, she begged me to understand. "So you see, I had no choice. My children—"

"Are the only reason you're still alive," I said, standing. Honestly, it was mostly a bluff. I couldn't kill her, not now that I knew the truth of who she was and why she'd created the Virus, but she didn't need to know that.

Dr. Wesley eyed me warily. "So you know."

"That Zoe and Jason are your kids? Yeah." I took a step closer to her desk and held out my hand, palm up. "You have a master key. Give it to me."

She ignored my demand. "Will you tell them I'm here?" Her eyes were filled with equal amounts of hope and dread.

"No. I hate lying to them, but the truth would hurt them so much more than if they go on thinking you're dead."

"They would hate me. Thank you for—"

My face twisted into an ugly sneer. "I'm doing it for them, not for you," I spat. "They'd blame themselves, because if you *had* refused the General and let them die, everyone else might've gone on living. At least, that's how they'd see it."

She flinched like I'd slapped her.

"Give. Me. Your. Key. If you don't, I'll tell the General about the other half of your Ability and the neutralizer," I said, an icy chill coating my words.

Dr. Wesley reached into the pocket of her lab coat and pulled out an inconspicuous key. She placed it on my palm without touching my skin.

"Does it open his office?"

She shook her head. "Only *he* has those keys."

"Do you know why he sent a Re-gen to my people's camp?"

"No, I—" Her face filled with worry. "Are they alright?"

"They're fine." Reluctantly, I added, "Zo and Jason know you didn't die in the car crash. They found a letter you wrote to Tom—"

"Oh God," she whimpered as tears leaked from her eyes. "How…how'd you figure out who I was?"

I started stringing the key onto the cord with the red card and the guard's warehouse key. "You look like an older version of Zoe. I'm surprised I didn't suspect sooner, but you *were* supposed to be dead, so…"

"What are they like?" she asked softly.

I sighed, really not wanting to ease her pain, but I could hear Grams chiding me in my head: *I didn't raise you to be so heartless,*

Dani-girl. "Zo and Jason are…they're two of the best people I've ever known. Strong, smart, stubborn…I love them both very much. I'd die for them, and I'm pretty sure they'd do the same for me."

"They might, when they try to get you out of here. Then I'll have a reason to hate you as much as you hate me."

God, I hope not. Their deaths were my worst fear. *Wait—how does she even know about the escape?* I narrowed my eyes. "Gabe told you." *That little…argh!*

She shrugged. "I'm not the enemy, Danielle."

I raised one shoulder.

"You didn't have to blackmail me for that." She pointed to the key resting against my chest. "All you had to do was ask, and I would've given it to you."

I almost said, "I don't care," but I caught myself. I *did* care, and I suddenly felt monstrous for blackmailing her. *It's too late to take it back now.* "I'll do whatever I can to keep them safe."

"If your actions kill my children, then everything I've done to keep them safe will have been for naught. *That's* on you."

Ouch. I shook my head, irritated at myself for letting her get under my skin. "Zo and Jason might blame themselves for everyone's deaths if they knew about you, but I don't. I blame *you.*" I turned and headed for the door.

When my hand was on the doorknob, she asked, "Would you rather I'd killed myself, thus killing the two people you love so dearly? Gregory would have found another geneticist to engineer his virus, and everyone would've died anyway."

I opened the door and exited the office without responding, not on principle, not to give her the cold shoulder, but because I didn't have an answer. I hurried down the hallway, around a corner, and leaned my back against the wall. Slowly, I slid to the ground, and cried.

22

ZOE

MARCH 21, 1AE

I flung my bent arm up to block Sanchez's elbow strike. When sparring, I was required to focus on something other than the thoughts jumping around like pesky, filthy fleas trying to distract me. I stepped into Sanchez, hooking my left leg directly behind her right, and before she had a chance to react, I shoved her shoulder, throwing her off-balance. She started falling backward. Knowing my weakness was not moving away in time, she clutched my thick braid and pulled me down with her.

"You're such a bitch," I joked, panting on the ground beside her. We'd been at it for over an hour, and I was feeling it…everywhere.

"I told you to chop it off. It's not my fault you keep it long enough to pull." She flung her hands above her head and tried to catch her breath.

I'd thought many times about cutting my hair, but I was reticent. It was the only "old" part of me I had left.

"I think you'll get those achy muscles you wanted," she said as she rubbed her thigh. "You did a number on me today. Those knees of yours are knobby."

I only laughed.

A small smile tugged at her lips and she shook her head slightly. "You did good. You're quicker than you used to be and definitely stronger."

That was a relief. I wanted to be better. Beyond that, I wanted my body to be as sore and heavy-feeling as my mind. I wanted physical exhaustion to help me fall asleep without trailing, wistful thoughts bothering me before my brain finally turned off for the night. We'd been practicing our Abilities, too—stretching and flexing them as much as we could.

I sat up. "How are you feeling about your telepathy?"

"It is what it is. I doubt I'll ever be able to hear responses like Dani."

"Yeah, but one-way communication is better than none, and it seems like there are no distance barriers. That's even better."

"I'm sure there's a limit to how far, I just haven't found it yet."

I shook my head. "Whatever. At least your Ability's easy to control. It's straightforward."

"Maybe," she sighed. "But your control's been getting better."

"Yeah, I guess. I mean, I can turn it on and off. There are some people it doesn't work around very well." I thought about Jake. "But that might be more of a *me* thing than an Ability glitch."

Sanchez took a long, deep breath and held it. "I'm…concerned for you, Zoe."

My eyes snapped to her. "Why?"

"Your Ability is a saving grace in a lot of ways. You can tell when danger is coming now, or at least you're getting better at that. You know when someone's lying and when they're sad."

She was right. Feeling what my friends were feeling and seeing their most sacred memories was becoming increasingly easier.

"But you'll see things about people that you'll wish you hadn't. To me, that sounds more like a curse than a gift."

I thought about it for a minute—about Jake's private memories of his sister and of the intimate feelings Biggs and Sarah had whenever they were around one another. I thought about Sanchez's memories of her abusive childhood and how she'd come to be the woman she was—I agreed with her. My Ability *was* problematic and exhausting, but deep down I knew I probably wouldn't change it if I was ever given the chance…even if I couldn't really explain why.

We sat quietly for a moment before she jumped to her feet. "Come on. One more round before we head back."

It was my first day riding Shadow, so we only ventured a couple miles away from camp, far enough to give him some exercise and a change in scenery. Much to my apprehension, I didn't use a saddle because the clanking sound of it frightened him, but Carlos had helped me create a padded halter for his face, so I didn't worsen his healing wounds. Shadow had clearly been ridden before, making the experience a good one even though I worried I was hurting him half the time.

Sanchez and I rode between the rocky cliffs of a canyon, through a long-forgotten mining community. The sound of clomping hooves accompanied us up the rocky hillside as we made our way back to our little western town. The steady sound of the breeze and the frequent cawing of a hawk off in the distance lulled us into a lazy silence.

I thought about life a million years ago and how untouched everything had been. Then humans came along and cut everything down, took over, and corrupted most things that were natural and beautiful. But not anymore. I almost laughed as I considered the unexpected twist of fate. We were the minority again. We were the outnumbered visitors in a place that would continue to thrive. *We* were the ones fighting to survive.

A few paces in front of me, Sanchez sneezed, and I watched her for a moment, realizing how much she'd changed in the months I'd known her. While I found myself hardening into someone I barely recognized, she seemed to soften. She was still the epitome of feminine strength, but she also seemed more compassionate and vulnerable than before.

"I'm starting to think we might actually have a chance," she admitted as she leaned forward to pat Delilah's neck. "Between all our Abilities…" She shrugged. "I definitely think we have a chance."

"As long as Jason doesn't null us all in the middle of everything," I scoffed.

I immediately regretted saying his name. Sanchez's relaxed expression hardened, and she stared out at the grassland that stretched out before us as we kept moving in the direction of our camp, settled beyond the next bend of trees. Jason seemed to be her own form of kryptonite. She struggled to shrug off his indifference toward her, but she never seemed fully able to do it.

"Stop staring at me." She glared, but I knew her irritation was only a defense mechanism. She trusted me with her privacy the way I trusted her with my life.

The corner of my mouth lifted in sympathy as I felt her vulnerability surface for the second time since breakfast. She'd had another unpleasant run-in with Jason while he and Jake were gearing up to go hunting.

Their past was one she'd cherished before, but now it ate away at her. Years ago, they'd been friends who could grab a beer when they had a free evening or sit casually outside of a pool hall getting lost in conversation, completely forgetting about the time. Sanchez wasn't typically like that. Neither was Jason, and that's what had made their friendship so special to her. I wasn't sure if they'd ever been lovers, but the years they'd spent together on the same base had shown her that he was someone she could have grown to love if circumstances had been different.

None of it mattered anymore…at least, not to him. He never so much as glanced her way unless he had to, practically treating her like a leper. His cold shoulder and one-word responses created tension so thick that we all grew anxious when the two were in close proximity. The longer Dani was away, the more palpable the tension became.

"I wish we had a better idea of what sort of Abilities they have access to at the Colony," I thought aloud. "So we really know what we're up against…so that we can form *some* sort of a plan." I thought about the programs Dani was learning about, and the altered "people" she was meeting. *What else is going on that she* hasn't *seen?* The possibilities frightened me.

Sanchez took a swig from her water bottle and slid it back into her saddle bag before looking over at me. "We know more than we did," she said frankly.

I nodded, and we plodded through the scant woods and into the ghost town, heading for the stable. When we were finished with the horses, I took advantage of the sunlight to finish a sketch of Shadow I'd been working on, while Tavis, Chris, and Sanchez went to get a fresh batch of water. Jason and Carlos were probably at the sheriff's office, whittling like they had been the last couple days, and Harper and Jake were playing fetch with the dogs. Sam seemed to be the only one unaccounted for.

Setting my sketchpad down, I gazed around. I noticed Sam-sized Nike footprints in the dirt and decided to follow them. The closer I came to the Sheriff's office, the clearer I could hear a quiet whoosh and thunk coming from the shooting range we'd created behind it. We'd been using the cowboy cutouts we'd found in the General Store as targets and hay bales and sacks of fake sugar and flour as obstacles.

I wandered over, only to find Sam standing in the last patch of sunshine in the center of the shooting range, his stance wide and his arms upraised; one arm pulled a bowstring back to his ear and the other held the bow extended in front of him. He was aiming an arrow at one of the bullet-riddled cowboys furthest from him.

I remained quiet, watching Sam's deep concentration and

feeling the focus radiating from him. "I can feel you watching me," he said without looking in my direction.

Just like he could see the blood covering my clothes in the darkness? Interesting. A smirk lifted the side of my mouth, and I took a step toward him, arms crossed over my chest. "You look like you know what you're doing," I said playfully.

Sam let go of the bowstring, and the arrow flew straight through the air, piercing where the cowboy's heart might be. He readied another arrow, and I watched him go through the same motions again—he let out a deep breath, shifted his feet, aimed, took another deep breath, and then released the bowstring. The arrow sailed off to the left, piercing a cowboy's groin area.

"I like the way you think," I said, laughing. "Where did you learn archery?"

"Tavis." Sam readied another arrow and, again, aimed and released. When he let go, he hit his target spot on—another cowboy, right in the chest.

"Why a bow and arrow?" I asked, half knowing the answer already. He was young, and I assumed Tavis hadn't wanted him to carry a gun. There was something unsettling about making a child shoot to kill, no matter the situation. Even though it was awkward and harder to carry around, the bow seemed less imposing and more…civil in some strange way. It made sense to me. I hated the feeling of cold metal in my hands and the sound of cracking gunfire.

"I don't like guns," he answered.

"Me neither," I said honestly. I stood and watched him while he walked to retrieve his arrows a few dozen yards away.

"Then why do you have one strapped to your leg?" he called.

"I need to be able to protect myself," I said with a grin. "Unlike you, no one's ever taught me to use a bow."

Sam looked at me as he returned. He was considering something; I could see it in his appraising eyes. "Want to make a deal?"

"Perhaps," I said, tilting my head in curiosity.

"I'll get Tavis to get you a new bow from the archery place in town, and we'll teach you how to use it, if you'll teach me how to draw." He stood there, watching my thoughtful expression, waiting.

"You like to draw?"

He nodded. "I saw your sketchbook in the house. I liked the one you started of the pregnant lady with crazy hair."

It was the sketch of Sarah I hadn't finished in her absence. "Well, thanks. But that seems like an unfair deal, don't you think? You'll give me a bow *and* teach me how to use it, and all I have to do is give you drawing lessons?" As I finished, I saw a memory of his mother painting in a room scattered with paints and rags and canvases. She'd been an artist.

"Take it or leave it," he said sharply.

I stifled a laugh. "Do you know how to defend yourself if you don't have your bow?" I asked, an idea forming in my mind.

His face was expressionless.

"How about you practice hand-to-hand self-defense with me when I train during the day, plus you help me with the bow, and then in the evenings we'll draw?"

He nodded in agreement. "When do we start?"

I smiled. "How about now? But we'll have to make this one a short session. I've been training all day, and my body aches. Sound good?"

He eyed me skeptically.

"What can I say, I'm old," I said with a smirk. "Humor me."

He handed me his bow and an arrow from his quiver. "Here you go."

I stared at the bow for a moment before accepting it, surprised by the weight of it in my hand.

"You have to hold it like this…" Sam maneuvered the fingers on my left hand around the bow's grip and then showed me how to hold the arrow between my index and middle finger with my right. "The fletching has to be lined up like this," he said, rotating the arrow in my grasp. "Otherwise the arrow will shoot off in that direction." He pointed to a pine tree off to my right. "Stand with your feet spread apart a little…good. Now raise it up." He stepped away to demonstrate with an invisible bow of his own.

I did as my young instructor commanded and allowed myself a smile. *I'm getting archery lessons from a ten-year-old.*

"Don't smile," Sam chided, and I cleared my throat to stifle another laugh. "Pull the string back to your cheek," he said, observing me. "No, further." Sam huffed and groaned as he guided my arm back further. "Okay, now let go."

Taking a deep breath, and then another, I squeezed my left eye closed to focus on the painted target. My fingers released the string and it snapped back into place. A grin spread across my lips as I watched the arrow glide past the target and land somewhere behind it. I was far from hitting my mark, but I felt victorious nonetheless. "I did it."

"You need practice," Sam said dryly. "But that wasn't too bad."

We continued practicing, and after sighing at me a couple times, Sam finally smiled with pride. After each shot, he had me back up a yard or two, testing me. When I'd let my seventh arrow fly, he crossed his arms over his chest and smirked. "Good," he said, walking beside me to retrieve the arrows.

"I kinda like this," I admitted.

"I knew you would."

I pushed his shoulder playfully. "You think you know me so well, Sam?"

He nodded. "Yep."

"Having fun?" Tavis called as he pushed away from the side of the sheriff's building.

I jumped. "Jesus! I didn't know you were watching."

He laughed, clearly amused. "Not long. How'd you do?"

"I think I did pretty good, actually," I said, handing Sam his bow. I tied my hair back into a knot to keep it out of my face. "But you'll have to ask my teacher for an unbiased opinion." I looked back at Sam.

"Zoe did better than you," Sam interjected with a subtle smirk, and I winked at him in gratitude as my own smile grew.

"I wasn't going to say anything," I said with a teasing shrug.

Tavis pointed to himself. "Better than me? This guy right here?"

Sam peered up into the sky, squinting and ruminating like he wanted to make absolutely sure. "Yep."

Tavis's mouth was gaping in mock horror, and then he gave Sam a wry look. "Well, we can't all have perfect aim like you, Sam." He ruffled the boy's brown hair.

Having collected all of Sam's arrows, the three of us headed back toward the boarding house. "Did you guys bring back more water?" I asked, realizing I was thirsty.

Tavis nodded, his thumbs hooked in the pockets of his jeans. "We did, and Harper's making rabbit stew, so I hope you're hungry."

"Ravenous, actually. How about you, Sam?"

"Meh, I could eat," he said casually right before his stomach grumbled.

I nudged his shoulder with my elbow. "'Meh?' I don't think your tummy agrees with you." I laughed, and when I glanced up, I noticed Jake and Sanchez watching us from the stable. Sanchez acknowledged us with a nod and turned toward the paddocks, but Jake's eyes lingered on the three of us. His eyes met mine before he turned and followed Sanchez.

23

DANI

MARCH 21, 1AE

I twirled my fork, making a nest of noodles and tomato sauce on my plate. This evening was the first time I'd been in Gabe's house, but it wasn't much of a change in scenery. His kitchen was much like mine, filled with taupe counter tiles, walnut cabinets, and an asymmetrical island. We were sitting across from each other at the small, square oak kitchen table.

"Are you sure?" I asked after chewing and swallowing my latest bite. It tasted of garlic and tomato sauce from a jar. Gabe wasn't a bad cook, but his skills didn't come close to Cam's. *I was spoiled in my previous life.*

"I'm too recognizable to be out after curfew. It's an impossibility…and you shouldn't go either. It's too dangerous." He watched me, his pale blue eyes pensive. "Maybe you can just tell those Re-gens—"

"Camille and Mase," I corrected. I was getting tired of everyone—except for Dr. Wesley, I acceded reluctantly—treating the Re-gens like dogs. They were trained, experimented on, and kept ignorant in the most ludicrous, disturbing ways, and though I knew their brains worked a little differently, they were still human, more or less. They had human emotions and human reactions, and I wanted Gabe to treat them like…well, humans.

Gabe took a deep breath and gently set down his fork. "Maybe you can tell Camille and Mase what you're looking for, and they can carry out the search for information for you." After a pause, he added, "I really don't think you should endanger yourself, especially not with everything going down tomorrow night."

I not-so-softly dropped my fork. "Oh, but I should let *them* risk their lives because they're what…not *real* people? They have feelings like you and me, Gabe, you just have to give them the chance to show you."

"But they're *not* like you and me, Dani," he snapped. He lowered his hands to his lap, but I could see his arms tensing as he clenched and unclenched his fists. "Not anymore. I know they look like normal people and they talk like normal people and, hell, they probably really do have normal human emotions to some degree, but they're not the same as us…they're not the same as they used to be. She…their brains are different…closed off to me." Running his fingers through his blond hair, he sighed. "I don't trust them."

"Maybe you're right, maybe they are different, but you're right about another thing that's more important—they *are* my friends, as much as you are." *More so, even,* I thought. *They haven't betrayed me.* Pulling a folded-up piece of paper out of my jeans pocket, I said, "Any information you can give me to answer these questions will help us plan our escape better."

"*Our* escape…" Gabe repeated as he reached across the table to snatch the paper from my fingers. It was filled with the many questions I'd written to gather information about the Colony after my mind-convo with Zoe and Jason the previous afternoon. After several long, silent minutes, Gabe stood, strode over to the sink, and pulled a lighter out of a nearby drawer. He held the piece of paper over the sink, and with a flick of the lighter, set it aflame.

"What are you doing?" I screeched, jumping up as I watched the paper shrivel into an ashy ball.

Gabe dropped it before the tiny flames burned his fingers, and shook his head. "It's evidence against you—against both of us. I'll gather as much information as I can tomorrow morning, but no list. Someone might find it," he told me.

I forced myself to reclaim my seat. "Why'd you say '*our* escape' like that?" I asked softly.

"Like what?"

"Like you aren't actually planning to join me. We've been over this. You promised," I reminded him.

He didn't answer immediately. "Why do you even want me to leave with you?" he finally asked into the sink. "After what I've done to you—"

"Because I care about you!" I blurted without thinking, and it was true. *I do care about him...probably more than I should.*

He spun around, facing me, his look hopeful. "What are you say—"

Before he could finish, I added, "I'd hate to see you stuck here forever, or worse, hurt because I left you behind. I couldn't live with myself knowing I'd done that." I shrugged. "Besides, I'd like you with me while I plot to take *his mightiness* down. You know things...you're useful."

Gabe leaned back against the counter. "It might also be useful for me to stay here...for you to have someone on the inside. I can do more from in here."

What's his deal? Why could he possibly want to stay? Is it Dr. Wesley? "I already have someone in the belly of the beast, and she's far closer to the brain than you are. You're, like, down in the intestines, but she's working her way up the esophagus."

I'd hoped my ridiculous analogy might wipe some of the torn expression off his face, but it only deepened it. "Wes shouldn't have to—"

"Why not?" I snapped. "She owes us. She owes everyone."

He held my eyes for a moment longer, then looked away as he walked around the island to reclaim his seat at the table. "She's not the monster you've made her out to be in your mind. She didn't have a choice. Maybe she can come with us, too."

Bad, bad *idea.* There was no way I was letting Jason and Zoe find out the truth about their mom…about what she'd done to protect them. "She's seeking redemption, Gabe. I highly doubt she'd ever agree to leaving"—desperately, I hoped I was right about that—"but if it makes you feel better, ask her. Invite her, whatever. I don't care," I lied.

Gabe was silent for a long time, looking into my eyes like he was studying my soul. "Fine, I will. And I *will* leave with you, regardless of her answer." He looked away, staring down at the table like he was trying to burn a hole in it.

"How long have you been working with her?" I asked.

He said nothing for a while, then finally, "I knew of her, but I didn't *know* her until the Virus started spreading throughout the base."

So he didn't help kill everyone. My relief almost choked me. "Good to know." I watched him for a few heartbeats, wondering what he was thinking about. *Is he making plans for tomorrow…for the escape?* "Do you have a way to get your friend out?" I asked. Gabe was always very guarded when he spoke of the woman who was "like a sister" to him—I knew next to nothing about her.

"I, uh…I'm taking care of it." Before I could ask for clarification, he said, "You, uh, probably need to leave soon to get ready for your excursion tonight, but before you go, I want to give you something."

Wait…what?

Meeting my eyes, Gabe stood. He walked around the table, pulled out the chair nearest mine, and sat. As he reached into the pocket of his slacks, he said, "I wasn't sure I wanted to give you this, but…"

I had no idea what he was talking about, but I was getting the very uncomfortable feeling that he was about to cross the just-friends boundary I'd carefully constructed. My eyes were wide.

Gabe set a small digital camera down on the corner of the table. "Take this with you tonight," he said, looking into my eyes as he nudged the camera closer to me with his fingertips. "It's fully charged and has a sixty-four-gig memory card, so you should be able to take pictures of whatever you find. Just…" His eyes squinted, his expression turning pleading. "Just please be careful with it. If anyone finds it on you…"

"Gabe, I…thank you," I said, picking up the little camera and turning it on to get a feel for its various settings. "I mean it. This'll be a huge help."

"I wish you weren't going at all."

"I know."

Before she left the previous afternoon, Camille had given me the address of the location where I would meet up with her and Mase at midnight. It was an empty house in an unoccupied part of the expansive residential area.

At a quarter to midnight, I slipped out the back door to my house as quietly as possible. Ten minutes later, I'd made it a block to the south, flitting from shadow to shadow, grateful that the moon had waned to a little less than half its full size. The house where we were to meet was on my right, looking almost identical to both mine and Gabe's. It was a two-story, modern craftsman painted a deep earth tone I couldn't make out in the darkness. As I stepped onto the overgrown lawn, I heard a soft whisper coming from the front porch and froze.

"It's too dangerous," a male voice whispered. I was fairly certain it was Mase.

"Nobody's going to catch us," Camille countered.

"That's not what I meant."

After a brief pause, Camille whispered, "I have to know. I only know what you told me before…which wasn't much." Again, she paused, and when she continued, her soft voice held a plea. "Giant, I *need* to. Don't *you* want to know?"

"I'm afraid."

Camille cooed soothingly. "You'll always be my Giant, no matter what we find out, okay?" I heard nothing for a few seconds, then Camille's, "Thank you."

Feeling awkward, I took a few more steps and cleared my throat. The noise sounded obscenely loud, and I cringed.

"C'mon," Camille whispered, stepping out of the impenetrable shadows and onto the porch steps. She was wearing military gear —fatigues and a few weapons—which made her look more like a girl playing dress-up than a soldier. "We've got stuff for you to put on. You can change inside."

Camille reached for the door handle, and I started up the steps. I could finally see Mase in the inky darkness. Only after I stopped beside Camille did I hear a click, and she twisted the knob. She'd unlocked the door, but she hadn't used a key.

"Uh…Camille?" I said quietly.

"Yeah?"

"What exactly is your Ability?" I was pretty sure I'd just watched her pick a lock with her mind.

She turned her face to me, and her eyes appeared to be half-dollar pools of night. "I control metal."

"So…why'd you need me to get Dr. Wesley's key?"

Camille opened the door and ushered Mase and me inside the house before answering. "We needed to know how committed she was. She won't talk to me, not really, and she almost never interacts with Mase. She still sees us as, um…"

"Puppets?" I offered. The three of us stood clustered together in the entry hall. "Someone she can control, sort of like how the General controls everyone else?"

She nodded enthusiastically. "Yes, exactly."

"And the key?"

“Oh, right. If she gave you the key—an action that could pretty much seal her death—it meant she was fully committed.”

Committed to what? But before I could ask, Mase thrust a black duffel bag at me and said, “Put this stuff on.”

It took me nearly ten minutes and Mase’s help to shuffle through all the clothing and gear in the bag and get myself fitted up. When I was finished, I was pretty sure I looked as out of place as Camille. Beside Mase, we looked like a couple of elves who’d escaped from the North Pole and bedecked themselves in combat gear. Regardless, I figured it was a better disguise than running around after curfew in black hoodies and jeans.

“Alright,” I said once my pistol, combat knife, and assault rifle were situated. I shifted my shoulders and cringed at the noise. “There’s no way I can move silently wearing all this.”

“Silent isn’t the goal,” Mase said, looking down at me with no hint of amusement. “We want to look like we belong, not like we’re sneaking around.”

Hide in plain sight? It made sense, so I didn’t argue. I glanced at the door. “So, uh…where to first?”

“We’re only going one place,” Camille said, grinning wickedly.

“And that place is?”

“Headquarters.”

I stared first at Camille, then at Mase, before taking a deep breath. “Shit,” I said as I exhaled. Headquarters was where the General’s office was located, and there were bound to be guards posted at all hours.

“Please tell me you have a plan,” I said weakly.

Camille’s expression melted into innocence, and it was Mase’s turn to grin. His smile was even more wicked than Camille’s had been.

The plan, as it turned out, was comprised of Camille using the metals that saturate the human body to hold any guards we came across temporarily motionless while Mase and I injected them with a chemical compound that would both knock them out for several hours and cause short-term memory loss. By the time they could recall their attackers—if they ever could—we would be long gone. Or we would be dead. Either way, we would be out of the General's reach. *Unless he brings me back as a Re-gen...*

We took out the two soldiers guarding the main entrance without complication, and Mase even managed to prop them up against the building so the unlikely passersby wouldn't suspect foul play simply by seeing the out-of-commission guards. Two more men were stationed in the dark hallway just outside the General's office, and they went down just as easily. My Ability to observe and keep track of the minds around me like a built-in radar was priceless.

Mase searched the downed guards while Camille and I waited patiently by the door. Neither had the three keys required to unlock the deadbolts barring the door. Fortunately, we had Camille, who was better than any key. She closed her eyes and concentrated. After two achingly long minutes, she glanced at me over her shoulder, her lips spread into a self-satisfied smirk.

It was my turn. I concentrated, and, not sensing anything beyond the door, gave Mase a go-ahead nod. He shouldered between us and opened the door to the dark office. All clear.

"Next shift change is at two," Mase whispered. "Nobody should be walking around the building until then." He glanced at the high-tech watch on his wrist and pushed a button to light up the face. "We've got about an hour until we need to be gone."

"Okay." I closed my eyes and focused, searching the night sky with my Ability. I couldn't find what I was looking for in or over the Colony, so I reached beyond. My consciousness expanded, an undetectable sphere of mental awareness, and I found my quarry less than a mile to the east, soaring over a prairie as they hunted.

For the briefest moment, I felt like I was flying with them…like I *was* them. *What the hell was that?*

The three owls were confused when they felt my touch, but curiosity convinced them to heed my call. They flew across the starlit sky with incredible speed, agreeing to keep watch over the building I showed them mentally—headquarters—while we were inside it. I could've used my Ability to observe the movement of minds around me, but then I wouldn't have been able to concentrate fully on the search for information.

"I've called in some friends to keep watch from above. They'll let me know if anyone's coming our way," I told Camille and Mase.

They said nothing and simply stared at me, clearly confused.

"Oh, um, my Ability works on animals, too," I explained. I watched as understanding lit their features in the darkness. "So… I'll take the desk, I guess, if you guys want to start searching the file cabinets?"

I reached into the neck of my fatigues and pulled the camera Gabe had given me out of my sports bra. "Let me know if you find anything important and I'll take a picture."

Again, their faces filled with confusion.

Crap…they don't know what a camera is… "Just let me know if you find anything that looks important or like it could help us get out of here, okay?"

Finally, they nodded and turned to the wall of file cabinets, clicking on their flashlights before opening neighboring drawers.

With a sigh, I looked down at the General's desk. It took me a moment to figure out why it looked so odd. There was no computer, not the laptop or tablet I'd seen General Herodson using the only other time I'd been in his office. Instead, all that cluttered his desktop was a stack of trays labeled *IN, OUT,* and *URGENT*, a cup holding writing utensils, the usual office supplies—stapler, tape dispenser, and notepads—and a stack of manila file folders.

One of those folders was labeled *DANIELLE O'CONNOR. Has the General been checking up on me?*

I opened the folder. My face stared up at me from an eight-by-ten photograph I'd never seen before. I wasn't positive, but it looked like it had been taken *inside* my borrowed house. *Creepy.* There were only a few sheets of paper beneath the photo, so I quickly flipped through them, taking a picture of each to read later.

The rest of the folders were dossiers devoted to individuals, just like the one with my name on it. *Why is mine here with these other people's?* Unwilling to waste time searching each and every paper, I photographed the profile sheet contained within each folder. It gave a good overview on each individual, including their personal identifying information, a small photo, basic characteristics, Ability, and an "Additional Notes" section at the bottom. *They must be important to the General too.*

Underneath the stack of dossiers was a black, leather-bound organizer. I unzipped it carefully, not wanting to disturb any loose contents. My caution proved fortuitous—several dozen loose papers, tabbed and color-coded, had obviously been organized in a specific order; messing up that order could easily clue the General in to what his nocturnal intruders were searching for, and I was determined to do everything I could to avoid that. He couldn't know my plans, couldn't know my intentions, until I was long gone. Not if I wanted to make it out alive.

I scanned the top sheet, then the three beneath it. It took my brain a few seconds to register what my eyes were seeing. It was a detailed outline of the General's schedule for the next two days, including start times, end times, and locations for each appointment. His schedule was packed, even in the evening hours. I took pictures of the four pages before moving on.

The next set of papers had been paper-clipped together, and a small green sticky tab had been stuck to the upper right corner of the top sheet. *DAILY GUARD ROTATION* had been printed neatly on it. I barely glanced at the words written on the pages as I snapped pictures of each. The remaining papers related to other day-to-day matters, but none seemed significant to my escape.

I almost squealed with excitement, and my heart most definitely skipped a beat, when I set all of the loose papers aside. The first item bound in the organizer was a detailed, laminated map of the Colony. I didn't hesitate before taking a picture.

"Dani?"

I jumped and looked up to find Camille standing on the other side of the desk, holding a folder out to me. *PROJECT EDEN.*

"Sorry," she said softly before waving the folder back and forth. "This looks important. I thought you'd want to see it."

Smiling, I laughed nervously and accepted the folder. "Thanks. Don't worry about me…spy work always makes me jumpy."

Camille cocked her head and shrugged before returning to the file drawer she'd been searching. I spared the briefest moment to watch her and Mase as they searched, side by side, stealing momentary glances at each other.

The breeding program, Project Eden, wasn't on the top of my to-learn-more-about list, but I appreciated Camille's help anyway. "I'd love to find anything that tells us more about the Controllers, or the Tabula Rasa program," I said quietly. "*Please* tell me if you find anything like that."

Quickly, I flipped through the papers in the Project Eden folder and found that it was a log of some kind, though I had no clue as to why Camille had thought it important. I returned to the top sheet and started skimming.

"Camille, I don't understand…" My eyes widened as I trailed off.

01.13.GT01 SUBJECT #0001 F26CO0021
Pregnancy failed—2 weeks
Spontaneous abortion, cause unknown

01.15.GT01 SUBJECT #0002 F30MT1534

Pregnancy failed—1 week
Spontaneous abortion, cause unknown

01.15.GT01 SUBJECT #0003 F21CO0372
Uterine hemorrhaging, fetus stabilized

01.16.GT01 SUBJECT #0004 F32OH1839
Pregnancy failed—2 weeks
Spontaneous abortion, cause unknown

01.17.GT01 SUBJECT #0003 F21CO0372
Pregnancy failed—4 weeks
Spontaneous abortion, cause unknown
NOTE: Fetus autopsied, appeared far older, possibly 12 weeks. Was fertilization date miscalculated?

01.17.GT01
Evidence indicating dire circumstances. Extreme measures required. Project Eden instituted.

"Oh my God," I breathed. *But Sarah's pregnant, and she* seems *fine…more or less.* I flipped to the last sheet in the folder and read the three log entries there. They were from the previous day.

03.20.GT01 SUBJECT #0103 F23CO0112
Pregnancy failed—3 weeks
Spontaneous abortion caused by genetic incompatibility

03.20.GT01 SUBJECT #0106 F26NV2315
Pregnancy failed—4 weeks
Spontaneous abortion caused by genetic incompatibility

03.20.GT01 SUBJECT #068 F29CO0834
7-week checkup—fetus and mother appear healthy

NOTE: Fetal growth extremely advanced. Would place at 27 or 28 weeks if pregnancy hadn't been monitored since fertilization.

TREATMENT REC: Switch to daily checkups.

"Camille," I whispered without tearing my eyes away from the documents. "Did you find anything else about Project Eden?"

When she didn't respond, I glanced at her. She and Mase were sitting on the floor, each with an open folder, the contents of which they were reading intently.

"Camille?"

24

MASE

MARCH 21, 1AE

Mase watched Camille's silhouette as she handed Dani a folder, replaying what Camille had told him about normals—about the things they did that were forbidden to Re-gens. Dani had offered the use of one of the rooms in her house in exchange for the two Re-gens' help. When Camille relayed the offer to Mase, his mind had screamed *NO* while his mouth had formed a single word: yes. He hadn't meant to agree, but something uncontrollable inside him had taken charge.

It was becoming difficult for Mase to focus on the files in front of him. He kept imagining doing what Camille had described and forgetting his current task. He wondered how—or *if*—it could even work. They were just so different. Camille was small and delicate, while Mase was…not. He was her Giant. She was soft, light, and fragile, while he was hard, dark, and prone to fits of uncontrollable strength and violence. But mostly, he thought Camille just seemed too small for what she described to work. Not that he wouldn't give it a try…

Shaking his head, Mase closed the drawer of supply lists he'd been searching and knelt to open the bottom drawer. As soon as his flashlight illuminated the labels on the tabs of the folders, he knew what he'd found.

AJ-01. AJ-02. AS-01. BM-01. CA-01. CL-01.

Re-gen identifiers, just like the tattoos on the inside of his and Camille's wrists. Each folder had to be devoted to an individual Re-gen. Mase pulled out the CL-01 folder, his hand shaking. CL-01 was Camille's Re-gen identifier, what everyone besides Dr. Wesley, Dani, and Mase called her.

Setting it on the carpet nearby, Mase scanned the tabs in search of another identifier—his. About halfway back, MA-01, thicker than Camille's folder, awaited him. He claimed it and shut the drawer, then turned to sit with his back against the file cabinet. He stretched out his legs in front of him just as Camille returned. When Mase handed her the other file—*her* file—she joined him on the floor.

Mase's fingers itched to open his folder, but his stomach twisted into knots. He felt like he'd swallowed a bucket of rocks and they were churning around and around inside him. He had no idea what he would learn about himself, about who he'd been, once he opened it. He only knew what Camille had told him.

Father had found Mase and his men trying to help Camille when she'd become trapped in one of the warehouses. Because Mase had tried to hide her, Father realized Mase was no longer trustworthy and decided it was necessary to enroll him in the Re-gen program—to control him and his Ability—and killed the men with him.

Camille had relayed everything that Mase had told her in the warehouse: that he'd known her before she'd been made into a Re-gen, that he'd taken care of her when she was younger, that he would take care of her still, rescue her. But in the end, it hadn't mattered, and *Camille* had been the one to rescue *him*. With truths about his past, Camille had freed Mase from the prison of control

Father forced on his newly made Re-gens. But she hadn't known much. Now he could learn more.

With a deep breath, Mase opened the folder, shone his flashlight on the top paper, and began to read.

His full name was Mason Kyle Atwell, and he'd been twenty-one years old. He was African-American, not that he understood what that meant, and was from Minneapolis, MN, which he also didn't really understand. As far as Mase knew, there was only the Colony and outside the Colony. His Ability was described as "physical enhancement through the manipulation of hormones and neurotransmitters, namely epinephrine." He frowned; instead of explaining his past, the information contained within the folder only generated more confusing questions.

Near the bottom of the first page, there was a short paragraph written in a hand Mase recognized—Father's. The rest of the information had been typed. Curious, he read:

01/03/GT01—It has been brought to my attention that CPL Atwell shows resistance to mental manipulation. If his resistance leads to the beginning signs of disobedience, he should be seriously considered for the Re-gen program. Drs. Wesley and McLaughlin agree that his Ability is too important to warrant a simple execution, and they seem certain that the Re-gen process would bring him back under my control. It is worth noting that CPL Atwell has been with me on this base for over two years and has never displayed overt disobedience. I will talk with my advisors and explore possible assessment scenarios.

Mase glanced at Camille out of the corner of his eye. He was tempted to ask her if she could explain any of Father's words, maybe tell him what he'd done to warrant Father's suspicion, but Camille was equally immersed in learning about herself. Remotely,

Mase heard Dani muttering something, but he turned his attention back to the folder containing pieces of his past life.

Beneath the first page was sheet after sheet of service records. Mase knew he'd been in the Army, but now he had proof. He scanned the information, paging through the stack until he reached something new: a handful of lined pages stapled together, each filled with handwriting—*his own* handwriting, it seemed. He started at the beginning.

Your name is Mase. Don't let anyone call you Mason—that name was for Mom and Nana, and they're both dead now. Fuck (that's your favorite word, by the way), I don't know how to do this. They told me to write down my life story, but I've never been much of a writer. Doc suggested that writing a letter to myself...my dead, future self...might make it easier. I don't know why it matters. You're probably never going to read this. Actually, I bet they're just trying to get more information out of me before they give me the juice.

Ha. The Juice. Don't drink the Kool-Aid. Dad used to say that. "Be your own man, Mase. Defend your country, your freedom, but for God's sake, don't drink the Kool-Aid." That's what he said when I told the family that I'd signed the Army recruitment papers instead of enrolling in college. We needed the money...Dad just took a pay cut and the school district let Mom go, and we were about to lose the house. Didn't matter that Mom was one of the best goddamn teachers they had. Most of the teachers they laid off were the good ones...just hadn't been there long enough or didn't teach the right subjects. Maybe General Herodson's right, and the world will be better after the "Great Transformation."

Nah. I drank the Kool-Aid, and now I wish I hadn't. It's all turned to shit. I volunteered for some experimental trials a couple years back, right after basic training. The money was too good to pass up, especially with Mom's cancer coming out of remission and General Herodson's vision of a brighter future, a prosperous society filled with improved humans. His idea was visionary. At first the changes were great, like my shit had been turned into money and my piss into beer, but then I started to notice things. Sure, I was super fucking strong and fast—stronger and faster than anyone I'd ever met—but there were odd things happening around the base. Secrets being kept from superiors off-base and people disappearing.

About two months ago, I was given a yellow band to wear around my left arm and given orders to prevent any person from leaving the base, with force if necessary. People could enter, they just couldn't leave. And just like that, this place turned into Hotel fucking California. I was tempted to disobey, to inform someone off-base of the coup, but I'd been ordered not to, and I'd seen what Herodson does to people who disobey him. He likes to use family members when his freaky ability to convince people to follow his orders doesn't work. Now I know it's his <u>*Ability*</u>*, but I didn't understand it then.*

His mind control doesn't work on me as well as it does on other people. I pretended to go along with everything he said, not questioning when innocents were hurt or killed, first because I feared for my family's safety, and later, after I knew they were dead, for the simple sake of survival. And for my men...my poor, ignorant, mind-controlled men.

But then Camille showed up and the shit hit the fan. I tried to help her, to save her from the punishment General Herodson doled out to unidentified intruders, but the girl I'd once known was gone. She'd been replaced by a deceitful, dead woman. Maybe I won't care once I'm dead too. Or undead. I don't fucking know how it works, other than I die and they bring me back like a fucking zombie.

Maybe she couldn't help it because of what she's become, but her betrayal...fuck, it hurts. She was working with Herodson. It was planned, all of it, like some sort of a sick test. Somehow, Herodson figured out that we grew up together. For all I know, she flat-out told him. He used that connection to prove that I was disloyal, that I was a traitor. If I am a traitor, it's not for this. If I'm a traitor, I'm a traitor against humanity and I have been since I first signed up for the trials, since I first let them inject me with that gene therapy crap, since I first drank the fucking Kool-Aid.

I suppose it wouldn't be so bad, that I could accept my fate as what I deserve for looking the other way for so long, but my men are dead. I forced them to agree to keep quiet about Camille, and because they listened to me, because my command momentarily overrode Herodson's or his lackeys' commands, and because they didn't have useful enough Abilities to warrant bringing them back as Re-gens, they were killed. They're dead. He made me watch while they were executed...shot in the head. Punishment for my disobedience, he claimed. Apparently I needed to be punished, since becoming a Re-gen is supposedly a reward. Yeah, like being turned into a walking dead man is so fucking great.

Maybe I shouldn't be mad at Camille for what she did. I know she's not the same person she once was, that the Re-gen process wipes the memory slate clean or whatever, but it's hard not to blame her. Oh, I blame her, but I mean, it's hard not to blame MY Camille—the tiny, sensitive girl I watched over all of my life. That's where the feeling of betrayal comes from. But I have to remember that MY Camille is dead, no matter how much this thing reminds me of her. She's just...gone.

Good luck, man. Avoid the Kool-Aid and don't fucking trust Camille or whatever the fuck they call her...it.

Mase refused to look at Camille as he processed what he'd read. About her. She'd lied to him.

Dani was standing in front of them, asking Camille something, but all Mase could think about was Camille. She'd *lied* to him. She hadn't been trapped in the warehouse when he'd tried to help her, but had been intending to trap *him*. She'd been a part of the plan to make him into a Re-gen and to kill his men. He wondered if she took care of him afterward because she felt guilty, and then he wondered if it even mattered.

...don't fucking trust Camille...

Mase flipped through the rest of the papers, but his mind was too numb to make sense of any of it. With a quick glance at his watch, he realized he'd wasted enough time—they only had fifteen minutes left, and what he'd just read jump-started his determination to get out of the Colony. He needed out.

Rising, Mase felt off-balance. The world had rearranged itself around him with the reading of a single self-addressed letter. He snatched Camille's folder from her grasp, ignoring her protests, and carried both to Dani. Flashlight in hand, she was continuing the Re-gens' search of the file cabinets where Camille and Mase had left off.

"Dani?" Mase whispered, startling her.

He felt instantly guilty for scaring her, she who'd done nothing to harm him, and felt even worse when she looked up at him. Her face was filled with fear. Why? Because Mase was scowling, and his scowl has always been scary and cruel. It took an effort, but he managed to lose the expression.

"Can you take pictures of the papers in these?" Mase asked, holding the two folders out. "They're about me and Camille, and we don't have time to read everything right now."

Dani smiled and took the folders back to the desk. "Were there files on all the Re-gens?" she asked.

"Looked like it," Mase told her. Before he could turn away, Dani's face blanked. She was completely still, like she'd fallen asleep standing up and with her eyes open. "Dani? Is something wrong?" Mase reached across the desk and squeezed her shoulder.

For the briefest moment, she came to. She patted his hand and said, "Hang on for a minute...I'm asking someone a quick question," before returning to her waking sleep. That time, she closed her eyes.

Mase waited, wondering if he should be concerned. He was.

Suddenly, her eyes popped open, and her mouth curved into a victorious grin. "I'm looking for the file on Becca Vaughn, or maybe Rebecca Vaughn. She's supposedly a Re-gen. Can you look for it?"

"Yeah. C'mon, Camille." Mase could hear the other Re-gen sniffling on the floor and knew she was crying. It was a sound Mase would recognize anywhere, and hearing it nearly broke through his anger and resentment, through the echo of a betrayal felt by a dead man. It was a struggle not to go to her. His arms wanted to wrap around her, his nose wanted to inhale her scent, and his lips wanted to touch hers, but there was no way he would let himself comfort her, not after everything he'd learned.

Slowly, Camille stood and turned back to the file cabinet without wiping her eyes. Mase wondered what she'd read in her folder. But curiosity would have to wait. They had work to do.

25

DANI

MARCH 22, 1AE

I was sitting on one of the stools at the island in my kitchen, taking frequent sips from an oversized, brown-glazed mug. The steaming chamomile tea calmed me as I organized my thoughts. My priceless bounty—the camera containing all the illicit photos I'd taken in General Herodson's office—sat on the countertop in front of me. With Camille and Mase's help, I'd gathered far more information than I'd expected, and all that was left to do was to pass it on to Jason, Zoe, and the others. Thus the organizing of my thoughts.

Distractedly, I smiled. Camille and Mase were upstairs in the larger of my two guest rooms. *At least* they *can be with the person they love.* I forced the smile to stay in place when jealousy threatened to erode it. I was determined to be happy for them, even if what they had was denied to me. *Only for one more day*, I reminded myself.

I'd once told Jason that hope was the one thing that could keep us going when all else seemed lost. He'd just learned his father was dead, and had started unraveling right in front of me. I'd never seen him so distraught. But together, we'd worked through it. Now, hope was the one thing keeping me going—hope that I would see my friends again soon, hope that I would finally escape the mind-controlled hell I'd been dragged into, and hope that I would be brave enough to express the extent of my feelings for Jason...to his face. I loved him, more than I'd ever loved anyone, and I needed to tell him. He needed to know. *But what if he doesn't...*

No! Not now! It was minutes until the eleventh hour, the worst possible time for doubts. Of course, knowing that didn't stop me from having them; the very heated, very real argument that started overhead did.

Muffled by the floorboards, insulation, and drywall, Camille and Mase had just erupted into an epic shouting match. I couldn't tell exactly what they were saying, but I could hear the tone, a heated mixture of accusation, hurt, and anger. It definitely wasn't the sounds I'd expected to need to ignore.

Not too slowly, I crept toward the stairs and up to the second floor. As I headed down the hallway, the guest room door at the end opened and Camille burst out. She thundered past me, sobbing.

"Camille! Wait!" I chased down the stairs after her, barely managing to catch her wrist before she reached the front door. "What's wrong? Did something...did he hurt you?" I asked softly. Concern was washed away by a sudden rush of anger. *If he hurt her...*

Camille faced me, her cheeks tear-streaked and her eyes red, swollen, and filled with fear. "I thought I could at least have..." Closing her eyes for a moment, she shook her head. "You won't understand. You *can't* understand." She jerked her wrist from my grasp and choked out, "Just let me go."

She rushed out of the house, accentuating her exit by slamming the front door. She was gone, and I was still standing in the entryway, baffled. *What happened? What did he do to her?*

Simmering with accusation, I stalked up the stairs and toward the guest room. When I reached the doorway, fists on hips, I froze. Mase was sitting on the carpeted floor facing me, his hunched back against the side of the bed and his head lowered into his hands. His shoulders were shaking. *Is he…crying?* The biggest and strongest man I'd ever met was crying in my guest room.

My fists dropped from my hips of their own accord. "Mase? What happened?" I asked softly. When he said nothing, made no move to respond, I repeated, "Mase?"

He didn't raise his head, but he did speak. "She killed me."

"What?" I blurted, before I could stop myself. "I mean, you look pretty alive to me."

Mase dropped his hands and glanced up at me, then shook his head. With dull eyes, he looked ahead, staring at nothing. "Before, when I was a normal. She helped Father kill me and make me into this."

My heart seemed to drop into my stomach, leaden and chilled. I sat down beside him, cross-legged and facing him, and gently touched my fingertips to the fatigues covering his knee. "What are you talking about?"

He told me. Everything. After he relayed everything he'd learned from his file, he asked, "How could she do that? How could she lie to me?" The angst filling his eyes, the tears of betrayal spilling from them, broke my heart. His hurt was that of a small boy who'd just learned that the world wasn't fair and that bad things happened to good people all the time, or that of a man who'd been misled by the woman he loved.

I didn't know what to say. I didn't know how to help him. I'd experienced a hell of a lot of pain in the form of death and loss, but never such a personal betrayal, not even from Gabe. *That must be how Zo and Jason feel about their parents*, I realized.

"You said that whatever Camille found in her folder upset her, right? But that you didn't read it?" I asked.

He nodded, still staring ahead. His eyes seemed to have lost some of their life.

"Hold on," I said, jumping up and rushing out of the room. I ran downstairs, grabbed the camera, and hurried back up to the guest room.

"Okay," I said, a little breathless as I reclaimed my spot on the floor beside Mase.

He watched me, curiosity lending some spark to his deadened eyes.

"Let's see what she read that upset her so much. Maybe it'll help us understand why she did what she did." Mase's eyes narrowed infinitesimally, and I added, "I'm not saying there's anything that could excuse her actions, but…let's not judge her *too* harshly until we know the whole story. Grams, my grandma, used to say"—I adopted my best Irish accent—"'Every story has as many sides as it does people.'"

Mase frowned, looking reticent, but he eventually nodded.

"I'm pretty sure there was a letter sort of like yours in her folder," I said as I scanned through the images on the small screen. I glanced at Mase. "There wasn't much in there, not like your file, but yours was mostly service records and other military documents. I think hers was just a profile sheet, some medical records, and a letter." I pursed my mouth as I waded through the pictures. There were so many. There was no way I would be able to read all the documents before the breakout in less than twenty-one hours, but there would be plenty of time once I was on the outside. *Not that I know where I'll find the power to charge the camera, but still…*

"Ah—here it is!" I scanned through the images of Camille's letter to see how long it was, then met Mase's eyes. Anticipation gleamed in their depths. If I was reading him right, I was pretty sure he wanted Camille's letter to exonerate her, to prove that at least part of her was the woman he'd come to depend on…and love. "It's a couple pages. Do you want me to read the whole thing out loud?"

Again, Mase nodded, so I started to read.

My name is Camille Marie Lin, I'm 17 years old, and I want to die.

Last month, I went to my high school's winter formal with my boyfriend, Matt. I wore the dress of my dreams, and Mom even let me splurge to get my hair and makeup done. I'd never done that before. Mom hadn't known that Matt and I planned on spending the night after the dance in a hotel room together. She thought I was going to a sleepover with a bunch of my girlfriends, but I was really going to be with Matt…like, BE with him. And we did. It was okay, I guess, but not amazing like everyone pretends it is. Fireworks? Yeah, right.

The next morning, my life turned into a horror movie. When I got up, Matt wouldn't wake. I called my Mom and confessed everything. Okay, not EVERYTHING, but you get the point. It turned out that half the school had to be hospitalized the day after the dance, and Mom and I were admitted the next day. We were both really sick, and they stuck needles in us and hooked us up to IVs and packed us into a room with a dozen other sick people. I eventually got better, but Mom didn't.

There were too many bodies and not enough people to take care of them…like, bury them or whatever…so they just stacked them up outside the hospital and lit them on fire. I've never smelled anything so disgusting, and it probably didn't help that I was still puking every other hour. I watched from the hospital room window as they wheeled Mom out to the human bonfire and tossed her onto the pile. I don't know what was wrong with me, but I couldn't look away. I watched my mom burn. Why couldn't I look away?

Eventually it was done, and I couldn't tell her from the other blackened bones. I didn't want to end up in that pile with her, so I left. I hid in my house for a day, then wandered around my neighborhood, looking for any of the people I grew up with. There was nobody. I stopped by Mase's house. It had always been like a second home to me, but there didn't seem to be anyone there. I sat in Mase's room for a while, wishing he was there with me. He always knew what to do. I knew that he would take care of me, if he was even still alive.

I was so happy when his dad walked into the room that I ran to hug him, but there was something wrong with him. He wasn't sick, not like I'd been; he was mean. I'd known him my whole life, and I knew he was kind and gentle, but he started trying to kiss me and take off my clothes. I screamed and screamed and screamed, but nobody came, and before he could actually undress me, a metal baseball bat flew to my hand like it was magnetic or something, and I swung it. I hit Mr. Atwell in the head and he fell to the floor. He didn't get back up. I killed Mr. Atwell.

When I realized what I'd done, I ran out of the house and into the street. I was so stupid. I ran right in front of a car, and it should've hit me, but it just...stopped. It had been speeding and was really close, too close to stop with brakes or anything normal. And I felt it. It was like the bat. I *stopped the car.*

The driver looked scared, but I told her I wouldn't let her car move until she let me in. I promised not to hurt her if she just took me with her. She did. Her name was Kathy, and she was my mom's age. She'd heard a radio broadcast coming from some place in Colorado. It was on every station, apparently, and finally I heard it too. So, we drove, and made it here, to the Colony.

I was coping okay, but then I saw Mase. I wanted to run to him and fall into his arms, sobbing and begging for his forgiveness. But there's no way he'd forgive me for killing his dad. I know him too well. So, when Dr. Wesley told me about a new program she was in charge of, a program that would make me forget everything, I volunteered. So now I get what I want: I get to die, and Mase never has to know what I did.

"That's it," I said, clicking to the next image and finding the profile sheet for Jake's sister, Becca. I made a mental note to ask Gabe to search her out tomorrow—or, technically, later today—turned off the screen, and set the camera on the bed near my head. "Mase?"

His face was twisted into a mask of grief, but only a single tear leaked from his eye. "I don't…" He cleared his throat. "I don't know what to do now. She"—he squeezed his eyes shut and took a shaky breath—"became a Re-gen because she was afraid to tell me what she'd done. I know about the normals who went insane because of the Virus. *He* must've been one of them. Would I have blamed her for defending herself? Was I that mean?"

I shook my head and fought back my own tears. Watching a man cry, especially one as strong as Mase, was usually a surefire way to jump-start my own emotional waterworks. "I honestly don't know, Mase, but I'd bet she was just afraid of losing you—the old you—along with everyone else she lost back home. I think she panicked and took the only exit in sight."

"What do I do now?" he asked.

After a moment of thought, I said, "There's one more person who can shed some light on this story."

"Dr. Wesley?"

I nodded. "I think you should stay here the rest of the night, and we can go and talk to her first thing in the morning. I don't want this thing between you and Camille to get twisted into any more knots before we know everything." I watched him, waiting for his agreement. "At least you'll have plenty of time to work things out with Camille once we've made it out of here. You won't have to worry about people watching over you all the time or doing who knows what for General Herodson." A thought popped into my head. "I know you work with Dr. Max, but what does Camille do for the General?"

"She's one of his executioners, among other things," Mase said, but he sounded distracted…anxious.

I spluttered, "Executioners? I…what…that's…wow." I really didn't want to think about the implications, but I couldn't help but wonder how exactly the General used her to execute people. *Does she tear the metals right out of their bodies?* I cleared my throat, shuddering. "I, um, suppose we should get some sleep. It's going to be a long day tomorrow." When Mase didn't respond, I asked, "Are you okay?"

"I—" He met my eyes only briefly, then averted his gaze like he was ashamed. "I'm afraid."

"Afraid?" I reached for the hand resting on his knee and squeezed it, nearly giggling at how childlike my hand looked compared to his. I was filled with anxiety, and it was manifesting in unpredictable, inappropriate ways, as usual. "Worry and fear won't help us now," I told him. "All we can do is prepare."

Mase shook his head, looking like a scared little boy trapped in a huge man's body. "It's not the escape that I'm afraid of; it's after. I've never been…" He took a deep breath and tensed his muscles. "I don't remember ever being outside the Colony. I don't know what to do out there. I don't know what it's like. I don't know anything. This is all I've ever known."

He sounded so despondent that I felt compelled to ease at least this part of his unrest. I decided to tell him some stories. *My* stories. I started off by telling him about my journey from Seattle to Bodega Bay, about the time I spent alone with only Wings and Jack, and finally about the long trek to Colorado. I described my friends to him and shared what it was like to be a modern-day nomad. I told him what my average day was like, starting from waking up in a tent and sitting around a morning campfire, and continuing on through riding and searching for a good place to set up camp. Eventually, Mase stretched out on the carpet and his breathing slowed to a deep, steady rhythm. He was asleep.

I craned my neck to glance out the window on the other side of the bed. It was still fully dark; the sun wouldn't be rising for hours. Making as little noise as possible, I rose and gathered one of the pillows, the comforter, and a blanket off the bed. Mase was a huge, heavy block of solid muscle, but I somehow managed to ease the pillow under his head and cover him with the comforter, tucking it just under his chin. He let out a faint sigh as I pulled away. Wrapping the remaining blanket around myself, I huddled on the floor, leaning against the wall and watching over him. *I wonder if anyone has noticed he's missing yet.*

Asleep, he looked so innocent, like someone who needed to be protected, which was ridiculous because he'd saved my skin several times already. But there was just...something. Maybe it was my knowledge of what he was, or maybe it was my sympathy for what he'd been through, but I felt an almost maternal need to keep him safe.

With a deep sigh, I leaned my head back against the wall and closed my eyes. I was exhausted, but sleep proved too slippery for me to hold on to at the moment. Exasperated, I reached out with my mind, searching my friends' camp for Jason. I wasn't surprised to find him awake.

"Hey," I said, putting as much tenderness as I could into the single word. *"Can't sleep?"*

I had the impression that Jason was smiling. *"No, but neither can you."*

"True...a lot's happened. Want to hear something crazy about my Ability?"

"Always."

Biting my bottom lip, I considered the best way to explain what I'd experienced for a few seconds in General Herodson's office. *"I had some lookouts tonight—some owls. When I first connected with them, I sort of* became *them for a few seconds. I don't know if it was an accident or what, or if I can even do it on purpose, but it looks like I can slip into some minds completely...experience what they're experiencing...know every thought they're having at that moment."*

"Can you do it with me? I have a few thoughts I'd like to share with you..."

My cheeks heated, and I stifled a giggle. *"I don't know. It only happened that once with the owls. People might be totally different, although...I wonder if that's what happened before, when I contacted you the first time."* I was *really* tempted to test that theory. *"But, before we get too distracted, I should probably share everything I discovered tonight."*

"Nobody caught you? You're still safe, right?" he asked, his tone transforming effortlessly from seductive to protective.

"I'm fine. I took pictures with a camera I, uh...found. Want me to go through them with you?"

"Yes," he said intently. *"Tell me everything."*

I did.

Hours passed, and the sun was just making its first attempts at climbing over the horizon when we said our farewells. Tempted as we were to have some long-distance hanky-panky, Jason had information to relay and breakout plans to finalize. I agreed to check in at noon to coordinate the final plan between the insiders—Gabe, Mase, Camille, Gabe's mysterious "like my sister" friend, and potentially Dr. Wesley—and my friends outside the Colony.

But noon was hours away, Mase was still fast asleep, and I had nothing to do. I figured there was no better time to try out the new facet of my Ability. Closing my eyes, I rested the back of my head against the wall and sought out a companion. I found her circling above my friends' camp, a falcon who identified herself as *Ray of Sun that Melts the Winter Snow.* Slipping into her mind was almost effortless. Ray was more than happy to share her morning hunt with me.

On her powerful wings, we soared.

26

DANI

MARCH 22, 1AE

The first rays of the sun warmed my outstretched wings as I circled above the female two-legs. She was walking like she was stalking prey, but I could see no prey. Though I found the sight boring, she-who-flies-with-me wanted to watch her. She-who-flies-with-me intrigued me, the way she could meld with me, flying with me, not just beside me. As I showed her what we could do together, she exalted in the joys of flight like a youngling, hooting and squealing with pleasure. She claimed to be a two-legs like the one below, but I was sure she was a wind-rider like me.

I swooped lower, calling out to the female two-legs.

"Dani?"

Screeching, I pulled up from a dive, the movement more clumsy than I'd intended.

"Dani?"

I shook my head and felt she-who-flies-with-me start to pull away from me. How could she want to leave the crisp morning air…the feel of it streaming between my feathers?

"Dani?"

She separated further and thanked me.

"Dani!"

I opened my eyes and took a startled, shuttering breath. Mase's concerned face was inches from mine, but he moved away as soon as he realized I was awake. Not that I'd really been asleep, but he didn't know that.

"Holy crap, Mase! There are such things as personal boundaries, you know."

He moved further away to sit on the edge of the bed and stared at his feet, shame drawing down his eyebrows.

"Hey," I said softly as I stood, stretched with a groan, and sat beside him. "Sorry. You just startled me. It's cool…no big deal. I'm not mad."

Sheepishly, he met my eyes. "You wouldn't wake up. I thought something was wrong. You…"

It was my turn to be embarrassed, and heat flushed my cheeks. "I was, uh, flying with a falcon," I told him. "I couldn't sleep, so…"

"It's first thing in the morning," he prompted.

I nodded, not quite grasping his point.

"You said we could visit Dr. Wesley first thing in the morning."

"Oh, right. I was thinking about that last night. I don't think you should leave this house until it's game time." Mase looked confused, so I clarified, "Until it's time to leave the Colony tonight. I mean, won't the other Re-gens have noticed you were gone all night? What if they tell someone? But if you stay here, you should be safe. The only people who've seen us together have either had their short-term memories wiped or are people we can trust, so there's no reason for anyone else to search for you here."

Mase didn't look entirely convinced. "But…Dr. Wesley…"

"*I* can talk to her without looking too suspicious. I promise I'll tell you every single thing she says," I told him, pleading with both my eyes and my voice.

Reluctantly, he nodded.

"Great! Why don't you wash up? I'll head downstairs to make us some breakfast." I didn't tell him that me making breakfast only went so far as opening a box of granola bars and, if he was lucky, making some tea. "Take your time in the shower. It might be the last one you get for a long, long time."

He nodded again.

By the time I made it downstairs, had the teapot on the stove, and was rummaging through the pantry for anything even remotely resembling breakfast, I could hear the shower running upstairs.

The doorbell rang. *It's probably just Gabe*, I told myself, ignoring the flutter of nerves trying to convince me otherwise. Luckily, the peephole confirmed that it *was* just Gabe at my front door.

"What's up?" I asked as I let him in.

Instead of responding, he glanced up the stairs and said, "About to hop in the shower?" I could almost see his mental struggle to hide a leer.

"Uh…"

His eyes narrowed. "Is someone here?"

"Uh…"

He raised a single eyebrow, telling me my idiotic responses weren't cutting it.

"It's Mase," I told him. "He stayed over last night."

His second eyebrow joined the first.

"Not like that!" I hissed quickly. I reached for his arm and dragged him into the kitchen. "He and Camille had a little tiff after spying last night—which was crazy productive, by the way. Did you know that nobody's been able to carry a child to term since the Virus?" I didn't give him a chance to answer. "Anyway, I passed on all of the pertinent info to Jason, and he's powwowing with the others right now. We came up with a pretty solid plan, but I still have to contact him in a few hours to hash out the final details. Want me to do that in your office so you can be in on the discussion?"

When Gabe nodded, I asked, "Did you find out anything else I need to pass along before then?"

Gabe frowned and shook his head.

"Did you find out *anything?*" I asked skeptically.

The look he gave me told me it was a stupid question. "Yes, but nothing essential for the moment. Right now we just need to focus on tonight. What did you and Jason come up with?"

I crossed my arms over my chest, raising my pointer finger to my lips as I recalled the specifics of the rough plan Jason and I had come up with in the wee hours of the morning. "Let's see…Jason thought it would be wisest if we disguised ourselves as a patrol team, like Mase, Camille, and me did last night. That way we'll look as inconspicuous as possible. He also thought that golf course just outside the fence at the southern border will be the best extraction point. There's a window of about three minutes every half hour when there's a lapse in the guard rotation there, so we'll have to time our escape around that." I glanced up at the ceiling, thinking. "Hmmm…did you know the fence bordering this place is electric?"

Again, Gabe shook his head. "It didn't used to be."

"Well, it is now, and it's charged with enough juice to fry even a Re-gen's brain. Anyway, Camille can cut a big enough hole through it with her Ability that we won't have to worry about it."

Gabe was still frowning, but the expression appeared contemplative rather than disapproving. "Are they planning any kind of distraction? Anything would be a big help."

"That's one of the things he's discussing with the others right now. But they're all super-tactical military-trained people, except for Zo and Jake, so I'm sure they'll come up with something good." I meant what I said; if anyone could come up with a distraction devastating enough to Colony forces to enable our successful getaway, it was Jason and Chris. I trusted them with my life… which was why I was *entrusting* them with my life.

"I hope so," Gabe commented. "What are your plans for the rest of today? Please tell me you're lying low."

I bit my lower lip. "Well…I was actually planning to pay a little visit to Dr. Wesley. I've got a few things to ask her before we leave. Unless…did you talk to her? Is she coming with us?"

"She's not, but I don't know if you should—"

"It's nonnegotiable. I'm going to talk to her," I told him. "I inadvertently caused a mess that I need to clean up, and she's the only one who might be able to help."

Gabe didn't look happy, but he didn't forbid me or anything ridiculous like that. "Fine, but you're coming to the lab with me and not leaving until I do. We can't risk screwing the pooch…not now."

"Honestly, I don't think you should *ever* risk that."

With a sly grin, he smoothed his hair back into a ponytail and secured it with a hairband. "Just try not to screw things up. Sound good?"

"Much better," I said approvingly. All of a sudden, something I should have noticed far earlier smacked me in the hypothetical face. "Gabe…I can *feel* you! Oh my God! Something's wrong with the neutralizer; it's not working on you anymore! He'll be able to control you! You'll become his slave! He'll—"

He reached out a hand and squeezed my shoulder. "Calm down, Dani. I *let* it wear off. I didn't think we could afford you not being able to communicate with me this evening."

"Oh…that's good, I guess."

He smirked. "You were worried about me."

I turned away from him so he wouldn't see my smile and

started down the hallway. "Shut up." I stopped halfway to the kitchen. "Shoot, I forgot to give Mase a towel," I told Gabe as I rushed past him toward the stairs. "Be right back."

As I snagged a mauve towel from the linen closet, I heard a dull thump from the guest bathroom. I tapped on the door. The shower was still running. "Mase? I brought you a towel. Sorry…I forgot that there aren't any in there."

There was no answer.

I knocked on the door with more gusto. "Mase? You okay in there?"

There was still no answer. *What the hell?*

I tested the door handle. It was unlocked. Slowly, I eased the door open and called out again. "Mase? Everything okay?" I poked my head into the bathroom and glanced around from the sage- and cream-striped shower curtain to the toilet to the open window to the sink. He was nowhere in sight, which meant he was in the shower. *Why isn't he answering? Did he knock himself out or something?*

I moved toward the shower curtain and reached out to pull it aside. "I'm not trying to be stalkerish or anything, but you didn't answer and please don't be mad at me for invading your privacy, but—"

The shower was empty. And the window was open.

"Shit."

Less than fifteen minutes later, I'd changed, stuffed the little camera in my jeans pocket, and dragged Gabe to work early, parting ways with him just down the hall from Dr. Wesley's office. I was fairly certain that was where Mase had run off to. Before heading up to his lab, Gabe warned me that my dose of the neutralizer would have worn off already as well—it tended to last only four or five days—and told me to be *very* careful about who I spoke to and what I said.

I entered Dr. Wesley's office without knocking. Unsurprisingly, Mase was standing in the middle of the room, his back to me. He glanced over his shoulder as I walked in, and I raised my eyebrows irritably.

"Sorry," he mouthed, and his eyes held such desperation that I couldn't stay annoyed.

He just wants to understand. I approached him and reached up to pat his shoulder, letting him know we were okay. We would have a chat later, but we were okay.

"I assume you're here for the same reason as Mase," Dr. Wesley said. Again, she was sitting in the chair behind her desk.

I just smiled and tugged her key from the neck of my shirt. It only took me a few seconds to remove it and the guard's key from the cord. "Thanks. As it turned out, I didn't actually need this," I said, setting both keys on her desk with a thunk. Once I was gone, I wouldn't have a use for either of them.

The doctor returned my humorless smile, and I had to remind myself that her resemblance to Zoe didn't mean I had to like her. "Had you told me who would be with you, I would've informed you that any key was superfluous."

So she knew Camille could pick pretty much any lock. *I guess that's not surprising.* "Camille told you about our late-night fun."

Dr. Wesley frowned the barest amount. "No, she didn't. I haven't seen her since yesterday." She motioned toward Mase with her chin. "He filled me in, a bit. At least, when he wasn't making demands."

I sighed. I could only imagine how Mase's anxiety and unsquashable protectiveness of Camille had manifested while he'd been trying to get the rest of the story from Dr. Wesley. She had, after all, been the person responsible for Camille's death and rebirth via the Re-gen process. I doubted *that* was something Mase would easily forgive. At least, not without proper motivation…like the truth.

"Why?" I asked.

"Why, Danielle? I think 'why' must be your favorite word."

Laughing softly, bitterly, I shook my head and closed the final few feet to her desk. I pointed my right hand back toward Mase without breaking eye contact with Dr. Wesley. "Don't you get it? He's in pain. He's heartsick because of something you had your hands in—or, *another* thing you had your hands in—and you have the information that might make him feel better. But no, you're holding out." I dropped my arm and glowered at her. "Your kids would be ashamed of you. Zo always said she thought her dad's oddities were caused by a broken heart, though she used to think it was because he'd lost the love of his life in a tragic car wreck, not that it matters now."

I expected her eyes to flash with rage, but hurt was all that filled their jewel-blue depths. Whatever her faults, Dr. Wesley loved her family. Unfortunately for humanity, she loved them too much.

"He was a good man," I added softly. "I never knew my dad, and I always considered Tom to be sort of my surrogate father. But he *was* heartbroken. He wasn't right in the head, not completely." Briefly, I glanced back at Mase and then returned my eyes to the doctor's. "*He* doesn't have to go through the same thing. You can help him understand why Camille did what she did. You're the only one who can do that."

Dr. Wesley's features tensed, turning the planes and angles of her face more severe, but then her expression softened. She sighed, a long, drawn-out exhalation of breath and emotion. It was a sound of letting go. Her eyes shifted to Mase, and she began to explain. "Camille came here…she came here for revenge, and although you might not agree, she was lucky that I intercepted her before Gregory learned of her. I know you read her backstory from her file. Well, it's not completely…complete."

Her brow furrowed in thought. "Let's see…if I remember correctly, Camille's mother was a nurse, and she noticed a correlation between the people she'd administered a certain batch of flu vaccine to and the first victims of the epidemic in her area—some part of Minneapolis, I believe." Dr. Wesley waved her hand in front of her dismissively. "It was the same in every large city. Mrs. Lin noticed the correlation and suspected it wasn't a coincidence. She checked the batch number and unusual place of origin, and made a complaint to the CDC. They told her they would take care of it—which was a lie, as they were already under Gregory's control. He's always been very strategic. His Ability can be expended, you know, so he has to be selective about who he controls."

Dr. Wesley paused for a moment, her gaze flicking back and forth between us. "Mrs. Lin fell ill soon after and died quite quickly, but not before she told her daughter to *never* go to Peterson Air Force Base in Colorado, that the base was where the faulty vaccines had originated. The rest of her story plays out much as you read it"—she waved her hand in Mase's direction—"with Mase's father attacking her, Camille killing him, and eventually her ending up in the car with the woman headed straight for the one place her mother begged her to never go. She was looking for answers."

Suddenly, exhaustion filled the doctor's face, along with wariness verging on fear. "I found her crying in a corner of the hospital shortly after her admittance exam. She'd spotted you, Mase, and couldn't face you knowing what she'd done. She spilled her whole story to me, along with her knowledge of the false vaccine, and in turn, I informed her that spreading such a tale here would mean certain death for her. She was so hysterical that I wasn't surprised when she said she would rather die than keep living with the knowledge of what she'd done. She was just so miserable…so I told her there was another option." The doctor's eyes turned pleading. "I know you think me heartless, but I could see it written across her face: the girl would've killed herself before the day was over. She'd given up."

"So you killed her and brought her back to life as your own puppet instead of Herodson's?" I clarified harshly.

Dr. Wesley shook her head, telling me she'd known I wouldn't understand. "I told her I could transform her, end her current, pain-filled life and give her another one. I told her I could help her avenge her mother's death. I told her the truth, and *she* believed me." The way Dr. Wesley said "she" told me Camille had believed her in a way she knew I never would, and that she appreciated Camille for her openness. "We started the process the evening of her arrival, and she was reborn the following day."

"And me?" Mase asked. "Before she was remade, did she know you were going to make me into a Re-gen, too?"

"What?" the doctor looked taken aback. "Of course not. The original Camille had no idea of what would happen to you. That was…that was partially my fault, and partially yours. Your letter was also not quite the truth. You see, you were using the neutralizer, like Dani. You were one of the first who was truly awake, truly free of Gregory's control, even before Gabriel."

For some reason, the revelation shocked me. *The original Mase had used the neutralizer like Gabe and me? Did Gabe* know *Mase before—the original Mase, as Dr. Wesley would have said? If so, why didn't he tell me?*

"Unfortunately for you, that freedom of mind led to your downfall. But that's where my fault comes in as well. Gregory believes me to be under his control completely"—her lips twisted into an ugly sneer—"but he commands me to behave as though I am not, wanting to give his fantasy more reality. This means I must give in sometimes to lend credence to my ruse. When your susceptibility to his mind control came into question, he asked his advisors, including me, for ideas on how to test your loyalty. I suggested he use Camille, a young woman who'd recently become a Re-gen, who you just happened to have a close connection with growing up. Gregory thought it was the perfect idea. He used Camille to prove your disloyalty, and the rest is history."

I could do nothing else but stare at her, dumbfounded. The whole situation was a mind-boggling, convoluted mess of coincidence and bad luck.

"Just when I think I've dug as deep as I can, I sink the shovel in again and make the hole deeper," Dr. Wesley said softly. "You must hate me even more now."

But before I could answer, before I even knew *how* I would've answered, I sensed Camille's mind signature. She was walking down the hallway leading to Dr. Wesley's office. I grinned and peeked over my shoulder at Mase. "Camille'll be here in five, four, three—" Suddenly, I noticed five other minds moving along with hers, and my grin withered. One of those minds belonged to General Herodson.

"*He's* with her," I hissed, my eyes wide. *What did he find out from Camille?* I looked from Mase to Dr. Wesley and back. "What do we—"

The door swung open. Apparently, like me, General Herodson hadn't felt the need to knock. "My darling Anna, I hope I'm not interrupting anything important."

Simultaneously, Mase and I turned to face the newcomers. General Herodson, dressed exactly as he'd been the first and only other time I'd met him, in a dark blue officer's uniform, stood behind two guards, both male, both wearing yellow armbands, and both armed to the teeth. When the guards stepped aside to flank the doorway, Camille came into view. She had a black eye, a fat lip, and seemed to be favoring one of her legs.

"Oh my God, Camille! Are you okay? What happened?" I asked her silently, terrified both for her and for me.

Images flashed through my mind, and I was only partially grateful for her adeptness at communicating with me in the odd, Re-gen form of telepathy. What she showed me was stomach-churning.

Camille sobbing as she ran back into a room with row after row of bunks.

A guard catching Camille by the arms and asking her something.

Camille lying on the floor, unconscious.

Camille, waking up tied to a plastic chair with plastic restraints in a room stripped of all metal.

A small child—a girl—strapped to another chair directly in front of her, crying.

A guard, hitting the child.

Camille mouthing, "I'm sorry."

My heart raced. General Herodson, in all his perverseness, had threatened Camille with the well-being of a little girl in exchange for information. I knew his manipulative Ability didn't work the same on Re-gens as it did on what Mase and Camille called "normals," but I hadn't guessed the heinous alternatives the General would use to get his way. I should have.

Oh God...what did she tell them? What could *she have told him?* Frantically, I searched through my memory for every interaction I'd had with Camille. Had I told her anything about Jason and Zoe? What did she know, besides enough information to damn Gabe, Mase, Dr. Wesley, and me?

"Gabe," I said silently, reaching out to my friend's mind. He was still upstairs in his lab. *"They know. Get out. Get out now!"*

"Are you okay?"

"Probably not, but don't you dare come down here."

"Dani—"

"I mean it, Gabe! If you care about me at all, get somewhere safe right now*!"*

"Danielle O'Connor. My new communications specialist," General Herodson said. He was trim, slightly handsome, and easily the evilest person I'd ever met. He blew Mandy right out of the water, if only for the sheer scale of what he'd done. Why did the mind-manipulation Ability turn people into the worst versions of themselves? "What are you doing here, my dear?"

Adjusting my telepathic aim, I found Jason almost instantly. My heart sank. He—all of them—were still at their camp, over fifty miles southwest of the Colony. *"Jason,"* I said to him alone. *"Don't panic, but we need to hurry things up a bit."*

"Dani?" he responded, sounding furious. *"What are you saying? Are you in trouble? Are you hurt?"*

General Herodson asked what I'm doing here...right. I pulled the cord over my neck, glad I'd already removed the keys, and held the red card proclaiming my health status as "not suited for work." I forced a smile, trying my hardest to make it appear genuine, and said, "I was just returning this. My sleep wasn't at all disturbed by my headache last night, so I figured I'd start work today."

"I'm fine for the moment, but I think they know," I mind-spoke to Jason.

"Tell me what's happening," he demanded.

"Lie," a woman said from behind the General. Like the guards, she was wearing fatigues, but she didn't appear to be armed.

Silently, I told Jason, *"Oh yeah, they know."*

"Fucking...fuck! Okay, listen. We're about to leave. We'll be waiting for you by the pond at the southern tip of the golf course south of the base. Carlos will signal our arrival and provide a distraction."

"How?" I asked.

"An electromagnetic pulse. When the lights go out, you'll know we're there. Do what you have to do to stay alive, Red. I mean it.

Anything. Just stay alive…for me, for you, for whoever. I don't care so long as you stay alive.*"*

"A pity," General Herodson murmured. During the entire exchange, his eyes never left me. "I had hoped CL-one's information was wrong. Restrain the telepath and the Re-gen," he ordered, and his guards took a step forward.

"No!" Mase bellowed. He stepped in front of me, blocking me from the guards. Predictably, they paused. With his Ability, nobody sane would confront him, but the mind-controlled guards were more living zombie slaves than sane humans. Still, they paused. Mase could be pretty goddamn scary.

"Stop, Mase!" Camille cried out. "You'll both live if you just do what he says. He promised. Let them restrain you."

"Camille? Why?" Mase asked, his voice breaking as his posture relaxed. No matter what, he would do what she asked.

"I had no choice."

"Did you hear me?" Jason asked in my head.

"Yes," I said. I was having a hard time following both conversations. *"Sorry. About to get restrained."*

"It's fine, Mase," I told the behemoth—my friend—protecting me from the General's lackeys. I rested a hand on his shoulder blade. "We'll do as they say. We don't want anyone to be hurt any further." In his head, I added, *"Especially not Camille."*

His muscles tensed beneath my fingers, but he eventually backed down, following their commands as they bound his wrists behind his back with handcuffs. I was next.

"Okay, I'm officially restrained now," I told Jason.

"How?" he asked.

"My hands are handcuffed behind my back."

"How many?"

"Handcuffs?"

"Men," Jason said, no hint of condescension accenting his tone.

Oh, duh. "Two guards, the General, a woman who's like Ben, and another man I don't know. And they have Camille with them. She's been beaten. And Mase is restrained like me. Oh, and Gabe was upstairs, but I warned him already."

The General turned his attention to Dr. Wesley, who was still sitting at her desk. "I sincerely hope you had nothing to do with this, Anna." With his statement came the realization that Camille had managed to hold at least a few things back. Maybe more than a few. There was still hope, and where there was hope, there was still the possibility that things might work out.

"No," she said calmly, and when the Truth Guard nodded, confirming Dr. Wesley's truthfulness, I knew the doctor was using her nulling Ability to prevent the other woman from feeling her lie.

"Okay," Jason said. *"Sit tight for now. We'll be there sometime this evening. If you haven't found a way out by midnight, I'm nulling everyone in the whole fucking state and coming in."*

"Jason, don't! It's too dangerous!"

"If you're not out by midnight..."

"Sir," the other man, the one I'd yet to identify, blurted. "Someone's using an Ability, a really powerful one."

"I'm using my Ability, Gregory, to augment yours as usual," Dr. Wesley said.

The man shook his head. "There's another."

"Knock the telepath out," the General said quietly. "We can't have her calling for help from God knows where."

"Jason, I—"

Pain. Blackness. Nothing.

27

ZOE

MARCH 22, 1AE

I stood by the dusty, cobweb-infested window in my room. The inky sky steadily brightened over the jagged tops of the Rockies as dawn neared, and from the sound of it, everyone was still asleep downstairs. *Is Jake down there?* It was strange not waking up beside him. *I've succeeded in pushing him away.*

I peered down at the street of dilapidated buildings stretching out on either side of the house. It was like I was living in an alternate dimension where everything was slightly off. I felt like my life had become a giant pinball machine, and around every corner there was another obstacle waiting to bounce me around. The world ends—ricochet to the right; get Dani back—launch upward; Dani's abducted—recoil to the left; learn how to fight—win more time; a Crazy jumps out—bounce to the right; find out Mom didn't die in a car accident—roll down to the bottom; another Crazy jumps out—careen to the left; fall in love with Jake—double points; Becca shows up—drain ball.

Becca's vision—the bottomless pit of dead, discarded Re-gens —had been replaying in my mind since I'd inadvertently witnessed it a few days before. I hadn't told Jake about it; there hadn't been a decent time. I wasn't sure he needed to know, not if we were planning on breaking her out of the Colony anyway, changing her fate. For Jake's sake, I hoped Dani had been somewhat successful in finding her, in somehow convincing Becca to come with us. But I knew that was a long shot; Becca didn't *want* to leave the Colony, and I knew Dani wasn't willing to risk her own life in order to convince Becca we could protect her.

I sat down on the edge of the bed, the morning chill biting at my ears and nose and fingers. I ignored it and lowered my eyes to my hands. My skin was darker, tanned from spending so much time in the sun, and my nails were short, uneven, and dirty.

I shook my head at the implausible direction my life had gone—that all of our lives had gone—and I glanced over at the picture on the vanity. It was the one Dani had brought from my childhood bedroom, a photo of us sitting on the edge of the deck, her telling me a secret. I'd been arguing with Jason, and she'd come over to console me. To distract me, she'd admitted to having a crush on the new boy in school—Mark, or Mike, or something like that. As always, I'd felt better having her there. Only she could make me laugh and feel like a normal kid.

A few days later, Dad had developed a roll of film—all pictures of his woodwork to add to his portfolio. Like me, he'd been surprised to find the photo of Dani and me mixed in the stack, and as I'd stood there, my teenage self in complete shock, I'd put two and two together: Jason had taken the picture. Even though he'd said I was a burden and that he wished I would just go away, he'd cared enough to snap the photo of us.

I'd snatched the glossy picture out of the stack in my dad's hands and run up to my room to frame it. I'd been happy my brother had made the effort to do something nice for me.

I smiled at the memory.

Cooper stirred from sleeping on the floor on my side of the bed, yawning as he stretched before curling back up into an oversized ball of fluffy fur to resume his slumber. I figured Jake had sent him into the room at some point during the night. My chest tightened and my eyes burned at the thoughtful gesture.

I tried unsuccessfully to reduce our relationship to physical attraction. *We don't* really *know each other.* I told myself we were just shells of who we'd once been, and therefore, there could be no depth or true connection between us. But in my heart, I knew I was wrong. Our old selves didn't matter—we weren't them anymore and never would be again. What mattered was that Jake had saved my life, that he'd been making it his mission to protect me ever since. He clearly cared about me. The hurt in his eyes every time I pushed him away *mattered* to me. How despondent I would be if he left me…*mattered.* My chest ached when I tried to diminish our relationship to something less than it was.

Then why'd I put so much effort into distancing myself? I could have been savoring our time together. *Why'd I work so hard to make everything harder than it already was?*

As if she was sitting on the edge of the bed beside me, her head resting on my shoulder and her wild hair tickling the side of my face while she patiently waited for me to gather my always-churning thoughts, I could almost hear what Dani would say to me, her words honest and her voice kind. "*You're scared, Zo. You've always been afraid you'll lose me, and you did…and now you're afraid you'll lose Jake. I know you think you're protecting yourself, but you're not. You're only hurting yourself. You can't keep pushing people away.*"

A despondent, hysterical laugh escaped from my throat, and I threw myself back on the bed. *I'm losing my mind.*

Taking a deep breath to steady my trembling chin, I rubbed my hands over my face in an attempt to scrub away the mounting pressure behind my eyes. Jake was right, too; I wasn't like Jason. I couldn't keep pushing everything beneath the surface and expect to remain in control.

I couldn't be who I once was, the guarded, almost friendless starving artist. Too much had transpired between Jake and me to simply push it all away and hope for the best, and realizing that made my heart swell with a sense of urgency. I *needed* him. I *wanted* him. Now.

Not bothering to take the time to change, I pulled combat boots on over my sweatpants, leaving the laces untied, and hurried out the door. I left Cooper to resume his morning slumber and hoped I didn't trip on my shoelaces as I rushed down the stairs.

I half expected to see Jake lounging in a chair beside the fireplace, but nobody was sitting by the dying fire. Tavis and Sam were sleeping on their pallets on the floor, and Sanchez and Harper were asleep in the opposite corner of the parlor. I didn't see Jake anywhere.

I tiptoed to the front door, careful not to let it creak too loudly as I opened it, and stepped out into the pale light of the early morning. Easing the door to a close, I strode toward the weathered stable across the dirt road. Shadow and Wings were among the horses out in the attached pasture, grazing on dewy grass. They raised their heads, only partially acknowledging me before refocusing their attention on their morning meal.

I'd had my hair in a ponytail, but it suddenly felt too tight. Anxiously, I pulled the rubber band out, and my scalp sang in relief as my hair fell from its snare.

Jake wasn't outside by the horses, or in the wagon area attached to the paddocks, but I heard a dull thud inside the stable, and then another. Assuming it was him, I meandered inside. A violet hue saturated the stable's interior, and I inhaled the comforting scents of leather and alfalfa. I heard another thud. The noise was coming from the tack room a few doors down from the stable entrance, so I headed toward it.

Leaning through the doorway, I peered inside. Jake was sitting with his back to me on the edge of an old, wooden bench that ran through the center of the room. His long sleeves were pushed up, his elbows were resting on his knees, and his face was lowered into his hands.

I opened my mind to his, trying to gauge his mood. When I felt his overwhelming frustration and sadness, my eyes pricked with tears.

"Hey," I squeaked and cleared my throat.

Surprised, Jake lifted his head, confusion and concern warring on his rugged features.

"I've been looking for you," I said as my eyes took in every inch of him. His scruff was thicker than usual, and his hair was disheveled, like he'd been running his fingers through it over and over again. He looked exhausted, and I wondered if he hadn't slept all night.

An invisible band tightened around my heart. *I did this to him.*

Jake sat on the bench, appraising my face. The corners of his eyes wrinkled as he squinted, but he didn't say anything.

"I'm sorry," I rasped. Unable to watch the increasing uncertainty in his eyes, the uncertainty I'd caused, I looked at the saddles on the racks and at the blankets hanging on the walls. I looked anywhere but at him. "I know I've been—"

A tennis ball dropped to the ground as Jake shot to his feet, surprising me, and he took a step toward me. "Do you love me?"

My eyes widened and my skin heated. "Um—"

"Do you love me?" he repeated. The fierceness in his eyes and tense set of his jaw startled me.

Do I love Jake? I took a hesitant step inside the room. "I… yes." The moment I said it, any remaining doubt in my mind cleared. I was certain that things between us could—no, *would*—work out. I took another step closer to him.

Jake seemed taken aback by my admission, but only for a split second. He strode toward me, confident and determined, and I could feel the flurry of his unusually impulsive emotions swirling around me: need—anticipation—excitement. They were like smoke invading my senses, making me feel feverish with desire.

His eyes were keen and wild with growing impatience as he moved closer, his gaze shifting from my mouth to my eyes and back. Without ceremony, his rock-hard body forced me backward and pinned me against a saddle blanket hanging on the wall.

"Don't ever do that to me again," he growled.

Before I could respond, he was tugging off my sweatshirt with one hand and gripping my waist with the other. His mouth covered mine with a frenzied yearning. My boots and sweats were gone within seconds, and I was left to stand in my black boy shorts and tank top, and Jake in his jeans and untied boots.

I jumped into his arms, my legs coiling around his hips, tightening to bring him closer. His mouth was rough and urgent against mine, pulling my bottom lip between his teeth. His hands caught in my hair, and my body arched against his. I gasped for air and licked my lips as he nipped and kissed the sensitive flesh beneath my jaw.

Moaning, I tilted my head to the side, providing ample skin for him to ravage with his mouth. Everything about him was lust and desire, and the acuteness of what he was feeling devastated my composure, making me feel nothing but need—his need and mine. I needed his hands and lips on every inch of my body. I needed him to take me until I had nothing left to give. I could barely breathe…I didn't *want* to breathe…I just wanted *him*.

Craving more than Jake's mouth, I wrapped my arms around his neck and leaned into him to steady myself as I lowered my legs to the ground. My nails raked over his shoulders and down his back as they skimmed toward his pants. I unzipped his jeans, letting them fall to his ankles, and grabbed on to his butt. The muscles flexed against my hand. He fumbled with his boots and kicked off his pants, while I shed my tank top and underwear. When I looked at him, he was completely naked.

Jake's hands were on me again, all over my body. I quaked under the power of his fingertips as they moved up my arms and over my shoulders to my back. He pressed harder into me, making my breasts ache and my body burn with an invisible fire. I could feel his arousal against my abdomen, and I gasped.

He tightened his greedy hands around my waist, but took a step back, his possessive eyes raking down the pale peaks and valleys of my trembling body. An unruly hunger possessed him as he examined every visible inch of me.

Unable to tolerate any distance between us, I pulled him closer. My arms wound around his neck, and I stole another taste of his deliciously curious tongue. I shuddered.

He gripped my loose tresses once more, pulling my head back against the wall with an arousing jerk. His urgency only spurred my own desire, and my insides warmed and clenched in excitement as I thought of really being with him. *Finally.* Pure bliss escaped from my lips in the form of another breathy moan, and my fingernails dug into his back.

Jake growled as his teeth grazed the top of my shoulder. One of his hands dropped to my lower back and continued downward, tracing the curve of my butt…my thigh…and finally the crook of my leg. He lifted my knee and was inside me with a single, possessive surge. He was raw, unrestrained power. I craved more of it… more of him. My heart raced with the thrill and astonishment that we were finally together—no thoughts, no words, just his flesh against mine.

As he pulled back to look at me, his body gleaming and straining in the dim sunlight leaking through the wall, his overwhelming desire for me became my complete undoing. I gripped his shoulders harder to steady myself and cried out. The tension in my body melted into a warm, tingling pleasure that filled every part of me. My senses winked in and out of focus, confused between his feelings and my own. Comfort—passion—relief—love—they all washed over me in a chaotic rush. I'd never felt so uninhibited or intoxicated; every kiss, every needy touch was more abandoned than the last, and I never wanted it to end.

But it *had* to end.

When it did, Jake's unwavering hold was the only thing preventing me from collapsing to the floor. "Promise me," he whispered into my ear through heaving breaths, his chest slick against mine.

I nodded, unable to form coherent words, and reached for his face. I pulled his mouth to mine, stealing one more deep kiss. "I'm so sorry," I breathed against his lips, trying not to sob. "I'm so sorry."

His eyes held mine, their savagery softening. Gentleness replaced his urgency as he brought his hand up to cup my cheek. He placed his lips against my forehead and moved down to the tip of my nose before he settled a tender kiss against my mouth. "I'm sorry too."

We stayed in each other's arms for what felt like only moments, but eventually, I noticed the sun shining brightly through the open doorway of the tack room, and I could hear the others hustling around in the house.

I was about to suggest that we head inside when I heard the front door to the house fling open. "Zoe!" my brother roared. "Where the fuck are you?"

I gave Jake an apologetic groan and wrapped my arms around his broad shoulders, wishing I could have just one uninterrupted day with him.

"Damn it, Zoe! Dani's in trouble!"

Dani? I could hear Jason walking away from the stable, and I hurried for my clothes. *Oh, shit.*

28

DANI

MARCH 22, 1AE

Pain was the first thing I noticed when I came to. It lanced the back of my skull, making me feel dizzy before I even opened my eyes. My head was drooping, my chin resting against my chest, and I seemed to be sitting up. *Yes*, I confirmed after assessing the rest of my body, *I'm definitely sitting up…but I can't move my arms or legs.*

I tugged both of my arms backward, but something cold and hard was clamped around my wrists, immobilizing me. All I received for my effort was a pulse of pain in the back of my head from the jarring motion. I groaned. My poor brain had been taking a lot of damage lately…I was hoping none of it ended up being permanent.

"She's waking up," an unfamiliar female voice said softly. "Tell the General."

Slowly, I cracked my eyes open and raised my head. Mase was the first thing I saw, the only thing I saw for several long seconds. He was hanging by his wrists, a thick metal chain stretched taut between him and the ceiling, and his feet were barely touching the ground. He was standing on his tiptoes, probably to alleviate some of the strain the metal cuffs placed on his wrists and shoulders. The top of his fatigues had been stripped off, leaving him in only a gray t-shirt and camouflage pants. His massive arm muscles twitched with the effort to maintain his position as his eyes tracked something else in the room. Based on the soft sounds of footsteps, he was watching whoever was moving around behind me. *The woman who spoke?*

"Mase," I whispered, and his eyes snapped to mine. *Why hasn't he broken free?* I was certain he was strong enough. "You okay?"

His face softened a little, and he nodded.

"Oh, MA-one is doing just fine, aren't ya, big guy?" It was the unfamiliar female voice again, only this time it carried a sadistic edge. She laughed, low and throaty. "For now, at least."

Ignoring the pain as best I could—which really wasn't all that much—I turned my head to catch sight of the woman behind my chair. She moved too quickly, and all I saw were the wispy ends of her long, golden blonde hair. *She doesn't want me to see her...fine.* I scanned the rest of my surroundings instead. I wasn't overly excited by what I found.

I was in a concrete room—the walls, floor, ceiling, and even my chair were all formed of concrete. *Comfy*, I thought sarcastically. I guessed the room was larger than the average bedroom, maybe twenty feet on either side, with me in the center and Mase several feet away in front of me. Above us, florescent lights flickered and buzzed, washing out everything in the room. The space had the feeling of a bunker or a basement…or a dungeon. *Oh come on, who even has dungeons these days?* Unfortunately, part of my mind answered, *General Herodson.*

The room was suffocatingly enclosed, and unless there was a door in the wall behind me, the only thing breaking up the unrelenting stretches of dirty, gray concrete was the metal door behind Mase. Well, that and the handful of guards lining the walls, armed just as heavily as the two who had accompanied General Herodson into Dr. Wesley's office. Each had an assault rifle, a sidearm, a combat knife, and who knew what else hiding on their persons. It was starting to make sense why Mase hadn't pulled his bonds free.

Suddenly, dizziness forced me to close my eyes or risk throwing up on myself, and I really didn't think vomit would improve the room's ambiance. I considered using my Ability, but if even opening my eyes pushed me to the verge of nausea, communicating telepathically might knock me out completely, and I couldn't afford that at the moment.

With a metallic clang and the screech of rusty hinges, the metal door swung open, and several sets of footsteps marched into the room. I finally attained enough control over my roiling stomach and spinning head to reopen my eyes. I wasn't surprised by who I found standing off to one side of the door—General Herodson and his human lie detector. I took a deep, apprehensive breath.

Shuffling footsteps preceded the entrance of four more people, including Dr. Wesley and Camille. Camille was the source of most of the shuffling. She was being forced into the room by another guard, his unyielding hold restraining her arms and torso and her feet dragging on the ground as she was unwillingly hauled inside. The man who'd informed the General of my telepathy use earlier—a lanky, scruffy-haired man—entered alongside them, gripping Camille's upper arm so tightly he had to be hurting her. Nobody else entered behind them.

Complete and utter relief flooded me, temporarily easing my headache. Gabe wasn't there. I hoped it meant he'd managed to get away…to hide…to do *something.*

"Delightful," General Herodson remarked quietly. He reached out a hand toward the door. "Come here, dear Anna. Come see the future of mankind—it's a beautiful thing."

Dr. Wesley wound around the others to his side and linked her arm with his. Her face was absolutely blank. If there was one thing I was certain she'd passed on to her children, it was a knack for hiding her emotions.

"I'd hoped this wouldn't be necessary," General Herodson

began, "but it would seem that some people are more resistant to my power of suggestion than others." He looked from me to Mase and back again. "Take MA-one, for example. He'd been on this base for over a year and had always been loyal and obedient. But once the Great Transformation began, every once in a while he showed small displays of defiance. Now, *even* as a Re-gen, he defies me." General Herodson smiled congenially. "So you see, when you started displaying similar signs of defiance, I could hardly make the same mistakes I made with him."

What's he saying? That he's not going to turn me into a Re-gen? So is he just going to kill me?

He paused and watched me thoughtfully. "I would just kill you, but I find myself in need of your rather unique talents. Telepaths I have—practically more than I know what to do with—but none like you. They're all one-way radios, only sending, never receiving, but you send *and* receive." He dropped Dr. Wesley's arm and took several steps closer to me, skirting around Mase with reasonable caution. The Re-gen's feet weren't secured to the ground, and I didn't doubt he could lash out with his legs, chained wrists or not.

Stopping barely a foot from my chair, General Herodson cocked his head from side to side, studying me. "Tiny little thing, aren't you? Where do you keep all of that power, I wonder?" He reached out with one hand to tilt my face upward. "Pretty, too, if you like redheads. Myself, I prefer dark hair." His hand shifted, seizing my jaw, and he squeezed.

I didn't want to do it—I hated doing it—but his grip grew too painful, and I couldn't help it. I cried out.

Mase's chains rattled, a dull clanking, and concrete dust rained down from the ceiling. It took me a moment to realize that the low, deep rumbling I was hearing was Mase…growling. It sounded so similar to Jack's vicious growl that I half thought a dog had found its way into the room. It's funny, the random thoughts you have when you're pretty sure you're about to die.

Without warning, General Herodson released my face and

hammered his fist down on my left forearm. There was a crack and a moment of bright, glittering white light, which was instantly eclipsed by the sharpest pain I'd ever felt. I howled in agony and squeezed my eyes shut, again fighting nausea.

"If you do anything like that again," I heard the General say, sounding far away and tinny, "I'll cut off her hand completely. A telepath doesn't need hands—at least, not both. Now, where was I?" Fingertips touched my cheek, patting gently. "Open your eyes, Danielle. I wasn't done speaking to you."

Gritting my teeth and panting, I somehow managed to peel my eyelids open.

"Good!" General Herodson turned away from me, returning to Dr. Wesley's side. Was that a hint of strain I saw around her eyes? "Why do I need you so badly, you must be wondering. Well, I'm having a bit of a problem drawing people to me, and you seem to have been designed for exactly that." He smiled faintly. "I view it as destiny."

I was tempted to tell him I hadn't been *designed* for anything, let alone his sick plans, but I was terrified of adding a second broken arm to the count…or a missing hand. *I'll kill you. I'll kill you and feed you to the animals, you sick fucking bastard.*

General Herodson continued, oblivious to my silent defiance. "The whole point of the Great Transformation was to scour the earth clean of the cancer of humanity and start again—here. We'll build a clean, stable, crime-free civilization where this next evolution of mankind can thrive in peace."

"*Your* peace," I managed to rasp.

The General patted Dr. Wesley's hand and nodded sadly. "It is the only peace there is…or at least, it will be, once we work out a few kinks. Which brings us to our current task. There's someone I'd like you to meet."

He motioned for someone behind me to approach him, and the blonde woman rounded my concrete throne. She was tall, slender, and pretty, in an ice princess kind of way, but there was something about her piercing blue eyes that seemed off.

"This is one of the gifted people who make our new T-R program possible. With her remarkable Ability, I can completely erase all of your memories and implant new, useful ones that will promote our cause and make you more…pliant." He paused, then smiled. "Ah yes, I forgot to introduce you. Danielle, this is Clara."

Clara. I stiffened. *Is it possible?* The age, the hair, the oh-so-creepy eyes. *It's her—it has to be.* Clara—the woman who'd poisoned Zoe, who'd killed several of Zoe's friends in a fire meant to destroy them all—was here, staring at me. *Oh shit…oh shit…*

Panic and pain flooded my body with adrenaline, and my mind cleared momentarily. I had to get word to the others. I knew I didn't have much time—minutes at the most—and probably not even that, with the Ability-sensing guy in the room.

I found Gabe's mind almost instantly. He was above me and a little ways off to the right, but not too far. I described my surroundings to him and told him, if he could, to figure out some way to contact Jason and Zoe and coordinate the rest of the escape with them. I didn't wait for him to respond, instead using my dwindling time to search for any of the rescue party's minds.

"Sir, she's doing it again. I can tell it's her this time."

"Dose her. We'll have to finish this later," General Herodson said. He sounded irritated.

I hadn't noticed Clara leave his side, but suddenly she was beside me, sticking something into my upper arm. In seconds, my world ceased to be. *I* ceased to be.

"Wake up," someone sang softly.

My head spun, and my eyes refused to open.

"Wake up," the voice hissed.

I moaned.

"I said, 'Wake up!'" the person—a woman—repeated, immediately before she slapped me.

Groaning, I managed to crack one eyelid open. Clara's face was inches from mine.

She smiled sweetly, an expression that should have looked angelic but fit on her face about as well as a lullaby in a horror movie. "I sent the guards outside, so it's just us girls," she murmured conspiratorially. She shot a glance over her shoulder, presumably at Mase. "Well, *him* too, but he doesn't really count, does he? I mean, it's not like he's a real person."

She tilted her head to the side as she studied me, reminding me of a vulture. "I have something I've been *dying* to share with you." She giggled, sending a wash of chills over my skin. "I was with the team that stole you away, and guess who I saw?" She paused, her eyebrows raised as though she actually expected me to guess.

Again, I groaned. Her voice was making my vision swim, and I just wanted her to shut up.

"You're no fun!" she pouted. Her expression shifted instantly, her mouth curving into a gleeful smile and her eyes alighting with delight. "While we were hiding from your frantic little group, I spotted none other than my dear, dear friend Zoe! What a small world!" she exclaimed. Her voice turned razor sharp. "So you know what I'm thinking? You're that bitch she was always whining about—the one who was supposed to be with her brother." Her upper lip curled into a sneer. "She's out there, isn't she? Her and the others…and *Jake.* They're coming for you, aren't they?"

My sluggish mind finally processed what she'd told me. While my friends had been searching for me in the woods, Clara and who knew who else had stood by, hiding, and watched. *How? How had they gone undetected?*

"How?" I said, voicing my thought.

She snorted. "How should I know?" I had the feeling we were talking about two different things, but my brain felt groggy enough that I couldn't connect the dots. With a supremely sinister grin, she said, "Even if you *ever* get to see that whiny, sanctimonious bitch again, you won't know her. When I'm done with you, you won't remember anyone…you won't even know who you are."

Go to hell! In the back of my mind, I wondered what would happen if I never escaped, was never rescued, and ended up as the General's personal PA system. Death—my death—was a better option for everyone.

I started mumbling nonsense, hoping to lure Clara closer.

She leaned in. "What was that? It's okay, you can tell me."

"At least…she'll have…Jake…you psycho…*bitch*."

Clara screeched like a banshee and slapped my face repeatedly until, finally, the world faded away…again.

❂

"I'm not pleased," I heard the General say from far, far away. *Is he talking to me? What'd I do to anger him now?* "If I didn't need you as much as I needed her, you'd already be dead." *Is he talking to someone else?* "There are other ways to make your life very unpleasant. Pull a stunt like this again, and I'll show you," he said.

"I'm sorry, Sir."

Ah…Clara.

"Apologies prove nothing. Just don't do it again," General Herodson snapped.

"Yes, Sir."

There was a long pause, then the General said, "Good. Now wake her up."

I felt another prick in my arm, followed by a burning sensation that spread outward through my body. My forearm flamed with pain, as did the back of my head and various spots on my face. I turned to vomit over the side of the chair.

"Clean that up," the General said. I heard movement beside me. "We expected as much, what with your many injuries." His voice sounded matter-of-fact with a hint of kindness. "I didn't intend for this to turn so ugly, Danielle. The nausea will pass in a few minutes, once your brain has a chance to equalize the pain."

Slumped sideways in the chair as far as the arm restraints would allow, I simply breathed. In and out. In and out. In and out.

I hurt so badly. But the pain, I soon realized, was both a blessing and a curse. When I focused on it—embraced it—my head cleared a little. The pain drove away some of the haze of whatever medications they'd injected me with, and my Ability flared to life, just out of grasp. I needed a little more time, a little more clarity. *Just another minute*, I thought desperately, *just one more minute...*

"Can you sit up?" I felt hands on my upper arms, righting me before they let go. "There we go. Better, no? I would gladly drug you further to prevent such undue suffering, but alas, Clara can only work with your mind when it's awake and unclouded with medications. So, we have a bit of a dilemma. I need your mind clear enough for Clara to begin the T-R process, but I can't have you communicating with whoever it is you keep communicating with. I've had a little chat with my advisors, and they all agree that since my influence worked on you in the beginning, it should work on you again, at least for as short of a time as we need it to, so—" When he spoke again, his words were laced with will-bending power. "—open your eyes."

I did, instantly. *I want to tear out your throat with my teeth.*

"Good. One more little test." Again his voice filled with the power of undeniable influence. "When I touch your broken arm, you will not make a noise."

I watched as his hand slowly neared my broken forearm, dreading the pain I knew would accompany his touch. When his fingertips pressed down on skin that was swollen and just starting to show hints of bruising, my lungs tried to force a scream, but the sound caught in my throat.

"Wonderful," General Herodson said. "Now listen very carefully. You will not talk to anyone telepathically, you will not try to escape, and you *will* answer all of my questions truthfully." He offered me a fatherly smile and added, "And because I'm not a monster, you will not feel any more pain."

Blessed relief—the lack of pain—blanketed my body. The aches and throbs weren't gone, exactly, but they were distant, almost like memories of pains long past. Freed from the burden of pain, I was able to notice the other people in the room. Mase was still dangling in front of me on trembling muscles, and Clara was skulking in a corner. There were even more guards lining the walls than had been there before, making me feel claustrophobic. The Truth Guard was back, along with the guard holding Camille and the man who could tell when Abilities were in use—who was still grasping Camille's arm in an iron grip.

"Better?" General Herodson asked.

I nodded, grateful despite myself. *I hate you. You* are *a monster.*

"Good. Now, tell me all about your little rebel friends on base. Who are they?"

Compelled beyond personal restraint, I answered. "Mase and Camille, and Gabe." Somehow, I hadn't felt the need to provide Dr. Wesley's name. *Is it because she's not my friend? Or is it because the neutralizer is still working, even a little?*

"Gabe? Gabriel McLaughlin?" General Herodson asked skeptically, frowning. "Why didn't I see that coming?" He turned away from me and barked several hurried orders at the guards nearest the exit. Two of them rushed out of the room, practically slamming the door.

I squeezed my eyes shut as the clang resounded in the room.

"Eyes open, Danielle," the General commanded, and I obeyed. He met my eyes, seeming to see inside me. "What about your other friends, the ones outside who are supposedly coming to rescue you? How many are there? What can they do? Where are they?"

"I'm not sure how many are coming…maybe a couple, maybe a dozen or more." I wanted to bite my tongue off to stop the words from tumbling out of my mouth. "They can do many things: walk, talk, jump, shoot gu—"

"What are their Abilities?"

I considered how to order their Abilities to hide the most dangerous, but then I realized that in his hands, they were all dangerous. "Visions, telepathy, changing the magnitude of others' Abilities, something with electricity, empathy, mental healing, regeneration, lie detecting, sensing volatility, and some we're unsure of. Oh, and I don't know where they are." I smiled.

"Have you come across any other large groups of survivors?"

"Yes."

He pressed his lips into a thin line. "Where?"

"One near Lake Tahoe and the other on the California coast a little north of San Francisco." Again, I'd been able to answer truthfully without revealing everything. He hadn't asked for any names of towns, he'd just asked *where*.

General Herodson sighed. "I see that there is already some resistance to my influence. Very well; I'll have Clara search for the things I want to know while she's erasing your memories." Gone was the pretense of kindness, and his steel-gray eyes turned to ice. "Sometimes the T-R process requires several swipes of the hard drive. You should know that to test your obedience I'll be ordering you to kill your sweetheart."

My heart skipped a beat. *Does he have Jason? Oh God, no!*

The General backed up and looked at Mase. "An interesting choice. I wasn't sure if Re-gens were still sexual creatures, but I know this one spent the night at your house and you seem quite concerned about his well-being, so I can only assume you two… it's quite enlightening." *He's going to order me to kill Mase…*

A thrashing and screaming Camille drew my attention. "You promised! You said you wouldn't hurt either of them if I told you! You promised!" But Camille was as small as me—half the size of the soldier restraining her—and she hadn't had any combat training. She didn't stand a chance of breaking free. Hell, were I in her place, I wouldn't have either. *Wait…why isn't she using her Ability to—*

"If you're hoping she'll mentally gut us all, don't hold your breath," General Herodson said, seeming to read my mind. He'd turned to watch Camille's struggles as well. "Frank, the man holding her arm, has a very unique Ability. Not only can he sense when others are using their Abilities, but through touch, he can suppress others from using theirs." He sighed, sounding wistful. "Unfortunately, Camille will also be disposed of when this ugly business is completed. She was useful, but…you can't always get what you want." Turning, he beckoned Clara from the corner. "Come, start the process. I'm tiring of this. I want to be done with it."

I watched Clara slink closer, watched her reach her slender fingers out to touch my temples. Her presence in my mind felt like an oil spill, toxic and clinging. Defensively, my Ability kicked in, and I sought out the nearest familiar mind.

Ray was circling in the sky above the Colony, swooping and soaring along currents of wind. Slipping out of my mind and into hers was the most welcome relief imaginable.

29
ZOE
MARCH 22, 1AE

It was a couple hours past nightfall and we'd ridden nearly fifty miles. Our horses were worn out by the time we made it to the south end of Silver Spruce golf course. We hadn't been willing to linger any closer to the Colony than necessary for fear of running into patrolling black-bands, so we'd settled for our tucked-away ghost town and exhausted horses instead.

Thankfully, having known we would be leaving, we already had most of our belongings packed by the time Jason received Dani's panicked communication. Tavis and Sam had decided to stay with our group, riding with us to Colorado Springs to rescue Dani, and then on to Durango to meet up with the others. Shadow was still healing and putting on weight, so he was ponied behind the brown mare I'd saddled up to ride on our journey.

As soon as we reached the pond, the place where Dani was supposed to meet us, Carlos, Chris, and Jason dismounted and moved a few yards away from the rest of us. Carlos needed to focus on sending out an electromagnetic pulse strong enough to shut down the ever-stretching sea of electricity. We needed to signal to Dani that we'd arrived and were ready for her to make her escape, and the disorientation caused by the blackout would aid her breakout.

Anxiously, I stood beside Jake, Harper, and Sanchez amidst the overgrown green, taking in what we could see of the infamous Colony. The very idea of its existence festered in my mind. The place seemed alive, radiant even. It had been months since I'd seen something so inexplicably awe-inspiring…and obscene. The longer I stared at it, the hotter the deep, septic hatred burning inside my gut became. *Killing people? Kidnapping them? And for what purpose, exactly?* I knew there was no acceptable reasoning behind it, and I wanted to hurt everyone responsible for causing so much pain and heart-wrenching grief—the doctor, maybe, or Gabe and the General.

In fact, knowing the General was responsible for creating the two Re-gens that were with Dani made me restless. I'd witnessed how loyal Becca had been to her "Father," how much she feared his wrath and how desperate she was to please him. *What makes Dani's Re-gens any different?*

But every time I thought of Dani stuck inside that glowing, mind-controlled encampment with the General, who wanted her Ability so badly he'd probably waste no expense to retain possession of her, I knew my *only* choice was to trust the Re-gens…and Gabe. I had to believe they would keep Dani safe and get her to the electric fence in one piece. I had to believe that Camille would not only use her metal-controlling Ability to successfully cut through the deadly fence, but also to detain any guards who crossed their path, and that Mase really would use his superhuman strength and speed to fight off any who made it past Camille. And I had to believe that Gabe, using his knowledge of how the Colony worked, would get Dani out of there once and for all…that he wouldn't betray us all again. I *had* to believe that together they would help keep Dani safe until we met them outside the fence, and I *had* to believe that tonight was the night we would all ride away and never look back. I sighed. *God, I hope they know what they're doing...*

Jake leaned into me, nudging my shoulder with his. Apparently my mental scowl was readable on my face, too.

I shook my head in disbelief at the glowing city spread out before us, but quickly my determination resurfaced. *We're getting Dani out of that fucking hellhole.*

There weren't walls lining the perimeter like those of a castle, nor were there machine gun stations atop battlements like I'd half expected; there was only a heavily charged electric fence. *It's not so impossible*, I mused. Then again, I guessed the General didn't need towers and tanks if he was mind-controlling everyone so expertly and had walking weapons at his beck and call.

Dani had told us that guards weren't scarce along the Colony's border, and that they patrolled the roads and the buildings surrounding the base, watching and waiting for any possible dangers. The Colony was well equipped, to say the least—they had electricity, and from the intense aura of light around it, they had a lot of it. We didn't stand a chance. At least, not without Carlos's Ability.

Unexpectedly, shooting and distant yelling echoed from inside the Colony, and my heart seemed to stop in momentary dread. *What the hell's going on? Is it Dani?*

I glanced over at Carlos's shadowed form kneeling on the grass. Even in the darkness, I could tell he was shaking. Chris's silhouette crouched on his right while Jason's stood to Carlos's left, each with a supportive hand on his shoulder. We were relying on the darkness and the weeping willows to shield us from any watchful eyes. Hearing another burst of gunfire, I grabbed Jake's hand, clutching it tightly while I squeezed my eyes shut. *Please work.*

As if Carlos himself had heard my plea, the humming sound of electricity faded. My eyes flew open in time to see a wave of darkness flowing away from us...away from Carlos.

30

DANI

MARCH 22, 1AE

I was Ray.

It was moon-time. I spotted my prey again, flitting from branch to branch in a tree with budding leaves. It squawked once before launching itself into the air. I dove, striking at it as I crossed over its back, and watched it fall to the earth. Lazily, I sank through the air, landing beside my prey with a victorious cry. I tore into it, savoring its warm flesh.

Sated, I extended my wings fully and launched back into the air immediately before she-who-flies-with-me withdrew.

I slipped out of Ray, and like I was sloshing across an ocean of tar, crawled back into my own mind. Instantly, I regretted it. Despite the General's power-laced command to not feel pain, a deep ache pulsed through my body, and the fact that I was still strapped to the damn concrete chair by shiny steel restraints wasn't helping my comfort level.

But...yes! I'm also still me! I'm not a T-R! I didn't understand it, but somehow, fleeing into Ray's mind had protected me from Clara's Ability. *Thank you, Ray!*

Opening my eyes, I glanced around the room. Camille was still there, standing with her wrists handcuffed in front of her and Frank at her side, suppressing her Ability through his touch. I could hear someone moving around behind me and figured it was Clara. Mase stood in the same place in front of me, his arms still extended over his head by heavy iron chains, and sweat streamed down his face and neck. General Herodson, on the other hand, was gone. The only other people in the room were two yellow-armbanded guards watchfully flanking the door. *Where'd the General go? Why'd he take most of his people?*

"Where's Herodson?" I croaked.

At my question, Clara skipped around to the front of my seated prison, blocking only some of Mase's massive body with her slender frame. "You're awake! That's a relief!" she exclaimed, sounding genuinely relieved. "General Herodson was super pissed. He thought I did something that broke your mind, but I knew I didn't. *You* did something." She balled her hands into fists and placed them on her hips in an exaggerated motion. "You made me look like a fool in front of him!" She glared at me. "What did you do?" I half expected her to stomp her foot in indignation.

What did I do? "Ah…what?"

Clara's eyes narrowed to slits, and she moved closer to me, setting her hands beside my wrists on the wide cement armrests. She leaned in so far that she was almost close enough to kiss. I was tempted to spit in her face.

Instead, I whispered, "You're in my bubble."

Slowly, a sly grin turned up the ends of her mouth, making her eyes glint with malice. "You know, *he* won't be back for a while. He has some crisis to deal with…something with those Re-gen freaks. But that doesn't mean we can't play while he's gone. I may not be able to wipe your mind—yet—but there are other things we can do for fun." Clara smiled sweetly. "And who says you're the only one I can play with?"

Turning, she took several steps in Mase's direction and placed a hand on the side of his ribcage. Ever so slowly, she walked a circle around him, tracing her fingers along his sweat-soaked t-shirt. "A bit damp for my tastes, but he's definitely burly enough." When she was behind him, she reached her right hand around to his stomach and slipped it down to the waistband of his fatigues. "I bet I could have a *lot* of fun with him." She traced a line along the coarse fabric, barely dipping her fingers lower.

Mase jerked away from her touch as much as possible. His eyes were squeezed shut, and his face was locked in a strained grimace.

I looked past the disturbing scene and met Camille's eyes. They were wide, imploring with me to pay attention to her…to the words she was mouthing, slowly and deliberately: "Use your telepathy on me." Her eyes widened further, demanding.

Use my telepathy on her? But I can't! The General commanded me not to…oh! He'd said I wasn't allowed to use it to *talk* to anyone, but he hadn't forbidden me from listening to—or, in Camille's case, seeing—what other people were trying to tell me. She wanted me to connect our minds telepathically. I jerked my head in a single, minimal nod.

"Don't look at her!" Clara screeched. "She's not a part of this. This is *my* game!"

I shifted my gaze back to the psychotic blonde, settling a bland expression on my face. It was harder than it sounds. Her left hand was clutching Mase's arm just above the elbow, her fingernails digging in deep enough that several thin streams of blood were sliding down his arm.

I leeched all emotion from my voice, doing my best to look bored. "What do you want from me?"

"I want you to watch…just watch, that's all," she cooed.

Keeping my eyes locked on Clara's, I reached out to Camille with my mind. I had to swallow a cry of relief. I could connect with her mind even if I couldn't actually say anything because of the General's damn command.

I saw myself in Gabe's empty lab, lying on the floor while he injected me with the neutralizer. And then I saw myself start screaming. Camille, peeking through the door from the hallway, dropped to her knees, clutching her head in her hands.

I saw myself as I currently was, restrained and broken. The rest of the concrete prison was in place, guards and prisoners alike. Again, I saw myself start screaming, but only Frank, the man touching Camille's arm suppressing her Ability over metals, seemed affected by my outpouring of power.

I saw myself running down a dark corridor with Camille and Mase. We were free and fleeing together.

Blinking, I refocused on Clara and Mase. Only seconds had passed since I'd started receiving images from Camille's mind, but Clara's hand had dipped further into Mase's pants. It wouldn't be long until she'd violated him completely. With renewed determination, I focused on my Ability. Camille wanted me to use it like I had after receiving my one and only dose of the neutralizer and remembering all of the memories and pain of the last few months.

Wait—she was there? I shook my head. *Focus!*

But I'd had heartbreaking memories, an aching sense of loss, to fuel my scream the last time. None of that was as fresh now. All I had was...artificially dulled pain. *Will that work?*

In a surreal moment, I stepped outside of myself, assessing my emotions. *What else do I have to work with?* Anger. Panic. Fear. I had an overabundance of fear. I was terrified of never escaping from the Colony, of being wiped clean and remade into someone else. *And what if something happens to Zo and Jason?* My gut-wrenching terror was so powerful that once I started screaming, I feared I might never be able to stop.

But that was assuming it would work at all. I didn't know if the General's command not to use my Ability to talk to anyone telepathically would extend to mind-screaming.

There's only one way to find out.

Shifting my attention to Frank, I opened my mouth and focused all of my mental power on my unrestrainable fear. I let it nourish me. Consume me. Transform me. I embraced it, and when I pushed the air out of my lungs, I used that fear to make my scream as mind-shredding as possible.

Oh God! It felt like shooting a never-ending laser of pure telepathic power into Frank's mind. I strained under the force of it, watching him convulse as blood leaked from his nose. Nobody else seemed to realize what was happening to him—nobody but Frank and Camille. Probably because everyone else was staring at me.

My scream cut off almost as abruptly as it began, and I hunched in on myself, panting.

"What's wrong with you?" Clara asked me warily, drawing my attention back to her.

I risked the briefest glance at Frank. Blood was leaking from his ears, too. Crimson tears started streaming from the corners of his eyes right before he stiffened and sank to the floor, releasing Camille…freeing her Ability. She didn't hesitate in unleashing it.

"What the hell?" one of the guards at the door exclaimed while his counterpart simply struggled in place. Their bodies weren't frozen—they could still move, a little, so I knew Camille wasn't restraining them by the metals in their blood—but they appeared stuck enough.

Stunned, Clara still stood behind Mase, one hand partially submerged in the front of his pants.

Camille pointed to her and said, "She doesn't have any metal on her. I can't hold her in place."

"Mase! Pull!" I shouted. He didn't falter.

At the exact instant my steel restraints snapped open, chunks of concrete rained down on Mase from the ceiling and the heavy chain clattered to the floor. Clara followed almost immediately, collapsing into a limp heap. There was blood on her temple.

I stood, cradling my broken arm, my legs shaking. Camille's fingers were hovering over the locks holding the manacles around Mase's wrists. Keeping an eye on an unconscious Clara, I approached my friends. "What'd you mean about the metal? Why can she still move?"

Camille was clenching her jaw. She didn't look up as she said, "The low concentration of metals in the body…takes a lot of effort to hold someone that way…but almost everyone has metal *on* them…and holding that in place is easier…a lot easier. I can do… more…that way."

The iron that had been around Mase's wrists clanked to the ground, and he rubbed his raw skin. "Thanks, Camille," he said softly before striding around the room, knocking out each of the guards quickly and efficiently. At least, I thought he only knocked them out.

Camille crossed her arms over her middle, her eyes narrowed with strain as she watched Mase. All of a sudden, a thick stream of blood started leaking from her left nostril.

"Crap, Camille, did you get hit in the nose?" I lurched forward so I could get a closer look at her face.

She turned wide, gray eyes on me. "What? No."

"You're bleeding."

Tentatively, she raised a hand to her face and touched her shaking fingers to the blood. Looking at her crimson-coated fingertips, she frowned. "I wonder…it must be because…I'm holding so much metal in place…right now."

If her Ability's making her nose bleed, what's it doing to her brain? "How much metal, Camille?"

She glanced around the room. "All of it."

"In here?"

She shook her head. "In the Colony…at least, all that I can reach. Except what's on us."

My heart sank, and I reached for her good arm with *my* good arm. "We need to get out, now, so you can let go."

Mase hurled his body at the door, and after several failed attempts at breaking it down, Camille asked him to stop. There was a low, metallic click. "It's unlocked now, but…"

"But what?" I asked, stopping midway to the door.

Camille sagged in place, remaining on her feet for a few seconds before falling to her knees. "I can't go with you. I can't do anything else. I'll lose concentration." Raising her eyes to mine, she made a silent plea. "Leave me. I'll hold on as long as I can."

"No, Camille—"

Mase had apparently heard enough. Having already opened the door, he stomped back to Camille and hoisted her up, flinging her over his shoulders in a fireman's carry. He turned to me. "Let's go."

All of a sudden, Clara was on her feet and sprinting out of the room.

"Mase! She's—" I started to say, but his hands were full with Camille, and the sadistic woman was gone before he could do anything to detain her. *Damn it!*

"Forget her," Mase said. "We need to go, now."

I followed him to the door…and froze. I couldn't move.

No, that wasn't quite right. I could move backward—back into the room—but I couldn't step through the doorway. My stomach soured and bile rose to my throat when I realized what was going on. General Herodson had *also* commanded me not to try to escape. So far, everything I'd done had been to help free Camille and Mase as much as myself. But leaving the room—that was definitely *me* trying to escape.

"Shit!" I hissed.

In the hallway, Mase turned, his eyebrows drawn down in confusion.

"I can't leave...the General's commands—"

There was the sound of a throat clearing in the hallway to the left of the doorway. "I believe I could help with that...if I could move more than my mouth, fingers, and toes." I didn't need to be able to see him to know it was Gabe. I wanted to collapse to the ground in equal parts relief and frustration. I couldn't get to him, but he was alright...for the moment.

"Ah, thank you, Camille." Looking harried, Gabe stepped through the doorway and into the interrogation room with me. His eyes flicked around the room, taking in the five motionless bodies, but he shook his head and returned his attention to me. He scanned me from head to toe, shock and fury pinching his features.

"I thought you might need this," he said, holding up a small metal case. I desperately hoped it held the neutralizer. Without pretense, he removed an inoculator and a glass vial, fitted them together, and injected the neon liquid into my neck.

Within seconds, I felt the General's influence erode until it released me completely. Luckily, it wasn't like the previous time, when all my old, painful memories had resurfaced at once. Unluckily, it was physical pain that threatened to drown me. I stiffened, shutting my eyes tightly while I struggled to hold on to consciousness under the sheer agony. I gritted my teeth. *I* won't *give in!* Slowly, it abated, fading to a more manageable level.

I reached for Gabe's hand with my good arm and gave it a squeeze. "Thanks. Let's get out of here." Tugging on his hand, I pulled him through the doorway, took a single step into the hallway, and froze again. At least that time it wasn't because of the General's commands.

A pretty, dark-haired woman wearing jeans and a navy-blue hooded jacket waited with Mase and Camille, her words speeding and her gestures emphatic as she spoke to them. I caught snippets of what she was saying...*had a vision...slaughter...warned them... uprising...all Re-gens...so much blood...*

She looked familiar, but I couldn't place her. "Gabe, who...?"

"Ah, yes," Gabe said. "This is the woman I told you about… RV-one. I mean, Becca."

"Becca," I repeated, and her familiarity slipped into place. I'd recognized her from the photo in her dossier. I was staring at Rebecca Vaughn, the formerly dead sister of Jake Vaughn. I'd forgotten all about her, about trying to find her and taking her with me when I fled. "How'd you—"

"Not now. Right now we need to run."

As if our friends on the outside heard him, the power flickered several times, then failed completely, leaving us in total darkness. It was my signal.

"Aw…you've got to be kidding me," Gabe muttered.

"No, it's good. It's Carlos," I told him. "It's my people. They're here."

"I've *seen* this," Becca said off to the left, her voice raspy. The way she said "seen" reminded me of her Ability—prophetic visions. "We must go now. The rebellion will only distract Father and his guards for so long, and not all are restrained by CL-one's power. They will be here soon. I know the way; I've seen it. Come. We must hold hands."

Gabe didn't give me a chance to protest. One second I was standing, holding his hand and gaping into the darkness, the next I was pulled into a fast walk.

Mentally, I found Ray, who I was still connected to by a thin tether. I pictured Jason and showed her the image. By the time Ray reached him, drawing me to his exact location, we were outside and running down the street, the half-moon glowing like a beacon in the night sky. I was surprised to discover that my concrete prison had been in the basement of the communications building.

My telepathy was slipperier than usual, making it almost impossible to lock on to Jason. Finally, after multiple failed attempts, I made contact. *"We're on our way,"* I told him, barely managing to complete the thought before my telepathy sputtered and winked out of commission. I'd burned it out—again. *Shit!*

But I didn't have time to worry about my damaged Ability. I needed to focus on my feet, on keeping them moving. Each step jarred my arm, making invisible shards of glass stab into the swollen flesh.

At least I'm not dead, I told myself.

31

ZOE

MARCH 22, 1AE

Jason shot up from his squatted position. "She's coming," he said as he started pacing.

With a sporadic, increasingly loud hum, the electricity flickered back to life, once more illuminating the darkness beyond the golf course. My head snapped to Carlos, who was still unsteady on his feet from overexerting his Ability for the first time.

"Fuck, they're back in business," Jason spat. A few seconds later, the humming dissipated and the Colony faded back into blackness.

Carlos dropped to his knees, his breathing labored and his palms seeming to be the only thing keeping him from falling completely over.

Without hesitation, Chris ran to his side. "Carlos! Why would you…" she asked, her words trailing off as she wrapped an arm around him, trying to soothe him.

I began to feel strange…foggy. *Is it his exhaustion? Anticipation?*

"They're going to be looking for the source of that, now," Harper said.

I glanced around at the others. "What do we do?" I was

growing dizzy, and I blinked the sensation away. A splitting pain shot through my mind, and I stumbled forward.

Jake caught me by the arm and pulled me against him. "Are you alright?"

I nodded, squeezing his hand in reassurance before pointing to a willow tree a few yards away. "I think Carlos's emotions are getting to me. I just need to sit down for a minute."

Although I felt his apprehension, Jake helped me over to the tree, easing me down to sit at its base. "I'll be fine," I said, leaning my head back against the trunk, trying to breathe away the dense fog creeping into my mind.

"Zoe!" Harper called from over near Carlos. "Bring me the med-kit from my saddle bag."

When I tried to stand, Jake's arm eased me back against the tree. "I'll get it." I could feel his concern and conceded.

Jake jogged toward the horses, who were drinking out of the pond.

"Zoe." In my muddled mind, I thought I heard Dani's soft, frightened voice. "Zoe."

I tensed. *It* is *her*.

The voice wasn't in my head, though, like her normal telepathic communications, but echoing all around me. I couldn't hear the others, my mind too fuzzy to concentrate on anything other than Dani's voice.

"Dani?" I whispered.

"Zoe!" I heard the acute panic in her tone. "Where are you, Zoe? I need your help…please!"

Oh my God, Dani! I rose unsteadily to my feet as I looked for her in the darkness—running toward me, sending me a signal, something…anything. I squinted, trying to see her, as my heart raced.

"Come find me, Zoe!" With her words, an image of Dani hiding in a copse of trees at the border of the Colony came to mind, and I *knew* where to find her.

I turned to call for the others, who were all huddled around Carlos. *Can't they hear her?* But before I could call to them, I was distracted by Dani's urgency and fear. It felt like I was the one hiding, scared and alone. I needed to get to the trees. I needed to help her.

Without a second thought, I ran straight for the Colony… toward Dani.

32

DANI

MARCH 22, 1AE

Our crazed dash from the communications building to the golf course was the longest mile I'd ever run. It was as though the laws of physics chose that moment to rearrange, expanding distance and slowing time; the distance was endless, the time it took to cross it, eternal.

Exhaustion clawed at my hamstrings and quadriceps while pain-induced adrenaline raged through my body, keeping me from collapsing into a trembling, twitching pile of limbs. My heart pounded, warring with my lungs for space, and my vision narrowed to a dark tunnel seeming to accent my route with silver and red starlight.

Swollen and bruised, my face slowly stopped aching. The shards of pain shooting up my arm dulled, and my feet turned leaden. They belonged to someone else, someone who had the will to keep moving…fleeing…surviving.

We were getting closer to the south end of the Colony, closer to the golf course and my friends and safety…so close.

Two men dressed in brown long underwear and wearing yellow armbands sprinted directly across our path only a few yards ahead.

Three more people—Re-gens, based on the scrubs they were wearing—followed them, close on their heels.

"What—" I gasped and stumbled.

Gabe's arm latched around my waist, gripping so tightly that it was almost painful. Or, it would've been painful if I'd been able to feel a single thing in my body. I could use my limbs, clumsily, but they didn't follow my brain's commands well enough to keep me moving ahead. If it hadn't been for Gabe, I would've been on the ground.

"Doesn't matter," Gabe grated hoarsely as he dragged me along beside him. "If they're not after us, we just ignore them and keep going."

"But…who—why—what's going on?" I managed to ask between several short breaths.

"The Re-gens rebelled. Becca had a vision of Herodson ordering and carrying out their mass-execution…and told them about it. There are enough of them to give Herodson's forces a good fight."

I was shocked, or as surprised as I could've been on the verge of passing out from exhaustion. A Re-gen rebellion on the night of our escape was an eerie coincidence. "Good…for them," I breathed. And then for minutes, or maybe hours, all I did was run.

With the power down, passing through the usually electrified chain-link fence surrounding the Colony and into the overgrown golf course was easy enough. Camille was able to multitask with her Ability enough to tear a man-sized hole in the fence, allowing the five of us passage, and surprisingly, the border patrol guards were absent. *They must have been called away from the fences to help squash the rebellion.* It was weirdly convenient, but I wasn't about to complain.

Suddenly, shouting surrounded me, a chaotic miasma of sound that sent my head spinning. I couldn't make sense of it.

"Hurry!"

"Get to the horses! They're here…"

"Dani? Holy fuck, what—?"

"Help her! Please!"

"What's wrong with her? Let me see…"

I scanned the darkness ahead of me, but all I could see were shadows. There were too many voices, too much confusion. I couldn't tell who was saying what.

"We need to go—now!"

"No! We find Zoe first!"

"What's *she* doing here?"

"Becca? How did you—"

Hands jerked me away from Gabe's supportive hold, jarring my broken arm. The new hands shook as they traveled over my face and clothes, searching.

"Can you ride?" Belatedly, I realized the question had come from Jason. It was his hands that examined me, tender and trembling.

"Her arm's broken, and she almost dropped on the way here. I'd guess she's on the verge of passing out."

That's Gabe, I realized. No matter how hard I focused, coherent thought slipped further away.

"Uh, guys? This one's not looking so good."

"What are you talk—" Jason started to snap, but his words cut off as my knees gave out. He eased me to the ground, cradling me against his body. "Dani." If he said anything more, I didn't hear it.

There was only silence…and darkness.

In the past four months, I'd lost consciousness more than I had in the previous twenty-six years of my life—knocked out, drugged, or fainted. It was getting old.

"Dani?" Jason whispered softly, his warm breath brushing my face. I wasn't surprised to find his eyes inches from mine, sapphire turned midnight-blue in the dark of night. They held so much emotion, so much fear and elation. Too much. They swallowed me, becoming my whole world.

Heart soaring, I raised my left hand to his face. Before I reached him, before I moved my arm a scant inch, pain enveloped me, and I whimpered. But I didn't look away from his beautiful eyes.

"It's okay," he murmured as he brushed a sweaty curl out of my face. "We'll get you fixed up as soon as we get somewhere safe. No one else is going to hurt you. I've got you now." Featherlight, he pressed his lips against mine.

Someone else licked my cheek. *Not someone...Jack!*

"Help me up?" I asked, pushing off the overgrown grass with my good hand. Beside me, my dog wagged his tail excitedly.

Jason's arms were gentle as he raised me to a sitting position and ran a hand up and down my spine. I maneuvered my feet under me, and carefully rose first to my knees, then my feet. I wasn't standing for long.

"Oh my God! Camille!" I wailed.

Chris, Gabe, Harper, and Mase were kneeling around Camille, her body stretched out on the grass. I stumbled the several yards separating us and fell to the ground beside Mase, who was holding her head on his lap. Silvery moonlight made her paler than usual. She looked almost dead.

"Is she okay?" I asked.

Shocking the hell out of me, Camille's eyes snapped open and focused on mine. "Dani," she breathed. Dark, thick blood streamed from her nose, staining her lips and teeth a ghastly crimson. "Come closer." Her voice was thin, strained.

I did as she asked, leaning in so all she had to do was whisper. Dread solidified in my stomach when I noticed that her nose wasn't the only thing bleeding. Less intensely, but no less frightening, blood leaked from her ears as well. *Does that mean her brain is bleeding...like Frank's?*

"I had to let go. I'm sorry." She took a deep breath and squeezed her eyes shut.

"Let go? It's fine, Camille." I hadn't noticed the tears leaking from my eyes until a sob bubbled up from my chest. "We did it… we made it out. We're gonna be okay…*you're* gonna be okay."

She smiled, and her gaze shifted to the man stroking her dark hair with intimate delicacy. "Giant?"

"Yeah?" Mase's voice was hoarse.

"I have to tell you something…come here."

Mase leaned over her, turning his ear to her lips. I could see her jaw moving, but her words were too faint to hear. Mase's eyebrows drew down, and he frowned as she spoke, but when she was done, his face hardened with resolve. He nodded and pulled away.

Camille's eyes didn't leave him as she mouthed, "I love—" Abruptly they rolled back into her skull, and her mouth formed a small "O." Her body starting jerking violently.

"Hold her down!" Harper exclaimed, securing her legs. "She's seizing!"

Someone nudged me out of the way with careful forcefulness. Jason, I realized as I scooted off to the side, only to have Carlos crouch down and wrap a sturdy arm around me. Huddling together, we watched as Jason helped Gabe restrain Camille's shoulders while Chris sat astride her, holding down her midsection, and Mase cradled her head. I'd never felt so useless.

Almost as suddenly as they started, the tremors ceased. Camille was absolutely motionless. The others froze in place, seeming to hold their breath.

"Is she…breathing?" I choked out. Shock had interrupted my tears, but the sorrow swelled anew in my chest. *I did this…this is my fault…I asked her to…it's my fault…*

"No pulse," Harper said. He'd reached up to her wrist, though I hadn't noticed him move.

"Camille?" Mase sobbed, bending over her head. "Camille!"

Chris shoved Jason's shoulder and shouted, "Move him! We have to open her airway!"

Jason met Gabe's eyes and nodded once in Mase's direction. They moved behind the Re-gen, crouching to drag him back several feet. He dragged Camille with him.

"You have to let go, Mase, or they can't help her!" I cried. His eyes met mine, pleading, and I crawled closer. "Let go, Mase, please. *Let go*."

After a breath—a lifetime—he did. Jason and Gabe tugged him backward, and Chris rose up on her knees, lifted Camille's neck so her head tilted back, and swept a finger into her mouth, making sure her airway was clear. Locking her hands together, Chris placed them on Camille's chest and glanced back at Harper. "I'll do the chest compressions, you do the breaths?"

Harper nodded and crawled around Camille's body until he was kneeling by her head.

"Now," she said, then waited for him to act as Camille's lungs before resuming compressions.

Three times they went through the cycle with no change. Three times Chris barked, "Now," and three times we all watched as Harper touched his mouth to Camille's, offering her his breath. On the beginning of the fourth cycle, a strange, cackling sound rang out above us, breaking through the repetitive sounds of CPR.

"Kak-kak-kak. Kak-kak-kak."

I stared up into the starlit sky, searching for the source of the sound. A shape, white against the darkness, swooped down. It glided past, barely a few yards from my head, and repeated, "Kak-kak-kak. Kak-kak-kak."

"One of yours?" Jason asked, catching my eye. "It's been following us since early this morning."

Understanding almost brought a smile to my face. "Ray!" Before I could reach out to the gleaming falcon with my mind, before I could even find out if my Ability worked, gunshots cracked in the not-too-far-off distance in the same direction Ray had come from. *Is she warning us?*

An instant later, two people coalesced in the moon shadows between the trees separating our current stretch of grass from that of another hole.

"Chris! Harper!" Jason hissed in warning as he rose to his feet. "Jake and Sanchez are returning. Sanchez says there's no sign of her. You've got until they reach us to bring the girl back or call it." He paused to study the two people sprinting toward us. "I'd say you've got thirty seconds, max."

I glanced around at my companions and then back out at the approaching runners, realizing Zoe was nowhere in sight. "Where's Zoe?" I asked, gut clenching.

Jason's jaw tensed, but he *did* answer. "We don't know." It wasn't much of an answer. "Can you ride?" Jason asked Mase, tossing him a pistol.

Mase caught the gun and shrugged.

"What do you mean? You don't know where she is?" I shrieked. I shot a look at Chris, who was pumping Camille's chest with renewed fervor. *C'mon, Camille, breathe!* "Zo came with you guys, right?"

"She wandered off. Now we can't find her." Suddenly, Jason's night-darkened eyes pinned me in place. "Can you feel her?"

I opened myself up to my telepathy—or tried to—but I couldn't reach it. "I can't…I can't feel anyone. Oh God, Zo!" I started to wring my hands but winced at the sharp stab of pain the motion caused. "Burnout. My telepathy's not working at all," I whispered, terrified. "We have to keep looking for her! We can't just leave her!" *Zoe…gone. Camille…dead. And why? So I can be with my friends again? My life's not worth theirs! How could I be so selfish? How could I let them risk themselves for me? How could I—*

A gasp, soft and stuttering, broke my mental flogging. Wide-eyed, I spun to stare at the trio of people still sitting in a cluster on the overgrown grass around Camille…who was alive.

Camille isn't dead!

Chris was hanging her head, and Harper was running his fingers through his hair.

An encore of gunshots from multiple directions shattered the anxious tableau. Jake and Sanchez reached us seconds later, Sanchez calling out, "We've got to move, now!"

Pain, exhaustion, shock, and fear immobilized me while the others moved around me. I should have been doing something, I knew, but I just…couldn't. "But, Zo…"

Again, gunshots cracked through the night, dangerously close. Hands were on my hips, lifting me, and instead of standing in the untrimmed grass, I was sitting in a saddle. Wings's saddle. She nickered softly and looked back at me, nodding her head in greeting.

"Are you fine to ride?" Jason asked from the ground. I nodded dumbly, watching as he mounted his chestnut gelding and turned him in a prancing circle. "Follow me," he called softly and kicked his horse into motion.

Glancing around at my companions, I noted that everyone had a mount, with Camille riding in front of Carlos. She was seated across his lap, unconscious but alive. I spurred Wings into motion and rode away from the Colony…from hell.

Without Zoe.

33

ZOE

MARCH 22, 1AE

I was standing—no, I was on my knees. They were damp, I was cold, and my body felt lethargic. My mind was a jumbled mess of partially coherent thoughts and pain…a searing pain centered in my brain and radiating to the base of my skull. I tried to open my eyes, but I couldn't, and uneasiness replaced my grogginess.

Where am I?

I heard the rustling of leaves and felt a slight breeze on my cheeks. *I'm outside.* I heard the leaves again. *Footsteps?*

When the sound stopped, I could feel the warmth of someone near me. My fingers twitched at my sides, yet I couldn't lift my hands or ball up my fists. *Why can't I move?*

I vaguely recalled trying to help someone, hurrying to get somewhere to help… "Dani," I squeaked.

It felt like I was teetering on the edge of something, about to plummet into a void. Yes, it was a fissure between something full and chaotic and something foreign and desolate. There were memories and images in it, muddled with blackness.

"Dani," I breathed again as an emptiness swelled inside me. I felt like my soul was being sucked from my body.

"Guess again," a familiar, sickly saccharine voice cooed near my ear.

Clara.

Hysteria crept over me. "Jake," I whispered. I wished he was nearby, but I knew he wasn't. *What have I done?* The muscles in my arms and legs clenched, and all I wanted to do was sleep…and cry. *What's happening to me? The voice…the images…she implanted them. She manipulated my mind…just like she did with Tanya.* A whimper escaped from my throat.

The pain in my head worsened, and the hot tears that rolled down my cheeks felt like liquid fire against my cold skin. "Clara… please," I whispered, begging for relief from the surmounting pain.

"I don't think so, Zoe," she said, and I could hear the smile on her lips. "I finally have you all to myself." She began humming.

I felt more tears spill down my cheeks, followed by a dull pulse of sadness and fear. *But why am I sad?* I suddenly couldn't remember. Chilled fingertips brushed my temples tenderly, and I couldn't recall why I'd been scared in the first place. *Why am I crying?* My clenched jaw relaxed, and an emptiness trickled into my mind. As the soft, angelic humming continued lulling me into a rolling wave of sleep, I felt lighter…*than what?* Lighter than I'd felt a moment before, I was sure. I didn't know why, and I didn't care. Sleep was all I wanted.

A woman's cold, hard tone pulled me back from the precipice of darkness. "What the hell are you doing?"

Growing panic filled the void inside me. I strained to open my eyes, but it was pointless.

The gentle hum ceased. "Dr. Wesley? How did you—"

"*What* are you doing?" the new woman—Dr. Wesley—enunciated evenly. "You're supposed to be in the interrogation room, working on the T-R candidate. I don't recall the General giving you leave."

"I…" The other woman sounded nervous as she struggled to find the words.

Slowly, my eyelids began to peel open. I could just make out the blur of the two women's outlines. The one who was standing further away was wearing a white lab coat. *That must be Dr. Wesley.* The other woman was standing beside me, dressed in something so dark she seemed almost hidden in the shadows.

"Get away from her," the doctor ordered, her eyes narrowing on the petite blonde before veering to me with what looked like concern.

Do I know these women? I thought I should, but the more I tried to recall them, the more severe the shooting pain in my head became. My hands flew to my temples, and I doubled over in pain.

The blonde turned to me, her sharp inhale audible even through my own cringing and gasping.

"How are you doing that, Zoe?" She bent down to me, twined her fingers around my braided hair, and yanked my head back. *Why is she doing this? Why is she hurting me?* "How are you fighting my Ability? I swear to fucking God, if you—"

"Get your hands off her!" Dr. Wesley demanded.

"You!" the blonde woman screamed. "You don't get to tell me what to do. I don't care who you are. She's mine!"

"I'm warning you, Clara. Get your fucking hands off my daughter or I'll—"

Her daughter? Me? My eyes landed on the doctor in time to see her swing a large, gnarled branch at the blonde's—Clara's—head.

When Clara fell to the ground, the invisible fingers digging into my brain retreated completely and the remnants of fog in my head dissipated. Although shaken, my mind felt amazingly clear.

"Zoe, are you okay?" Dr. Wesley crouched down beside me, her fingers tentatively reaching for my face and her eyes filled with an emotion I didn't understand.

She's my mom? Rubbing the back of my scalp, I nodded, wondering how the hell I'd gotten myself in my current situation to begin with. *What* is *the situation?*

Out of nowhere, a fist-sized rock grazed the side of the doctor's head, making her stumble to the ground.

"Your *daughter*?" Clara laughed demonically from beside a tree trunk. She dry-washed her hands and sighed. "Interesting. And how did you know I was out here? I know the General rarely lets you off your leash."

The doctor rubbed the side of her head, momentarily stunned, and I tried to stand.

Clara's interest shifted to me. "And what did you do? Why isn't my Ability working anymore!" she screamed in frustration. "What the *hell* is going on!"

"RV-one," the doctor grunted with what appeared to be a smirk on her face as she staggered to her feet. "RV-one told me where you'd be; she wanted me to protect Zoe."

"Why would she care about Zoe?"

"Well, I suppose that has to do with who her brother is. She said you might find his identity interesting."

Sneering, Clara crossed her arms and rolled her eyes. "I can barely contain my curiosity," she said snidely. "Please, Dr. Wesley, tell me. Who is her brother?"

"His name is Jake."

I watched the color drain from Clara's face. *RV-one? Jake?* My heart was thundering in my chest. *Why can't I remember anything?*

"Jake?" The shrill pitch in Clara's voice was gone, replaced with astonishment.

Taking advantage of Clara's momentary surprise, the doctor rounded on her, backhanding her across the face and sending Clara sprawling to the ground. As the doctor reached for the branch again, Clara grabbed on to the tail of her lab coat and yanked her down to the ground beside her.

Clara did this to me. Whatever's wrong with me, she did it. Dr. Wesley tried to save me. She called me her daughter. Before I realized what I was doing, I picked up the branch the doctor had been reaching for and swung it at Clara's head with all my might.

Clara's body went limp as she fell to the ground, but she'd done that once before and gotten right back up again. My body trembled with a surprising surge of adrenaline, and I hit her in the head again.

Dr. Wesley motioned for me to stop and crouched down to check Clara's neck for a pulse. "She's dead." When she stood, her eyes were on me and filled with sorrow.

Why is she sad? Shouldn't she be relieved? Happy, even?

"Thank you," she said quietly, tucking a loose strand of hair behind her ear.

I nodded, still shaking. "Thank *you*." I brought my hands up to my face to study them. "I'm—I'm not sure what would've happened if you hadn't shown up." I looked down at Clara. "I don't even know who she is or what she was doing to me." Panic began to resurface as the adrenaline running through my veins reduced to a simmer. "I don't—I don't even know who *I* am. I don't—"

The doctor idly stroked the edge of a rolled up manila envelope that stuck out of her coat pocket before she took a hesitant step closer to me, her own chest still heaving. A million unspoken thoughts seemed to dance in her eyes.

"I don't understand why I can't remember anything. Where am I? What—"

"Shhh," the doctor murmured, and her warm, trembling hand cupped the side of my face. "They'll find you. You'll be safe." She stroked my cheek with welcomed affection, and I wondered if we should hug, especially if she was, in fact, my mother. But I was glad we didn't. It didn't feel right to hug a complete stranger.

The doctor blinked, and a few tears escaped from the corners of her bright blue eyes. "I'm sorry I didn't get here fast enough. I couldn't get away from—I'm so sorry, Zoe."

34

MASE

MARCH 23, 1AE

Camille's tiny, fragile hand was limp in Mase's grasp. He was kneeling on the carpet at the side of the bed where Camille lay, watching her. Like her hand, the rest of her was limp. Mase studied Camille's angelic face, looking for any sign that she was still in there. But she didn't twitch, didn't moan, didn't sigh; she just lay there, still as the dead.

Camille *had* been dead, but she wasn't anymore. Because of Chris and Harper. It was a debt Mase wouldn't soon forget, and it wasn't the only one. The man named Jason had guided them all to an enormous house on the outskirts of a settlement—a city, Mase remembered from his lessons—that dwarfed the Colony. They had yet to reach the wild lands Dani had spoken of, the lands untouched by man's structures. Mase wondered what it would be like, and he feared he wouldn't be able to take care of Camille in such an unpredictable place.

"Trust her. You must promise me, Giant. You will listen to her and trust her."

Mase didn't understand the words Camille had whispered to him before she'd had her seizure. She already knew Mase trusted Dani and that he would listen to her. It didn't make sense to him.

He heard quiet footsteps and looked up to see RV-01 enter the bedroom. She stopped on the other side of the bed, hesitating for a few seconds before gingerly sitting on the edge.

"Will she make it?" Mase asked, surprised by the hoarseness in his voice. "Will she come back to me?" RV-01 had been the most powerful of Father's seers. If anyone knew Camille's fate, it was her.

RV-01 studied Camille for several long minutes before finally meeting Mase's eyes. "She will. But she will not be exactly as you know her. She will be both what she was before and what she has become. And she will be neither."

Mase shook his head and stroked his thumb across the back of Camille's hand. "I don't understand."

"You will."

"RV-one—"

"Please, call me Becca."

Mase felt himself frowning. RV-01—Becca—had been made into a Re-gen before either him or Camille, and to his eyes, she'd always acted like a model Re-gen. She'd never shown any signs of the differences he and Camille displayed. Was she changing? Would she start having the memory-dreams too? Was she reverting back to who she once was?

"Becca," Mase said, enjoying the rebellious feel of using a normal's name for another Re-gen. "Why did you leave with us?"

"I started the rebellion. I could not stay."

"What?" Mase asked, sounding as shocked as he felt.

"It had to be," she answered. "Our options were Re-gen rebellion or death to us all. We'd shown ourselves to no longer be suitably reliable to Father. Since he cannot control us with his Ability, losing his conditioned control meant we had to be eliminated. He would have replaced us with T-Rs in time."

"Will any of our brothers and sisters survive?"

Becca shrugged, averting her gaze. "Time does not share all of its secrets with me."

Mase was pretty sure that meant she didn't know. But…what if she was lying? What if she was really there to track Mase, Dani, and the other rebels for Father? Mase felt a sudden pang of fear and reached across the bed to capture Becca's neck. "How do I know you're telling the truth? You're his favorite. How do I know you're not here on his orders?"

"I…told…Camille…how…to…escape…the…interrogation… room…before," she managed to gasp.

Mase relaxed his grip, and Becca collapsed over Camille.

"Trust her. You must promise me, Giant. You will listen to her and trust her." Mase wondered if it was possible that Camille had been talking about Becca, not Dani. "Dani's friend is missing. Do you know where she is?" Mase asked, testing Becca's loyalty.

Before Becca could answer, there was muffled shouting and a loud crash from somewhere else in the house. It sounded like it had come from downstairs.

Becca sprang up from the bed and sped out of the room, and Mase followed close behind her. It didn't take them long to find the source of the commotion. Side by side, they froze on the bottom stair.

Jason had Dr. McLaughlin pinned against the front door a few yards beyond the foot of the stairs. Jake, a man Mase hadn't heard speak a single word since they'd arrived at the house, was trying to pull Jason off the doctor before he could strangle him to death. Jake wasn't being very successful.

"Mase!" Dani called from a doorway to another room. "Please, help Jake!" It was all she said before stepping into the battle zone.

35

DANI

MARCH 23, 1AE

"Mase! Please, help Jake!" I called, never taking my eyes from the terrifying scene playing out in the entryway. I rushed over to the brawling men, glass from a broken mirror crunching under my boots.

Luckily, Mase didn't hesitate in following my request. Together, he and Jake pulled Jason off Gabe and held him back by the arms and shoulders. Jason was struggling and glaring at Gabe, but I thought I spotted a self-satisfied glint in his eyes.

Gabe's back was against the front door, and he appeared remarkably unscathed aside from the ring of raw, red skin circling his neck. I wondered if he'd said or done something to goad Jason, though I didn't think it was strictly necessary; Jason was, well, Jason. He was also stronger and fifty times the fighter. Gabe didn't stand a chance against him—ever.

I stalked to Jason and hissed, "What the hell are you doing? Zoe's out there, somewhere, and you're wasting time picking fights?" I wanted to scream at him, to hit him, to do something to relieve my mounting anxiety.

Jason's eyes were filled with heat as he glared at me, and not the good kind. "He almost got you killed," he ground out through clenched teeth. His saliva was tinged pink. *Maybe Gabe's not as helpless as I thought...*

I stepped closer until I had to tilt my head back to look him in the eyes. I returned his glare. "He also saved my life...several times."

The bandage crossing Jason's face bunched along with his features as his eyes traced every visible bruise and cut marring my skin. Finally, he lowered his eyes, and I watched the tension leave him.

"Please let him go," I told Mase and Jake. When they did, reluctantly, I reached for Jason's hand and led him to the stairs.

"Jake, I—" Gabe started to say, but his words cut off with a loud smack, followed by a thunk.

Jason and I spun mid-step. I wasn't surprised by what I saw. Not much surprised me anymore. Gabe's back was still against the door, but he was no longer standing. He was slumped on the floor, his head lolling forward. A few feet away stood Jake, shaking out his hand and scowling.

Ignoring the drama, Jason and I turned and resumed our walk up the stairs. Only once we were enclosed in an unoccupied bedroom did either of us speak.

"Dani, I—" Jason said as he strode away from me, toward a wide window. He looked out at sprawling grounds, the scattered lodgepole pines and vast expanse of scraggly grass covering the rugged landscape. The house was on a big enough lot at the western edge of Colorado Springs, about ten miles west of the Colony, and deep enough in the foothills of the Rockies that we were fairly well hidden from prying eyes, at least for a little while. I just hoped we would be safe long enough to find Zoe and *finally* get the hell away from the Colony.

"Don't apologize, please." I sat on the bed, sinking into the fluffy down comforter. An elaborately carved dresser and matching nightstand fashioned from some dark wood were the only other pieces of furniture in the room. Sitting on the foot of the bed, I stared at the dresser. "He did deserve to be knocked around a bit, but…he doesn't deserve to die."

For a long time, Jason said nothing. He just held a floral brocade curtain out of the way and stared out the window. "He has feelings for you."

"Sanchez has feelings for you," I countered. It had been a guess, but from the way his head hung as soon as I said it, I knew I'd guessed right.

Jason turned to face me, his eyes burning with hatred, but not for me. "He fucking took you away from me."

"Yes," I said, standing. With a sigh, I joined him at the window. "But I didn't choose to go with him, and I came back to *you*."

Raising his hand to my face, Jason almost touched me. His fingertips hovered millimeters from the bruised, swollen flesh of my cheek. I hadn't had the courage to look in a mirror yet, but I knew it was bad, if only from the way everyone winced when they looked at me.

"The man who did this will die," he promised softly.

I smiled, and promptly winced at the dull ache. Harper had given me some pain meds, but they didn't mask it completely. "It was a woman, actually—Clara. The same one who poisoned Zoe. She's the one they use to wipe memories, to make T-Rs," I told him, knowing he would recall the information I'd passed on early the previous morning.

Jason's gaze sharpened, his calculating intelligence showing through. "Are there others like her?"

"I think so."

"Is she still alive?"

I nodded and was suddenly sick of thinking about Clara, General Herodson, and the Colony. I was beyond frustrated that I couldn't use my Ability to search for Zoe, I pretty much hated myself for the role my escape played in her disappearance and Camille's comatose state, and I was on the verge of diving into an endless ocean of hysteria. I needed a distraction. I'd been away from Jason for a week, and for a few stolen moments, I could allow myself to focus only on him.

"Take it off?" I asked, brushing the edge of his bandage where it reached his jawline. I'd known about the injury, but I hadn't expected the dressing to be so large. The bandage crossed his face, covering an inch-wide strip from hairline to jaw. *How bad is it?* He and Zoe had definitely played it down. I needed to see how seriously he'd been injured.

He flinched, turning away so I only saw the unmarred side of his face and the corner of the gauze and tape on his forehead. *Does he think I'll be disgusted?* I shook my head. *He can be such an idiot sometimes.*

"Come on," I said, reaching up to trace my nails along his neck. Goose bumps rose beneath my fingertips. "I showed you mine"—I pointed to my battered face and kept my words light, flirty—"so you have to show me yours."

The hint of a dimple shadowed his cheek, and Jason murmured, "Tease."

"Only for a little while. Once I'm healed enough…"

The full dimple made an appearance as Jason's delicious, sultry grin curved up one side of his lips. When he met my gaze, his eyes were again filled with heat—this time, the good kind.

I took his mood change as assent and again raised my hand to his face, tracing the bottom outline of the bandage. I hadn't known undressing a wound could be sensual, but the heat in his eyes flared. As I slowly peeled the bandage away, the heat dampened, turning to worry. My eyes flicked to Jason's periodically, letting him see the concern and affection I felt for him.

Finally, I reached his hairline and uncovered the last of his wound. I set the tape and gauze on the windowsill and studied his face, committing the changes to memory. His face, however it looked, was the one I loved.

Raising my fingers to his forehead, I hesitated before touching him. "Does it hurt?"

He shrugged, never looking away from me. Lightly, I touched my fingertips to the skin above the top of the wound and began tracing around the edges. It was red and a little puffy, and the stitches had yet to be removed.

Jason's breath caught.

I jerked my fingers away. "Did that hurt? Did I hurt you?"

"No." His voice was rough and deeper than usual. "It's just a little sensitive." He reached for my hand and raised it back up to his forehead. "Please, keep going," he said, and I saw in his eyes that he needed me to do it, to show him that his altered appearance didn't disgust me.

I started where I had before, just above the place where the red, angry gash began about halfway between his right eyebrow and hairline. Using my fingertips, I traced the skin around it as lightly as possible as it angled toward his nose, turned back to slash over his eyebrow, just barely missing the inner corner of his eye, and cut down his cheek, from cheekbone to jaw, almost touching the edge of his mouth.

Standing on tiptoes, I brushed my lips against his in a gentle, wordless claiming. Jason didn't deepen the kiss, didn't pick me up and ravish me against a wall, but he did smile. His lips curved against mine.

"Red…" he breathed.

Dropping my heels back to the floor, I sighed. "Lay down with me?" I moved to the bed and scooted into the center, waiting.

Jason joined me instantly, lying on his back and letting me figure out what position was most comfortable for me to snuggle against him. When I finally settled on my back with my head resting on his outstretched arm, he turned his head to the side and just watched me.

I looked into his sapphire-blue eyes…*so much like Zo's eyes.*

"You're thinking about her, about Zoe, aren't you?"

My mouth fell open. "How'd you know?" I narrowed my eyes. "You haven't developed some new mind-reading Ability, have you?" I was only half joking. The results of such a development could be disastrous. *If he finds out about his mom...*

A soft chuckle escaped from his throat. "No, but I can read your face." He frowned, and again, almost touched the side Clara had beaten. "Even like this," he added quietly.

"Oh." I studied his expression, trying to read *him*. "I just wish my stupid telepathy was working. I wish I could find her." I took a deep breath, holding back tears. "It's just so unfair. Everything is so ridiculously unfair."

"I know," Jason said, bending down to press the gentlest of kisses against my forehead. "Sanchez will keep searching for her. She's not as good as you with the telepathic radar thing, but…" He frowned, the expression pulling on the lower portion of his wound. "She's better than nothing."

"I know," I said, offering him a small smile.

"Rest now, Red. Wearing yourself out won't do Zoe any good."

I sighed and closed my eyes. "I missed you."

I started awake, cringing as I jostled my broken forearm. Jason's arm was still beneath my head, but he'd propped himself up partially with his other elbow and was staring at the bedroom door. Which someone was gently knocking on.

"Jason? Wha—"

"Shh…" he murmured, easing his arm out from under me. "I'll take care of it." He stood, stretched, and strode over to the door. "What?" he asked as he jerked the door open a few inches, irritation evident in his voice.

I could hear Mase, but he was speaking too quietly for me to make out his words.

"She's resting," Jason said.

I sat up and groaned. "No, no, I'm up. What's going on?"

Looking over his shoulder at me, Jason said, "Mase says he needs to talk to you. Becca's with him."

I ran the fingers of my good hand through my tangled curls and frowned. Yes, I was injured, but I didn't need to be treated like I was made of glass. "Just let him in, Jason."

At least he didn't argue.

Mase entered the room first, Becca trailing right behind him. They both stopped at the foot of the bed, neither speaking.

"Uh…so, what's up?" I asked, feeling awkward.

Mase nudged the other Re-gen, who was staring at me with a curious smile. For several long seconds, nobody said anything. And then Becca opened her mouth.

"I had a vision. I saw where Zoe is. It is not far from here."

"Wait—what?" I asked, scooting to the edge of the bed as quickly as I could. Which wasn't very quickly.

"Why didn't you just tell me that to begin with?" Jason snapped. Even as irritated as he was, he still hurried to the side of the bed to help me to my feet.

"Is she okay?" I asked before they could respond to him.

"She is somewhat changed, but she is unharmed," Becca said.

"What do you mean, *changed*?" Jason's voice dropped in temperature to well below freezing.

"Her memory has been wiped. She has no idea who she is, and you will definitely be strangers to her."

"Oh my God…" But I managed to stop myself from freaking out completely. I couldn't afford to lose it—not right now. Finding her, making sure she was safe and sound, and getting the hell away from the Colony was all that mattered. I took a deep breath. "We need to go get her—"

With barely a glance at me, Jason turned away.

I squeezed his arm, holding him in place. "Wait. I think it should just be me who goes to get her…with Chris and Sanchez. You boys can, you know, hold down the fort."

"No."

Damn, he can be so stubborn! I gritted my teeth. "She's more likely to be afraid of you or Jake. You're big, scary men who she doesn't know…not anymore. I mean, c'mon Jason, we don't want to traumatize her more than she already has been."

"She'll get over it. I know my sister."

"But that's just it—" I was nearly shouting in exasperation. "If what Becca says is true, she's not our Zo anymore!"

Jason shook his head. "She may not remember who she is, but she's still my sister. Deep down, she'll still be Zoe." I wanted to believe him, to agree with him, but even his own statement held a hint of uncertainty.

I glanced at the Re-gens, then back at Jason. "You don't know that," I said, my voice small.

Turning back to me and leaning down, Jason pressed his lips against mine. "C'mon. Let's go get her." He snagged my hand and led me to the door, Mase and Becca close on our heels.

"Jason, I still don't think—"

"I know," he said over his shoulder. We were in the upstairs hallway, heading for the stairs to the ground level. "But we're all going."

Single file, we led our horses through a gate in the fence wrapping around the back of the house Becca led us to. Sanchez and Harper stayed out front with their new companions, Tavis and Sam, keeping watch, while Mase—holding Camille—Gabe, Becca, and Carlos settled themselves in the backyard with the animals. Jack came into the house with me, along with Jason, Chris, Jake, and Cooper. I led the way, Jack at my side and Chris and Cooper right behind us. The ladies and dogs were taking point on Operation: Rescue Zoe. At least I'd won *that* battle.

We entered the house through a sliding glass door leading from the back patio.

"Zo?" I called out. To my right was a carpeted, slightly shabby living room, and to my left was an open, outdated kitchen. The house was single-story, with maybe two or three bedrooms. I didn't think we'd have to search for long.

As we entered the second bedroom down the hallway beyond the living room, Cooper and Jack wagged their tails and barked. They trotted side by side to the giant mirror on the sliding closet door and whined.

"Good boys," I said, following them into the room. I scratched first Jack's scruff, then Cooper's, and gave them the hand signal to lay down—an open hand, palm down—partially out of habit and partially out of necessity. My Ability was still burned out, which meant I had to rely on good old-fashioned hand signals.

I glanced over my shoulder, meeting Jason's eyes. He was standing just inside the doorway, Jake blocking the opening beside him. "You're nulling her, right? I don't want her to, you know"—I waved my hands back and forth beside my ears, referring to Zoe's Ability—"and get freaked out by what she sees or feels."

Jason simply nodded. Chris, on the other hand, stepped up beside me and whispered, "I'll do what I can to calm her, but I've got to touch her first."

"Sounds like a plan. Okay, Zo," I called softly through the mirror. "I'm going to open the door, so don't be afraid. There's another woman here with me, and a couple dogs, who're real sweethearts." I glanced at Chris and shrugged. "Ready?" I mouthed.

She nodded, and I slowly slid the door open.

36

ZOE

MARCH 23, 1AE

I sat on the hard, creaky bed, almost too scared to move. *Why did Clara do that to me?* What *did she do?* I set the manila envelope on the mattress beside me and stared down at my shaking hands. I was on the brink of tears, but didn't know why. The tremors in my hands worsened as I tried to remember something… anything. Watching them tremble escalated the brewing storm of tears and unease. I did my best to will my hands to be still. I couldn't think while I was so scared. But I *was* scared, and I didn't understand why. *Dr. Wesley told me that I'd be safe here, at least until my friends came for me. She saved me,* I told myself. *I can trust her... she says she's my mom. It's not like I have much of a choice...*

The sound of multiple voices and heavy footsteps startled me. Holding my breath, I listened. There were so many footsteps…too many.

I jumped to my feet, frantically scanning the room for a place to hide. The footsteps were getting closer and the muffled voices louder. The closet was my only option. I panicked. Plunging into the darkness, I slid the door shut behind me, hiding my face in my knees and hoping the shadows would swallow me from sight.

"Zo?" a woman said timidly. I heard hushed voices outside the closet door and an ear-piercing barking. My fear increased, my heart beating so loudly in my ears that I couldn't concentrate on what the voices were saying.

Before I could think what to do next, the closet door slid open. I glanced up at the people staring down at me, hoping to feel some sort of relief at seeing their familiar faces, but there was nothing about them I recognized. *I know them?* Something about their appalled expressions and their stillness made me think I did. I studied my hands again, not wanting to meet their expectant, scrutinizing eyes.

These are my hands, I thought. *They're my hands, yet I feel like I've never seen them before.* I balled my fists, clenching them as hard as I could, and dropped them to my sides. I let my fingernails jab into my palms. I needed the diversion of physical pain. I needed a distraction from the horrified, unfamiliar faces that were staring at me as I huddled in the closet, confused. They were waiting for something.

"...Zoe," the curly-haired woman with the bruised face said. She was speaking to me, and I struggled to process her words. She seemed sad...uncertain. Something about her fire-red hair seemed familiar, but a sharp pain shot through my skull as I tried to recall why. I winced and reached for the back of my head, trying to rub the pain away.

"...name is Dani," she continued, holding one of her hands out to me. Her other arm was in a sling, and I wondered how she'd injured herself.

I glanced from the redhead's hand back into her wide, green eyes. Her eyebrows were pulled together, and her chin quivered a little. She squatted there, blinking, waiting.

Slowly, I reached for her hand, curiosity winning over any lingering reluctance. She clutched my fingers lightly in hers with a small smile and then let my hand go. When she released my hand, she nodded to the woman crouched beside her and said, "This is Chris."

Just like Dani had done, Chris held out her hand and waited for me to meet her halfway. I felt better—less afraid—as soon as my hand touched hers.

"This is Cooper," Dani said, interrupting my thoughts. She was petting the head of a large husky who was lying nearby. "And this" —Dani turned to the dog sitting beside her—"is Jack." She held her hand out to him and he raised his paw, shaking her hand just like I had. I couldn't help but smile. I pulled my hand from Chris's and reached for Jack, but hesitated.

My fear resurfaced, creating a knot in my stomach and forming a sudden lump in my throat. Chris touched my other hand, and I immediately felt better. *I like her*, I decided.

"Let's get you out of there, hmmm?" Dani said. "It smells like old people in there." She wrinkled her nose. It was a cute expression, and I felt my smile grow a little. With the help of the two women, I crawled out of the closet on shaking legs and stood between them.

The other dog—Cooper—was standing and wagging his tail excitedly.

"Cooper," I whispered happily and dropped both women's hands to bend down and pet his furry head. I heard a collection of inhales, and the feel of eyes on me made me self-conscious. I straightened and scanned their faces.

Dani's mouth was gaping open. "Zo?"

I felt my face scrunch, and I cocked my head to the side, unsure if I was supposed to answer her.

"Do you remember us?" The slight chirp in her voice made her sound hopeful, and I felt a pang of guilt.

I shook my head. When her face fell, I held my breath for a moment and my eyes shifted around the room. Two large, formidable men were standing in the doorway. The black-haired man was intimidating. He had brilliant blue eyes and a bandage crossing his face, and he was scowling. The way he concentrated on me with his arms crossed over his chest made me feel like I should be frightened of him, but for some reason I wasn't. I was uncomfortable, but not frightened.

The other was tall and equally unnerving, but in a different way. He stood in the doorway, one white-knuckled hand gripping the doorjamb. His eyebrows were drawn down and there was a sadness in his eyes that made me feel like I should comfort him, although I wasn't sure why or how or if I really even wanted to.

I felt inadequate. I didn't want them staring at me. "I'm not sure what to say." The sound of my voice was shrill in my ears, and I tried to swallow the growing bubble of panic inside me.

When the sad man realized I was looking at him, he ran his hands over his scruffy face, then turned and walked away. I could hear his footsteps, loud and quick as he headed down the hallway. The dark-haired man nodded at either Dani or Chris, a single, sharp movement, before following the sad man out. Cooper trotted behind them.

With a smile, Chris reached for my hand again, but my gaze stayed fixed on the empty doorway where the sad man had been standing. I wondered what had made his strong features so drawn and his eyes so empty.

"What now?" Chris asked quietly.

Dani sighed. "I have no idea." She turned to me. "How did this happen? Do you remember anything?"

I shook my head. "I don't remember anything, and I don't know why she did this to me."

"She who?" Dani asked.

"Clara."

Dani's mouth opened, then immediately closed as her eyes shut, almost like she was wincing in pain. "I should've made sure she was dead before she could run." She shook her head. "I'm so sorry, Zo. This is all my fault."

"Nonsense," Chris said. "You couldn't have known." She

reached out and offered me her hand. "Come on, Zoe. Let's get you out of here. We'll tell you everything we know."

"Wait," I said, and walked back to the bed. I picked up the manila envelope, wondering if I should know what was in it. I headed over to Dani and handed it to her.

She looked at me, confused.

"I was told to give this to you."

Her eyebrows rose as she reached to accept it.

"What is it?" Chris asked. She took a step closer, glancing between us.

I shrugged. "I have no idea."

"Dani?" Chris seemed barely able to curb her curiosity.

Dani stared at the envelope, her name written in block letters across it, and she shook her head. "There's only one way to find out."

EPILOGUE

Dear Danielle,

If you're reading this, it means you found my little girl. I don't have much time before I am missed back at the Colony, but there is much I must tell you.

I'm sorry. I'm so incredibly sorry. I didn't step in when Gregory took you to turn you into a T-R for a reason. RV-01, a Re-gen with the strongest prophetic Ability we've come across, assured me Gregory and Clara would fail in their attempt to transform you. She did not, however, inform me of the torture you'd be subjected to. For that I am truly sorry. I hope you believe me.

Maybe this will give you some comfort: Clara is dead. She took my little girl and turned her into... something. I was too late to stop her completely, but I did interfere. She was extremely frustrated with Zoe when I showed up, so I believe my daughter was somehow able to interfere with the process as well. I don't think she's completely wiped, but there's no way to tell. If there is any piece of her left inside, please, I beg of you, find it. If anyone can do it, you can.

I don't know what your plans are now, but you must run far from here. RV-01 believed she would end up in your company. Use her to keep yourselves safe. She may prove to be one of your strongest allies. She foresaw much over the past few days, including the Re-gen rebellion and your escape. She also saw the resurgence of the Colony. You are safe for now, though I don't know for how long.

Perhaps this will help you...I've included several invaluable documents in this packet. These things should help protect you from Gregory and others like him in the future. His control reaches so much farther than you could ever imagine. There is much that I didn't have time to tell you, but I have been assured that our paths will cross again.

I fear I shall anger you one last time. Included with this letter is another: one to my children. It explains much of what has happened over the past few decades and why I've made the choices I've made. As you know my children far better than I do, I trust your judgment as to whether or not my letter should be shared with them. I don't wish to hurt them any more than I already have, but I cannot pretend I don't yearn for them to know me. Whatever you decide, watch over them for me.

Until we meet again,
Anna

Thanks for reading *Into The Fire*! This marks the end of the book, but not the end of Dani and Zoe's post-apocalyptic adventures. The adventure continues in Out Of The Ashes.

Keep reading for a preview of book three.

OUT OF THE ASHES

THE ENDING SERIES BOOK THREE

MARCH 1 AE

I

JAKE

MARCH 23, 1AE

COLORADO SPRINGS, COLORADO

Body tense and heart racing, Jake scoured Zoe's face for *any* inkling of recognition. He couldn't allow himself to believe she had no memory of him or all they'd been through together. She'd admitted she loved him only hours earlier. Now, she was scared, casting furtive glances around the room at friends and family she clearly didn't remember—including him.

In the dying moonlight seeping through the undressed windows, Jake watched her, desperation making it hard for him to breathe. Her eyes…he couldn't tear his gaze away from her teal eyes.

Zoe studied the two women in front of her, taking in Chris and Dani before settling her gaze on her brother, Jason. Her wide, appraising eyes narrowed and her chest heaved, like she was frantically trying to remember him. Her gaze lingered a moment longer without a hint of recognition, and then landed on Jake. He could see the confusion and fear warring within their depths, making his heart ache and his conscience cloud with an undeniable guilt.

He shouldn't have left her alone on the golf course.

Her head tilted slightly as she considered him, and he prayed there was even the slightest nagging familiarity. *Remember,* he silently pleaded. But seeing no recognition of him—of *them*—reflected in her eyes, he knew the Zoe standing in the room, looking at him like he was a complete stranger, was only a shadow of the woman he'd fallen in love with.

His grip on the doorframe tightened so hard he thought the wood might detach from the wall. Zoe was terrified, and for the first time since he'd met her, there was nothing he could do to help her. He fought the instinct to go to her, knowing that if he did, he would frighten her more, and then he might risk losing her completely.

Unable to stand the tension any longer, unable to bear the feeling of loss and his encroaching devastation, Jake turned and strode out of the suffocating room. Each step provided distance, and the more distance he put between them, the easier it became to breathe. He couldn't get away fast enough.

Cooper, his loyal-friend-through-it-all husky, trailed behind him, panting and trotting to keep up as Jake made his way down the hall. He needed space…needed air. Continuing toward the kitchen, he hoped the fresh air beyond the sliding glass door would give him a clearer head. But regardless of how quickly he strode through the house, the image of Zoe's fearful eyes remained, permanently projected in his mind, a constant reminder of his failure to protect her.

His hands fisted at his sides. He'd known something wasn't right when she said she felt strange outside the Colony, and if he'd have just stayed with her instead of leaving her side to help Harper, she might not have run off…she might still be *her*.

With a roar, Jake spun toward the wall. His fist met the hard, textured surface in unbridled anger. His knuckles cracked beneath his skin as they barreled through a layer of drywall, but he barely noticed. Bracing his hands against the wall, he tried to catch his breath, to stop his mind from spinning out of control. They'd already been through so much…why was this happening?

Hearing Dani and Zoe's muted voices in the bedroom down the hall, Jake turned away from the hole his fist had made and continued into the small kitchen, then stopped. With a heavy sigh, he leaned against the Formica countertop, not ready to go outside with the others. Not ready to answer questions.

Almost immediately, Jason came through the doorway behind him. In two steps he was at the counter, gripping the ledge, and in the dim light pouring through the sliding glass door, Jake could see the hard set of his features.

"I can't blame the Colony this time," Jake said. "I knew something was wrong." Zoe was infuriating and stubborn, but she wasn't stupid; she wouldn't have just run off for no reason. But without her memory, there was no way to know why she'd done it.

With a yawn, Cooper lay down on the linoleum floor, his eyes angling up to Jake and then to Jason, ensuring that, even in their silence, they were still standing there.

After what felt like a few minutes, Jason grunted and shook his head. His shoulders were tense, and Jake could almost feel the apprehension rolling off him in waves.

Jake couldn't help but wonder if Gabe—his best friend turned traitor—was to blame for all of this. Despite their friendship as children, Gabe had brought soldiers into Jake's home, ready to take his sister, Becca, away from him, and then he'd lured Dani into the Colony for the General. Had he been involved in what had happened to Zoe, too?

"What a fucking mess," Jason said, shaking his head. "I guess I'll just keep nulling her, at least until—"

The sound of footsteps approaching brought both men's attention to the hall doorway. Chris spoke softly, Zoe's hand resting in hers as they entered the kitchen, Dani and Jack, her German shepherd, close behind them. Though Chris and Zoe were both grown women, the image of them walking hand in hand resembled that of a mother and child.

Jake's eyes met Zoe's as she was led past him; hers were shrewd and penetrating. They were the same eyes that had affected him so intensely the first moment he saw her, their brilliance and expressiveness capturing his attention—his soul—in a way no other woman ever had. Regret and anger gnawed at him; he'd never told her any of that, and now she might never know how he felt.

Her eyes fixed on him. He could tell from the way Zoe walked —with less fortitude and more uncertainty—that she was a poorly made replica of *his* Zoe. But she was a version of her, nonetheless, and like always, the bottomless depths of her eyes housed her every emotion: embarrassment—curiosity—confusion. Jake was grateful she didn't seem to be afraid, and he knew he had Chris's Ability to curb Zoe's unease with a single touch to thank for that.

Chris whispered something inaudible, and Zoe's gaze shifted to the sliding glass door. They stepped through and outside, heading toward the rest of the group and the horses waiting in the early morning shadows, Dani's dog traipsing after them.

Dani, however, hung back in the kitchen. She moved closer to Jason, her gaze darting between him and Jake. With her broken arm, swollen and bruised face, and hunched shoulders, she looked like she'd been the General's punching bag while held captive in the Colony. She gave him a sidelong glance.

Jake's blood ran cold. "What is it?" he asked.

"There was a letter," she said tentatively, fingering the edge of the sling holding her left arm. "It's from one of my Colony contacts. She brought Zo here after finding her in the golf course… with Clara."

Jake stopped breathing. His anger drained from him, his stomach knotting with fear.

Clara.

He exhaled slowly and rubbed his hand over his face harsher

than was necessary, fighting to maintain what semblance of composure he had left. Clara'd had it out for Zoe from the first moment they'd met. Back at Fort Knox, she'd poisoned Zoe in a desperate attempt to get rid of her, then attempted to kill them *all* in the barracks fire that had claimed several lives. And now she was here, in Colorado, trying to hurt Zoe *again*.

White-hot rage and self-loathing scorched through Jake, and he clenched his shaking hands into fists. He should've left Clara in the hospital where he'd found her, pleading and scared.

"She's dead now," Dani said, but Jake's anger lessened only slightly.

"Dead," he repeated hollowly. Clara might've been dead, but not before managing to strike one final blow.

Dani's eyes met his for a brief moment before settling back onto Jason's. "Did you tell them about the T-Rs and the memory wiping?"

Jason nodded.

"It looks like that's what happened to Zo…sort of. Clara started the process, got interrupted…at least now she's gone for good."

Jake studied Dani. "How do you know for sure?" he asked.

Dani smiled weakly and shook her head, wisps of her curly red hair escaping the braid it was gathered into. "My contact said so," she said. "I trust her…at least with this." She glanced between them once more, like she wasn't quite sure of something. "There's more, but we should probably get going."

Jason reached for her, lacing his fingers with those of her good hand, and nodded. "We'll figure the rest out on the way to Colorado Trails," he said. "We've got to get moving or Ky and the others will think something's happened to us."

The sliding glass door opened, and Becca stepped into the doorway. She glanced between Jason and Dani, and even though she still didn't seem to believe that Jake was her brother, her eyes found and locked with his. "We should go," she said, her voice raspy, as it had been since she was young. "I have had a vision. If we do not leave soon, the General will find us."

"Shit," Jason muttered, and Becca turned slowly and exited the kitchen, leaving the door open behind her.

Dani led Jason toward the sliding glass door, his imposing form dwarfing her petite, battered one. Part of Jake wished Zoe's wounds were as straightforward as bruises and broken bones; *those* wounds would heal. What Clara had done to her might not.

Feeling deflated, Jake followed after them. Once again, Zoe was right in front of him, but as unreachable as though she were miles away; it infuriated him. While Clara's first attempt to kill the only woman he'd ever loved had inevitably brought Zoe closer to him, Clara's *final* attempt might have succeeded in tearing her away completely.

2

ZOE

MARCH 24, 1AE

ROCKY MOUNTAINS, COLORADO

"Potty break," Dani said, halting her Paint horse, Wings, in the middle of the highway just ahead of me.

I'd been riding a brown mare named Mocha since leaving the house in Colorado Springs, the others taking turns staying close to me, since I had no clue what I was doing. Tavis was my current companion, riding on my right. I liked him; he was a funny Australian man who didn't talk much, but when he did it was playful and put me at ease. Becca, the woman sharing his saddle, seemed nice, though she hadn't said much to *anyone* during the five-plus hours we'd been on the road. She seemed almost as lost as I felt.

Dani struggled to dismount Wings using only her right arm, since her left arm was cradled in a sling. She was obviously in a lot of pain, despite the medicine the doctor, Harper, had given her.

I glanced up ahead at Jason, assuming he'd be charging toward us to help Dani in her flailing attempt to dismount and chastising her for attempting it on her own. But he was at the head of our parade line, talking to Chris and completely oblivious to Dani's self-dismount.

When Dani's boots hit the ground, she glanced toward Jason, then looked up at me, a sheepish grin on her face as she brought her index finger to her lips. "Don't tell him…"

I smiled and shook my head. I liked Dani, a lot. She was fiery and peppy, and the ease with which she spoke to me made it easier to cope with what was going on, like I had a friend who would stay by my side no matter what. When she'd tried to explain to me what had happened to the world, that we'd grown up together and had spent the last three months trying to get to one another only to be separated by the Colony again, I'd begun to freak out. The weight of reality and my lack of memories and sense of self were all too much to bear at once.

But Chris had been quick to wrap her arms around my shoulders, telling me that it would be alright, I just needed time to readjust, and for some reason, that had made me feel better. Dani had later explained that it was because Chris had the innate ability to comfort people. Although I got the distinct impression there was more to Chris than that—a nagging suspicion in the back of my mind—I liked the way I felt in her presence and savored the reprieve of unwanted emotions when she was around me.

"Come on, Zo," Dani said, holding her good hand up to help me climb out of Mocha's saddle. "Let's go pee. You never know…" She scanned the tall aspens on either side of the road. "We might not find another woodsy spot before we stop for the night. Might as well take advantage of the privacy while we have it."

I considered the image of the two of us standing side by side, best friends who, I'd been told, were so completely altered from the last time we'd seen each other. Tiny little Dani, with her bruised pixie face framed by wild, red curls, and me, tall, with an unmarred exterior but hollow interior. *I wish I could remember…*

But having been found inside the bedroom closet of an abandoned house the night before was as far back as my memory went.

"Zo? You okay?" Dani's brow furrowed. "Do you need me to get Harper?"

I shook my head. I had a million and one questions, but a pee break wasn't the time to ask them. Instead, I offered her what I hoped was a reassuring smile. "No, I was just thinking." I waved her proffered hand away. "I got it, Dani, but thanks." I didn't want to hurt her by jerking her body around as I dismounted. "It's only a couple feet." I'd decided it was much easier getting up into the saddle than it was getting down, an art I was determined to master if this was going to be my *spot* during our several-day journey.

While the others seemed all too excited to meet up with the rest of our group, it meant that *I* had even more people to "reacquaint" myself with. Dani had spent part of the morning filling me in on my relationships with them. Now I just needed to remember all that she'd told me: Sarah, apparently a friend I'd traveled with from the East Coast, was pregnant; her boyfriend, Biggs, was a military man we'd met up with along the way; Mr. Grayson was my high school history teacher and had been traveling with Dani for months; and Jason's best friend, Ky, and Ky's older brother, Ben, were waiting for us deeper in the mountains.

I stood up in the stirrups, prepared to fling my leg over for an awkward dismount.

"Here," Tavis offered kindly as he strode up beside Mocha. I hadn't even noticed him dismount his own horse. He wore an easy smile, and his blue eyes crinkled in the corners where his smile touched them. His dirty-blond hair was a little long and mussed from running his fingers through it so frequently.

Caught off guard, I felt my heart flutter a bit.

"Fling your leg over, and I'll help ease you down…"

Flashing him a brief smile, I did as Tavis instructed. With one hand gripping the saddle horn and the other gripping the edge of the saddle seat for leverage, I swung my leg over Mocha's rump, just like Dani had shown me. As I was about to lower myself to the ground, Tavis's hands grasped my waist, firmly but gently, and he helped lower me the rest of the way down.

"It's not mountain climbing, so you'll be a pro in no time," he said as I pivoted around to face him.

"Thanks," I chirped, and he answered with a nod before he turned and headed back for his horse.

Turning around, I found Dani eyeing me carefully. Jake, a man who hadn't uttered a single word to me since they'd found me but had taken to watching me with unnerving intensity, sat upon his horse behind her, his gaze equally assessing.

"Jason," Dani called ahead, startling me. I looked up toward the front of the caravan as Jason turned around in his saddle, his gaze questioning as it shifted between us. "We're gonna pee," she said. "It might be difficult for you to keep nulling for a minute, but we'll be right back."

Jason's eyes hardened. "Be careful."

"Come on, Zo," Dani said, biting her lip. There was a hint of uncertainty in her voice. "There's some stuff you should know." She hooked her arm in mine, and we headed toward the tangle of bushes a dozen yards away.

"Dani," Jake said, swinging his leg over his saddle, clearly intending to come with us.

Dani shook her head at him and patted the handgun in her shoulder holster. "We'll be fine, Jake. I need to talk to Zo for a sec."

Although Jake didn't seem pleased with the decision, he remained in his saddle, his gaze shifting between us as we turned away.

"Wait, Zoe—" Sam, a forward little boy I'd spoken to only a few times, called from behind us.

"We'll be right back, Sam," I said over my shoulder as Dani pulled me forward; I was practically stumbling as I tried to keep up with her. "What's—"

"Zo, I know you're probably exhausted and more than a little confused about everything that's going on, but you're super close to getting yourself into a mess that you'll regret later."

Trying to stay at least partially aware of where my feet were landing, I gave Dani a sidelong glance. Her bright green eyes were a bit glazed over in the sunlight. I could tell the pain meds were starting to kick in.

"What do you mean by 'a mess'?" I asked, near panting as we clumsily hurried through the underbrush and over uneven ground.

"You're with Jake," she said.

I blanched and stopped, the abrupt movement making Dani wince. "What?" A faint thrill wriggled down my spine.

"Yeah, for a few months now, I think…" She shook her head. "What's important is that you remember that, especially when you're chatting it up with Tavis." She urged me toward the berry bushes a few feet away.

Falling into step behind her, I frowned. "But Jake hasn't even talked to me."

She snorted. "That *might* have something to do with the fact that you don't even know him anymore." Pulling a wad of tissues from her pocket, Dani handed me a couple, and then looked down at her broken arm. "This is gonna be fun," she muttered, and I tried not to laugh, though I didn't do a very good job.

I found that preoccupying my mind with observing Dani, her little quirks that I was still trying to understand, was a good distraction from all the things I was *supposed* to already know, the things that threatened to overwhelm me and bring me to tears.

As we each squatted behind our own cluster of bushes to do our business, I allowed my mind to wander, if only a little. I considered what Dani had told me about Jake and me being together, and I found it impossible to picture. He seemed so quiet and capable, it was a little intimidating. I couldn't even imagine having a conversation with him, let alone *being* with him. But in spite of my reservations, there was also a mysterious air about him that was intriguing, and I was curious to discover what the old me already had. The number of questions ticking through my head increased exponentially.

Hearing leaves crunch beneath footsteps on the other side of the shrubbery, I sighed and finished up. "Geez, you're fast." I assumed I'd have to *help* Dani, not that she would leave me in the dust. Jumping up to my feet, I zipped up my jeans and stepped out from behind the tangle of leaves and branches. I froze.

Sam was standing a few yards away, his bow drawn and an arrow aimed at the figure of a small girl standing between us. Her back was to me, her blonde hair hanging in a knotted mess.

Sam's expression was one of pure horror—his pale eyes wide and his nostrils flaring—but his stance and aim were unwavering.

"What the hell are you doing, Sam?" I screeched.

"What's wrong, Zo?" Dani called from behind the bushes. But I was too focused on Sam and the little girl he was prepared to shoot an arrow through to answer.

"Sam," I said again. "She's just a little girl. Put your bow down."

Dark brown hair hung in his eyes, but he stared at her, unblinking, and I could see his uncertainty.

"Sam…"

As if hearing the scolding tone of my voice had brought the little girl to life, she slowly turned around. At the sight of her, my heart nearly stopped. The front of her nightgown was *covered* in dried blood, as were her arms and neck. Her face was doll-like, with crystal-blue eyes wide and gleaming in the sunlight, and her porcelain skin was hidden beneath what looked like weeks' worth of layers of dirt and blood.

"Mommy?" The haunting pitch of her voice sent chills up my spine.

"Jesus," I breathed. "Are you alright?" Although I had the innate urge to run away from the little girl, I took a hesitant step toward her, wondering what the poor child had been through.

"Zoe, get away from her!" Dani said from behind me.

The little girl took a step closer to me, her eyes narrowing and her lip curling into a snarl. Her body was suddenly trembling, like her muscles were coiling to strike. Gritting her teeth, she growled, "Mommy?"

As she lunged toward me, an ear-piercing crack resounded through the air, and before she could take another step, the little girl fell to a crumpled heap on the ground. A crimson patch blossomed on her nightgown, spreading across her chest.

My hands flew to my mouth and I screamed, tears trickling down my face. "Oh my God." Turning around, I found Dani, handgun drawn and still pointed where the little girl lay. Dani's eyes were wide, her face ashen, and her mouth hung open. "What have you done?"

Dani blinked several times, and her gaze slowly shifted from the small body to me. Her eyes were filled with shock and horror. "She was a Crazy," she said, lowering her gun. "She was a Crazy." I wasn't sure if she was trying to convince me, or herself. "I—I had to…she was a Crazy…"

"A *what*?" I turned back to the little girl and stared down at her. I was suddenly shaking uncontrollably. "What the hell just happened?" I asked no one in particular. "She's just a little girl."

I heard a rush of footsteps and calling voices, but I couldn't focus on anyone but the dead child lying horrifyingly still on the ground. Her eyes were open and staring directly at me. *She thought I was her mother…*

"I've never seen a kid one before," Sam said, and I looked at him. "I tried to warn you."

"This is gonna be bright," Harper said as he sat me down on a log beside the fire and clicked on a small, near-blinding pen light. He shone it directly into my eyes. On instinct, I tried to blink, but Harper wouldn't let me; his fingertips were warm and firm as he held my eyelids open.

"Sorry, Baby Girl, but I just want to check one more time…"

Still trying to understand the whole Ability thing Sam had explained during the last stretch of our journey, I decided now was as good a time as any to start asking more questions, especially since Sam was probably getting tired of being the one having to answer them all. "Harper?"

"Hmmm."

"Were you a doctor before, or is this, you know, just part of your Ability?" I had no idea what counted as an "Ability," only that Sam had said everyone who survived the Virus had one—at least those who weren't "Crazies."

Harper He smiled. "This doctor stuff is all training, Baby Girl. I was a medic in the Army. My Ability has to do with visions and seeing things that haven't happened yet."

I snorted, determined not to cry out in confusion and disbelief.

"I know it's a lot to take in, especially all in one day, but we can't risk another incident like earlier today."

I shrugged, figuring the more answers I had the easier it would be for me to fit in. "Yeah, Sam said he has heightened senses, that he can hear, smell, and see things that others can't." I shook my head.

"Try not to move, Baby Girl."

"Sorry."

Harper shifted his hand down to my chin, gently gripping it while he moved my head from side to side in tandem with the flashlight he waved in front of my face.

"What are some of the others' Abilities?"

"Well," he began, "let's see—I'm not sure what Tavis or Daniel can do, but Carlos can control electricity, Dani can communicate with animals, Sanchez is telepathic, Jake can regenerate…Chris and your brother, well, they're the reason you're dealing with things as well as you are; Chris is keeping you calm, and you're brother is keeping your Ability hidden. He can actually nullify *or* amplify other people's Abilities."

Regeneration? Communicating with animals? Telepathy? Controlling electricity? I was almost afraid to ask... "What's my Ability?" I placed my hand on Harper's, gently pushing the pen light down so I could look him in the eyes. "What's Jason protecting me from?"

Harper gave me a sympathetic smile. "You can see people's memories. You can feel what they're feeling. On top of everything that's happened today, we didn't think it was a good idea to add your Ability into the mix, too."

Jason and Chris had been shadowing me pretty closely all day. Part of me wondered if I should be offended that they hadn't told me about this sooner. But then again, the idea of having an Ability, especially one that was so intrusive, didn't seem like something I could handle on top of everything else.

Harper clicked the light on, blinding me once more.

"Is there something *wrong* with my eyes?" I asked a bit tersely. The more he wanted to check them, the more concerned I became.

"No. Sorry to scare you. There's nothing wrong, I just—" He gave me another sympathetic smile as he clicked the light off. "I was just making sure there's no brain damage, or...I just want to make sure I'm not missing anything that might help us figure out exactly what she did to you, or how bad it is." He sighed. "But I don't see anything, and I doubt I will without doing an MRI or—"

"It's only been a day," Dani chimed in as she walked by. It was the first time I'd heard her speak since the incident with the little girl...the Crazy. Dani stopped in the narrow clearing where everyone was setting up their tents for the night. "You might be back to your old self by tomorrow, Zo. Could be all you need is a good night's sleep."

Dani fought to keep a nylon sleeping bag from slipping out

from under her good arm. Although she flashed me a smile over her shoulder, I could tell it was weak and forced. I could picture a real Dani smile brightening her face to glowing, nothing like the halfhearted smile she gave me now, which had quickly faded.

I watched as she struggled to open a tent bag. "I'm sure you're right," I said and glanced up at Harper. "Tomorrow will be better. Can I be done?" I felt like I needed to be doing *something* to help Dani, since I was otherwise useless and she was having such a hard time after such a crappy day.

Harper nodded absently, not really staring *at* me so much as staring *through* me. He rubbed his jaw and took another deep breath.

I stepped toward Dani but hesitated the moment Jason appeared beside her, crouching to help. He muttered something I couldn't hear.

"Yeah…I just want to go to sleep," Dani said.

"This isn't even our tent, and you shouldn't be doing this on your own, Red. You'll just make your arm worse. Please…just ask me for help next time." Jason, a man of words that were few and to the point, continued to grumble as he pulled the tent out of its bag and unrolled it like doing so was second nature.

"I didn't want to bother you." Dani rested her hand on his shoulder, his body tensed and stilled. "I was thinking Zo and I could share a tent tonight. You know, since it would be weird for her…" Dani's gaze drifted to Jake.

Hurt flashed in Jason's eyes.

"It's alright," I rushed to say. The last thing I wanted to be was more of an inconvenience than I already was.

Jason and Dani both looked at me.

"I don't mind having my own tent. You guys share, really."

"I don't think you should be alone tonight, Zo. What if something happens?" I noticed Dani's eyes skirt to Jake again; he'd just dropped his own tent on the ground on the other side of the fire.

"What if your memory comes back and you're all alone?" Dani

said, bringing my attention back to her. "I should be with you... unless..." Again, her eyes drifted to Jake.

What does it mean that he can "regenerate"? A rush of anxiety filled me as I thought about sleeping in the same tent as him. Dani might've told me that Jake and I were *together*, but she hadn't given me any of the details, and I wasn't quite ready for that yet.

Becca walked past, startling me. Her face was soft and glowing in the building flames. "We can share a tent tonight, if you would like," she said. I hadn't talked to her much since we'd left Colorado Springs, so I was surprised she'd even offered.

I flashed her a grateful smile. "Thanks, Becca." Looking at Dani, I asked, "Do you mind?"

Dani shrugged and shook her head. "Only if you're sure, Zo."

"Yes, I'm sure."

"You can use this tent," Jason offered, prepared to pull the tent poles out of the pack.

"That's okay, Jason. I can finish. You guys can set up your stuff. Can you just point me to my things?" I hadn't needed them for anything yet, since we'd been riding all day. "I do have *things*, right?"

Jason nodded to Dani, and with a willing smile she picked up the flashlight he'd set on the ground and walked with me over to Mocha.

As I trudged along behind her, I noticed how many people were bustling around, chatting while they set up for the night. Our cramped little camp was in a wooded area off the highway, out of sight but not so far away from the road that I couldn't hear one of the horses clip-clopping lazily on the asphalt.

Stepping up to Mocha, Dani started untying the two long stuff sacks secured behind the saddle with one hand, tossing me each as she freed them. Both were black with a purple Celtic knot painted on the side.

"That's your sleeping bag and sleeping pad," she said, pointing to each before she peeked into one of the saddlebags, which were still on the horse. "Yep, your clothes and whatnot are in here. Give me a sec and I'll have these down for you."

"Don't worry, I'll get them," I said, not wanting her to struggle needlessly. As I fumbled to loosen the saddlebag, I stared at the knot painted on it. I had no idea what the heck it meant. "Apparently I really like this symbol," I said. "It's all over my stuff."

Finally unfastening the bag, I turned around. Dani eyed me a moment, her face cast in shadows; obviously it meant something important to her, too. I glanced back down at the bag, the knot glaring at me.

Assuming it was my confusion that made her expel a tiny sigh of sadness, I released a sigh of my own. "I'm sorry, Dani. I wish I could remember…"

She stepped closer and nudged my arm with her good shoulder, offering me a reassuring smile that didn't touch her eyes. "It's okay, Zo. We'll figure it out tomorrow. It's been a long day, and we all need our rest."

I nodded and turned to tug the leather bags off of Mocha's back, but grunted when they were heavier than I'd expected. "What the hell did I put in he—"

"Here." A deep rumble came from behind me, and an arm reached over my shoulder and grabbed the cross strap of the saddlebags. Jake pulled them effortlessly off the horse and asked me where I wanted them.

"Over by Becca," I said, pointing dumbly. I'd decided Jake was intimidating—alluring but intimidating—and it prevented me from putting on a show of calmness around him, like I could around everyone else.

A pained expression pinched his features, but without another word, he headed to the other side of camp, toward Becca.

Dani was watching me, idly patting Jack, his tongue hanging out of his mouth. She gave me a reassuring nod—the nod that I'd grown used to over the past twelve hours—before I followed quickly after Jake.

Feeling inadequate in our silence, I occupied my mind with observations of the rest of the campers, busy in their various stages of getting situated.

Chris, just finished setting up a tent for Camille and Mase, was pulling her blonde hair up into a ponytail, while Mase, huge, dark, and imposing, stood in front of the tent with Camille in his arms, her head resting on his shoulder. They'd been inseparable since she'd awoken right before we stopped for the day, and despite being unconscious since before they'd found me, she still looked exhausted. Mase stared at the nylon dome like it was from another dimension. He seemed constantly confused—even more than me, which I thought a little strange—but after a brief moment of hesitation, he ducked inside the tent with Camille.

Gabe, the tall, blond man who seemed to keep to himself, was setting up another tent beside theirs.

"What's his Ability?" I asked Jake. When he peered back at me, I pointed to Gabe.

Jake's jaw clenched, and I immediately regretted asking him. "He can manipulate people's dreams," he said. I didn't need to know the history between them to know it wasn't a good one.

"Oh."

Sanchez, who seemed to be leading the group with Jason, was stacking wood next to the campfire, while Sam and easygoing Tavis hauled over bunches of kindling. I enjoyed watching Sam and Tavis interact; they acted more like brothers than father and son—though I'd been told they were neither—and they laughed more than the others, which I found comforting.

But as much as everyone *seemed* to coexist easily enough, a cloud of tension hung over the group. I wasn't sure I wanted to learn the cause yet. Trying to remember everyone's names, their Abilities, and my relationship with each of them was chore enough.

Jake stopped short in front of me, and I ran into his back.

"Sorry," I said, unable to stop a nervous laugh from bubbling out of me. "I got distracted." I dropped the load in my arms on the ground near Becca.

Jake set my saddlebags down as well. "I'll be right back," he said and headed back toward the horses.

I watched him for a moment—watched the way he rubbed the back of his neck and the way his shoulders relaxed the further he was from me.

I turned to Becca, who was attempting to finish setting up our tent. "Thank you, Becca. I appreciate you offering to stay with me tonight."

When I realized she was practically wrestling with the tent poles, I crouched beside her to show her how they worked. "It's pretty easy once you get the hang of it," I said. I was surprised I remembered silly things like that—how to set up a tent, how to excuse myself when I sneezed and cover my mouth when I coughed. *Why can I remember those things but not others?*

"You have done this before," Becca said quietly, watching the way my fingers moved and how I maneuvered the fabric of the tent as I pushed the poles through the red nylon loops.

"Yeah, I guess I have. You've never been camping?" Slowly, I forced one end of the pole into the corner of the tent, and watched as Becca mimicked what I was doing.

"Not that I remember, no." Her voice was distant, as if her mind was somewhere else.

"Yeah, me neither…at least, not that I can remember."

Jake returned, dropping two more stuff sacks on the ground, what appeared to be another sleeping bag and pad. He looked at Becca. "Those are mine, but you use them tonight. We'll stop somewhere tomorrow to get you your own gear." Becca watched Jake, her mouth pulling into a barely-there smile. "Thank you, Jake." The way she spoke to him seemed deliberate, like she meant more than what she said.

He watched her for a moment, his head tilting slightly to the side before he nodded. When his stare shifted to me, he appeared uncertain and regretful. There was a long, awkward silence before he said, "Will you please let me know if you need anything else?" His tone was soft, beseeching, even. There was something warm and inviting about his deep, velvety voice. "*Anything*," he repeated, his eyes filled with a sadness I didn't understand.

"Yes, I promise. Thank you," I said. With a final nod, I watched him walk back toward his tent, which he had yet to finish setting up.

Becca unzipped the tent door behind me and I turned around, ready to follow her inside. But she just stood there.

"What's wrong?" I asked, stepping up beside her. The light from the fire danced around inside, illuminating the tent enough to see there was nothing wrong with it.

"I guess I will sleep in my clothes," she said so quietly I almost didn't hear her.

"Is that all?" I asked and snatched up my saddlebags before sidestepping her and heading inside. "I'm sure I have something you can borrow."

Becca followed me in, bringing the sleeping bags and pads in with her.

Fiddling with the ends of my hair, which were draped over my shoulder, I watched Becca as she just stood there. "Have a seat," I said and opened my bag. I rummaged through the haphazardly folded clothes tucked inside, trying to find something for each of us to sleep in. "Here," I finally said, handing her a long-sleeved thermal shirt and a pair of sweatpants. "These look comfy, and it looks like I packed…yep, two of each."

Becca smiled, or at least I thought it was a smile; it was the first time I'd seen her be very expressive at all. "Thank you, Zoe."

"Why don't you have any clothes?" I asked, zipping up the tent to change.

Slowly, Becca peeled her clothes off one by one, until her ensemble was piled on the floor of the tent. "I have only just joined the group, along with Dr. McLaugh—I mean Gabe, Mase, and

Camille. We were unexpected, so we are relying on your friends' kindness to take us in. Dani and the clothes on our backs were all we brought with us."

"Dani was with *you*?"

Becca made a noncommittal noise and pulled the sweatpants on. They were too long and very baggy on her, but I figured that meant they were perfect for sleeping. "Yes," she said. "Dani was with Gabe and Dr. Wesley…in the Colony." Becca's voice was distant, her demeanor instantly shifting from open to hesitant.

I tugged my long-sleeved V-neck on over my head. "Did you not want to leave the Colony with Dani?" I couldn't stop myself from asking. The more complicated things became, the more my curiosity amplified. "You don't seem happy to be here…" I glanced over at Becca in time to see the bruises on the side of her body before she pulled her borrowed shirt down.

"I am happy to be away from there. It is just that things are not simple for me." She looked at me. "Or for you."

I shrugged. "Hopefully my memory will come back tomorrow."

The look Becca gave me made me feel nauseous.

"You don't think it will?" I asked.

"I do not know everything," she said, offering me the slightest of smiles.

"Only some things?" I asked wryly.

Without hesitation, she said, "I have the gift of prophecy."

Still unable to fully process the whole "Abilities" thing, I paused.

Becca bent down and began folding her clothes so meticulously that I thought she might be in the military. I looked over at my saddlebags and almost laughed. The clothes I'd changed out of were tossed on top, no rhyme or reason or organization. Feeling self-conscious, I gathered up my dirty socks, jeans, and shirt, and after unwadding them, I folded them as neatly as I could. My attempt was pathetic compared to Becca's, but it sufficed.

Becca must've been watching me, because when I looked up at her, her smile turned genuine. "You are very different from the last time I saw you."

My eyes widened. "How so?" I unrolled my sleeping pad, then pulled my sleeping bag out of its stuff sack and laid it out on top. Unzipping it, I crawled inside to keep my feet warm.

Becca studied me and did the same with Jake's sleeping gear. "You and Jake were fighting."

"Really?" I hadn't been expecting that. "We were fighting?"

She nodded, her eyes fixed on mine like she was gauging my reaction. "He was going to leave you and your people and take me away; he said it was not safe. But Father sent a team to retrieve me, and I escaped during the gunfire." Becca looked down at her fingers, which were laced on her knees. "I had to return to the Colony…Jake did not understand."

"Did Father do that to you?" I asked, pointing to the bruised side of her body.

After contemplating my question for a moment, Becca nodded. "I had to get them out of there," she said to herself, and I assumed she was talking about Dani and the others she'd escaped with.

My mind filled with images of a distraught Mase and newly-conscious Camille. "The others are like you, too," I said, suddenly feeling an intense desire to know what had happened in the hours I'd lost my memory. "Mase and Camille, they're…different, like you. The way you speak, and how you see things like it's for the first time…they're the same."

Becca nodded. "Yes. We are called Re-gens at the Colony, though Jake says I am his sister as well."

My brow furrowed at yet another surprising truth. Jake didn't treat her like a sister—but then Jason didn't treat me like one either, at least not how *I* thought a brother should treat a sister. I was beginning to think that whatever remaining perception of reality I had was both misleading and impractical.

"I saw things," Becca continued, her voice a panicked whisper.

"Horrible things. Things that I could not let come to pass. I had to tell them. I had to get away from there." Becca continued to stare down at her hands. "I am not sure what to think anymore."

"No?"

After a depleted sigh, she said, "No."

Pulling the rubber band from my hair and letting it fall around my shoulders, I ran my fingers through the dark strands, wading through my limited memories, trying to determine how *I* felt… what I *thought*.

All I remembered were strange voices and surprised faces staring down at me as I huddled inside the closet. *Did I really forget* all *that Becca just described?* It seemed impossible, and a ravenous emptiness drained any optimism and hope I had left. A sick feeling settled in my stomach as it dawned on me: every single moment that shaped me into Zoe was gone.

I am no one.

"You are not 'no one,'" Becca said, and I stirred, not realizing I'd been thinking aloud. She rested her hand on my shoulder. "You are important."

"You've seen this?" My sudden curiosity to know more of what she'd *seen* was making me antsy; I twirled a strand of hair.

Becca shook her head. "No, I haven't seen your future, nor do I know your purpose, but your mother is Dr. Wesley, I know that much. If you are her daughter, you are important." She paused in thought. "Jake loves you, and he is important…I know that as well. So, you must be, too."

Jake loves *me?* I wasn't sure why I was surprised; Dani had told me much the same earlier. "He's barely talked to me all day," I said.

"All day, I have thought about two things," Becca began, her voice a bit softer than before. "I considered what I might do now that I no longer have a home, a place I belong. And I thought about Jake. If what he says is true, if I *am* his sister, then he has lost both his sister and the woman he loves. Now, here we are again, and neither of us remembers him. I cannot imagine how he might feel." Becca frowned. "I generally am not so…reflective, I think is the word, but much is changing…" She stretched out in her sleeping bag, staring up at the bouncing shadows on the nylon overhead.

We were quiet for a while, and I nearly allowed the crackling fire outside and the sound of crickets in the woods beyond our tent to lull me to sleep. But before I was out completely, I heard low voices by the fire.

"We've got to figure out a way to fix her," Harper said, his voice low and thoughtful.

"It's not like there are rules to any of this shit," Jason grumbled.

The sound of wood being tossed in the fire filled the momentary silence.

"There has to be a way." It was Jake's baritone, followed by retreating footsteps.

I glanced over at Becca to see if she was awake, but her back was to me, and all I could see was the outline of her torso rising and falling with each breath. I lay there, listening to my "friends" discuss my condition like it was simply an infection needing proper treatment. My mind reeled with questions and mounting fear until their voices fell silent, and I eventually drifted to sleep.

A slight breeze caressed my skin as I sat on a dock, gazing out at a lake—its glassy surface was illuminated with pinks and oranges, like it was set aflame by the sun sinking behind the rolling hills.

My chest grew heavier, and I was nearly suffocating under the weight of too many emotions.

"I know what I want," said a deep, rumbling voice.

I spun around to find Jake standing beside me, his luminous, amber eyes peering into the depths of my soul. He knew me; I could see it in the way he looked at me, those eyes filled with longing and uncertainty and need.

Like his emotions sparked my own, I felt the need to weep from the inexplicable love I felt for him.

"Jake, I—" I didn't have time to think, to say anything.

In seconds his lips were pressed against mine, his kiss fierce and blazing. My hands moved of their own accord, grabbing a handful of his jacket and pulling him closer to me as his fingers tightened in my hair. An overwhelming, frenzied greed consumed us both as my arms snaked around his neck and his hands explored my body.

We were panting, and a low groan resonated deep inside his chest. My body throbbed with a pleasurable ache I wanted to both last forever and go away, ridding me of my torment.

Jake froze, sending an unnatural anger and despondency simmering through me. He stepped away, leaving me to stand there alone, the cool breeze turning icy against my exposed skin. Panic riddled my nerves, and I tried fervently to grasp hold of him.

He was pulling away from me...

He was leaving me...alone...

With a jolt, I opened my eyes. I was surrounded by darkness, only the starry sky overhead visible through the rectangles of netting on the roof of the tent. There was no more campfire, and there were no more voices. All I could hear was the wind whistling through the trees.

As I lay there, my heart still pounding from the dream, I felt completely lost and alone. I didn't like the dangerous intoxication that settled over me as I remembered Jake's hot breath…the thrill that sang through me as I recalled the feeling of his fingers pressing against my skin…

"Zoe? Are you alright?" Becca asked quietly.

"Yes," I said quickly, not feeling comfortable talking to her about it.

"Are you sure?"

"I just had a strange dream. I'll be fine."

Becca was quiet for a moment. "Was it a dream or a memory?"

Rolling over, I studied her darkened outline. "A dream. At least, I think it was…"

"Do not fight it," she said. "If it *is* your memory, you should not fight it."

Had it been a memory? It had been so vivid, so charged with emotions I couldn't remember ever feeling before, that part of me doubted it was even possible.

MORE BOOKS BY THE LINDSEYS

THE ENDING WORLD

THE ENDING LEGACY
World After (Prequel)
The Raven Queen

THE ENDING SERIES
After The Ending
Into The Fire
Out Of The Ashes
Before The Dawn
The Ending Beginnings
World Before

SAVAGE NORTH CHRONICLES
(by Lindsey Pogue)

The Darkest Winter
The Longest Night
Midnight Sun
Fading Shadows
Untamed
Unbroken
Day Zero: Beginnings

ALSO BY LINDSEY POGUE

FORGOTTEN LANDS WORLD
(Can be read as stand-alones)

FORGOTTEN LANDS
Dust and Shadow
Borne of Sand and Scorn (Prequel)
Earth and Ember
Tide and Tempest

RUINED LANDS
City of Ruin
Sea of Storms
Land of Fury

SARATOGA FALLS LOVE STORIES
(Recommended reading order)
Whatever It Takes
Nothing But Trouble
Told You So
Memory Book Story Collection

ALSO BY LINDSEY SPARKS

ECHO WORLD

ECHO TRILOGY

Echo in Time

Resonance

Time Anomaly

Dissonance

Ricochet Through Time

KAT DUBOIS CHRONICLES

Ink Witch

Outcast

Underground

Soul Eater

Judgement

Afterlife

FATELESS TRILOGY

Song of Scarabs and Fallen Stars

Darkness Between the Stars

THE NIK CHRONICLES

(Patreon exclusive serial)

LEGACIES OF OLYMPUS

ATLANTIS LEGACY

Sacrifice of the Sinners

Legacy of the Lost

Fate of the Fallen

Dreams of the Damned

Song of the Soulless

Blood of the Broken

Rise of the Revenants

ALLWORLD ONLINE

AO: Pride & Prejudice

AO: The Wonderful Wizard of Oz

Vertigo

AO: LOOKING GLASS

(Patreon exclusive serial)

THE LAST

VAMPIRE QUEEN

(Patreon exclusive serial)

Season 1: Awakened

ABOUT LINDSEY POGUE

Lindsey Pogue is a genre-bending fiction author, best known for her soul-stirring, post-apocalyptic survival series, Savage North Chronicles and Forgotten Lands. As an avid romance reader with a master's in history and culture, Lindsey's adventures cross genres and push boundaries, weaving together facts, fantasy, and timeless love stories of epic proportions. When Lindsey's not chatting with readers, plotting her next storyline, or dreaming up new, brooding characters, she's generally wrapped in blankets watching her favorite action flicks with her own leading man. They live in Northern California with their rescue cats, Beast and little girl Blue.

Access VIP Vault Exclusive stories, audiobooks, and more!

www.lindseypogue.com/newsletter

About Lindsey Sparks

Lindsey Sparks lives her life with one foot in a book—so long as that book transports her to a magical world or bends the rules of science. Her novels, from Post-apocalyptic (writing as Lindsey Fairleigh) to Time Travel Romance, always offer up a hearty dose of unreality, along with plenty of history, intrigue, adventure, and romance.

When she's not working on her next novel, Lindsey spends her time hanging out with her two little boys, working in her garden, or playing board games with her husband. She lives in the Pacific Northwest with her family and their small pack of cats and dogs. www.authorlindseysparks.com

PATREON: https://www.patreon.com/lindseysparks

MAIN SOCIAL MEDIA

FB Reader Group: Lindsey's Lovely Readers
Instagram: @authorlindseysparks
YouTube: Author Lindsey Sparks
Discord: discord.gg/smTeDHQBhT

OTHER SOCIAL MEDIA

Facebook: @authorlindseysparks
TikTok: @authorlindseysparks
Pinterest: @authorlindseysparks

www.authorlindseysparks.com/join-newsletter

www.ingramcontent.com/pod-product-compliance
Lightning Source LLC
Chambersburg PA
CBHW050958180726
48291CB00006B/1879

* 9 7 8 1 9 4 9 4 8 5 0 2 8 *